BRAMDEN HOUSE

DARCIE MCGRATH

BRAMDEN HOUSE

DARCIE MCGRATH

ISBN: 979-8-9892451-0-9

To my teachers, mentors, and friends that have taught me so much......and to "Harold" who taught me more

Author's Notes

"Who doesn't love a good ghost story?"

Some would argue what this has to do with this book, but having been an avid student of parapsychology—among scientists and researchers striving to solve the mystery of human consciousness—I find it a good measure of my audience before I begin to speak at any venue. Reactions can vary from excited anticipation, to mild skepticism, to religious objection. Parapsychology attempts to pursue such matters in the dispassionate vein of science. Considering the 'organic' laboratory of the everyday world, regular scientific controls are not always possible. The most basic of data collection starts at the experiential level— observation, recording, and publishing to share among those of like-minded research. With the current atmosphere of using such collected data as *entertainment*, this subject here is being approached with care.

As a student of both parapsychology and history, to quote one of my favorite Civil War epics, "very little can be accomplished under the spirit of fear". Those expecting to find a 'horror story' within these covers may find themselves, woefully, unimpressed. Unlike what mainstream entertainment may convey, not all experiences within the category 'paranormal', equate fear. People have had these experiences regardless of race, gender, culture or creed since the human race began on this world, and it has been made somewhat apparent to those that have observed such events, that many people are *born* into these experiences with certain antennae switched on. Not all people have a direct trajectory toward financial gain or exploitation, but simply walk through life with these experiences being 'normal' to them. Those in current day research—ranging across many scientific endeavor—have attempted to approach such events with an eye toward 'normalization' rather than 'exclusiveness'. Since these people who have these experiences come from a wide spiritual background, it is not unusual for those experiencing such events, to apply their own brand of spirituality to such things to cope with it in their own way.

It is in this vein that this book has been written, with certain personal 'experiential' references applied across decades of experiences as a consultant in this unique field, and the author hopes this will be taken into consideration while reading.

In closing, the author would also like to extend special thanks to Julia at Fortune Literary Services for the tireless hours of poring over words and various topics within, via phone and chat. And also, to the countless members of the reenactment community and esteemed colleagues in the paranormal and parapsychology communities, without whom this author would have no stories to tell. Additional thanks is extended to the National Park Service, the Illinois Archives, the Army War College at Carlisle(Pennsylvania), the Missouri Civil War Museum at Jefferson Barracks, and the Van Buren County Historical Society(Iowa), for their invaluable information and passionate research.

And last, but not least—to those brave and honored souls who gave the last full measure of devotion, for the dedication of generations of those that have served, and for those still battling scars seen and unseen.

'Thank you' is not enough.

Music is very much a living part of this book. To hear the selections mentioned, and other music that has inspired its creation, see the Bramden House playlist on YouTube:

https://www.youtube.com/watch?v=tBKJRJ- M-A&list=PL9q3-EjOQKR3FTlLuM8BUdJ1vaMJYRYcf

or use the QR code below:

Prologue

September 1861, somewhere along the Missouri northern border

Senior 1st Lieutenant Charles Danforth snapped the gold hunter case of his pocket watch closed, placing the precious keepsake in his breast pocket. He cursed softly to himself, his dark eyes scanning both sides of the forest trail as he removed his blue cap-style Army-issued kepi from atop his head. He had lost count how many times he removed the cover to wipe the sweat forming along his thick dark brow with the sleeve of his blue wool shell jacket.

Wool. Whomever came up with the idea of wearing wool should be shot. Or, at least forced at full march through the height of a humid summer in Missouri. He really didn't care how practical the Army thought it was.

It was unseasonably hot, and the junior officer had long exchanged his regulation frock coat and high-crowned, wide-brimmed Hardy hat, for the shorter shell jacket and flatter-style matching kepi. Not only did it introduce less glinting brass for the enemy to aim at, the replacement ensemble was not as heavy to wear. It did nothing for his wavy dark brown hair that kinked in the heavy humidity, so the kepi was covering a multitude of sins. Good thing it was dark. But as he replaced his cover, one thing was for certain.

Someone up there hated him.

The artillery battery was just weeks away from getting federally-mustered in at Jefferson Barracks, when they got the call that they had been assigned to the 1st Northeast Missouri for border patrol duty. They were, originally, to back up the ragtag militia at Athens to take on a company of homegrown Missouri State Guard but arrived too late for action. Now, here they were—moving under the cover of night, in dense woods, looking for trouble. And knowing the reputation of the regimental colonel, it would likely find *them*. The colonel's temperament was the thing of legends. They said his own sons went as far as joining the other side, just to get away from him.

That placed Danforth, here, in a precarious position. Border patrol was tedious, yet, perilous duty. Tensions were high among the locals ever since the event at Camp Jackson last May. Before that, all the home guard had to deal with was the obstinacy of a few youthful rabble rousers from town to town. Most of the locals kept their political opinions regarding Confederate or Union sympathies to themselves, or at least in hushed tones at the local tavern. Now, after the *incident*, with the blood of St. Louis citizens on their hands, the United States Army moved with a high degree of vigilance and unease through the Northern Province aptly named "Little Dixie".

Lieutenant Danforth was of a rare height. He definitely stood out amongst his peers. However, his dark eyes beneath a heavy brow, along with thick sideburns and even thicker mustache was enough to send most of the enlisted elements scurrying for cover, but it was even worse when he scowled. Coupled with a brusque demeanor and salty disposition, it did nothing to remind others that he was a man of letters. Some would argue that was what kept him from rising in the ranks, but there were more than enough *other* reasons for that. His grandmother was suspected of Southern political leanings, while his father's apathy about the war spurred rumor of disloyal "copperhead" tendencies; neither fully supported his entry into the war.

However, within the lower ranks of artillery, it had the opposite effect on the men. Some had even marked him to lead the battery by popular vote alone. But somehow, as often happened, letters were sent, favors were cashed in, and the role went to another. Danforth was fine with it. He preferred the comradery of his army family over the prestige of command.

He touched the spurs to the ribs of his chestnut-colored Morgan, urging his mount to a more deliberate pace ahead of the limber and attached bronze Napoleon cannon. He preferred point, much to the chagrin of his section, but it was just as well. At 11:45 in the blessed PM, he had the best vantage to see what was coming. The contraption made an uncomfortable amount of din as it rolled across twigs, leaves, and branches on the forest floor. He winced at the grinding and groaning of the wood and steel, wondering if it might have been more efficient to use a bull-horn to announce their position.

His horse snorted, shifting beneath him, uneasily. It sensed something he could not see. Not in the blasted dark, anyhow. He leaned over to pat the stallion, whispering assurance that he didn't really feel. They were in vulnerable conditions; even the horse knew that. He, and the rest of the battery section, would be a prime target for bushwhackers. They were out there, like phantoms in the underbrush; a fleeting glimpse, but never enough to draw a bead on. Never fair in a fight. Never ones to take on a unit head on. That's what made them dangerous.

A local militia with Confederate sympathies would like nothing better than to get their hands on a cannon, and there was barely enough of a regiment to protect them if they did get hit. But the regiment had orders. They were to meet up with the 2nd Northeast Missouri Home Guard with all possible speed. If they could find them.

Danforth cast a sympathetic look over his right shoulder. There was Sam Callhoun, as if he even had to look. Sam hadn't moved from that position in over twenty years. They explored every inch of the Dry Run together back in Peoria. To his left was Fenton. He had been there for at least four months, joining up as soon as he had graduated from the Academy. His uncle was a colonel and promised him a fast rise if he joined the state volunteers instead of the bloated ranks of the federal units. The state of Illinois was happy to prove him right. His uncle was even happier that his nephew wasn't going to be used as cannon fodder in the eastern side of the conflict. Bringing up the rear was Batterson. The first sergeant was fresh off the farm, but Army through and through. They were thick as thieves, the lot of them. They all knew the high risks of tonight. But wherever their lieutenant would go, they would follow. Even if it meant to their graves.

Damn them.

"It's Batterson's fault," Sam's tenor voice floated up from behind him, referring to their skittish horses. "He shaved before breaking camp. The horses smell the blood."

"Was it a shave or a bloodletting?" Fenton quipped. "Who the hell shaves at the end of the day, anyhow?"

"If Batterson went home in a box less than clean shaven, his mamma would perch on the edge of his grave, and never let him hear the end of it."

"Don't let him fool ya," Fenton snorted. "He's probably got a date with his horse later."

Batterson sneered at the jibe. "My horse is way better company than the two a you!"

Danforth wasn't amused. "Quiet, alla ya! Or a box might be what we get."

And that's when he noticed it. Now that the others had ceased talking, it was more noticeable. He held up a white leather gauntleted hand to bring his section to a stop.

Batterson was the first to speak up. "Sir?"

He waved off the comment abruptly, straining to hear for what he hoped wasn't there. And yet…

"You hear that?" the first lieutenant noted in a hushed whisper.

Sam's mount shifted beneath him again, forcing the rider to reassert his grip on the reins. "Hear what?"

"Exactly."

A lead ball of fear churned in the pit of the older officer's stomach. It was wrong. It was all wrong. The forest should be alive with night sounds; crickets, the occasional bird or coyote. But there was…nothing. Nothing but half a cannon section anchored into position by a 2,400-pound piece of bronze.

A crash in the brush ahead caused all four to unholster their pistols. Some of the infantry that had wandered too far ahead, swung their muskets around, causing the battery officers to reign their mounts in sharply. One mistake, and they all could be taking on friendly fire.

Not even five yards ahead of the artillery group, a small form erupted from the greenery before diving face-down into the dirt. Danforth's Morgan reared in fright. It was all the junior officer could do to keep from being thrown.

"Help!" the small figure croaked. Small, child-sized hands fumbled for the dark slouch hat that had fallen off in the unceremonious landing. The poor thing couldn't have been more than ten. "Please…help me! The barn. It's on fire!"

The majority of the horse-mounted party relaxed momentarily, taking their gun sights off the new arrival, but Danforth was ill at ease. His dark, penetrating gaze swept around their perimeter, senses at full alert.

And those senses whispered in its voiceless voice, tickling the back of his intuition. *Ambush*.

He reached inside his coat, removing his silver St. Barbara medal; the patron saint of artillery. It was gift from his college mentor and fellow Catholic. He wore it attached to his watch fob. He, himself, didn't pray on a regular basis, but now seemed like a good time to consider it. He eyed the medal in the palm of his gauntleted hand, the faint moonlight playing across its raised features. He pressed the artifact to his lips before putting it away.

He wasn't alone. Batterson was in his own nervous state of alertness, lifting his weapon, the ominous click of the cocked Remington revolver announcing itself at the ready.

The sergeant's steel blue eyes darted for any potential threat in the shadows. Nothing felt right about this. "Sir…"

The first lieutenant swore under his breath, and despite his better judgment, swung down from his mount. The army didn't need any more bad press.

"Batterson. Cover me."

Danforth moved with a wary air toward the child, and dropped next to the youngster. He eased the child onto their back. Short, dirty blonde hair framed the freckled face, which grimaced in pain. A bad ankle? Shoulder?

"Gun!"

Danforth whirled about, hand dropping to the handle of his revolver. He staggered to stand upright, but failed as the silence of the night was interrupted by multiple explosions. Pain ripped through his left side, sending him backward into the hard-packed dirt of the trail. As a momentary silence fell, his ears still rang from the noise. It was short lived as gunfire peppered the party from the brush surrounding them. He gasped in agony, ears ringing as explosion after explosion continued. From his position on the ground, he could hear the agonizing screams of a horse. Unable to move, he couldn't see whose it was. Screaming, but this time human. Someone young. What was happening?

A triumphant male howl broke the silence as he heard a rider wheel his mount about. The sickening thud of two more bodies hitting the ground made him wrench his body, painfully, to see who it was. The vermin in the underbrush seemed to retreat as the horse rider took off at high gallop. Army militia musket fire formed a rapid response, but the continued fading hoof beats attested to their ineffectiveness. Apparently, the raiding party thought the better of it when faced with prepared militia, because as suddenly as the ruckus had begun, it stopped. The only sound in the darkened wood continued to be the labored breath and shrieks of the dying horse. Danforth pulled himself to his feet, feeling lighter than he should after such an impact. He examined his side but could make out nothing in the dim light.

"Sam?" he called out, finding his feet. "Fenton?! Batterson?! Report!"

The lack of an answer made him fear the worst, on top of the sudden realization that standing out in the open, shouting, was the last thing he should be doing.

But why was no one firing? Had their enemies simply hit and run with no time for the spoils?

As he stumbled forward, something blocked his forward progress.

The youth? No, even by the sparse light of the moon he could tell the form was much larger than that.

At his feet was a crumpled body in federal uniform. The figure had fallen onto his side with his back to Danforth. The man's regulation kepi had fallen from his head, exposing a thick head of dark, wavy hair. The tree-filtered light of the waning moon provided little visibility, but there was enough that he could make out the gold and red sardine box-style straps at the shoulders of the unfortunate man's coat. The only Army artillery officers with this militia unit were his own. It was all very perplexing.

Taking in an unsteady breath, the bewildered officer circled the figure to take in the stranger's face. The face was pale. Dark eyes open, his death stare gazed down the trail from which their party had just come.

No.

Panic seized him. He staggered back in horror as he stared, incredulously, down at the face. He could barely utter a sound.

"No…" his voice raspy with fear, raking his fingers through his dark hair as he trembled uncontrollably. "No!"

It wasn't real. This wasn't happening. He stumbled and fell into the dirt, scrambling away from the awful nightmare that presented in front of him. Away from the face. That face.

"Help…" he breathed, still not able to find the strength to be any louder, as if volume would bring the nightmare to stark reality. "God, no…please!"

Before him, undeniably, was the lifeless form of Senior 1st Lieutenant Charles Danforth.

The next thing that the lieutenant was aware of was a hazy lightness of being. He was completely free of any physical sensation. No pain. No hot or cold. No smell. No…anything. As his eyes became more accustomed to the light around him, it occurred to him that he had the most peculiar view of the river valley. Not observing it from the ground but from *above* it. He just seemed to be hovering far above the early morning mists, watching with fascination as they rolled and writhed throughout the river valley. The flow would inevitably branch out to snake through the trees that lined the winding river. Down below, against the northern shore, was a flat-bottom ferry made of lashed wooden logs. A wagon with a pair of horses was being pulled on board, along with two more cows and their owner. There seemed to be a disagreement between the ferryman and the cow's owner, as to price, the commotion causing the horse attached to the wagon to shift, uneasily. He was acutely aware of the huffing sound of the horses, as well as the hollow thud of the horses' hooves as they shifted on the wooden planking of the flat, raft-like vessel. After a moment, all passengers seemed to calm down, and the ferryman moved to the craft's edge and rammed his long pole into the thick sediment of the river bottom, and pushed.

He had to still be dreaming. He had the most frightening nightmare of observing his lifeless form on the forest floor. At least this dream was more pleasant. Of course, it was strange as to why he was choosing to dream this.

As if in response to his thoughts, he felt a sudden jolt roil through him before the world rapidly rose up to meet him. He was swimming through crashing waves of pain as his vision went eerily dim. It took a moment for his eyesight to adjust to his new location.

He was vaguely aware of the saffron glow of sunlight on canvas above him. He was in a wagon. By the sounds of the occasional thud reverberating beneath, he guessed he was no longer viewing the ferry from above but from inside the wagon being transported on top of it. A belligerent cow shifted restlessly next to the wagon, mooing in indignation at having been removed from the comfort of land. It was answered by the occasional snort of the horses attached to the wagon. He wasn't alone on the wooden floor of the wagon. Two or three other bodies were also crammed in with him. He recognized one soldier propped upright with his head bandaged as one of the militia men of the Home Guard unit to whom his artillery section had been attached. There was an older, gray-bearded gentleman to his right, bellowing in pain. The craft came to a jarring stop as it landed on the opposing river bank, causing the wagon to lurch. Dull pain became fresh as the bodies within the wagon bed were jostled by the impact. The older man to his right, shrieked in response. Upon spoken command, the wagon pulled forward, but by only a few feet. The wagon shook and creaked as it came off the ferry platform. Pain that Danforth hadn't even realized sprang to piercing sharpness in his left side and leg as the slack suspension of their transport offered nothing in the way of cushioned support for those on board.

Without warning, the back canvas flap was thrown open. Burly, dark-faced orderlies climbed inside, some dressed in vests of blue wool and the shapeless matching forage caps. Others wore civilian attire, shirts of different color choices, with the uniting color of either tribe being that of blood. The lieutenant did his best to stifle a cry as they heaved the canvas stretcher into the open light of day, his temples keeping time with the nearby heavy clang of a cast iron bell splitting the air. His left side was on fire; knives of pain stabbing through his side, groin, and upper thigh. An intense-looking, ruddy face hovered before his own, sporting a mop of white hair, thick brows and even thicker mustache. He was wearing what the wounded officer could only assume what was once a white apron. He quickly examined the soldier's side, practiced fingers picking through the shattered remains of his red checkered shirt and dark blue trousers. The ghost of fatigued disappointment flashed fleetingly across his face before his steely-gray eyes caught the attention of the nearest stretcher bearer. With a jerk of the inspector's head, the orderlies snatched up the stretcher and spirited the lieutenant away in the direction indicated.

Danforth let out a painful grunt through gritted teeth as they placed him on the grass beneath a tree, abandoning him for the next patient. Looking for a distraction—any distraction from the pain—his fingers found the grass on either side of the stretcher. They found purchase in the thick thatch, fingers curling to grasp the coolness the day was merciless in providing. From what he could tell, his fingers were the only thing that didn't hurt.

It was at that moment that another pair of stretcher bearers brought him company. The older man. The one that had called out earlier. They placed his stretcher in a cool spot next to him. The man was oddly silent. One of the bearers paused just long enough to gaze into the wizened face of the man. Noting his eyes of watery blue stared, unblinkingly, into the tree canopy above him, the boy reached down and tugged the man's beige threadbare blanket over his face. At least one soul here was no longer in pain.

He closed his eyes against the light of day that filtered down to him through the leaves of the young tree above him. The area about him was alive with activity. Nearby, he could hear the sound of someone retching and heaving. From the following sob, he could tell it belonged to a young female. The soft voice of a female companion offered words of comfort. In sharp contrast, the voice of an authoritative older male barked over them.

"You tell Ole Man Estus that he can bill the federal government for all I care. He brings that ferry as soon as he has wounded. I don't care if it's not full, yet. How many are there?"

"Twenty-one, sir," the voice of a younger male replied.

"See to it that only officers are taken inside. I don't want to tell you again!" The man seemed to reconsider his tone and exchanged it for one of quiet concern. "We're running out of beds."

"Yes, Mr. Bramden."

Danforth raised his head a fraction, and he could see he was next to a two-story Federalist-style house made of reddish brick, its black shutters starkly framing tall white window panes. Peeking through the swaying branches above him, he could make out multiple red brick chimneys. Someone had done fairly well for themselves, and to the soldiers' good fortune, seemed willing to share what they had. He collapsed back into the makeshift bed, the pain shrieking in a pulsing tempo behind his eyes. He didn't have enough energy to do that again. He let his head roll to the side. The scene sprawled out before him was one of a tent city, bustling with orderlies, soldiers in blue uniform, and other more civilian-styled attendants, both male and female. Doctors and stewards moved nimbly from patient to patient, the lawn littered with multiple stretchers just like his. But in the midst of the fray, one solitary, bespectacled figure stood out. Dressed in a tweed frock coat, gray wool trousers, and a brown slouch hat, he protectively held a black book under one arm. It didn't take much to discern his profession. The man stood completely still, as if the center of the universe and everything evolved around his fixed point. Despite being at a considerable distance, Danforth felt the man's sharp gaze singling him out with a precision that the lieutenant found unsettling.

The officer frowned, letting his head drop to the blanket, his eyes closing. *No, preacher man. I shall not be needing your services today.*

"Oh, you never can tell when you *might*."

The light tenor voice wasn't at all threatening, but the suddenness of it, right next to him, startled the officer in the uncomfortable and painful position of sitting upright against the tree behind him.

Danforth's dark brow knitted in confusion. "I never said…You were just over—"

"There…I know." The spry, youthful preacher smiled from beneath the thick brown mustache that was in great need of a trim. As he removed his hat to kneel down alongside him, the lieutenant could see the good humor in the young man's hazel eyes. "You know how it is. When the Spirit moves you, you don't dally."

As the adrenaline wore off, the pain returned with a vengeance.

"I had the…strangest dream, Preacher," Danforth said with a wince, his hands moving to his thigh as he adjusted himself against the tree. "I really don't understand it."

The preacher's hands went up to the black tie around his white collar shirt and pulled it loose, muttering a *tut-tut* as he moved the soldier's hands away from the affected limb. Tying the fabric around the mangled extremity, the holy man created a makeshift dressing with surprising swiftness and precision.

The man sat back on his haunches to admire his handiwork, wiping his soiled hands on his gray trousers.

"The pain no longer needs to continue," the preacher observed, dispassionately. "It serves a purpose no longer. You can stand, if you like."

"What?!" The lieutenant gave an indignant snort of disbelief. No person's dressing was *that* good. And by the look of the surgeon's face that had him abandoned beneath the tree… "That's impossible."

Something in the sternness of the holy man's look revived old memories in Danforth of his childhood schoolmaster; a look he would only receive when in for a painful lesson. It only lasted a moment. The preacher's expression softened, resting a hand on the officer's shoulder in a gesture of compassion.

"I can take you to where there is no more pain. Your fighting days…they are done. The pain is a ghost from another world. It's time to leave it, and to go *home*."

Danforth shirked off the touch as if it had burned him. Immediately, he regretted the sudden movement as a wave of vertigo swept over him. Home. Maybe that appealed to a lot of people here, but not him. Home was a place of dread. Of bitter words. Of fights and discord. Of constant disappointment. He had left that place behind to be here. To serve. Besides, the last thing he wanted to do was return and be someone else's burden.

But that wasn't the only thing that made the lieutenant uncomfortable. It was the way the preacher had said it. It carried such a note of…*finality*. And if Danforth went with him, there was no coming back. Back from…

The soldier pushed the thought aside. No. He had to find Sam and the others. Once he found Sam, everything would be fine. Be…normal.

"I've got to find my men," Danforth muttered, struggling to set himself more upright against the trunk of the tree. "They need me…"

The preacher's face took on the shadow of disappointment as he renewed his grip on the officer's shoulder. "This is…completely unnecessary, you know. It doesn't have to be this way."

The lieutenant fixed him with a firm gaze of his own. He didn't like this. He didn't like the way the stranger made him feel. It was warm. Compassionate. Safe. Enticing. His rough upbringing and his years in the military had taught him not to trust that feeling. Besides, he had a duty to perform. Duty to his unit. His men. His *other* family.

"I wouldn't expect you to understand."

The holy man considered the lieutenant for a moment. Gently, he removed his hand from the soldier's shoulder. Instantly, to Danforth's displeasure, some of the queasiness of the earlier pain started to return.

The younger man winked; a secret wink, as if he understood more than the junior officer realized. "I'll be around."

As the preacher withdrew, Danforth felt the land around him start to tilt and whirl. Perhaps the man was supporting him more than he knew. He planted his hand in the grass next to him to steady himself. The vertigo began to ease. That was better.

With his free hand, he reached into the inside pocket of his shell jacket to remove his pocket watch. The watch was a gift from his uncle in Boston; the last remnant of family still speaking to him after his enlistment. He moved to refasten the chain to a brass button, the twisting of his torso causing a new series of shrieking pain.

His movement seemed to catch the attention of someone nearby. A slim, silver-haired gentleman marched toward him. The man's well-dressed look was ruined by his rolled up shirt sleeves and lack of a coat, but his black silk jacquard vest spoke as a person of some means.

"Why is this officer here?" the older man barked, his gray hawkish gaze falling, disapprovingly, upon two shiftless layabouts leaning against the brick wall of the house. "That wall will stay up on its own. Help this man!"

He immediately recognized the voice as the authoritative man giving orders earlier. Before Danforth could say a word, he was back into the stretcher.

"Take him upstairs to the spare room."

"But Dr. Maxwell—"

"I don't give a care what the surgeon said. Upstairs with him. *Now!*"

The older man rested a hand on Danforth's shoulder as the men moved toward the house. "Don't you worry about a thing, brother. We'll take good care of you here."

The last thing the lieutenant wanted was to be a difficulty; his bed could go to a healthier man. But he had no energy to argue. He would settle the affair later. At that moment, all he wanted to do was sleep.

BRAMDEN HOUSE

When the first lieutenant finally awoke, he realized he was in a bed.

After a fashion. Unfortunately, it was a small single-sized contraption, with the addition of a trunk needed at the foot to accommodate his unusual length. The room was no larger than a glorified store room. No windows. The bed filled the majority of the whitewashed space, but there was room for a small bedside table and a candle-lit lantern.

He felt the distinct feel of eyes upon him. Rolling his head to the left, he noted two small forms pulling abruptly back from the door frame. After a moment, the pale young face of a green-eyed little girl braved another peek. She couldn't have been older than twelve, her long, light-brown hair drawn back into a long braid. He offered a friendly smile, which coaxed her a bit more from the shadows. Her friend did, likewise. Her lanky companion was a head taller and considerably older than her. His dark skin and curly dark hair made him blend in with the shadows. He watched Danforth, carefully, with large brown timid eyes, even more nervous than she was.

"Abigale! What did I tell you about being upstairs?"

The older man's voice had returned. The two jumped to attention, the spell of curiosity broken as the lean, silver-haired gentleman appeared in the door frame.

"Go downstairs and help your mother," he ordered. "And, Nathaniel? You go with her and fetch some food for the lieutenant. And tell Dr. Maxwell he's awake."

The two scrambled away as the older gentleman returned his attention to his house guest. The dim light of the candle flickered across his hawkish features and added to the severity of his expression, but his piercing gray eyes seemed to regard him with warmth.

"Lieutenant, I hope I'm not disturbing you…"

"Not at all," the officer answered, wincing as he did his best to prop himself up a little higher on the pillows. "Thank you…for your hospitality."

The host motioned to an unused chair in the corner. "May I?"

"Please."

The older gentleman retrieved the rustic wooden chair and placed it next to the bed. "I'm Elias Bramden, but please--call me Eli."

"Charlie Danforth." The officer reached out a hand to his host, wincing as the twisting of his torso caused fresh pain.

Bramden clasped his hand, just as a look of recognition crossed over his face. " 'Charlie Danforth'…" He reached inside his vest. "Ah, this is fortuitous. You have…correspondence."

The officer blinked in surprise. "Here?"

"Well, we did not know you were here, but apparently, the Army did. Appears to be from…Springfield." He handed the folded paper to the bed-ridden guest. "I'm glad it's found its place."

The lieutenant was confused. "How…long have I been sleeping?"

The older man gave him a heartfelt smile. "You've been in an out of consciousness for a week now. You had quite a fever. The bloodletting must have done its job."

The junior officer examined the paper, mystified. Finally, he chose to break open the wax seal that secured the fold, but a wave of nausea came over him. The flickering of the candle in the darkened room sent the lieutenant's head pounding. "I'm afraid…I can't…"

"Would you like me to read it to you? Of course, I understand if you'd wish to read it in private."

Danforth weighed its possible contents before making a decision. "Please…if you wouldn't mind."

Bramden retrieved his wire-rimmed glasses from his other vest pocket and perched them on his hawk-like nose, holding up the paper for optimum light in the dim room.

" 'Illinois Volunteers. Head Quarters. Know ye, that this is to certify, that Charles E. Danforth of the Second Light Artillery Regiment, Illinois Volunteers, having received the recommendation of his Colonel as a fit and proper person to receive the appointment of Captain of Company E of said regiment. He is therefore hereby appointed accordingly, with all the rights, privileges, immunities and allowances appertaining to said appointment. He is, therefore hereby strictly charged, carefully and diligently to perform and execute all duties belonging to said appointment, in conformity with the rules and regulations of the service. And he is to be respected accordingly. Given at the Head Quarters of the Regiment, at Springfield, this 15th day of August, 1861. Thomas S. Mather, Colonel, Commanding.' " Bramden let the letter fall into his lap, a broad smile brightening his face. "Well, it sounds as if congratulations are in order—*Captain*."

Danforth sank back into the pillow in stunned silence. Captain. He'd have to start over with a new company. As captain, he was sure he could coax some of his trusted seconds to appointments, but…he would miss his Battery A.

"There is a notation included that goes on to say something about '…pending the completion of the company's federal muster at Jefferson

Barracks', which I'm sure is just a formality." Bramden removed his wire-rimmed glasses. "I'm sure your family will be quite proud."

Captain. He couldn't wait to tell Sam.

Sam.

Danforth moved to lay a hand on the older man's arm before his host could move away. "My men. I need to find them. They were with me when I fell."

Bramden's brow furrowed. "Well, I can make a note of their names and pass it onto the steward, but that would only be of benefit if they got off here. They needed to stabilize you. The rest likely ended up at the surgeon's hospital in Keokuk."

The older man gave the officer a reassuring pat on the shoulder, before drawing up from his seat.

"You best get some rest. I'll have someone stop by at breakfast and collect the names."

Danforth wanted to object. He found his mouth opening to do so, but Bramden had already done so much. Morning would have to do.

The peculiar thing that the captain was aware upon awakening was the smell of bread. He thought he might have been dreaming of home, until something cold on his brow jolted him awake. However, strangely enough, in that awakened state, he still smelled it.

A wizened face hovered scant inches before his own, no doubt belonging to the long-promised doctor. The concerned furrow of the older man's brow did not inspire confidence in the officer. Noticing his bedridden charge had come awake, the examiner feigned a quick smile of politeness. He patted the captain on the shoulder before removing himself from the small room.

Danforth's gaze caught a shadow in the door frame. There was the glint of light off silver spectacles in the sparse candlelight. The ever-present serene smile of the young preacher was the first thing to emerge from the darkness, his familiar floppy hat pressed to his breast.

"You have a guest," he announced, drawing back into the hallway.

And, in entered his second lieutenant, wearing his familiar lopsided grin. Sam Callhoun had his hat tucked under his arm, his face looking all the more youthful with his short, neatly combed auburn hair and a fresh shave.

He flipped his best friend a jaunty salute. "*Captain* Danforth. Or...should I just call you 'sir'?"

The captain chuckled, but winced. His side still pained him, greatly. "You do, and I'll put you on caisson duty."

Callhoun laughed his usual bell-like laugh, the kind of laugh that encouraged more laughter from those around him. "Well, it's time to move out, Captain. The crew is waiting."

Danforth looked at his friend, puzzled. He felt in no shape to leave his bed.

"The sections are assembled, awaiting inspection," Callhoun chuckled. "We've got to get moving."

"To where?"

The captain's gaze fell on the folded letter still on the chair next to him. Jefferson Barracks. Perhaps they could get on a steamer. He glanced down at his legs covered in wool blankets and a tattered quilt. His mangled, shot-riddled legs.

"I can't—"

Sam offered his hand. "I think you'll find ...you *can*."

Still bewildered, he reached out for his friend's hand, and just as his childhood acquaintance suggested, he, effortlessly, flung his legs over the side of the bed. He stood up, slowly, testing his balance. He, halfway, expected to reach out for Sam's shoulder to support himself. There was some mild stiffness, but he straightened to his full height with little difficulty. Baffled at his surprising recovery, he eased each of the dark blue braces up over the shoulders of his checkered shirt. He took a seat on the edge of the bed to pull on his cavalry boots as Sam handed him his officer's shell jacket. Standing up, he shrugged into it, taking a few slow and deliberate steps out into the hallway.

The early morning staff buzzed around them as the two headed down the corridor. They had only gotten a few steps toward the staircase when familiar voices floated out from a nearby room. Sam caught his arm and they paused to listen.

"How are you feeling, Abe?"

"Tolerable," the other voice said, tiredly. "Just grazed my arm. Better than…"

"I know." The second man gave out a beleaguered sigh. "Two in one week. You know what they're saying?"

"What?"

"The battery is cursed. We're not even fully mustered, yet."

"That's ridiculous, McGuiness!" the other man quipped. "I'd better not catch you saying anything like that. You'll lose your stripes. Superstitious nonsense."

"I'm not! But it just…gets you thinkin'—first Callhoun, and now, Danforth."

Danforth felt as if someone had shoved an icy spear into his chest. He staggered back a step. Sam caught him by the shoulder as the conversation continued, unencumbered.

"You gonna write his folks?"

"I already wrote one to Sam's family," the other man replied, punctuating the statement with a long sigh. "Is this supposed to get easier?"

Danforth's mouth opened and closed, but nothing came out, his dark eyes wide. His breathing came in short raspy draws as he, instinctively, turned back toward his room.

Sam doubled the grip on his friend's shoulder, doing his best to make his taller friend look him in the eye. "Charlie? Look at me. *You've got to look at me!*"

Sam's calm, steady voice did not help. It made no sense. None of it made any sense. He tried to wrestle free from his friend's grip to turn back toward the room where they had just come. Perhaps if he crawled back into bed, he could find another dream. A different one from this nightmare. Why did they all end in nightmares?

"There's nothing for you there."

Something in those words penetrated the wall of disbelief, shock, and fear. He finally saw it; the seriousness in his best friend's doe-brown eyes, penetrating to his very soul.

"I knew it was gonna be hard," Sam said, flatly, his gaze hard as flint. "It was hard for me. I knew it would be hard for you, so I waited. You have to understand. It's over, Charlie. Our lives. We're...done."

"I can take you to where there is no more pain. Your fighting days are done. It's over."

The preacher man. He had said that before. Was he trying to tell him? Prepare him? All of the people of his life flooded before him. The arguments. The regrets. He had to get back to them. This couldn't be it. What about... marriage? A career? Children? A father. Something inside him ached. He had always wanted to be a father.

Things he was going to fix later but never got around to. He was going to do it later. All of it. All of the intangibles swirled together, threatening to overwhelm him. It, eventually, dissolved itself in a tidal wave of grief. In a flood of tears he had no control over. He choked, stumbling backward to find support against the hallway wall; his hand rising to cover his eyes. To hide the emotion. Sam's expression eased, melting into one of sympathy and understanding. No judgment. No condemnation. No discomfort. After all, he had been there in that emotional space not long before him.

"The war is over for us," Sam said, closing the emotional and physical gap between them. "It's time for you to lead us out of it."

Danforth blinked at the man before him. " 'Us'?"

He took the captain by the elbow and led him down the stairs toward the front double doors of the house.

Callhoun's lopsided grin returned for a fleeting moment. "Leave the letter to Batterson. You know he writes a far sight *prettier* than both of us. Why they put him in charge of reports."

Sam continued to drag him along by the elbow, as Danforth continued to fight a flurry of emotion as his friend pushed the doors open. It took a while for his eyes to adjust. It felt as if he was emerging from a darkness he hadn't realized he had been residing in. The day was bright, but not so bright that he couldn't make out the figures in the dusty street.

And it was suddenly obvious who 'us' was.

"Hey, Captain!" Curtis Alderson hailed from the street. He hadn't seen Curtis since college. His forage cap and four-button blue sack coat had a layer of dust, but his smile was still bright.

" 'Bout time you got here, Captain!"

Danforth spun to his right, in surprise. Kevin Kettleman. He and his family had attended church together in their younger years. Sam, Kevin, and he managed to find a lot of mischief at the church socials. And here he was, like so many others, dressed in familiar blue wool.

A chorus of voices seemed to erupt from all around him. Familiar faces, childhood memories. All wearing Union blue, and all having one thing in common—being the subject of sad correspondence from back home. They were all…

" 'Dead'," Sam said, with his usual carefree grin, finishing his thought by tugging his army-issued kepi firmly over his own brow. "You can say it."

His best friend's demeanor shifted as he snapped a powerful salute, the fingers of his open palm touching the brim of his cap. "Orders, sir?"

Danforth took in the sea of expectant faces, trying to hide his uncertainty. *Orders, sir?* Lead them? Lead them where? He had just *died.* How was he to know where to go?

A few yards down from the collection of soldiers stood a lone figure. From the steps of the house, he could still make out the figure in the familiar floppy hat, and from beneath the brim, the familiar flash of glass in the wire-rimmed spectacles. Still in his tweed coat and gray trousers, and carrying his book, he seemed to be waiting, silently, expectantly. The same man that had been trying to tell him something all along.

The clarity of the moment faded as two individuals surged through the sea of calm souls before him. A fair-haired, lanky Union private stormed up before him, snapping to an overcorrected stiff attention that only came from those new to the service.

"Ca…Captain Danforth, sir!" a voice interjected. "I di…di-di-di..did..didn't know you waa…wwa...were up an' about! We…woowoo…would have ca-ca…ca…come to mmm…mm…mm-meet you…"

"Stand down, Private Hampden," Callhoun said, curtly, his demeanor showing more than a little impatience with the youth.

With a rushed enthusiasm, Corporal Hampden Number 2 met up alongside his brother and offered an excited salute. He was lanky, like his brother, but taller, a shock of wavy blonde hair peeking out from underneath his leather-trimmed forage cap.

"Capn', it's great to see you up and about, sir!" he grinned. "We've been waiting for you. We didn't want you taking off without us."

Danforth's brow furled. " 'Taking off'? Well, fall in, Corporal."

He didn't expect Sam to catch his arm. Puzzled, he watched his friend shake his head in a subtle, covert motion, as if for the young gunner not to see it. It clarified nothing, leaving the captain more confused. If the corporal could see him, then it was obvious that other members of the battery had expired, as well. Why couldn't they be invited to come along?

"We need to get back to the regiment," Corporal Hampden Number 2 said, enthusiastically. "They'll be waiting for us."

Sam looked uncomfortable. "Corporal, we've discussed this. There is no going back—"

It was Corporal Hampden Number 2's turn to look agitated. "No. No, I'm sure you've just forgotten. We need to get back to the regiment. We don't want them to think we're shirking."

Danforth blinked, incredulously. "Sam, don't they know—"

"Yes, they know." Sam sighed, resignedly, his gaze not leaving the unfortunate younger gunner. "They just…won't accept it."

More men in blue began to emerge from the side street, faces Danforth recognized from the battery and the regiment. Men he had served with over the last four months. Disturbingly, unsettlingly, they chose a different side. They chose to form up behind the Hampdens.

"No…that's crazy!" Danforth muttered to his friend, his voice edged with agitated sharpness. "They can't just *ignore it*!"

Sam's lips pursed in frustration. "They've been told, Charlie. It's their choice as to what to do with it."

"What are they going to do? They can't just…*stay* here!"

"They'll come. When they're ready."

"And, until then?"

Sam shook his head, pityingly, flashing the disorganized gathering a sidelong look. "They'll find something. Maybe, wander until they come to terms. They all do, eventually. Time moves differently here. They may even…keep fighting in a war that can't see them anymore. It's easier for them to do that than…"

"What?"

"…than to accept that they're never going home again."

The words stopped Danforth cold. Had the preacher or Sam not intervened, he wondered if he would have been looking at a similar fate. Fighting an endless war. No peace. No family. No home. No world that wanted any part of him.

"No," the captain rejected. "No, that's not an existence. They *have* to come with us."

"Charlie…"

"I'll order them to!"

"It doesn't work like that."

The officer looked his friend sternly in the eye. "You are not suggesting that I leave my men *behind*."

Sam's expression was unflinching. "For the good of the rest, you have to."

Danforth became aware of another presence at his other side. The preacher, his expression one of sympathy and duty. It was almost a mirror of Sam's own.

"It's time," the young preacher said simply.

The conflict tore at his very core. He would have liked to have thought it was his heart, but if all that was said today was true, he didn't have one anymore. All he could do was lead. It was up to them to choose, whether or not, to follow.

"Fall in!" he bellowed, his voice cracking, just a little.

Hampden Number 2, stepped in front of them, clearly agitated. "Surely, you are not going to follow *him*?!"

"Why not?" Danforth rebuked, sharply.

"He doesn't know where to go. He's…he's…"

"What?"

"He's crazy, that's what! He thinks we're supposed to follow him. We don't even know who he is." He pulled his commanding officer's arm toward him to whisper, conspiringly. "He could be the enemy."

The captain shrugged off the boy's hold, taking up position next to the men that had already organized into the familiar lines of four.

"He thinks we're…we're…"

It was Danforth's turn to step into Hampden's path, drilling the boy with a stern gaze. "What, Corporal? He thinks we're—*what*?! Say it."

Hampden Number 2's jaw set, stubbornly. "No."

"Say it!"

The corporal's blue eyes were brimming with tears of rage that he finally loosed in one word.

"NO!"

The captain did not flinch. His eyes rose to look over the corporal and the dozen or so men still standing with him. He looked for any doubt. Any confusion. But it was clear from their stern expressions who they continued to support.

The young corporal was practically shaking with rage. "You don't understand. I'm gonna finish this, and .go home to my family. They're gonna give me a hero's welcome. And, maybe then—my father—might actually see me. Treat me like a man. I'm *not* going to give up all that based on what a…a crazy preacher says!"

Danforth didn't turn around as he addressed the assembly. "Company—*march!*"

"We can't just…walk away from the regiment!" the boy countered bitterly. "We have orders!"

The captain ignored him, his jaw set as he turned away and fell into formation alongside the faithful. To leave those that were in his care, his responsibility…it tore at his very soul to do it.

For the good of the rest.

The unit moved on, leaving the remainder of the men in turmoil, but none more than Hampden Number 2. He ran after them with a few halting steps, dust kicking up in a cloud around him.

"Traitor!" the young boy declared, tears of anger streaming down his dirty face. "You…spineless traitor!"

1

917 LaVeta Drive, Aurora, Illinois. Current Day.

Catheryn Greye stared out the window of the attic, the September rain running down the rippled, antiquated glass like quicksilver. The dim light of the dreary fall day cast phantom tears down the high cheekbones of her pale face, her aventurine-colored eyes gazing out at the suburban street, the mature elm trees lining each side in perfect spacing. It reminded her of the picturesque backdrops of the old black and white family serials she used to watch after school. Memories of afternoons, just like this one, where her grandfather taught her chess. How old was she? Eight?

It was a complex game for a child, and it wasn't unusual that she would get grumpy and pout when her grandfather would claim one of her pieces from the board. There were several times she just wanted to give up, and her temper would switch to hot. But her grandfather remained neutral in his expression, even when she accused him of cheating. If it wasn't some trick, then how does someone get good at a game like this, she would declare.

"You play the game over and over," he would say with quiet solemnity, winking as if he was sharing some great secret. "You stay steady, when your opponent is losing their nerve. You stay grounded, calm. And, then, after a while, you can get so good that you can make your opponent move into traps all on their own."

"But how?" she asked.

"By putting obstacles in their path and forcing them to react. Or…" His wizened fingers picked up his bishop, and with practiced fingers, collected her knight, placing the bishop in its place in one smooth move. "Make them move with a false offering."

"How do you keep from making a bad move?" she asked.

"There's no such thing. Regardless to how you feel, you are never given more than you can handle. No matter if the experience is good or bad—there's a valuable lesson there. Life is like that. But you always have a choice; you can become a victim to it, or learn from it."

He picked up his queen and placed it before her king with a note of finality. Checkmate.

"Always learn from it."

It was exactly those kinds of conversations that always brought her back for more sessions. Even after she learned that her grandfather had passed away years before she was born.

It didn't bother her. Those conversations seemed like a tutorial. And not just restricted to chess. Lessons that came to serve her years later. She just assumed that everyone had visitors like that. Didn't they?

As she got older, new people came to visit her. They taught her new things, but strangely, after her grandfather, she never saw those that had crossed to the other side, again. With the exception of her guides, all of the other Dead she experienced seem lost in their own torment— needing to find the doorway to the other side. Some of them were quite frightening and threatening, but the guides were more than happy to help her guide those lost souls, no matter how complex their issues were. Somehow, it had never quite occurred to her to ask what had changed between the time she had talked to her grandfather, to now; why that situation had changed. She figured it was like he had always told her.

She was never given more than she could handle.

She felt a vibration in her pocket, her broken focus causing the memory to evaporate before her eyes. The image of the foggy window

pane materialized before her, as she blindly foraged in the pocket of her

green tweed jacket for her smartphone.

She tipped the device's microphone up to her mouth, resting her

waifish figure against the wall next to the window. "Yeah?"

"Hey," a male tenor voice responded to her through the speaker.

"How…it…over there?"

She frowned at the broken connection, slapping the side of the

device, hard, with her palm. It never improved anything, but she felt

better. She hated blasted electronics.

She tipped the mic-end of the phone back up to her lips. "I'm sorry.

Say again?"

"Anything…yet?"

Dr. David Faustus was her professional partner of over fourteen

years. It first started out as an arrangement of him overseeing her clinical

hours at his Chicago therapy office while she was completing her clinical

psychology doctorate. She had been nervous about working with him.

Clinical psychology was, very much, a 'by-the-book' methodology with

very little room for things outside the known world. The DSM 5—

otherwise known as "The Book"— was very much the basis for client fact-finding, compiled by professionals from hundreds of thousands of clinical hours and observation. She had to study "The Book" harder than most other students since the majority of insights she received had nothing to do with it. But she had to make it look good. Had to have answers, at the ready, just in case any of her professors asked where she had mined such data. Extrasensory perception had no place in their profession, although hundreds of thousands used their "gut" instincts inside their consulting rooms every day. When they first met, she wondered how long it would take Faustus to realize "The Book" had little use in her sessions, but as it was, fate had placed her in the right office. She was pleasantly surprised that Dr. Faustus had a keen interest in human consciousness studies, and as time went on, she felt safe in sharing her life-long psychic-related experiences with him. Instead of setting her through the paces of classic psychoanalysis, and writing her off, he put her through a series of field tests to discern her level of ability. There were times that she felt as if he treated her more like a lab rat than a co-worker, but over time, she was able to work past the irritant. It wasn't long after that he asked her to start attending *private* consultations outside the office, involving those having apparitional and haunting-type experiences. They were a fine and balanced pair; he brought the psychoanalytic grounding needed to observe, whereas she would be able to add her own particular insights to the situation. Although the day job could become tedious at times, *this* work was never dull.

Well, almost never.

Catheryn gave an exhausted sigh into the handheld device. "Nothing yet. If I don't make any contact with anything in the next hour, I'll just give you my notes and call it a day."

"Well…'nothing' is not always a waste of time…May be an answer…of itself."

"Sure," she said, trying to mask the disappointment from her voice. "I'll call you later."

She closed down the phone and stuck the infernal machine back into her pocket.

"You're not my mommy."

The little girl's voice came from directly behind her, snapping Catheryn's attention back to her physical surroundings. She felt the familiar tingle at the back of her head; the familiar static charge that raced up her scalp. No, it wasn't subsiding. Whatever the presence was, it was right behind her.

She closed her eyes, taking back a measured breath stolen from the sudden surprise. Grounded, the young doctor opened her eyes and turned slowly. Her brilliant aventurine green eyes dropped down to the face of a child, not much older than five. The freckled-face cherub gazed up at her with voluminous brown eyes. The child's dark hair was done up in classic ringlets, pulled back and secured with a large white bow. Her puffy, short-sleeve pink cotton dress was spattered with tiny print flowers, falling just below the knee; an adorable ensemble of a day gone by.

The young clinician smiled warmly, casually flipping her long auburn hair over one shoulder. "No, I'm not. Is she home?"

The child looked crestfallen. "No, I haven't seen her in a while. I thought you might be her. She was supposed to go to the store and get food for—"

"Dinner! Dinner for four people!"

Catheryn spun about to see a dark-haired woman in a small pillbox hat and camel-colored swing coat. A new arrival, an older woman, looked up at Catheryn with dark, intense eyes that suggested Catheryn should have understood her full meaning. But Catheryn was still struggling with the little girl. The doctor cast a look behind her.

But…where did the child go? She was just right…

"The very least that Frank could have done was call ahead to tell me!" the middle-aged woman said, curtly, tugging off the white polyester gloves from beneath the coat sleeves. "What if I hadn't had time to get all of that extra food? Why, he could have at least —"

"—had the decency to call and tell me he didn't wanna go out any more."

Catheryn spun about again, backing away from the third voice. This was getting too much. It had been so quiet all afternoon. The woman that stood before the medium now, had dark hair cut in a bob. This girl looked to be in her late teens. She recognized the gray sheath-style dress as something commonly worn in the late 1920s, or early 30s.

The adolescent looked completely heartsick, her doe eyes cast down to the floor. "To lead me on like that. It's not right! It's just—"

"—he shows no respect!"

The lady with the pillbox hat had returned, the teenage girl whisked away to who-knows-where. Catheryn felt dizzy as the middle-aged woman still appeared to be in a state of raving.

"He has no idea all I do around here…"

"I want my mommy!"

"How do I show my face at school?"

Catheryn squeezed her eyes shut, wincing in pain. The little girl was back again, much more disturbed than before. But the other women remained as well, their ongoing conversations bouncing around inside her skull, spinning her into vertigo. The clinician's jaw clenched in agitation.

"Stop!" Catheryn ground out, gripping both sides of her head. "You have to stop this…"

"…all the time it takes to properly prepare a meal?!"

"What do I tell my parents? They had such plans for the two of us!"

"… just because I don't have a job doesn't mean I should be invisible. I have needs!"

"Will they even let us back into the country club after this? All the rumors…"

"Mommy! *Mommy!* MOMMY!"

"Stop!" Catheryn felt her knees buckling. It was too much. "Just…*stop!*"

And then, silence. Sudden, abrupt, welcome silence.

Catheryn opened her eyes with apprehension, her breathing coming down to a more normalized state. Slowly bringing her hands down from her head, she felt her attention being pulled to the left of her.

The room was entirely empty now, except for this small, elderly woman. Her petite, frail form was trembling, huddling in the far corner, dressed in nothing but a simple white flannel nightgown and slippers. Her hair was cropped short in tight silver curls. She seemed so real—so present—that Catheryn doubted she would have given the older lady a second look passing her on the sidewalk. But the medium in her knew she was not from this plane of existence. Not anymore.

The elderly woman's attention was transfixed on the window pane, her confused brown eyes as watery as the rain-streaked glass. She looked so small, fragile and frightened, that Catheryn's heart went out to her. She seemed to startle slightly at the sight of the young medium, before looking up at her, her brown eyes filled with utter helplessness.

"Help…me," the older woman uttered in a tragic whisper. "I don't know where I am…"

Dr. David Faustus' gray eyes watched the middle-aged woman seated across from him with patient expectation. The neon "open" sign from the window of the small shop played unflattering shadows across his high cheekbones in the darkened room. She was a good twenty years his junior; her round face framed with a frizzy pile of curly, over-processed blond hair compared to his salt and pepper waves.

Her youthful hands rested on the tops of his that rested, palms-down, on the satin spread of the parlor table before them, eyes closed. It was strange, the doctor observed. All of the psychic practitioners seemed to have the same table; round, no larger than 20 inches in diameter. He wondered if all of the practitioners ordered from the same psychic merchandise catalog.

"Someone is coming through," she said, her whisper somewhat labored from some unseen effort. "I see…a woman. Gray hair. Short. Has someone…been sick, Mr. Smith?"

"You tell me…"

Her eyes snapped open, lines tightening around her large brown eyes. "I can't help you if you can't validate that we're on the right channel. You're only wasting your time…and mine."

Considering the one-hundred dollar price tag for the half an hour time slot, she was probably more right about him than her. She was being more than aptly compensated for her time. The grant was covering this, but it was money not spent lightly.

"Alright. My apologies. Continue…"

The woman adjusted more securely into her seat, closing her eyes once more.

"She's smiling at you. She's very proud. I'm getting an 'M' name around her. She has a very…motherly feeling about her."

The doctor kept his poker face a bland neutral expression. "Does she have anything to say?"

"She's just…smiling. You've come a long way in your profession. She's been watching. She's here today, because she knew you'd come looking for her." The soulful eyes opened to squint at him. "What profession is that, exactly?"

He squinted back, quizzically. "Is it relevant?"

He didn't need any ethereal abilities to tell her agitation was mounting.

"Let's try…a new direction," she sighed, closing her eyes again. "You are at a crossroads about something…"

It was everything Faustus could do to keep from rolling his eyes and demanding his money back. Instead, he expelled his emotion in a tight-lipped sigh. "You need a better script."

He pulled back his hands and stood up from the table.

The young practitioner mirrored his movements, a touch more abruptly. "I beg your pardon…"

" 'At a crossroads…'" He growled, collecting his discarded gray window-pane wool sport coat from the back of his folding chair. "Who doesn't come to a psychic at a 'crossroads'?"

He slid an arm into his coat, chuckling softly. " 'A woman, smiling'? No validation other than that? Could be…anyone."

The woman looked openly indignant. "Perhaps if you were more accepting of the process—"

"You've asked me more questions than I ever asked you. That's not how this works." He slipped his other arm into the coat. " 'M' name? No doubt you gauged my age and guessed I knew *someone* female with an 'F', 'M' or 'R' name…if male, it would have been a 'G' or 'J'."

"A skeptic," she snorted, her arms crossing defiantly over her chest. "Why you come in here and waste your money is a mystery to me. No proof is ever enough for you, is it?"

"Oh, I've worked with those that are the real thing." He twisted the old brass knob of the small shop door, and paused at the door frame just long enough to flash her a lopsided grin. "Just—not today."

He was about through the doorway when her words stopped him.

"There's a younger woman."

He paused, door knob in mid-turn. He glanced back at the woman through the reflection in the glass shop door, the neon glow of the "open" sign casting an unnatural pink halo about her image. Even with the distortion, he could tell there was no expression of a question in her eyes this time.

"Your greatest weakness. You underestimate her, don't you? She needs you. But you…" The mystic squinted at him as if it added to her insights. "You need her *more*."

Faustus paused. It was enough to make him do that, but he simply turned to throw her another self-assured smirk. "Wrong again. It's not that kind of a relationship."

"Men," she snorted, running a light sweep of her fingers across the vacant table top. "You always think it's only about one thing. She sees the world you cannot see. Not that you can't. You won't. It would reflect differently upon you if you did. You envy her, and you *need* her, at the same time. It's frustrating for you."

He turned back to the door and pushed it open, brusquely, the brass bell at the top ringing angrily with the movement. But it didn't stop the host from offering one more thing.

"Be aware, Doctor. Lessons come in all forms."

He shoved the door, pushing his slight form through the frame. It was at the point, as the door snapped closed behind him, that he realized.

He hadn't told her his profession.

He rolled the collar of his sport coat up about his neck, but he knew it would do nothing against the chill that rolled up his spine. He sped off into the dampness of the night to leave it behind him.

BRAMDEN HOUSE

2

The creeping rays of the early morning sun painted the dusky attic room with streaks of deep lavender, pink and orange. Captain Charles Danforth felt an odd tingle as the rays brushed across his sun-ravaged face, his dark eyes twitching as they adjusted to the brightness. The twitch was nothing more than one of a series of learned responses from a lifetime before. He, simply, no longer had the eyes to react, but just as reflexively, he ran his fingers through his thick dark hair. Danforth had grown the full mustache in his physical incarnation, almost as soon as he was able to maintain one, and his sideburns kept regulation length just below the ear. Even though it was nothing more than a projection of self-image, he saw to the care of it with the same duty as he saw to his current office.

Totally impervious to the beauty of the valley sunrise, he reached into his blue woolen frock coat for his pocket watch. As he gazed at it, he imagined the coolness of the metal, the subtle vibration of the carefully synchronized, geared mechanism clicking away as it kept time. All sensations against skin that once was. He pinched the release on the gold-filled hunter case and interpreted the Roman numerals on its face.

6:31 A.M. So noted.

The captain was chided, endlessly, for his nostalgia of time. Since his passing from one *world* to the next, the discovery was that time really meant nothing for all here, but for him, it was a tether to the mortal coil that he could not ignore. It wouldn't be long before the residents of this *mortal* plane would awaken and that required a certain diligence in order for him to do his job.

He felt a pull at the corner of his Awareness—his sense of universal knowing. It was gentle, but insistent. Never forceful or demanding. Always loving, patient. Many succumbed to that invitation in their last mortal days, much like he had done. He had dwelled there, for a time; that nameless place where mortals transition when their physical body could no longer hold them. It was beautiful and wondrous for a time, but he soon found himself restless.

For Charlie Danforth, there was no rest. Having worked on the family farm since he was six, he learned early that there was always work to be done. A task to be completed. A battle to be waged. And that nagging doubt in the back of his mind that he had never quite earned his keep. Mortal death, for him, was not a release, but simply, a means to be reporting to a different commanding officer.

In his good fortune, he found others, much like himself, in the next World. And others willing to hand out assignments to those willing to take them. Through it, he found a renewed sense of duty, honor, and purpose. That duty could have taken him anywhere—any time— yet, he chose to return here, to this plane. The return subjected him to similar sensitivities of emotion and ego as did his mortal life, but without the physical obstacles of sleep, food, or ailment. He also had the universal understanding of how things worked interdimensionally, allowing him to travel wherever, and whenever, he wished.

But no matter where he went, there was always the pull. The pull to return to that loving embrace that took him in before. He had always assumed that the reason for it had been to attract those reluctant to leave this work, back to the Source of All-That-Is, but now that he no longer had a physical body, and had completed that journey, he was mystified as to its purpose. It eventually became an event that he brushed aside as a nuisance to be dealt with on this plane. He didn't turn to acknowledge it.

But then, along the same current, he felt…something else.

The 'something else' seemed to come from a new direction. He turned toward the glow of dawn coming through the window, his eyes narrowing perceptively. The individual's consciousness brushed against his being, like the soft stroke of a feather. He could sense it even though the origin of it was miles away from the house. It wasn't cold or predatory, but simply *inquisitive* in its attention. The curious intelligence seemed to flow about the room before returning to him, probing with a curious innocence, not unlike that of a child poking him with a questing finger.

He pressed back with his Awareness to follow the current to its source. Where was it…ah! There. He would know where to find it, again. Each individual consciousness carried an energy much like a unique fingerprint. It didn't feel to be a threat of any kind, but he could tell that it originated from the mortal world. It was coming, and it would be there soon.

A more immediate presence forced him to break the connection. This one was firm and expectant, with a certain rigidity that only came from time in military service. Danforth knew who it was, even before the knock at the door came. All the same, his gaze fell to the face of the watch in his hand.

6:45 A.M.

Right on schedule, as always. He closed the gold hunter case and pocketed the timepiece within his wool frock coat, as he turned to end up nearly nose to nose with the young, fresh face of Corporal Moore. The man had blue eyes, a square jaw and dimpled chin, however, the length of his wavy blonde hair was slightly longer than regulation would, normally, allow. He presented himself, clean-shaven, although none of them needed to practice the ritual any longer. This morning, the corporal kept to his usual gray wool frock coat, his gray wide-brimmed slouch hat with creased crown tucked under one arm, his collar and sleeves trimmed with rank he had never earned in life. He could have given the youthful officer a hard time, but how could he fault the man when he still wore his own colors with the same sense of pride.

"Reporting for day watch, sir," the younger man announced, his open-palmed hand touching his temple in formal salute. "Here to relieve you."

The older man, respectfully, returned the salute. "I consider myself relieved."

"If I may be so allowed, sir; the mistress of the house wants to speak with you. It is…" His young face seemed pinched in struggling to find the appropriate words. "…uncertain what her mood is."

And, so much for a light-hearted day.

"Thank you for the warning," he replied, a tug of a smile working the corner of his mustache as he observed the younger man's newly-improvised sleeve insignia. *"Lieutenant."*

The senior officer abstained from using the door, or the stairs, although it often gave him much pleasure to stir the living occupants of the house with his booted footfalls reverberated down to the main floor. Best to get the unpleasantness over quickly.

Danforth gave no thought to the fine fibers of the ornate rug as he passed through it, or the molecular construct of the subfloor. Over a century of such travels dulled him to the fascination of it. His form passed through it with ease, barely managing his trademark announcement of, "Coming down," before entering the parlor below.

Abigale Bramden did not acknowledge his entrance. She was in her comfortable rocker, facing the window that offered a generous view of the river across the road. He reached out with his energy, sensing the ebb and flow of hers. He felt the usual unflappable sternness, uncompromising sense of duty, and her usual aloofness, with an undercurrent of disappointment in all that was. But today, there existed a touch of melancholy. And her dress; not her regular casual day wear. The lavender satin weave of her hair fall was pinned meticulously to her braided gray hair, and the matching silk-trim day dress was more appropriate for church wear.

It was not Sunday.

She addressed the two-hundred-year-old window pane, her voice benign of emotion. "Harry is ready."

He knew she would not have missed the flash of strong emotion that shot through his being. It was one thing that he still had trouble getting used to in this form. There was no hiding expression behind masks. No putting on airs. Existing in a form of pure energy created an emotional state of *transparency* between all that dwelled within. No secrets.

Damn it.

"You knew this day would come. It's what we work for."

Her robust form rose fluidly from the chair, her face as grim as her words. There was a dark wood cane in her left hand, constructed out of thin air as if an afterthought. Nothing she needed, of course. It was just a comfort to have it there.

She punctuated her words with a hard rap of the cane tip against the hardwood. "This should be a day of celebration."

The captain remembered the night he had met Harry, as if it were yesterday. Considering there was no sense of time here, it very well *could* have been yesterday. Harry had come to the house in the mortal world, when he was but eight years old. He was sick with fever, his mother bringing him to the doctor whose lodgings were upstairs.

The boy's near-death state drew attention. Unpleasant attention. The things they referred to as the *Coldness*, was not so much a temperature but a vibration. It had a predatory logic, and it had been stalking Harry. The captain knew of it all too well. He'd seen the cold, hungry things before; lingering on the lonely battlefields, sometimes near the hospital camps. It seemed to follow death. To feed. Calling upon some of his more advanced universal knowledge acquired from his existence on the other plane, Danforth saw to it that the Coldness stayed outside the residence. Since he could feel within his own Awareness that the doctor could do little for the boy, the captain saw to it that the child's passing was as comfortable as possible.

Upon crossing into his new existence, Harry struggled with the physicality of being apart from his mother and younger sister. The spectral officer helped Harry through the meticulous process of the boy's transition. It had to be handled carefully, patiently, so the boy's own personal grief and fear wouldn't bind his presence to that of his mother. Since Harry had, yet, to make up his mind on where to go next, Harry stayed at Abigale's house.

But the house was far from being barren of energetic life. Abigale fostered many other young souls like Harry. He made friends easily, and enjoyed the book-learning and other lessons that Abigale offered to him and the others. It gave them all a sense of normalcy, so that they would not be thrown into shock. It was the divine gift of Free Will that gave souls a choice on where—and when—to go. Young or old, Bramden House had become a safe haven, until those souls made up their mind.

And now, Harry had made up his.

Abigale moved to the doorway leading toward the dining room. "If you don't wish to take him—"

"I'll do it."

The abruptness from him made her pause, and she turned to look at him. In that instance he witnessed a rarity of emotions cross her face. What was it? Empathy? Sympathy, perhaps? It was always hard to tell the difference. It was gone as quick as it had appeared.

She turned to continue on into the hall. "Very well."

Little Harry was seated in the mauve, high-backed chair of the sitting room, swinging his tiny ankle-booted feet beneath him without even touching the floor. Children were not normally permitted in this room, but Abigale had made an exception on this occasion. His ginger hair was combed over, parted on the side. He was also dressed in his Sunday best. His white cotton shirt was starched and pressed; his gray suspenders matching his gray short pants. His mother would be pleased.

"Hi, Uncle Charlie." There almost seemed to be an undercurrent of shame in his voice, his expression cast downward into his lap.

"Hello, boy."

Danforth knelt down to his level, folding his arms casually across bended knee. He tipped Harry's freckled face up by the chin, so the boy's blue gaze would meet his. "You ready to go?"

Harry nodded silently, his eyes falling downward, again. "Mama has been visiting me. She says it's time. My little sister is there now, too."

The larger man tugged the boy's chin up, again. "You're making a big decision that you have every right to make. Some adults have a hard time doin' what you're doin'…even though, they should." He tweaked the freckled nose playfully. "Nothin' to be ashamed of."

"Are you going to come and stay with Mama and me?"

The taller man pretended to take a second to decide. "Not...yet. Who would watch after Allie and little Josie?"

Harry's lower lip quivered. Within a fraction of a second, his little arms were around the neck of the man he called 'uncle'. He lifted the boy effortlessly, giving him an affectionate squeeze.

"You've been a good boy, Harry."

The ginger-haired boy offered a weak smile, tears staining his cheeks as he slid out of the captain's arms to the floor. He took the soldier's hand firmly, with the assuredness that a child does with a trusted adult, and the two strolled into the privacy of the parlor to conduct their business.

Crossing was a private affair.

When the deed was done, the senior officer returned to the sitting room to find Abigale waiting for him.

"His mother was waiting," he reported, stone-faced. "She said to thank you."

After a moment of reflection, Abigale nodded with a note of finality. She rose from her perched position on the edge of her seat and brushed by him on the way to the remainder of her daily duties.

As close to a 'thank you' as he ever would get from her, the captain decided. He would miss little Harry.

His own regret vanished as his senses were alerted to another emotion, triangulating from the room from which he had just come. Bridgette's petite form sat in the corner window sill, dressed in her pretty pastels for the day. Frozen in time at the age of fourteen, she obsessed about her appearance, flouncing about the house in dress more befitting a pending social engagement instead of common day wear. He learned some time ago that the young lady craved attention, and even more recently, his. Even though they both shared the agelessness of the Afterlife, it still was inappropriate. She was still a charge in his care, and no matter how she wished that to change, that sacred trust could not be compromised.

Her wide brown eyes shot up to his gaze, mirroring the panic that her energy exuded. "People! Living people! And they're not the Roberts'."

No, it was not the Roberts'. He had not seen the Roberts' for over four calendar weeks now. This was too long for them to be gone on a casual vacation.

The young girl hopped down from the sill and *blinked* through the parlor room wall. Anyone living who had the capability to witness the Dead may have been astonished at the actions of the young girl disappearing through a wall, but decades of existence together had dulled the officer to Bridgette's flair for the dramatic.

Peering through the window, his gaze darkened as he observed the new arrivals. A slender man with short cropped salt and pepper hair was outside, standing next to a blonde-haired woman. By their body language and easy flow of emotion between them, he guessed them to be husband and wife. They were accompanied by another man. He was somewhat shorter than the husband, with short blond hair and wore a strangely-tailored beige suit. He had an air about him that Danforth didn't care for. Something akin to one of those…snake oil salesmen. And something else. Something else he couldn't quite put his finger on.

Andrew Baldwin was more than ready for this showing. He shifted his hazel-eyed gaze to the driver's side mirror of the agency's minivan. Yes, short blonde hair was perfectly styled with a generous amount of pomade, and nothing was in between his teeth. This had to go well today. Not only was the $12,000 dental bill due for all of his new veneers, but the mortgage payment was coming due on this place.

Normally, he would have this sale in the bag. The clients certainly seemed willing to buy, and their lender-of-choice had them cleared for houses in this ballpark. He had all of his details down pat. He'd certainly showed the house enough times for that. All he needed to do was to get through all of the details before anything…happened.

His pitch this morning was to a middle-aged couple from Leavenworth. They were insistent on an early morning showing since the husband had to get to a business appointment. It was interstate the entire way, but traffic was still hell at certain times of the day. He mentally filed that away as he turned his best Oscar-winning grin on them.

"So, as you can see, you get quite a lot for your money with this place. Three point five acres, to be exact. Hope you've got a riding lawn mower. You're gonna need it!" He started backing toward the front steps, not missing a beat. "The house has quite a bit of history to it. Bramden House was built in 1849 for Elias Bramden. Quite the entrepreneur from upper state New York. Wanting a fresh life for his growing family, but still craving a little adventure, he moved out here with his wife and three daughters; Abigale, Lillian, and Anna. They also had one son, Eugene—who was a little sickly. Breathing problems, if memory serves."

He turned toward the large, double-door entrance of the Federalist-style house. Fishing for the key out of his pocket, he took a deep cleansing breath.

Nothing is gonna go wrong this time. Nothing is gonna go wrong this time. You were Realtor of the Year five years running. You can do this!

His hand was shaking. Good Lord! Thank God his body was blocking the view of his hands from the clients. He used his other hand to steady it, sliding the key into place. He turned the lock and pushed.

The door did not budge. He flashed a bemused smile back to the waiting couple, and tried again, this time, putting his shoulder into it. That's when he became aware of the giggling.

He peered inside the Georgian cross hatching of the door window just in time to see two pairs of little eyes looking up at him. Two children, under the age of five. One was a dark-haired boy and the other a light-haired girl.

Neither of which should be in there.

Not *again*.

He spun around, trying to look casual as he fell back against the door, hoping his laughter didn't sound overly nervous.

"So, what made you consider a house in this area?" he inquired nonchalantly, still trying to fiddle with the jammed lock behind his back.

The petite blonde smiled, adoringly at her husband. "Oh, we've lived in the Kansas City area most our lives, and it's a great place, but the traffic of the morning commute was making my poor Marty here a bear!"

Her husband beamed back at her. "And if I'm going to continue to make use of that terrific 401K and survive to see it, I thought I'd better look at a less stressful solution. So, Beth convinced me that working from home, in the country, was the way to go."

His wife's giggle and intimate snuggle into her husband's side turned Baldwin's already nervous stomach, but he pushed through it, like a pro. Besides, faking it until he made it was how he achieved the United States Regional Realtor of the Year, two years running.

But nothing was going to allow him to fake his way through a jammed lock.

"Completely forgot! Bolted it from the inside last night. Sturdy dead bolt is a good thing, right?" Baldwin flashed his most disarming smile. "Let's go through the side door, shall we? It will give me an opportunity to show off one of the best features of the house—the kitchen!"

"You don't have a key for the dead bolt? Isn't the front door working?" the husband asked, somewhat concerned. He tried the brass handle for himself.

Baldwin took the man's elbow in a firm grip, steering him away. "Oh, best locks in the industry. Told you you'd be safe in here. Right this way!"

After a few moments of gushing over granite countertops and aged Midwestern oak, he moved the couple out into the front entryway. With an exaggerated twist of the dead bolt, he unlocked the front door and opened it with a dramatic flourish.

"Good brass fixtures with carbon steel bolting action. You can feel safe in here," Baldwin said with a subtle laugh. "Even from...me!"

The wife was already taking in the mahogany railings of the grand staircase but seemed distracted by the pocket doors leading into a side room.

The woman stepped toward them. "What's in here?"

"Oh, this would be the very spacious side parlor. Mrs. Bramden would entertain the ladies here. Mr. Bramden would conduct business in the library, oftentimes, with people of political influence from St. Louis, Galena, Dubuque, Keokuk..." the realtor continued on, sliding the pocket doors open with a dramatic movement.

And finding himself nose-to-brass buttons with a tall figure on the opposite side. The gilded ornaments were set against a wall of dark blue wool. His brown eyes followed the buttons up to a dark, formidable mustache and a pair of deep-set eyes beneath thick, surly eyebrows. Behind it all was an expression that was absolutely frightening.

"*Ohmigod*," he breathed under his breath, staggering back at the sudden sight of the dark, imposing figure glaring down at him.

The master salesman quickly asserted himself between his guests and the doors, quickly snapping them closed behind his back, much to the surprise of the clients standing before him.

"What's wrong?" the wife inquired, moving forward in an attempt to inspect the brass handle fittings. "Is there something wrong with these, too?"

Baldwin darted before her, back against the doors. He was still racing for a logical explanation of how a man in a blue uniform had come to be standing in the doorway of the parlor, when it slowly dawned on him that, as imposing as the figure was, Baldwin appeared to be the only one reacting to him. He searched the faces of his clients for any sign of abject terror, but there was only blissful ignorance, with an edge of suspicion that their realtor might be trying to hide something from them.

Baldwin only prayed that the sudden fright hadn't drained *all* of the blood from his face as he plastered on his best $12,000 grin. "See, work just fine. I just forgot that they were…refinishing part of the floors in here. Didn't want anyone to trip! Shall we go into the dining room?"

No sooner had the words gotten out of his mouth than the doors behind him started to shudder violently. Fortunately, the couple had already turned away in anticipation of the next part of the tour, missing the commotion of someone trying to open the parlor doors. From the inside.

Baldwin squeezed his eyes shut, perspiration starting to form on his cleanly-shaven upper lip, the muscles in his fingers straining with fatigue as he fought desperately to hold the doors shut. His fingers finally found purchase on the latch that locked the doors closed. The vibrating doors abruptly stopped. The realtor let out a long sigh of relief as he stepped away from the door, nursing the blood back into his overworked fingers.

Just as a silver saber blade sliced through the seam in the pocket door just inches from his side.

Nothing could stop the shriek that escaped his lips this time. He threw open the front doors and flew down the steps before the clients could even turn to see what the clamor was about. The only sign of their agent was the commercially-reproduced smiling visage sailing by them on the side of the company minivan as it took off at full speed down the driveway.

3

Dr. David Faustus leaned back in the oak-carved booth of the coffee shop, savoring his freshly-made Ethiopian blend. He closed his gray eyes as the rich taste rolled over his tongue. Oh, how he needed that. He didn't bother with a shave of his salt and pepper stubble before leaving the apartment. He barely took the time to run a comb through his thick wavy hair before getting to the coffee shop. Three late nights in a row were taking its toll. He was only forty-five, but he felt eighty.

The sound of the heavy folder dropping on the table in front of him startled him to the point that his precious nectar almost went flying. Instead, only a few drops fell on his dark pants, which he brushed away quickly. He almost let out a curse until he looked up to see his partner's triumphant grin.

Catheryn slid into the booth across from him, flashing him a wry smile. "You need a haircut. You're beginning to look like some of your college students."

Seeing that he wasn't about to get an apology, the psychologist picked up the report before him.

He flipped to the back for the conclusion, and his thick dark eyebrows arched upward in mild surprise. "Dementia."

"I didn't think I was going to get anyone to talk, but they finally did. I actually did some research, and I only found one historical inhabitant that matches. Cecelia Banks."

Without permission, she opened the folder in his hands. With another smooth movement, she snatched up the coffee in front of him and took a draw from the cup.

She winced. "How do you drink that stuff? I think you could clean an engine with this."

"Those are finely-crafted African beans." He could tell by the look on her face that it failed to impress her. He conceded for the short version. "Medicinal value."

"Cecelia grew up in the house. Her father died when she was six, leaving her alone with her mother," she explained.

Catheryn looked down at the table, her body language changing noticeably.

"I…think I'm going to need some help with this one."

His eyebrows, and his gaze, shot up with surprise. "Why?"

"Her personality. It's too…fractured," Catheryn frowned, waving for one of the wait staff to come over. "She keeps going from her childhood, to teenager, to middle age… I can't talk to her quickly enough before she jumps to the next persona. I don't know how I'm going to get her to cross over."

He stroked his chin, thoughtfully. "Can you arrange for an…intervention? A relative that's still living?"

"She has one grandchild. Portland, Maine," she said. "But how do you get someone convinced to come all that way from Maine for something like this? Mrs. Banks may not even have been lucid enough to remember *having* a granddaughter."

"Well…" He ran his fingers through his thick wavy hair and scratched the back of his scalp as if to bring some idea to the surface. "We might have to put this one on the back burner for a little while. We have another client."

The psychologist reached into his leather satchel next to him and pulled out another file for her. She took the manila folder from him and opened it.

"A *paying* client this time," he clarified.

Her eyes looked up at him over the file, her face darkening. "Just because they're paying doesn't mean *this* one—"

He flourished a hand in an artful gesture to cut her off. "I realize this one's important, too, but…"

She sighed into the folder, her eyes dropping. "…we need the money."

Of course, as if the bad news about their failure to capture the parapsychology grant wasn't bad enough, they were raising the rent on their office suite. The parapsychology work, albeit fun, was going to have to kick in its fair share of the rent if they were going to keep their psychology practice in the prestigious Therapist's Row.

"And he's offering to pay us. Well."

"And what is he expecting for his money?" she mused, her eyes drinking in the information of the dossier before her freckled nose wrinkled, distastefully. "I know this guy. Isn't he that slimy real estate guy I keep seeing on TV? Buying 'distressed houses'?"

"*Select* distressed houses." David corrected. "High-end historical distressed houses. Apparently, this one turned out to be more *distressed* than most."

It was her turn for her eyebrows to go up. "This one is out in the middle of...nowhere."

"Anything particularly...special about the activity there; battlefields...burial grounds?"

She brought up the map in her mind, her brow furrowing. "That area is so rural...I can't think of anything right now."

He leaned back in his seat, fingers coming to form a tent against his chest. "Comes with airline tickets. We fly out of O'Hare at 8 A.M."

She fell back into the booth with a groan.

Great. And likely a puddle jumper to boot. She was suddenly very grateful for the coffee the barista slid in front of her. That meant the TSA would require them to be at O'Hare by...ugh. She was not, nor had she ever been, a morning person. And certainly not where the TSA was concerned.

"This better pay *extremely* well," she mused, cradling the coffee cup in her hands, praying to the coffee gods that the Zen of the drinking experience would improve her mood. "And they'd better have a coffee shop nearby."

Catheryn wrapped anxious fingers around her mug of chamomile tea as she took in the artificial shadows cast by the garish lights of the street below the oversized picture window of her apartment. She had pulled up her auburn hair on top of her head hours ago in preparation for bed, but it was way past midnight. She could not sleep.

The picture window was her favorite feature about the place; her 'window on the world' where she could observe it in safety. She'd owned the 1,400-square foot apartment for years now. She had fairly good security in the building, and her neighbors were nice, so she was rarely concerned about the living occupants. The Dead were the original concern. It took her over a year to get the energetic formula just right to keep out the constant churn of generations of birth, life and death that had consumed the land beneath her in this area of Chicago. It was a recipe that took time to develop, which was why when she settled in a spot, she stayed put for a while.

She had also chosen the location of the apartment for its conveniences; minutes from the market and less than a block to the 'L' train to whisk her off anywhere she desired. The symphony hall was 2.3 blocks away. And yet, she never went. The food and grocery delivery service was a mere message away, and there wasn't any entertainment she couldn't 'order in' on the convenient streaming service.

People, in general, bothered her. Well, except for the chosen few that were almost as close as family. People posed a problem. They had thoughts and feelings. Oftentimes, those they wished to remain hidden screamed out at her the loudest in that all-too-unique way she had to pick information out of the air. She found honesty in short supply. Integrity, even more so. And God help her if the random stranger caught onto who—and what—she was. The anxiety that exuded from those people only fed her own. As if she didn't have anxiety in ample supply already.

But tonight...

A chill ran up her spine. Perhaps her body was registering the temperature difference between the room and her recently ingested chamomile tea. Maybe the bone-numbing chill of the autumn rain was finally wearing off. Maybe it was time to re-caulk the windows against drafts. No. She knew it was none of those things; just her over-rationalization used to shield herself against fear.

And then, the 'chill' brushed against her.

She jumped, the cup of chamomile falling from her grip and breaking into shards on the hardwood floor. There was no mistaking the intrusion against the nape of her neck. Such an intimate intrusion of space.

"Who are you?"

The voice was deep in its timber. She froze, her eyes darting around the room. The voice was distinctly, male, but she could see no one. She paused, reaching out with her senses, wondering if this was what a blind person felt like when cornered.

"Who are you?!!"

The voice was a demanding growl, right at her ear. Every hair on the back of her neck was already standing at attention, but the proximity of the presence pushed her anxiety to the maximum. She yelped, jumping instinctually away from the sound. Her back found purchase against the bedroom wall. She cursed herself, immediately, for doing so. No. She needed to stand her ground.

"You don't belong here!" she said, firmly; a slight quaver of insecurity in her voice. "Get out of my space!"

A hurricane of the voice swirled about her, assaulting her ears, probing her personal defenses. She wrapped her arms around her head, trying to shield herself from it.

"Who are you?!"

"What do you want?!"

"Why are you coming here?!"

"Leave us alone!"

"Stay away!"

She flung her arms down to her sides, her hands balled up into fists, digging deep down for as much assertiveness as she could muster.

"GET OUT!!"

With that, the assailing voices came to an abrupt stop.

With the sudden silence, another sound became more apparent. A rapping. An all-to-familiar rapping. Knocking, as if at a distant door. No, she was not going to answer. The insistence of that knocking was almost as frightening as the whirlwind of voices around her. It was at that point she knew. Knew all of this was just a...

The thunderclap sent her bolting upright in her bed. A dream. It was all just a dream.

Lightning painted the room in garish shadows, not setting her any more at ease. She wasn't going to be able to just go back to sleep. With the lightning and the thunder happening, she knew what would be happening next. She knew she would have discarnate 'guests'— disembodied visitors waiting out the energetic chaos of the storm until it passed. They no longer had the insulating layer of flesh to protect them from the disruptive, charged environment outside. It usually started with slight whispering coming from the darkness, like a poorly planned surprise party. Most were courteous enough to keep out of the way, grateful for the shelter, but there would be the occasional two or three that would be drawn to her, like moths to a flame; excited, to finally, have someone to converse with. It made her wonder if every structure in the city was like her place; full of unseen guests. She just had the unique personal mechanism to be aware of it.

Knowing it would do no good to lay in the bed, she swung her legs over the side, her feet feeling around for the slippers she kept there. Easing into them, she ventured across the hardwood floor and into the bathroom.

The vanity light was on, as it always was at night. It cast just enough light into the bedroom to give her a sense of comfort. She couldn't recall a time when she didn't have a light on when she slept. It always seemed to alert her when the shadows came to play. She hated absolute darkness. Absence of light allowed them to get too close with little to no warning. How often parents would tell their children there was nothing in the darkness that wasn't there in the daytime. They were right.

But at least in the daylight, she could see it coming.

The unflattering light of the harsh vanity LED only accented the haggard look around her eyes. She ignored it, flipping open the mirrored door. Among all the normal toiletries—razors, eye drops, band aids—sat an amber plastic bottle. Something David had recommended to her for anxiety. She had the prescription renewed every 30 days, even though she never used it. She just wanted it there, just in case. On nights such as this, it called to her, in quiet whispers, goading her, urging her. But no. Everything was under control. As much control that could be mustered under such conditions anyway. Besides, it messed with her…other sight. Part of her wondered if it would bring relief or simply create a different anxiety driven by what she could no longer see. Closing her eyes, she exhaled sharply and closed the cabinet door.

"You don't need me to tell you that you don't need that."

The soft tenor male voice floating to her from over her shoulder made her start violently, her hand falling to her chest.

"Ralph," she said, breathlessly. "You scared me!"

The spirit guide smiled serenely through the reflection of the mirror, the effect reaching his magnificent blue-green eyes. He was casually perched on the edge of the bathtub with a foot planted on either side of the fiberglass wall. His outfit of choice was a pair of taupe linen trousers and white collar shirt. The faint, but harsh, light of the vanity made a soft halo of the collar-length, light brown hair framing his pale face and drawing attention to his high cheekbones. Despite his feminine attributes and soft tones, she had learned through their lifelong association to never mistake that for weakness. She had seen the power that lay behind that calm visage, and she trusted him with her life.

"Sorry," he said, a touch of the mischievous in his grin, making her wonder if his sudden appearance wasn't intended to make her jump. "You seemed anxious, so I came."

She turned to take in the newly-arrived company in her apartment, her hands resting back upon the white sink behind her. "I hate lightning storms."

"So do they."

She didn't have to ask who *they* were. She didn't have to go looking to know they were there. She could feel them.

"Things will quiet down when the storm passes," the enlightened being mused. "May I ask a question?"

Catheryn looked up at her spiritual mentor, a touch surprised that he would even bother to ask permission. "Of course."

"In your dreams. Why do you never answer the door?"

It didn't surprise her in the least that he was aware of the content of her dreams. They spoke of them often enough. She shifted her stance to allow her back to rest against the wash basin. Folding her arms across her stomach, she studied the grout of the tiny tiles at her slippered feet.

She blinked, thoughtfully. "I guess…I guess I'm afraid of what might be there."

The knocking had been a feature in her dream as long as Catheryn could remember. She couldn't quite explain it, but the thought of turning the knob of that door seemed to fill her with anticipation, as well as dread. Wasn't her life complicated enough without letting in more…complications?

"Do you know?" she asked, her arms forming more tightly about her, as if it would protect her from the answer. "What it is, I mean?"

Ralph merely smiled his serene, compassionate smile. "That's for you to find, in time."

She shifted her weight, uncomfortable, casting a look out into the room as it illuminated with another lightening flash.

"Could you…could you stay with me until the storm passes?"

"You know I will."

Using the vanity light to assist her, she shuffled back to her bed. Sliding in between the covers, she rolled onto her side, keenly aware of her guide's calming presence behind her. With the renewed sense of security, she drifted back into a more peaceful night's slumber.

4

Catheryn awoke to the flipped-stomach feeling caused by the car's sudden descent into the river valley. After processing where she was, she rolled her head to look out the back seat window. David had been kind enough to allow her to sleep off her short night in the back seat, rolled up in the coziness of a gray fleece throw. The pillow was wedged at an angle somewhere between the top of the back seat and the side door frame, offering her a comfortable view.

The roadway to one side was lined with the rough-hewn limestone of the bluffs, its sun-bleached pale surface interrupted frequently with rolling streaks of rust-colored oxidation. Through the opposite window was a sight that nearly took her breath away. The ground sloped down away from the road but was thick with woods. The trees were on fire with deep red, orange and gold leaves of fall. As they descended further into the valley she could spy the meandering waters of the Des Moines

River below. She had taken some time before coming down to study the origins of the area and could easily picture Native Americans blazing the hunting trails along its banks and fishing from its waters. And then, of course, was the magnificent bridge.

Built in the familiar steel-through truss bridge-style, with its cross-steel side pattern and horizontal girder cap, it started its life as a bridge for pedestrians only. Fitted with wood planks, it allowed for foot traffic to and from the local village across the way. Now, more of a tourist draw than anything, it was a beautiful feature to augment the scenery of the river valley. Its rusty red beams blended perfectly with the fall pattern of the trees around it. Definitely, picture worthy. Maybe later.

The car turned, lurching off the highway onto the unkempt gravel road of the town. The termination of the asphalt seemed to be the end of the modern world and a step back into time. Dodging a plentiful number of potholes washed out by the late season rains, the car rounded the bend before coming to a complete stop.

"We're here," David announced, snapping open the driver's side door.

She popped her door open and immediately regretted opening her eyes. She squinted into the late morning sun, pausing in the middle of the street to take in the rolling rapids of the broad expanse of river.

Amazingly, there was no levee. The town was literally one with the river

with nothing standing between the winding water and itself. The

entrance to the pedestrian bridge was right there, almost as if the bridge

was put there to lead right up to the house they had been called to

explore. She turned the opposite direction to examine the structure

before her. Where in God's name were her sunglasses?

Finding her feet, she raised a hand above her eyes until they could

adjust. "Wow...that's...old."

He took up a likewise pose next to her, using his hand to shield his

eyes from the late morning sun. "It's on the National Registry,

so...yeah. Eighteen hundred and...something."

It was the largest building in the little town; its red brick rising to an

impressive three stories with a solitary black-shuttered window at the

peak of the gabled roof. Her eyes were, strangely, drawn there. There

was something...*someone* watching. She could feel it.

The cold shudder of it helped shake off the haziness of her sleep,

but it did not stop her from nearly tumbling into the water-filled pot

hole in front of her.

"Looks like they haven't done anything with the roads since then either…" she murmured, side-stepping the hazard.

"I think GPS forgot about it, too. It had a hard time finding the place," he muttered, hiking the shoulder strap of a bag onto each shoulder.

She frowned, heading up to the house's double doors. She ran an inquisitive finger down the chalky white door frame before turning outward toward the river view. There it was. That pull again. That pull of someone's attention on them. She gazed up from underneath the window, straining her inner Awareness to probe the space above.

And nearly fell back into the door that suddenly opened behind her. Catching herself in the door frame, she spun about.

"Catheryn?" Without warning, someone caught her in a tight embrace. "Catheryn, it *is* you!"

Her jaw dropped, even as the man's hug tightened. "Peter?!" Even after he released her, it took her a moment to recover from the shock. "What are you doing here?"

"I was invited," the younger man answered, pushing his astute-looking horn-rimmed glasses more securely on the ridge of his nose. He rested a hand against the door frame with an awkward sense of forced casualness. "Same as you, apparently."

His body language read volumes. He was trying to exhibit confidence with his open body display, but the foundation of it wasn't secure. They were not expected, and their arrival gave him a sense of unease, creating a need to assert dominance, even if it was unconscious. Competition. His body language, literally, screamed it out loud in the way he was blocking the doorway. Some things never changed.

Catheryn shook her head to clear it. "Peter, this is Dr. David Faustus. David, this is Peter Elgin from the…Society of the Paranormal Institute Team."

David had only a moment to drop the travel bags to the floor before the light-haired man stole possession of the doctor's hand, pumping it eagerly. "A pleasure. I thought I saw something on Catheryn's social media that she was going, you know…legit. I knew Catheryn from the good ole' days."

The older doctor's eyebrow went up, inquisitively. " 'Legit'?"

"You know…making a serious study of it. We're still in the experiential stage ourselves," the younger man clarified, jerking a head indicating deeper into the house. He stepped aside, ushering the pair in with a dramatic flourish of the hand. "Come on in, *Doctor* Greye."

David paused just ahead of Catheryn, throwing a casual look back at her. "SPIT? Their name is SPIT?"

She frowned. "I wasn't there the day they voted on it."

"Dr. Faustus! Dr. Greye!"

The two turned in the direction of the voice in time to see a shorter, middle-aged man with short cropped blonde hair. It had been displaced by too much pomade in an attempt to look stylish. He charged across the hardwood floor of the entryway with a gait of excitement, no doubt a practiced attempt to make up for his small stature. He flashed the artificially-whitened smile of someone that had spent too many hours in a dental chair. Immediately, Catheryn didn't trust that smile.

"Andrew Baldwin. I'm the realtor," he greeted, not asking for permission as he grabbed each of their hands, pumping them, vigorously. "The architect of all this, you might say."

Before either could blink, a business card was forced into both of their palms. Catheryn fought down the impulse to go wash her hands. He had years of practiced insincere sincerity. Perhaps, that explained her unease.

"I'm so glad you could both make it," the host beamed.

Catheryn gazed around the room at the generous amounts of electrical wiring tacked up along the plaster moldings of the ceiling, oak baseboards along the floor, and writhing around the beautiful railing of the main staircase that led up to the second floor. The entry way looked as if the old house was being devoured in the tentacles of some vinyl-coated monster.

Before she could mourn what was happening to the fine craftsmanship of the building, she stumbled over a taped bundle of wires that got under foot. This was not the day for heels.

Catheryn caught herself on a section of white chair railing along the wall. "Are we…going to be wired for sound?"

Andrew's gaze followed hers for a second before the meaning sunk in. "Oh! I hope you don't mind. What's better than one set of ghost hunters than…two?"

"We're not ghost hunters."

It was unclear who said it first—David or Catheryn –but it was clear from their unison that they were both in agreement that the distinction needed to be made. And quickly.

"We're parapsychologists," the elder doctor corrected.

The realtor offered a nervous chuckle. "What's a parapsychologist?"

"We study anomalous human experience, or what we refer to as *psi*. We hope, through that, to help find the origins of human consciousness," Faustus explained. "Where it resides…what it is capable of. People like Catheryn, who can interface with the Dead, is what we call *receptive psi*. She was born with the capability of hearing and seeing in a way most people can't."

The realtor looked a bit perplexed. "And…ghosts? How does that fit in?"

"Studying apparitions and hauntings cover both the potential for spontaneous receptive psi experiences people have with them, as well as examining the potentiality of the *survival* of human consciousness—or, as we call it, *survival psi*."

Catheryn observed the realtor's hazel eyes looked a bit tight around the corners, as if struggling to absorb all that her partner was saying. Of course, she had also seen the same effect on people with too much Botox. With Baldwin, it was difficult to decide which was at play.

"Well, if you came looking for…*anomalous experiences*," their host said, turning to motion them deeper into the house, "there will be plenty to be found here."

David hiked the straps of their bags back onto his shoulders and followed the salesman through the hallway, looking less like an academic and more like a Sherpa. She moved to follow, when she caught Peter's eye, still watching them closely. Assuming her partner had the luggage situation under control, she moved over to mirror the team leader's posture as he rested his back against the parlor wall. Realizing his curiosity had been discovered, he suddenly found something more interesting on his smartphone.

"So," she drawled, casually. "How is the house in St. Louis?"

He frowned in discomfort, taking in the whirling activity of his team before him, while he thumbed, furiously, through the social media in the palm of his hand. Virtually, anything he could do *not* to meet her gaze.

"Catheryn, do we really have to talk about that, again?"

She didn't look at him. "I'm just making conversation…and trying to guess at the meaning of your presence here."

Hearing the realtor's overzealous voice float down from the second floor, she pinned him, with what she hoped was, an uncomfortable side-long glance as she launched her body away from the wall, making it clear that the conversation was to be continued. Tracking the voice of her partner from below, she wandered out into the entryway.

"What are you doing here?"

The deep male voice next to her made Catheryn start, a hand falling on her chest. Years of entities popping in and out of her vicinity, and they still never ceased to surprise her. But in particular, it was more the voice.

That voice.

The demanding, interrogating presence that had been in her bedroom the night earlier. It wasn't coming from the environment through her *physical* hearing. It was more of a psychic impression in her head; an unwelcome intrusion into her personal space that she disliked immensely. She rolled her head, slowly to her right, keeping the motion casual as to not draw unwanted attention.

A tall, dark-haired man in a blue woolen military uniform glared down at her, his dark, deep-set eyes putting her ill at ease. He was taller than Peter, which was intimidating in itself. In addition, he was so solid. So…*there*. It took her a minute to realize he wasn't a living human. His energy was so *grounded* in this place.

"I thought I told you to stay away!" his voice projected, menacingly, into her head.

The fact that his anger was channeled directly into her, threatened to throw her off balance. She set her jaw, putting on a bravado that she didn't really feel. It was the best way to deal with the aggressive types.

She strolled casually into a secluded corner of the empty entry way, sparing a casual glance over her shoulder to gauge if anyone in the next room could see her. The last thing she wanted anyone to know was that she had already established mediumistic contact with someone in the house. Who knew what kind of gadgets and gizmos the paranormal team would come rushing over with.

His dark presence shifted with her, his visage appearing before her in the blink of an eye.

"Who are you?" she spat at him in a harsh whisper, "...and what were you doing in my house, uninvited?"

"You are one to talk..."

"This is not *your* house!"

"Like you would know anything about it," he growled. *"It belongs to the Roberts'. Make him tell you what he's done with them!"*

Her eyes narrowed as she fired her own thoughts back at him. *"You don't order me around!"*

Before she could get any more out of the spectral officer, the physical presence of the insincere smile was back, with David bringing up the rear.

"Everything...okay out here?" the realtor asked, his expression a touch bewildered.

"Oh, fine," Catheryn said, pretending to take interest in the wainscoting and chair rail that lined the hallway. "This house is beautiful! The woodwork is exquisite. A lot of care went into this place. Can you...tell me a little about who owned it?"

"Oh, the Roberts'," he offered, rocking on his heels. He seemed a touch more nervous than the question warranted. "He taught at the local school system here with his wife—"

"Emily," the apparition finished.

"Emily...yeah," the host blurted out. Something in his demeanor seemed to shift, as if someone, backtracking. Someone...dishonest. "Yeah, that was her name. It...it took me a minute to remember. They got tired of the winters. You know. Moving someplace warmer."

"That's a lie!"

Catheryn nearly jumped at the brusqueness of the entity's words. Choosing to ignore him, she turned to look at the young realtor and sparing a sidelong glance at the commotion coming from the next room. There was a haunted house up for sale *and* Peter was here. The ghosts of past experiences with the paranormal coordinator were beginning to float up in her memory, and she didn't like what this appeared to be adding up to.

Baldwin now appeared openly nervous, his jubilant façade now cracking. His hazel eyes seemed to dart from hers to a point just beyond her left shoulder.

"Make him tell you what he did with them!"

Just tell me they're not in the basement, she thought to herself. Tell me they're not in the basement!

"Don't you think we would have looked there?!"

Before she could *think* the ethereal officer to be quiet, something clicked. She turned to Baldwin once more. His eyes were still shifting. Tracking, from left to right. It was more than just social awkwardness at play. It was almost as if…

"You!" She squinted down at the little man. "You can *see them*, can't you?!"

The emotion broadcasting from the entity was more than a touch irate. *"Oh, look who's finally catching on…"*

Catheryn took a bold step toward the realtor. "…and *hear* them?!"

Her partner was becoming lost in the banter. "See *who*? Hear *what*?"

"He's a bit slow, though."

Faustus turned on the young man, his demeanor changing from

bewilderment to suspicion. Baldwin was beginning to look more and more like a cornered rat, taking a cautious step backward.

"I...yes—maybe! Sometimes! Maybe—"

Faustus frowned. "Catheryn, what is he talking about?"

"Yes, yes...okay! Yes!" His hands went defensively up over his blonde messy hair, much like a child about to be stricken.

The young doctor's green eyes flashed with heat. "I think you'd better explain yourself. Fast."

"Make him tell you what he did with them!"

Catheryn was at the end of her rope. "Ask him yourself!"

Faustus was reaching the peak of confusion overload. "Ask who...*what*?!"

Baldwin's hands were still up, as if the fear of being beaten was not over. "I specialize in certain...distressed properties."

Faustus glowered at the little man. "What kind of 'distressed properties'?"

"You know...you know...ones...hard to move!" the little man divulged, reluctantly. "I've been able see and hear them since I was a child. Can you blame a guy for making the most of his...*talents*? It's a very competitive industry I work in!"

Realization was now beginning to dawn on the older doctor. The investigators. Catheryn's incorrigible, unseen tormentor. The shiftiness of the real estate agent.

"Oh my God…" Faustus muttered under his breath.

Catheryn's eyes went wide with incredulity. "You specialize in distressed *haunted properties?!*"

"Wait a minute! This house is haunted?"

The roiling energy coming off of her was enough warning to the specter that he should stop firing any more thoughts in her general direction.

"You say it like it's a bad thing," the small man whimpered, defensively. "They were getting too old to take care of the house, and word came down the grapevine they were looking to sell. I knew a good deal could be made."

"So, you took it off their hands for them," David concluded, distastefully. "At a good price, I'm sure."

"I didn't expect to carry a mortgage," Baldwin defended, his tone turning into one of frantic defense. "It usually doesn't take this long—"

"What do you mean 'take this long'?"

"You know…" Baldwin made an exasperating flapping motion with his hands. "To...move them *along*."

"Move them..." Faustus took a moment to let the conversation sink in. "You mean you've done this *before?!*"

"I had...you know...to weigh my options! If I couldn't move the house, then maybe I could market it to..." The realtor's hand flailed out in the direction of the commotion in the other room. "...other *interests*."

And just as she thought the little human couldn't sink any lower.

Catheryn was at a loss for words, shaking her head. "I can't...I...where's my stuff?"

She turned on Faustus, casting a threatening finger in his face. "I don't want to hear you say anything more about my 'non-profit cases'."

After a very short moment's consideration, the silver-haired doctor nodded in defeat as she blew by him to charge up the stairs.

"Good riddance!"

She ignored the ghost soldier. She had no time for it. For *any* of it. She just wanted her bags.

Baldwin blinked after her, incredulous, before turning to the elder mentor. "She seems...upset.?"

Faustus found Catheryn in the suite at the top of the stairs, thrusting her loose travel items into other bags in hurried attempt to consolidate.

"Catheryn…who are these people?!" When she failed to respond, he caught her elbow to still her. "Isn't it about time you explained what is going on? Who is this…Peter?"

"Peter and I were…involved." The young therapist exhaled, her gaze falling into the bag before her. "It was a long time ago. A part of my past I'd rather forget."

Reading the discomfort and shame in her body language, he released her elbow. She threw herself into a seat on the edge of the bed, not looking at him.

"I was volunteering at a historical mansion in St. Louis; giving tours, things like that. I liked old buildings. I liked their…character. My special skill set came in handy there," she explained. "Peter was interested in the *unique* activity in the place, so the management directed him to me. As you can imagine, I was more than a little familiar with the house's…*character*. I knew the board was interested in exploiting the activity there to make money—to augment their financial bottom line— but I kept finding ways to deflect them from doing it. I explained how it

112

would change the atmosphere of where people worked and visited. How it could actually make the place more unpleasant, harder to keep volunteers, and high-dollar events."

When she met her partner's gaze, her eyes were hardened. "I knew every entity in that house. I knew their triumphs, their sorrows…To think that people would come in…strangers…and *torment* them for their own personal amusement…"

She shook her head, frustrated at the memory. "I threatened to quit. We were the custodians of that family's legacy! To use the entities like that…I couldn't think of a worse betrayal of their trust."

Her partner rested his back against the flowered wallpaper behind him, taking a moment to ponder her words. "…and, Peter?"

She chuckled at some hidden irony. "Little did I know, they hired him as a 'consultant' to create a ghost hunting program. He cozied up to me to learn what he could to forward that agenda. By the time I found out what he was up to…we were already involved. He insisted that he never meant for things to go that way. He said he always meant to tell me."

"I can…imagine the rest. I'm sorry. If I had known…" Faustus sighed through pursed lips, turning toward the bedroom door. "It's an obvious conflict of interest. I'll tell Baldwin we're bowing out."

"No."

The word of finality from his female partner surprised him, causing him to pause mid-turn. His brow furrowed, searching her face for some explanation.

"He's not getting his hands on another house," she said, flatly, her green eyes flashing. "Not while I'm around."

BRAMDEN HOUSE

5

Catheryn hovered close to the short, heavy-set man with the grizzled dark beard. She frowned openly as he fiddled with the tiny knobs of a small wooden box situated on the ornately-carved Eastlake-style parlor table.

Faustus had spent nearly an hour negotiating the situation with Baldwin. It was only after Baldwin offered to throw in return airfare on a flight the next day, did Catheryn agree to come downstairs, at all.

"You've got to be kidding," she muttered, distastefully. "You brought that thing with you? Do you even know what you're dealing with in this house?"

"Why do you think we brought it," he muttered from under his thick mustache. "Tuning it to the AM band. We get better results that way."

The doctor was unamused. She rolled her eyes and returned to her partner's side, arms folded, curtly, against her chest. "This is ridiculous."

"What's going on?" her partner asked, somewhat mystified.

"Oh, we've got a real *specialist* on our hands here. He's being all scientific, and stuff," she nodded, her arms folded, with an air of exaggerated smugness, "…with a broken radio."

"Does he…know it's broken?"

Catheryn shrugged. "Pretty sure he's the one that broke it, so…they usually 'break' the tuner lock on the circuit card, so it, freely, sweeps up and down the radio band at a rapid pace."

"…and, what is it supposed to do?"

She rested her back against the wall with an exasperated sigh. "If you listen between the stations—in the white noise—you can sometimes hear voices."

Faustus' brow furrowed. "Doesn't that mean the radio's…working?"

"The theory is they're spirit voices."

"How do they know that?"

"They don't," Catheryn frowned. "They're using a device that still receives live broadcast, so the results will always be questionable as to what is causing the output. Even then, if they're lucky, they might understand a word or two, but there's no solid understanding of what it means, or who is saying it. It's all conjecture. Before the designer of the first box died, he admitted that even he didn't know how it worked. No one had mastered the box. Not even himself."

"So, there's nothing to it, then," her partner mused. "Right?"

The medium pursed her lips. "I'd like to think so. However, I've seen the anomalous activity in many places actually get *worse* after using them. And there are times…"

Faustus raised an inquisitive eyebrow. "What?"

She looked at him, her expression, unsettled. "I've heard things. Things that were coming from the box. And then, those same voices…were in the room with us. Almost like a predator, using the device to hone in on our location."

The older doctor blinked, incredulously. "How is that any better than a spirit board?"

"Tell that to them."

Peter Elgin clapped his hands for attention. "Okay, everyone. Quiet! Recording Session One."

The team lead pressed his lips to the microphone of his digital recorder. "Session One. Bramden House Parlor. September 23rd, 1:37

PM. Box session to commence."

Peter leaned toward Catheryn, conspiringly. "Catheryn, are you getting anything?"

"No," she whispered, glancing briefly around the room. "Not yet."

"What is that?"

The young medium tried not to look startled as the image of the dark-haired officer suddenly appeared just opposite of Peter Elgin. The spirit's gaze sunk to eye-level with the table, scrutinizing the box with his usual scowl. It was somewhat comical to observe, sending Catheryn to wonder what Peter's reaction would be if the researcher suddenly saw the spectral officer like that.

"It's a ghost box," she fired at him in her mind.

"I don't like it."

"Why not?"

"I don't like it."

"Don't do anything," the medium strategized, silently. *"Maybe they'll shut it off. They won't be interested if they don't find anything. Don't. Say. Anything."*

"I don't intend to."

The box popped to life, emitting a steady, repetitive, static sound, not unlike that of a steam locomotive, but at a much quieter scale. The sound was unsettling, grating against Catheryn's already sensitive nerves. There was a cold queasiness settling into the pit of her stomach.

The noise continued like that for almost two minutes as she observed with increasing unease. Maybe nothing would happen. Maybe they would shut it off and give up. It would be the best case scenario if none of the entities gave them anything at all. Her heart sank when the device gave an audible squawk in between the steady cadence of static.

"There!" Elgin offered in a hush tone. "Did you hear that?"

The ethereal officer looked unimpressed, his dark brows knitting. "*Hear what?*"

Catheryn, not wanting to draw attention to his presence, did not answer him. Her head was really killing her.

"What am I supposed to be hearing?" she inquired of Elgin, pinching the bridge of her nose, wincing in pain.

"The distortion in between the waves," the team leader answered, leaning into the operator's personal space to fine-tune a setting. "You hear it?"

There was a slight break in the locomotive sound as another sound spat from the box.

"….hi…"

Elgin's eyes lit up like a child at Christmas. "Did you hear *that?*"

Catheryn was growing more and more puzzled. "What was it?"

"A voice!" The burly, bearded technician was back, hovering close to the box at eye level. "It said, 'hi'."

Catheryn frowned. "Who said 'hi'?"

The army officer took a step back from the device, his dark gaze looking more suspicious, taking in the air around them. "*It wasn't me…*"

"The ghosts," Elgin smiled, not taking his eyes from the device. "They're talking to us!"

" '*They' who?*" the specter scowled. "*It wasn't us.*"

Now it was Catheryn's turn to look uneasy. It wasn't lost on her that the ethereal soldier was suddenly speaking plural. She looked about the room, but the only presence she picked up on was the glowering male apparition.

"What ghosts?" she muttered, still scanning the room. "Where?"

"Well, here, of course!"

"*It wasn't us!*"

"….hi…open…"

" 'Open'," Peter mimicked, his eyes aglow as if the words had some sacred meaning. He took a more authoritative posture, challenging the air with a booming voice. " 'Open' what?"

"….door…Please?"

Peter appeared puzzled. " 'Door'? What 'door'?"

The officer's response was quiet, but firm. "*No.*"

"…Please? Open… Want…to…play!"

"You are NOT invited!"

The young doctor took a step back from the device, feeling as if suffering from a technologically-induced hangover. This was not good at all. The room felt as if it were spinning.

"Turn it off," she muttered, a hand going to her forehead, uncertain if it was the incessant chatter of the box, or that of the belligerent entity causing it.

Elgin turned her way, abruptly. "What? Are you crazy?!"

"Turn it off!" Danforth issued, forcefully. *"NOW!"*

"Turn it off!" Catheryn repeated, weakly, stumbling toward the box.

The unsteadiness of her steps knocked the parlor table over, sending the box careening to the floor. The husky technician dove for it, but missed, the device hitting the hardwood floor with a sound crack. The locomotive had come to an abrupt halt, filling the room with awkward silence.

"Catheryn, what are you doing?!" Elgin wailed, picking up the damaged broken radio from the floor, inspecting it.

Now that the device was off, she was finding her feet again. The room stopped teetering, and her head stopped swimming.

She grabbed the team lead by the elbow in a brusque manner that invited no argument. "Peter—"

Elgin put up no resistance as she dragged him to a private corner of the room. "What is going on, Catheryn—"

"Do you know who you are talking to when you turn that on?"

"Whatever's here, in the house—"

"You don't know that." She turned away, running her fingers through her dark reddish hair in agitation, shaking her head. "Complete conjecture. *I* can tell you that's *not* who you were talking to."

It was Peter's turn to scowl. "You've never been crazy about us using this thing."

"It gives you nothing!" she countered, sharply. "Bits and pieces for you to string together. It says…whatever you want it to say!"

"You just don't like it because it keeps us from needing *you!*" he retorted, closing the space between them. "We can cut out the middle man…er, woman."

Catheryn glowered, observing him. Encroaching on her personal space. Using his considerable height to his advantage. Threatening behavior. Yes, she was getting to him. It wouldn't be long before this whole scene devolved into something ugly.

Catheryn leaned toward him, attempting to keep her voice down. "*I come with years of experience, developing communication skills of symbols and language, and a little thing called *discernment*. Turning that box on does not make you an instant medium. You have no idea who you are talking to, or where they are—if it's even anyone at all."

Peter's eyes scanned her face, searching for some chink in her emotional armor that revealed any sense of doubt. There wasn't. But then, it dawned on him.

"How else would you know it wasn't anything from this house, unless…you were in contact with them! Why didn't you say anything—"

She slammed a hand down on the parlor table, glaring at the team lead. "I owe you *nothing*. Only that they…"

She wasn't sure why she said it. Was there more than just the spirit soldier? She only had the entity's word that there might be more. It didn't matter how she knew.

"...they seem to know more about that...thing there than you!" Catheryn challenged. "Where did you even get that?"

"It was built for us," he muttered defensively, his voice tinged with sheepishness. "No one really knows how it works..."

"The 'great scientist' is using a device without knowing how it works?!"

Peter's body language was shifting defensively, the chinks in his own armor beginning to show. He had nothing to attack her with and he knew it.

Faustus stabbed a finger at the silent device being cradled in the grizzled tech's arms like a precious child. "How many of these *boxes* are there?"

Peter shrugged. "The beginning designs were huge, clunky. Now that the design has been refined...they're down to the size of a handheld radio."

" 'Refined'?" Catheryn looked wary.

"They're mass produced. You can order them off any home shopping site online."

Catheryn pursed her lips tightly, feeling the lump in the pit of her stomach beginning to grow. New psychic tech for a new age. And similar to the spirit board, no one had a clue how to use it, or even how it worked, but that didn't seem to stop it from being mass-produced.

Catheryn fixed Peter with a sharp glare and a more threatening finger. "*Don't* turn that thing back on."

The bearded tech threw up his hands in a half-hearted attempt at defense. "Since your latest 'refinement'—no chance of that. It's broken."

She snorted quietly to herself. It was 'broke' before she even touched it.

She turned toward the hallway, only to find herself nose to brass buttons with the dark, agitated entity. She didn't jump as much this time. Perhaps she was finally getting used to him.

"I want it out of my house. I want you ALL out of my house!"

"It's not *your house!*" she whispered sharply.

"Who are you talking to?!"

Peter and the male doctor blinked at one another, uncertain who said it first.

Between the ghost shouting in one ear, and the nausea-inducing box in the other, she just wanted to find her bedroom and lie down.

"Never mind," she sighed. "I'm just…going to settle in."

She returned to the front foyer and to the stairs heading up to the second level. She just needed to get away from everyone for a while. It didn't take long to realize that, in this house, it would be a difficult task.

"Isn't it about time you leave?!"

She stopped abruptly at the foot of the stairs as the figure loomed before her on the third step. Didn't she just leave him in the parlor?

"What is your *problem*?!," she snapped.

"The problem is that you weren't invited any more than that thing was!" the male entity fired back, haughtily.

"If *you* hadn't caused such a ruckus then *I* wouldn't have to be here!"

"Oh, so the great Saint Catheryn is here to save us all, is it? Move us troubled souls onto where we'll find redemption?"

For the first time since she arrived, his aggravated thoughts gave her pause. He knew exactly why she was here. Of course, he did. He was the voice in her bedroom that night.

Well, who here needs saving?! Maybe it's already handled. Did you ever think of that?" He loomed large in her face, his darkened eyes on fire. *"Ah, you didn't, did you? Not sure who you're used to dealing with, but the Dead are quite capable of handling things without your…blasted interference!"*

She blinked. In all honesty, she hadn't come close to considering it. In her experience, they had always been confused, lost. Reaching out to her for help, day or night. Disturbing her sleep, or plaguing her dreams with chaotic nightmares. But not this one. This one seemed firm. Quite *aware.*

"The Dead in my house are under my protection. My care!" he said with sharp rebuke, stabbing his chest with his finger. *"I keep the Chaos at bay. It stays outside. I keep order around here. Even if that means I have to protect the Dead from the Living."*

Now, it was Catheryn's turn to get indignant. "What the hell is that supposed to mean?!"

"Those here have been through quite a lot, and they don't need the likes of you to be…poking and prodding them with your flashy boxes and your…Christmas lights. This ain't a…goddamn circus!"

The energetic brunt of his anger made her stagger back against the railing, fingernails digging into the dark varnish of the wood. The energetic grounding effect of the wood under her fingertips made her vaguely aware of someone at the foot of the stairs.

"Catheryn?" It was her partner's voice floating up from behind her. "Are you alright?"

Her hands went to her head, fingertips massaging her fatigued brow. The whole thing was adding up to one catastrophic headache.

"I…I just need a break. Lie down for a bit," she muttered. "I'm gonna get settled in. I'll see you in the morning."

Catheryn returned to her suite, pushing the bags from the bed and dropping onto the mattress, exhausted. She wrapped a forearm over her eyes to block out the fading light of day. It did little to dull the pain.

Thanks to Baldwin's stellar staging technique, the house was halfway livable; almost a hotel, in itself. However, she wasn't exactly sure how much sleep they would all be getting since Peter's team would likely be fumbling around in the dark until early hours. The understanding that a house being haunted meant any time of the day or night, was lost on them. The group was insistent that their equipment was more effective in the dark. She left them to their resources with the warning that should any of them stumble into her bedroom, expect something to be hurled at them, and by someone with far better aim than a ghost. And most likely, heavier than anything the spirits could muster.

At a point where she felt that movement wouldn't cause her to lose her lunch, she rolled out of bed to rip back the comforter from the full-size antique four-poster bed. Retrieving her favorite Celtic band t-shirt and a set of yoga pants from her discarded travel bag, she crawled into bed. Turning to the marble-topped side table, she fumbled for the switch of the pink antique banquet lamp to turn it off.

She mused that, with the exception of Baldwin's staging touches, the house seemed just as if everything had been left in its original place from long ago. She gazed out the picture window of her small room. And quite a picture it was; it afforded a beautiful view of the river across the street, the light in the sky receding to pinks and scarlets over the peaks of the river bluffs, streaking what clouds that were in the sky with purplish hues. Without a power line or light pole in sight, if someone had told her they had fallen back into the 1800's, she might have believed them.

She wasn't used to the quiet. Years of living in an apartment building in the middle of the bustle of Chicago, where noise was the norm, it still explained away the odd sound or two that might keep her up at night. Unlike the sleepless city, she could hear every creak of this house, the rustle of the trees in the late-night breeze, and the rolling of the water along the rapids below.

And the unceremonious stumble and crash of someone tripping over a piece of furniture in the dark.

Catheryn stifled a giggle at the long string of curse words, before rolling over onto her side. Yeah, that was more like it. It comforted her more to hear the noises of the living than other unidentified ones that came in the night.

But of course, if today was any judge, there was an increased likelihood, that those may just materialize, also.

6

Upon emerging from the depths of her slumber, Catheryn heard the long, frustrated sigh first. Her green eyes snapped open in alarm before it came flooding back to her where she was. Sunlight streaming into the picture window caused her to raise a hand against the brightness. As her eyes adjusted, she took in a form silhouetted against the window. It was a tall male figure with his back to her. She didn't have to guess who it was.

"Get out of my room," she stated, more than a little cross.

"Get out of my house," he traded, blithely.

"You've really gotta get over that."

She threw back the comforter, swinging her bare feet onto the soft pile of the burgundy area rug on the floor; grateful that she had chosen more modest night time attire. She needed caffeine. Immediately.

"They've already started a pot of chicory downstairs."

His ability to read her thoughts was annoying, but she needed the caffeine more. Catheryn fumbled for a hair scrunchie she had left on the bedside table and tied her auburn hair up in a loose bun.

Slipping her feet into her flats, she started out the door. She paused when he didn't move. She watched as he made note of something in the palm of his hand before placing an object in his breast pocket.

"You're lucky that sunrise comes later in the valley," he said to the window pane.

She rolled her eyes, uncertain what that meant as she trudged out into the brown-painted barn wood floor of the hallway.

As the young therapist continued down the hall, she allowed her fingers to trace the dark oak of the spindle-style railing that wrapped around the hall to the staircase. She liked the cool feel of the ancient wood and was grateful for its support as her tired steps landed heavily upon the stairs. Continuing into the parlor, she stifled a yawn as she found her partner, David, seated at the large oak Duncan Fyfe dining table. Even on his day off he opted for business casual; dressed in a beige sweater and gray slacks. He sat with his legs crossed, sipping from a delicate china cup. Baldwin was there also, dressed down in a pair of blue jeans and faded blue hoodie. Despite his appearance, every hair of his bleach-blond head was meticulously in place with styling product.

Just beyond him, leaning against a primitive, pine-planked door, was Danforth, still dressed in his familiar woolen blues, arms folded leisurely across his chest.

She flashed a pinched, insincere smile at the specter before shuffling over to claim her own cup and saucer from the table. Her cool expression of social acknowledgement was enough to draw David's attention over his shoulder. Seeing nothing, he exchanged a quizzical look with her. She shook her head, rolling her eyes in exasperation. It was all the answer he needed as to what, or who, she was responding to.

Filling her cup with coffee, she marveled at the delicate fine bone china in her hand. She threw a look over at the realtor, who was working on a mug of his own, emblazoned with the gauche gold and red logo of his realty business.

"Did they leave *everything* behind?"

He shrugged, taking a last swig from his vessel. "Pretty much. The stuff kinda goes…you know…with the house."

Catheryn took a long draw from her cup, her eyes keeping the figure across the room within eyeshot over the delicate rim. He stared back at her with an air of nonchalance. It was at that particular moment that the door at his back began to vibrate from the effort of someone trying to open it from the opposite side.

The thumping increased, drawing the attention of all in the room. No longer able to keep his casual air, the soldier moved away from the door, allowing the contents from the other side to spill, unceremoniously, onto the floor like a large sack of potatoes.

Peter Elgin got up to his feet, along with one of his fellow teammates. The team lead brushed the remnants of the dusty floor off of his black team polo, trading sheepish grins with all observers. His scrawny colleague retrieved his fallen ball cap from the floor as he found his feet, also.

"Latch…must have fallen down and locked us in," Elgin chuckled.

Catheryn's eyes were fixed on the entity beyond them, a look of none-too-convincing innocence gazing back at her.

"Uh huh," she muttered, discarding her cup and saucer onto the table. "Are you guys about finished?"

The young researcher's face brightened. "Oh, well…yeah! We got lots of great stuff!"

"Really great stuff," his partner echoed.

"Audio. Video."

"Really great video."

Baldwin looked mystified. "Well, great! And…"

Elgin shook his head, smiling. "You are most definitely…haunted."

"Yeah," his twin chimed in.

The realtor looked, decidedly, underwhelmed. "And…what do I do about it?"

"Oh, uhmm…" Peter muttered, eyes moving from Catheryn to Baldwin, and then, back to Catheryn. "You need to talk to…ah…them."

Baldwin turned his back to all of them, running frustrated fingers through his carefully coifed hair.

"I mean…we can pull all sorts of audio, and…and…video, but…" But with that, the leader of the Paranormal Research Institute couldn't help but look dejected. "Yeah…"

The disappointment of the host was easily felt by all there, so it wasn't a surprise when the team swiftly put themselves to task collecting cables, routers, microphones, and cameras. The van was hastily packed, and Elgin barely got a grateful handshake with the exasperated host before the large double doors of the entryway were closed in his face.

Baldwin pressed his forehead to the door as a sympathetic Catheryn and David looked on.

The realtor found a comfortable, yet, subtle rhythm as he banged his forehead on the antiquated woodwork. "I'm ruined."

"Not…yet."

Her own voice surprised even Catheryn. Both David and Baldwin turned to look at her. Feeling the weight of their expectation, she wasn't sure what she could do, exactly. But she knew what she hadn't done.

"I haven't walked the house, yet," she mused. "We need to gain their trust. And I'm sorry, but …bringing in ghost hunters is not the way to do that. This is going to take some time."

"How much time?" Baldwin asked, his hand reaching down to claim a black garbage bag containing the previous evening's investigative rubbish.

David Faustus had another bag, doing what he could to help clean up. It was the only thing he could think to do. With all that he had witnessed, there was only one thing the doctor knew for sure. By the number of taurine-laced drinks he had disposed of, he was certain the majority of Elgin's team would have kidney stones by the time they were in their mid-thirties.

David paused. " '*Their* trust'?" You think there's more?"

Catheryn glanced up, expecting to trade glances with the ghostly officer, but for the first time since she had arrived, she found the room empty of presence.

"Oh, there's more of them," Baldwin snorted. As he felt their eyes shift to him, he held up his hands in mild defense. "Let's just say…I'm never having kids."

"The soldier," Catheryn frowned, thoughtfully. "He was really brutal as to wanting us out. He's protecting something. We just need to figure out what."

The realtor collapsed into a dining chair, dragging the garbage bag with him.

"Thirty days," he sighed, trying not to look too defeated. "I just made another mortgage payment. We're good for thirty days. After that…"

He let them draw their own inferences from his trailing words.

So, they had thirty days, Catheryn thought to herself. Thirty days to unravel the mystery that was Bramden House. They couldn't justify shutting down the practice just for this. By the sound of it, they'd be lucky to get what was owed.

"I could probably move some money around to pay you for another week, or so," the realtor mused. "Please…just…don't go!"

Catheryn allowed her intuitive sense to draw her up the servant's staircase behind the kitchen. The narrow, thinly-placed steps made her nervous, stepping carefully and clinging to the makeshift mid-century railing. She wondered just how many people had tumbled down them, by accident.

As she reached the second floor, she continued down a narrow hallway that led to an open area at the top of the main staircase. A sound. What was that sound? Strains of…music? A violin.

The music wasn't coming from below. Her attention was drawn to a doorway to her left; a doorway she had failed to notice before. She placed her hand on the white ceramic door knob and turned it. The narrow oak door opened on antiquated hinges, squeaking with more volume than she felt comfortable with. And as she suspected, it was loud enough for the musician to hear, because the music came to an abrupt stop. The stairs before her were wood, and just as narrow as the servant's stairs. She gingerly tested her weight on the first step and winced as it squeaked. So much for the element of surprise. Even so, she edged up the staircase slowly and deliberately.

The upper area of the house was not as elegantly-designed as the rooms of the first floor. It was obvious to her that these accommodations were not meant for guests. The rafters were bare and undecorated. Cobwebs joined the spaces in between. The mustiness of mold and rot hung in the air from unattended leaks, but there was enough light to see by. Ahead of her, she could see the daylight spilling into the landing ahead of her. A window. Recalling the outside view of the house, she guessed she must be entering the attic.

She paused, uncertain as to whether she should proceed. It was at that point that she could hear the bow resuming its play across the resonant strings of the violin once more. If there was any doubt before, the whereabouts of the musician was now clear.

The run of the musical notes started and then stopped. Then, they started again, as if their originator was not satisfied with the results from before. And then, repeated once more at a more confident pace, vibrato intact with a more practiced flourish.

But as quickly as it had resumed, it stopped again, followed by an impatient male sigh.

"And they say the Dead are creepy. Would you quit skulking in the stairway and get up here?"

Catheryn smiled sheepishly, the familiar voice echoing in her head. She continued up the stairs at a less covert pace.

The barn wood floor of the attic was dusty. Her movement churned clouds of it up to dance in the rays of sunlight spilling through the tall cathedral-style window before her. Standing before it, booted foot perched on an old trunk, was the spectral captain. He frowned, his eyes glowering under his heavy dark brow. The instrument whose voice she had been following, was still tucked beneath his chin, and supported with his right hand. Curious, she thought. He played left-handed.

"Regardless of what the schools thought, it can be done," he muttered, drawing the instrument away from its perch on his clavicle. *"They tried to beat it out of me, but found I attended more lessons when they didn't."*

She didn't know what surprised her more; the fact that he had so clearly read her mind, or the fact that he was no longer speaking in it.

"Was wondering where you'd gotten off to," she muttered, brushing off some of the dust from the window seat before sitting down.

He frowned distastefully before depositing his instrument in the old-fashioned, hand-made wooden case splayed open on top of the closed trunk. *"Was rather hoping you'd left with the morning's entertainment."*

She stopped in abrupt surprise. Looking up at her with curious green eyes, from the other side of the trunk, was a gray tiger-striped cat.

It was not young; white tufts of hair peeking out of patches giving away its seniority, but it still met her with a warm trilling meow.

"Well, hello!" Catheryn greeted warmly, bending down to offer her hand to the creature's tiny nose. It accepted her offering with an exploratory sniff.

The soldier's eyes darkened at the furry animal. "You! Get!"

It was difficult to know who started first, the cat or Catheryn. It was the first time she had heard him use his full audible voice. The cat's face withdrew from Catheryn's hand and switched its attention to the spectral officer. It bared its fangs in a distasteful hiss.

The doctor winced at the officer's tone. "Was that really necessary?"

"That cat has been here for years!" He stabbed an infuriating finger at the beast. *"You know how frustrating it is to live alongside that? Knowing it can see you, and it still acts like...like..."*

"A cat?" Catheryn smirked, stooping over, making baby talk noises to try and lure the creature back. "If you acted like this all the time, I'd pretend not to know you, too. Besides...is that any way to treat guardians of the Underworld?"

She mused, silently, for a moment as she scratched the animal behind the neck. It purred in reciprocity. "It makes sense why the ancients thought that. Their vision can see you better than the Living can. They also have a sympathetic nervous system, which means they are hypersensitive to energy shifts; whether that be electromagnetism or human emotion."

"You really like the sound of your own voice, don't you?"

She sat back on her haunches, watching as the calmed feline rubbed up against her pant leg. "They can interact with you. And you with them. One of the few creatures that can."

"No thanks." He scowled, openly. *"With all this worldly knowledge that you possess; what is it that you do, anyway?"*

"I'm a doctor," she answered, rising to her feet. "David is my partner."

"Oh," he uttered, looking somewhat taken aback. *"So he's...?"*

She had no trouble picking up on his thoughts. She shook her head, brushing her hands off on her thighs.

"We share a *practice*."

"Oh. Is that what they call it now?"

"A *doctor's* office," she corrected. "We are not...*together*. Not in that way, anyway."

"Great. Another 'doctor'," he snorted. *"And what kind of quackery do you do?"*

"It's a doctorate of Behavioral Science. We help people get in touch with their feelings; in order to heal, emotionally. To improve quality of life."

"Sounds like something a quack would say."

She pushed against the floor, stretching the crick in her back as she rose. "You don't like doctors much, do you?"

"Only met one once, and I died right after. What do you think?"

Catheryn planted her hands on her hips, forcing her shoulders back into a stretch. "Now you know more about me than I do about you."

"How's that?"

"I don't even know your name."

A pained expression seemed to pass over his countenance, as if being forced to give up more than he wanted. The moment was brief.

"You can call me 'Captain'."

"Glad I caught you in a *giving* mood."

"If you don't care for the accommodations, you are welcome to leave any time."

He picked up his instrument once more, tucking it under his chin before pausing to nod in the direction of the feline.

"Feel free to take that *with you."*

The pale light of the moon made long shadows of Catheryn's bedroom. Sleep was long in coming. Comforter drawn up to her chin, her mind rolled through strategy.

Thirty days.

Taking off work for thirty days was impossible. Baldwin would have to find a way to reimburse them more. But at the same time, they had to move things up, rapidly. That meant taking short cuts. That meant doing things that made her uncomfortable.

She rolled over, watching the swaying branches of the bare trees casting spindly shadows along the bedroom floor.

"Ralph," she whispered, intimately, to no one in particular. "I'm going to need you."

Her eyes closed. She underestimated how tired she was. It was almost impossible to tell how long she had been sleeping, before she was...

Aware.

The lights of her small, octagonal-shaped room seemed to light instantly. Her hands still had a firm grip on the comforter as her eyes darted around the room. In the distance, she thought she could hear the light stirrings of music. At first, she thought it was a music box, before she realized it was coming from the room below her.

I'm dreaming, she thought.

She raised her hands before her face, pushing the fingertips of her right hand into the palm of her left. Her breath caught as they phased right through. That was it. That was the tell-tale sign. She was lucid.

She studied the nails of the back of her fingers. The lines of her palms. No, she mustn't give into the excitement of it, or she would wake up. Lucid dreaming was tricky business. Giving in to emotional excitement could cause her to awake, but this state of psychic exploring could reap enormous benefits if she could stay in the zone. Feeling more in control, she didn't bother with pulling back the comforter. She simply *floated* up from the bed. She alighted on the carpet, her bare feet feeling the plushness of the rug beneath them.

Now, the music seemed intermingled with voices. A party? She looked down at her nightclothes. Well, this wouldn't do for a party.

She turned toward the tall walnut wardrobe against the wall of the bedroom.

Open, she demanded through thought.

To her satisfaction, the double doors of the walnut wardrobe flung open as if automated. Inside, were the most delicious selection of dresses she could have ever dreamed of. She couldn't help but note that they were of a period from years past. Silk taffetas, fine lace, the most delicate of wools. All would require suitable underpinnings to make the look complete. It would take some time getting into one.

Of course, it wouldn't. This was a dream. She simply had to choose one.

She flipped through them; and like a watercolor wash, all turned perfect for her hair and skin coloring. What to wear?

Ralph moved through the crowded dining room, dressed in his black long coat, white shirt and silver vest. He chose a silk burgundy cravat, and styled his light brown hair back into a matching ribbon for the occasion. Happily, no one seemed to pay him any mind as he took in the changes made to the brightly-lit dining room. All of the furniture had been pushed back against the walls to make room for a sizable dance floor. The 'occupants' of the house had seen fit to set up a small platform for the musicians to play. From the look of things, the instruments were well represented among them. They had a banjo, a guitar, two fiddles, and a lively upright piano.

The dance floor was alive, with barely an inch to spare. Adults ranging from sixteen years to seventy were taking part in country reels and waltzes.

The ladies were dressed in long, floor-length dresses made of everything from the finest silks and lace to the lightest homespun cotton. Some had shorter sleeves with a generous neckline, while others sported longer sleeves of a more modest nature. All of them featured the wide, expansive skirts of an earlier age.

Many of the men were dressed like Ralph, but some opted for more of a military dress for the occasion. Some wore fitted Union frock coats of blue with gold-framed shoulder boards, while others wore Confederate gray with sleeves of generous gold brocade. Neither seemed to mind the presence of the other. Some even shared drinks, toasts, and swapped stories. There were others of a more conservative dress, but they were definitely in the party spirit. That included a little man in a tweed coat and bowler hat that had more than his share from the punch bowl. He found Ralph more than amiable company.

"You know, with the exception of typhoid, cholera, consumption, yellow fever, scarlet fever, measles, dysentery, and smallpox," the elfish little man mused, "it really was a great time to be alive!"

"I have no doubt," the spiritual guide commented, doing his best to sound agreeable while casually sipping from his glass punch cup.

The smaller man gave the enlightened being an impish wink. "I don't suppose you'd be interested in a drink a little *stronger*."

The guide smiled his usual serene smile, his fine bone structure accentuating the good-humored twinkle in his blue-green eyes. "Alas, no. But thank you all the same."

"If I may say, you seem a touch...*familiar*. Have we met before?"

"I'm told I have that kind of face."

"Most likely mistaken," the little man muttered, stroking his chin, thoughtfully. "I believe the other lad was a touch *taller*."

With a departing pat on the shoulder, the small man withdrew. As Ralph's gaze followed him into the crowd, his attention was captured by a door opening at the end of the dining room.

Catheryn entered in a beautiful dress of slate blue silk. The bodice was a generous open neck, trimmed and tucked with the finest white lace. The short sleeves were also trimmed with white lace as well as fine black velvet ribbon. Her auburn hair was braided into a low bun, but sported the severe central part so popular with the style of dress. A plume of a black feather peeked up from the back of her crown. Albeit, a woman out of time, she still looked striking.

But even Ralph was surprised when everyone, even the music, came to a disorganized halt. They all turned to stare at her. Some faces were curious. Others wary. Some were masks of outright suspicion. It made him uneasy, and he took the opportunity of momentary confusion to *blink* across the room. Although surprised at his sudden appearance, Catheryn was relieved to find him at her side.

"Uh oh," she breathed, trying to get a read from the room. "Bad idea?"

"I would like to stay around to find out," the guide mused, his gaze lingering back to his former company who was already perusing the punch bowl, "but I feel I may need to limit my presence here among the Dead."

"Why?"

Ralph seemed to nod in the direction of a very familiar, brooding energy. "Longer story than we have time for, at the present."

As her guardian *blinked* to who-knows-where, the physical incarnation of the approaching energy made its way through the crowd, toward her.

The captain held the fiddle by the neck in one hand, his bow was in the other. She felt it curious that the scent of citrus-scented hair cream mixed with tobacco preceded him. The hair cream kept his dark wavy hair in a neat side part. His full thick moustache was also neatly trimmed. Dressed in a blue wool vest and matching pants, the sleeves of the underlying white collar shirt were rolled up to his elbows. Even though he hadn't donned his standard blue officer's coat, his demeanor was all business.

"What do you think you are doing here?" he demanded, his dark eyes flashing.

His voice was no longer in her head. She could hear him as any normal person. Whether it was an illusion from the dream, or something else, it felt alien to hear him like that.

"I thought it might be a good opportunity to introduce myself to everyone," she replied with an aloofness she hoped was convincing.

"As if you were even invited—"

"What is this?"

It was a woman's voice. A slightly older voice, but one that still held weight with the crowd as it parted, once again.

The older woman wore a burgundy organza peach tree gown that opened at the neck; the v-shaped opening lined with generous amounts of pleated trim that terminated at a black belt accentuating an even more generous waistline. Filling the space in between was a white collarless dickey, punctuated at mid neckline with a beautiful black broach of dark mosswood. The fringes of the dress were trimmed in fine black lace, her long full sleeves buttoned at the wrists. Her gray hair was swept up in a well-constructed chignon, the severity of the hairstyle seemed augmented by her lips drawn in a thin line. She regarded Catheryn down the end of her nose, her green eyes pinning the therapist where she stood. Everything about her screamed control, and Catheryn had no doubt that she was finally meeting the lady of the house.

"I am Abigale Bramden," she said, cavalierly, offering a white-gloved hand to her. "Who are you?"

BRAMDEN HOUSE

7

Catheryn took the hand of the hostess and bowed, slightly, at the neck. She breezed through her limited rolodex of older customs. The hostess's bluntness could be seen as rude, but Catheryn was, after all, present without a proper invitation.

"I am…" She stopped just short of using her professional title. Did the majority of this crowd even recognize female doctors? "…Ms. Catheryn Greye. A pleasure to make your acquaintance, Ms. Bramden."

"And your people?" the older woman asked. "Where are they from?"

'Her people'? She wasn't expecting that, but fortunately, she was more than acquainted with her family's genealogy.

"Michigan. Houghton County."

"You've come a ways to see us then," the stern woman commented, collecting her gloved hands in front of her. "I see you've met our caretaker, Captain Danforth."

The doctor offered her hand, expectantly. Knowing he would be rude to refuse it, he took it, and bowed stiffly at the neck. Feeling all eyes in the room on them both, she curtseyed in polite response.

" 'Caretaker'?" Catheryn repeated, inquisitively.

"Watching after the day-to-day operations of the house," the hostess replied. "Making sure we are not infiltrated by…ruffians." The hostess's attention shifted to the captain. "Perhaps, after our evening's amusements you could show Ms. Greye the house?"

Catheryn could see his brow furrow in agitation. Not to contradict the hostess or insult the guest, he bowed at the neck, again. As close to agreement as the young doctor would probably get from him. He chose that opportunity to withdraw to the comfort of the musician's platform. He took a casual half-standing posture, a booted heel upon the rung of a tall stool. He rested his backside upon the seat as he retrieved a block of resin from a black, homemade coffin-style case and proceeded to rosin up the bow. The instrument found its regular position under his chin, resting against his clavicle. As he drew the bow across the strings, he slid effortlessly into the opening strains of a country reel.

The stately lady turned, in response, to a hand on her shoulder. A shorter, middle-aged gentleman gazed up at his hostess, the only apparent communication between the two of them being a deliberate nod. Catheryn watched, in bewilderment, as the man withdrew into the crowd. The older woman's attention, briefly, returned to her young guest.

"If you'll excuse me," the older woman said, flatly.

The mistress of the house disappeared into the crowd only to reappear at the musician's platform. To her side, stood the funny little man that had been Ralph's social companion earlier that evening.

"Ladies and gentleman!" Ms. Bramden announced. "We have someone to provide sport this evening; a challenger to our dear comrade, Captain Danforth—Mr. James McCreary!"

The crowd erupted in spirited applause as the elfish little man in the tweed suit doffed his bowler hat, revealing a mess of gray hair. His height stood in comic relief to Danforth's towering form, but the new arrival seemed drunk on the attention of the party. He bowed with a dramatic flourish of his arm, to the crowd, before reaching behind him to draw up a fiddle.

The mistress of the house smiled, benevolently, at the little man. "Since you are challenging, Mr. McCreary, feel free to name the tune."

Mr. McCreary couldn't have looked more confident. " 'The Special'?"

Danforth offered the man a sidelong look, and responded with a rare smile, nodding in acceptance.

The lady of the house raised her hands to the crowd. "We have a match!"

With that, the mistress bowed out from between the two men and withdrew to the back of the stage.

The captain tightened his grip on the fiddle beneath his chin and soundly passed through the first round of the old railroad tune with the elfish man following at a deliberate pace that brought the crowd to their feet, cheering for the two to best it with chants of "faster!"

Smiling confidently, the little man launched in to the second round, without missing a beat, driving the speed of the tune to new heights, but masterful enough not to lose the melody. Danforth was more than up to the challenge as the speed increased. The crowd went wild, chanting for the tune to go faster, yet. Catheryn observed that even though Old Man McCreary looked pleased with his performance, his smile did not match the self-assuredness of the captain's.

McCreary matched note for note of the third round up to the

central movement when it became apparent to all in the room that the spectral officer was holding back. And, just as the young medium thought the tune could not possibly go any faster, it did.

Danforth sped up, leaving the little man without a hope, and McCreary dropped his bow from the bridge of his own fiddle, stepping back in defeat. The captain finished out the round, alone, proving why he was the one to beat. Ms. Bramden smiled proudly, applauding the champion as she stepped down from the stage to an open-mouthed Catheryn.

"That…" she muttered, the words coming out before she could stop herself. "That was astounding!"

Ms. Bramden smiled, tightly, a touch of mischief in her green eyes. "You don't think we keep him around for his warm personality, do you?"

The guest was taken aback at her host's rare humor, but before Catheryn could reply, a young, blonde-haired officer dressed in gray pulled her hand, with gentle insistence, as the band rolled in to the next reel. It was magnificent! He was as light on his feet as she was, and she twirled and danced down the line of party-goers, exchanging a pleasant smile at each turn. She couldn't think of a better way to meet them all, and yet, she couldn't comprehend there being so many of them in one place.

As the reel wound down to an eventual end, she found herself back with her original partner. He bowed, kissing her gloved hand, gratefully. His eyes looked up at her over her hand; a dazzling shade of blue that made Catheryn's cheeks flush, just a bit.

"May I fetch you a glass of punch, Ms. Catheryn?" he offered, his accent carrying a touch of the Old South.

"Please," she smiled, taking the arm he offered. "I'm afraid you have me at a disadvantage."

He took it, but released her just long enough to retrieve a cup from the refreshment table. "Forgive me for taking liberties. I overheard you with Ms. Abigale. I'm Lieutenant William Moore, but…" He held out a white-gloved hand to her. "You can call me Bill."

"Well…Bill," she smiled. "Do you serve here at the house, as well?"

"Yes, we're all quite on intimate terms here."

"And the captain? You know him also?"

His smile turned a touch bemused. "I've…lost track of how long. I know it's not possible, but…" His voice trailed off as he brushed imaginary lint off of his gray wool coat. "I have trouble recalling a time when we…haven't served together."

"That's a unique arrangement," she mused, nodding toward his uniform. "…considering your past *affiliations*. However, he seems quite…" How could she put it without being insulting? "…talented."

"Well, you know what they say," he said, leaning in conspiringly, flashing her a flirtatious grin laced with Southern charm. "They play the music, because they can't dance."

"Is *that* what they say?"

The young man snapped straight at the sound of the voice behind him, charm evaporating from his face and replaced with one of disciplined duty. "Captain."

Catheryn couldn't help but giggle as it was the lieutenant's turn to blush.

The captain offered a gloved hand to her. "Ms. Catheryn?"

Not quite ready to leave such pleasant company, it took her a moment to accept. If she recalled her manners guide for the era, it would have been a grave insult not to. And she was, obviously, trying to work in to his good graces.

The makeshift band fell into a waltz, and Catheryn assumed the stiff anatomical frame, doing her best to recollect dance lessons from her college days. It had been so much easier for her to dance before.

Perhaps, it was his brooding behavior that had her so distracted. He

entered the position with a practiced step; keeping polite distance

between the two of them; hand at her waist, his gloved hand

outstretched, supporting hers.

Despite the lieutenant's jibe, she was surprised to find the surly

officer quite light on his feet.

"You are quite at home with the waltz," she complimented.

His eyes seemed somewhat distant over her left shoulder. "When

you play the fiddle, you receive quite a few invites to dances. Especially,

when at school."

"School?"

"State College. At Columbia," he answered, stiffly. "Civil

engineering. Or, as much civil engineering one could get there at the

time. My grandmother on my father's side wanted no 'country

bumpkins' in the family tree. Wasn't exactly West Point, but it was the

next best thing."

"I'll bet they were proud of you."

"No," he said, flatly. "They were not."

Catheryn was more than a little surprised, searching his stolid face for further explanation. She could tell by the set of his jaw that the topic was now closed for further consideration.

The medium felt it best to change the subject.

"I have to say, I was surprised by the choice of music this evening," the young medium stated. "Some of it seems to be from more *recent* selections."

"You think we would be content playing 'Dixie' forever?" he snorted, his eyes remaining riveted to a point on the wall behind her. "There are some songs we can only play by express written permission. You no longer have to wish to be in "Dixie"; you just *go*. No one cares if the Federals are coming, and the Soldiers have *long* lost their joy."

Catheryn recognized the play on words of the common Civil War tunes and chuckled softly. "So, I suppose you've had to…expand your song portfolio."

The waltz came to an end, and she pulled back to honor her partner with the traditional sweeping curtsey. As she prepared to move on to a new partner, she was surprised when he offered her his arm. Somewhat puzzled, and against her better judgment, she took it.

"Might as well start with the first floor," he muttered with an air of resignation.

The two of them moved away from the revelry and into the spacious parlor. She half-expected him to turn on one of the many lamps in the room, but he did not. He offered her a seat on the Federalist-style settee upholstered in a pale, Greek-revival striped print. She watched, curious, as he moved into a shadowy corner of the room behind the small parlor piano forte.

"It appears to be quite an affair out there this evening," she mentioned, a little ill-at-ease in the darkness. "I didn't mean to cause such a stir."

"You used the door," he murmured, curiosity causing him to move deeper into a darkened corner of the parlor.

"None of you uses a door?"

"Not for over a century."

She felt her cheeks grow warm. Of course, an energetic being would not trouble themselves with physical barriers that they could simply pass *through*. That was for the Living to deal with. She had to remember that she was in their world now.

The shadows of the room seemed to absorb him for a moment. Even though some of the din from the party spilled over into the parlor, she could still make out that he was whispering something, unintelligible.

To her amazement, in the dim light, a silhouette emerged from the darkness, as if in answer to his summons. She couldn't hear it, but she observed a momentary exchange between him and the shadowy figure. Concluding the conversation, he returned from around the other side of the small piano forte.

He came back to her side, turning to face the direction he had just come. His hand rose from his side, as if in a receiving gesture. Her eyes widened in astonishment as a small crack—a splinter of light—began to form in the space next to the piano. It widened, brightening into a large disruption, looking much like a crack in glass. An inner light gleamed, augmenting the boundaries of the artifact.

Catheryn was mesmerized. "What…*is* that?"

"It's a dimensional fracture. Damage." He continued to hold his hand high, not removing his eyes from the splendor. "When Ms. Abigale was a young woman, she and her mother held séances in this parlor. It was the late 1880's. It was popular. The opening and closing of the celestial door caused a crack to form between worlds. It's weakest here. It has to be guarded at all times. As long as we stay here, it has to be watched."

"Why?"

"Things…can get through. Things attracted by our presence," he frowned, his eyes not wavering from the spot. "Unpleasant things."

He dropped his hand, and just as abruptly, the rupture sealed as if someone had drawn a zipper closed.

"Remarkable," she breathed, shaking her head as she turned to his stone-faced visage. "Why are you showing me this?"

"Remember the box from earlier?"

The box. The broken radio. She nodded.

"In a séance, it takes the concentrated effort of multiple people to open one door, and as you can see, not very well," he replied, his eyes still riveted to the spot where the schism once appeared. "That box doesn't merely open a door."

His words sent a shudder through her. She recalled her feelings that afternoon. The vertigo. The suddenness of not feeling stable.

"What does it open?" she asked, her voice edged with concern.

Without a word, he moved toward the side door that led out into the entryway.

"Captain," she said, more insistently. "What door does it *open*?"

Even in the dark she could feel the intensity of his seriousness in the weight of his energy.

"All of them."

C atheryn followed Danforth up the stairs. The heaviness of the

moment before still plagued her mind, the words reverberating in

her head.

"It has to be guarded at all times..."

Guarded, from what? Before she could consider the matter further,

he made a motion with his hand. To her surprise, an unlit lantern seem

to conjure from thin air, swinging from an arched handle of brass held

tightly in his grip. As she watched, he waved his hand over the candle,

and without so much as a spark, it sprang to a saffron glow. She

recognized where they were. They were only a few steps from the room

Catheryn had claimed as her own. Instead of that direction, they

followed the railing along the other side of the stairs. The light was a

beacon in the dark hallway. It was hard to make out any features on the

walls. The light only cast a yard ahead of them. It was in that candlelit

casting that they saw the feet. Tiny, bare feet.

As the soldier raised the lantern, there were legs, and the fringes of

a little girl's white nightgown. Raising it higher revealed a child, no older

than five, with shoulder-length blonde hair. Her pale, round face was

downcast, as if she knew she was in trouble.

Danforth sighed. "Lottie, what are you doing up?"

He handed the lamp off to Catheryn, and, effortlessly, the soldier scooped the child up with a tenderness Catheryn didn't realize him even capable of.

"I couldn't sleep." The child rubbed her sleepy eyes. "Uncle Charlie, can you read me a story?"

Catheryn stopped short of laughing out loud. *Uncle* Charlie? The descriptor just didn't seem to fit so draconian a figure.

If Danforth heard her thoughts, he didn't acknowledge them. "You know Ms. Abigale would be displeased to find you out and about."

As if in response to the imagined vision, she wrapped her tiny arms around the officer's neck, burying her face into the curve of it.

Hefting her onto his hip, he turned toward a closed door nearby. "Back to bed with you."

He paused before the door, waving Catheryn ahead to turn the white ceramic door knob, stepping into the room. Her jaw dropped for the second time in one night.

The room was long; each side lined with four extraordinarily tall Victorian-style windows. Four dark-painted wooden chests were set up along its perimeter. A few were open; offering the glimpse of a spare doll or other toy. An upright bookshelf was set up against the far wall with six neatly-arranged shelves full of books. It was set up, very much, like a child's nursery. That alone didn't shock Catheryn. Set up on the old barn wood floor were two sets of six single-sized beds; one set on each side of the room.

And in eleven of them, sleeping children.

Their ages seemed to range from three to mid-teens, the girls and boys from diverse ethnicities. Catheryn stared in awe of them as she followed behind Danforth. They stopped at a cot that was unoccupied, the sheets cast back.

The soldier put the child onto the bed as if it were a precious parcel. Lottie loosened her grip and gently fell on her back, her head landing on the pillow. He pulled the sheets over her, and Lottie grasped them with her little hands, pulling them up the rest of the way.

He tweaked her little nose, playfully. "You stay in bed now, missy."

Danforth rejoined Catheryn, who was raising the lantern to take in the twelve sleeping forms.

"Where did they all come from?"

"Everywhere."

He motioned, silently, for her to exit with him. As he closed the door behind them, she turned to him for an explanation.

"All of these children are still very much grounded here," he said, quietly. "For reasons only they know, they chose not to move into the next dimension."

Catheryn blinked, incredulous. "They had no parents? No loved ones to come and claim them?"

"Either they were unable to see them, or they chose not to follow. Every conscious being has free will, no matter their age or experience. They choose when the time is right."

He moved to a chair at the end of the hall, pale moonlight shining in the one lone window. She couldn't read him well, but there was the proverbial weight of something on his shoulders. He looked out the window, not meeting her gaze.

It suddenly became clear in Catheryn's mind. "You brought them here."

"There are predators out there—just like in the world of the Living. I've seen 'em." His eyes met hers, etched with the most solemn expression of responsibility. "Dark, awful things that feed off the innocent. They need protection."

"And, Ms. Abigale? Is she aware of all of this?"

"We share the same mission."

It all made sense. His aggressive demeanor. His threats. His cajoling. The constant probing of her purpose here. The overwhelming sense that he was protecting more than just the house.

"Tell me something. I don't understand," she muttered. "They are all...asleep. They're dead. What need do they have for sleep?"

"Many of these children don't understand death. Putting them in a sleep cycle gives them a sense of normalcy like the life they had before. But it also serves another purpose," he explained, keeping his voice in a hushed tone. "When you dream at night, your consciousness is no longer here. Consciousness is quantum. It knows no time or place. Sleep is that moment where the walls between worlds fall away. Only then can their loved ones come to them without them being in a state of confusion or fear. It offers a moment for...visitation."

"Do they ever leave here?"

"Eventually. We keep them safe here until they decide it's time to go."

"But how do they leave?"

He rose from his seat. "We best get back downstairs."

There was a note of closure in his statement. She realized that was all she was going to get from him tonight. Taking the lantern from her, they prepared to descend the staircase when she caught his elbow.

"Thank you," she said, "for showing me."

The importance of what was shared needed no more acknowledgement than that. They, all those within the house, were taking a risk bringing her into their confidence. She felt humbled by that.

There seemed a brief pause in the offering of his arm, as if considering the weight of what he had just done. She took it as they headed back down. They were only a few steps from the entryway, when there was a rapping at the front double doors.

They exchanged startled looks of surprise.

"Are you expecting anyone?" he muttered.

Catheryn's eyes were riveted to the large oak doors, her throat tightening. The rapping. That steady cadence. The density of the thud. She wasn't certain as to why, but it, somehow, filled her with a feeling of dread.

"Don't answer it," she breathed.

Danforth's voice was edged with concern. "Ms. Catheryn…"

8

Catheryn found herself gasping, bolting upright in her bed.

Damn it. She hated when that sudden surge of emotion broke her free of her lucid dreaming.

She took in the early morning light streaming through the picture window of her room as her breathing returned to more of a casual rate. Her heart rate bounced as she heard an audible snap to her right.

Danforth, pocket watch in hand, was leaning against the far wall of the room. "You're up early."

She stretched her arms above her head, noting she was back into her familiar t-shirt and yoga pants. Her mind still struggled to process everything from the night before. She toyed with the idea of heading down in just her slippers. Thinking the better of it, she grabbed the riding boots from the floor at the foot of the bed.

She started to pull one shaft over the cuff of her yoga pant, when she paused. "Was it real?"

"What?"

"Last night. Was it real?"

He moved toward the bedroom door. "Dr. Faustus is waiting."

She slowly trudged down the oak stairs, drawn by the smell of brewing coffee. As she reached the bottom of the stairs, she felt, embarrassingly, underdressed. Dr. David Faustus was dressed in his trench coat and slacks, sipping from his cup while holding a matching saucer. His travel bag was next to his chair.

The elder doctor placed his cup on the saucer, his gray eyes looked puzzled. "I take it...you're not leaving, then?"

Catheryn found herself at a loss for words. After the evening's events, she wasn't sure what their next course of action should be. But 'leaving' wasn't one she had considered.

As if reading her body language, Faustus placed the cup on the Duncan Fyfe table. "Should we get some air?"

Catheryn and David stood out on the cement steps of the house, taking in the roiling waters of the mini rapids on the opposite side of the road. Both had managed to dig through the kitchen cabinets, finding some kitschy mugs for taking their coffee out of doors. It was a welcome warmth to take the edge off the cool autumn morning.

David took up a comfortable position against the wrought iron railing, studying Catheryn's face, carefully.

"So, what happened last night?"

She gave him a smirk. "Am I that obvious?"

"Only to someone who has worked with you for nearly twenty years."

Her eyes returned to the chaotic churn of the river. "I've never been to a location where there were…so many entities."

"How many?"

"Not sure," she muttered, taking a sip from her mug. "There were over sixty last night."

Faustus stood abruptly away from the railing. "Sixty?!"

"Oh, it was difficult to determine the 'permanent' residents here. Some may have been just passing through…" She shook her head, incredulously. "But to see them all in one place. What would draw them here?"

"Well…there's a thought…" her mentor muttered, rubbed his freshly-shaven jaw. "Look across the road. What do you see?"

Catheryn frowned, thoughtfully. "A river."

"A river; that's large enough to have movement, even in times of low precipitation or cold temperatures. The rocks create water shearing, producing negative ions."

The Lenard Effect. She studied the energetic principle in college. "Sure…"

"Combine that with the high water table, rich calcium deposits, and plentiful underground springs…"

He let his voice trail off, but she got the message. He stepped down into the grass, retrieving a small branch. "You are also in a river valley, which creates perfect conditions for fog and mist. Additional negative ions could be created by the coronal discharge from the plentiful forests nearby. Negative ions created by those two kinds of events are the most stable generation of ions."

"A potential energetically-rich 'feeding ground'…for the right kind of entity," she mused.

"Completely theoretical, of course. Considering the age of this community—the multiple generations of life and death—such a feeding source could support a colony of entities…" the scholar mused, taking a swipe at the grass with his stick. "…indefinitely."

"Keeping it historically-preserved would make it very attractive for them to return. Nothing changes for them," she supported. "Prime real estate. For the Living and the Dead."

"Unfortunately, the Dead don't pay rent."

Catheryn opened her mouth. She thought about telling him about the children. About the entities' mission here. She closed it. No. She wasn't even sure if she fully understood it all, yet. How could she expect him to?

She studied the pattern of dead leaves on the ground, stirred by the sweeping wake of her partner's stick. "I...think I'm going to stay."

Even though she didn't see his face, she felt the intensity of his gaze, probing her details.

She smiled, wryly. "...for a little while, at least."

"I can't stay," Faustus responded, flatly. "I have clients...and you as well, if you recall."

Nowhere near the number the older doctor had accumulated over years of practice. Not yet. Talk about not 'paying rent', she thought to herself.

"I know," she muttered. "I can talk to Baldwin. Maybe negotiate a larger fee for staying."

David was uneasy. "You feel comfortable staying here? With him?"

She hadn't even considered the real estate agent even being an issue. Andrew Baldwin didn't bother her. The other 'him' was another concern. She didn't want her partner to worry.

"I'll call you mid-week to let you know if it's worth staying around."

She could read the discomfort in the older doctor's taut expression as he took in the small town surrounding them. She didn't need to be psychic to know he didn't like the idea of leaving her here.

As she could sense his mind rolling through the fifth or sixth unpleasant scenario of what could happen, she took him firmly by the shoulders.

"Mid-week," she said firmly, looking him dead in the eye. "I'll call you."

As if in response, Andrew Baldwin trotted down the steps in his signature faded blue hoodie and hair wax.

"What's going on?" he said, stifling a yawn.

David took a hard look at her. Seeing no falter in her expression, he gave a sigh of resignation before addressing the realtor.

"I have to head back to town. Catheryn's got a few more things she wants to check out." Faustus opened the door to the rental car and paused just long enough to catch her gaze. "Mid-week."

She nodded, smiling at him, assuredly. "Mid-week."

"So what do we do now?" Baldwin asked from across the kitchen table, stifling a yawn as he raked his fingers through the sides of his bleach-blonde hair.

The young doctor scrutinized the cup of coffee on the table, forcing an irritating strand of her auburn hair over one ear that refused to stay in the ponytail she fashioned. She left the legal stimulant on the table, arms folded in contemplation.

"No more ghost hunters," she said, firmly, with a look that invited no argument. "We need them to build rapport—and trust—with us. We can't afford them being distracted with shiny gadgets."

"No more ghost hunters," he echoed, in agreement. He threw his hands into his lap with tired resignation. "What then?"

"I'm going to go look outside."

"Suit yourself. But watch it; the town goes into full swing about high noon," he quipped sardonically, pushing himself up from the table. "And if you see the village idiot crossing the road against traffic around three, he has right-of-way."

She rolled her eyes. "I'll consider myself warned."

She opted for the kitchen door off the east side of the house. Just a few steps away was a concrete garden bench not far from the side road running alongside the property. No doubt prime positioning to take in the colorful townsfolk. Or, the lack thereof. Across the street was a copse of trees sheltering another antiquated, two-story brick house. It seemed to have no signs of life; no car, no trash cans, no modern mailbox post. She made a mental note to ask Baldwin about it later.

She took a seat on the cool bench top, placing her feet flat on the gravel/grass surface beneath her. Closing her eyes, she breathed in the generous bright autumn sunlight, feeling its warmth against her skin.

Calm. Breathe in. Breathe out. She felt the slight stir of a warm breeze against her cheek. The singing of birds. Relaxing. Controlling the breath. Breathing in. Breathing out.

It was at that point that she became aware of a buzzing sound. Her first thought was that someone was mowing their lawn. But the buzzing became louder, almost more of a sensation. A sensation in her skull. The air around her skin seemed to vibrate. The hair on her arms started to prick. Something was going on. Something was about to happen. Her eyes snapped open.

The buzzing stopped abruptly, but she was starkly aware of the change in her surroundings. The house opposite of her was gone. So was the copse of mature trees. The only thing that remained in their place was a small collection of saplings. And spread out on the acreage before her was a sea of bleach white canvas. Tents. Tents of different configurations. Some were large wall tents, while some were smaller A-frame tents. Colors of various flags planted in the ground were fluttering in sharp contrast against the white. The sound of a horse's whinny drew her attention across the street and off to her right. A pair of brown horses with white markings were hitched to a nearby fencepost. On their backs were blankets of a familiar navy blue, trimmed with gold. Military horses. But not any military of the modern age. One of the steeds turned from its gentle grazing, its soft brown eyes taking note of Catheryn, which confirmed to her that she wasn't just observing this scene—she was part of it.

"What are you doing out here?"

She didn't have to turn to see who it was.

"Captain," she answered, curtly, not bothering to look at him.

Danforth took the spare seat next to her. He was freshly-shaved, but still sported his thick moustache and side burns. He was dressed in a clean red-checked collar shirt and navy wool frock coat. Resting his hands on the knees of his navy pants, he took in the sprawling tent city across from them, not bothering to spare her a glance.

"Someone reported one of the lady folk bothering the horses. I could only assume they meant…you."

"How would they know I was bothering the horses?"

"The horses know when they're being bothered."

Catheryn shook her head, uncomprehendingly, losing count of the number of tents spread out before her. "When did all these people get here?"

"They've always been here."

"No, they haven't," she challenged, looking him full in the face. "There were trees. And a house."

"Oh, yeah," he muttered. "I see that sometimes."

Her irritation was growing. "You 'see that sometimes'? What does that even mean?"

"They both exist. It's a shared reality," he muttered with a shrug. Don't you have something else better to do?"

"Like what?"

"Anything. Anywhere else."

Before she could drum up a response, there was the sound of approaching horse hooves on gravel. A tall, magnificent-looking brown stallion trotted up to them from just down the road. Mounted on top of him was a soldier in the familiar signature blue wool in a short shell jacket, the braided gold trim at the collar, sleeves and front signifying his cavalry sergeant status. His face was mostly covered by the navy wool kepi-style cap he wore, but she could still make out that he was of African American descent.

White leather gauntlets tugged on the reigns, the forced movement causing the horse to snort in challenge. Dismounting, the non-commissioned officer marched up to the captain, saluting sharply. Danforth rose to meet him, answering his salute.

"Sergeant Solomon—report."

"The evenin' scouts have returned, sir," the rider reported.

Catheryn could tell there was some unease in the cavalryman's demeanor. She could tell by the abrupt sidelong glances that the sergeant saw her, but seemed unsure whether to acknowledge her.

The new arrival kept his gaze riveted forward. "The perimeter is secure. Nothing to report."

If Danforth noticed the oddity in his behavior, he didn't mention it. "At ease, Sergeant. You and the men fall out. Get some breakfast."

After another exchange of salutes, the scout mounted his horse, urging the animal into a trot toward the tent city.

"I made him uncomfortable," she observed.

"You're new. It's been a time since there was anything *new* around here."

There was a question on Catheryn's mind, but she wasn't sure how to phrase it.

He released an exasperated sigh. "Out with it."

"Well…Sergeant Solomon," she stammered, still not sure how to, politely, put it. "He…reports to you?"

"Of course," he replied, his voice edged with impatient bristling.

"I didn't think the units crossed…ethnic barriers."

He snorted, the kind that hinted more at insult than amusement.

"You talk funny," he said, continuing to observe the early stirrings of the soldiers across the street. "All the units work together. Nathaniel Solomon is a good soldier. Earned those stripes. Knew him from when he was just a boy. He runs patrols for me. I would trust no other."

She eyed the red markings on his jacket and pants. "But if I'm not mistaken, you're…artillery. He's cavalry."

For the first time that morning, he regarded her with a sharp look of directness.

"Yes, you are mistaken," he said, bluntly. "He is cavalry, while I—am in *charge*."

She set her jaw as he swept past her, her disposition a mixture of anxiety and forced sternness. No, he could be as brusque and uncouth as he liked. She was not going to show fear. All the same, she released her tension in a long, unsteady breath.

"You okay, miss?"

She blinked, not at all expecting the voice to her right. Standing before her was a boy, no older than fourteen. He had brown eyes and dirty blonde hair. Unlike Baldwin's meticulous coif, this boy's hair stuck out from beneath his brown slouch hat like a scarecrow. He wore the butternut color of a Confederate private. His jacket had been mended a thousand times over, but the knees of his trousers were not so fortunate. His brown leather brogans were also in dire need of repair, his wool socks poking through random holes in the toe.

She smiled at him, cordially. "I'm fine. Thank you. What's your name?"

The polite removal of his hat did nothing for his hair. "Andy. Private Andy Jones, ma'am. Everyone else…they call me Rooster."

"Why do they call you that?"

"Because, half-pint makes a lot of noise for his size," a male voice answered over the young one's shoulder.

A big meaty paw landed on top of the private's head, mussing up the hair even more. The brown-haired man with a bushy beard came up from behind the youth, his broad shoulders and sun-kissed, weathered face spoke of hours in the field. His red sleeves of his pullover shirt were rolled up exposing a hairiness only challenged by his beard, but his shawl-collar front and numerous pockets sported beautiful needlework. Even though he wore Army cavalry trousers, they seemed a bit mismatched with the other accessories.

The man let out a good-natured guffaw from deep down in his plentiful belly. "Hair never did stay down worth a dang."

The little private made a face, shrugging off the unwanted attention, and the man moved on about his business.

"I noticed the captain was cross with you," Rooster commented.

"Don't pay it no mind. He's cross with everybody. He's better with the men than the womenfolk."

"You know him, too?"

The young soldier offered nothing more than a downcast nod, suggesting a similar discomfort with the fairer sex. "We all work together."

It was the second time she had heard that this morning. "Doing what?"

"Whatever needs protectin'." His eyes rose from the ground, but only for a second. "Right now, we protect the house."

"From what?"

Something seemed to shift in his demeanor. Like he had already said too much. "I...I gotta go. I can't be missing from my post."

"Wait!"

Before she could form another question, he was off across the road, disappearing among the tents.

Protect the house. Protect the house, from what?

She had no sooner formed the question in her mind than she began to feel somewhat dizzy. Lightheaded. What was that? The buzzing...It had returned. Growing louder and louder. Her eyes blinked.

And then, it was gone. The tent city. The horses. The soldiers. All she found was her staring down the mature copse of trees and familiar house across the street. She sighed, frustrated. She would have to make progress, another way.

9

Eight-year-old Jimmy Talbot put the small black box on the rough, barn wood floor of the children's room. His freckled nose was only inches from it while his two other compatriots crowded around. The redheaded Billy Crankstop put his toy horse down to squeeze in a closer look, forcing his African-American friend, Josiah, to jostle for position next to him.

Bridgette Talbot let out a resigned sigh and stood up from the rocking chair. She sported dark braids on each side of her head, and much like her younger brother, she had a sprinkle of freckles across her nose. Since she was the eldest in the room at fourteen, it was her, indirect, responsibility to watch over all there. She dropped her needlepoint in the rocking chair, and came over, as well.

Billy's wide blue eyes were mesmerized by the gadget. "What is it?"

Jimmy's brown eyebrows knitted together in recollection. "The men brought it. The ones that left. I think they broke it. I found it in the trash."

Bridgette placed fists on the scrawny hips of her knee-length cotton brown and white calico dress. "Maybe it should have *stayed* there…"

"What does it do?" Josiah asked, shouldering in for a closer look.

Jimmy ventured forward, reaching out a finger toward it with the utmost caution. "I don't know…"

Something happened. None of the children knew what, exactly, but something in Jimmy's touch sparked the small box to life. Voices emerged from the box; scrambled, stuttering voices.

Bridgette stumbled backwards, her brown eyes wide. Before anyone could stop her, she turned and ran, vanishing right through the closed door of the nursery.

They all sensed the urgency, anxiety feeding upon anxiety. Bridgette's abrupt departure was a sign that adults would be coming soon.

"How do you turn it off?!" Billy shrieked.

"Turn it off!" Josiah demanded.

Before Jimmy could take any action, a blue coronal light opened up behind the box. It was taller than any of them, resembling a sort of…doorway. All three of them jumped to their feet, unsure whether to be amazed or alarmed at the object's sudden appearance.

Billy stood frozen, exchanging anxious looks between the squawking box at his feet and the looming bright opening. He wasn't certain which to be more terrified of. "Jimmy, we have to turn it off!"

Much like before, Jimmy was more curious about the thing most were afraid of, and he took a cautious step toward it.

Josiah's big brown eyes mirrored panic. "Jimmy, don't touch that!"

All of the pleading in the room went unheeded as the brown-haired boy took another uneasy step forward. Their voices seemed to fade away in the background as his eyes seemed taken in by the hypnotic churning of light before him. He reached out with a tentative hand.

Josiah lunged forward. "Jimmy! No!"

A strong arm wrapped around the child's waist from behind, and dragged him back away from the whirling energy, just as a black, and dubious-looking shape projected out from the brilliant abyss toward where Jimmy had once stood. Tentacles grew from the ominous mass, causing the children to shriek in terror.

Danforth used his remaining hand to hurl unseen energy at the box on the floor. The small device took to air, striking the far wall of the nursery, smashing into pieces. The vortex collapsed immediately, and the room took on a foreboding silence. All the young eyes in the room looked up fearfully at the towering officer.

The captain dropped to one knee before his rescue, the boy's little body still trembling from the close call. "Jimmy—"

Everyone expected a stern tongue-lashing. A sound paddling wasn't out of the question. But to their surprise, the officer pulled the boy into a tight embrace. Danforth noted all of the astonished looks over Jimmy's shoulder.

"If you *ever* see a box like that again, you don't touch it— *understand!*" he ordered, sharply.

The wide-eyed children nodded in immediate compliance. At the open doorway stood Bridgette, looking somewhat shaken, herself.

"Bridgette, would you clean that up, and dispose of it, please?" the officer requested, firmly.

She swallowed hard. No doubt, after seeing what it had done, she didn't want to go anywhere near it. With a reluctant nod, she went to work.

Danforth turned his attention back to the boy, clutching him by the shoulders, his eyes a mixture of subsiding panic and agitation.

"Jimmy…what if I wasn't here in time? Your curiosity not only puts you in danger, but everyone here! What if that had gotten into the house?" He clutched the little body to him, again. "What if it took *you?*"

"I'm sorry, Uncle Charlie." The boy rested his cheek, wet with tears, against the shoulder of the wool uniform. "Please don't be mad."

Danforth was a mixture of emotions. The anger had no outlet. He couldn't be mad at the child. The protection of the house, and the protection of all in it, was his responsibility. He only had one person to be mad with.

That was, until a second opportunity came sailing into the door.

Catheryn Greye, alerted by the noise near her room, rushed in, sweeping past a startled Bridgette.

She noted the smashed device against the far wall of the room. "What the…"

Danforth rose from the floor. Catheryn's eyes widened. She could feel it in his presence before visually confirming it. She took a step back toward the doorway. His anger radiated from him, permeating the room.

His dark eyes pinned her to her spot. "You! This is all your *fault!*"

She stumbled back, catching the door frame. His rage took her breath away.

192

"I told you not to come here," he growled, taking a menacing step toward her. "I told you, but you wouldn't listen!"

Fearfully, she stepped back into the hallway, her eyes not leaving his smoldering gaze.

"You all think we are just part of a game. A source for your amusement. Not once do you think of the pain and misery you cause with your poking and prodding!" His eyes lit with fury. "You…go pack your things…and get…*out*!"

Unassisted by any human hand, and with a force that rattled all of the windows on the second floor, the nursery door slammed closed in her face.

Catheryn sat on the edge of her bed, fumbling with the smart phone in her lap. David's number screamed back at her from the bright screen in the dim light of the room, taunting her. Should she call? What would she say? What did she expect him to do? Drop all of his appointments to come up and rescue her?

Her jaw tightened at the sound of footsteps. The long shadow of booted feet passed underneath the closed door of her bedroom. It wasn't Baldwin; he had opted to go into town for some business. She fought down the urge to reach over and lock the antiquated oak door.

As if it would do any good.

She became aware of a presence standing at the foot of the bed. She could barely make out his silhouette in the dusky backlighting of the window. As jumpy as she was, she could feel immediately that it was not the spectral soldier.

"Why didn't you protect me?" she asked, sternly.

"He felt vulnerable and exposed. You just happened to be a target. You know the type," Ralph said, passively, unmoving, the dim lighting playing off his angular face. "You didn't need defending. He didn't hurt you."

"He *could* have," she snorted back at the enlightened being.

"He didn't."

She didn't know what was more infuriating; her adrenaline rush spinning her out of control due to the close encounter, or her guide's grounded sense of calm.

Fuming, the medium threw the phone onto the bed. "What is this; some crazy restraining order I can't file until he does something?"

"He lives by rules, too. If he breaks them, the repercussions are severe."

"You didn't see his face."

"I did," he said, blithely. "You are safe in here."

"And tomorrow?"

"That," he sighed, "…is a new day."

Charles Danforth was on his fourth pacing of the second floor. He was forcing the house into, what was probably, unnecessary precautions. He had Sergeant Solomon run the scouts along the Outer Defenses, again. Extra sentries were at the point of every portal leading into the house, and to the outer property. No telling what attention the box could have attracted.

And then, there was the living being on the second floor. What to do with her? A new light had emerged from beneath the slit of the door. Was she finally packing? He was more than slightly agitated to find her still present. He was rounding the railing when he stopped abruptly. In the corner of the hall was a red velvet high-backed chair. It had been empty on his last three passes. Now, it had an occupant.

The tall, lean figure was dressed in dark clothes, his long limbs resting on the carved cherry arms, pale fingers draping over the elegantly-carved lion's head stylings at the ends of the armrests.

The soldier frowned. "And, who are you?"

The presence tilted its head, slightly to the right, in

acknowledgement of the voice with an unsettling lack of alarm. "No one of consequence."

The figure rose from the chair, the single window lighting the hallway giving the sentry more detail of the new arrival's features. He had almost four inches on him. He was of a very lean build, his skin like fine porcelain. The senior officer wasn't sure what unsettled him more; the stranger's exceptional height or his startling blue-green eyes that almost seemed to glow with an otherworldly intensity.

Danforth felt the tiny tendrils of suspicion playing at the back of his neck. "State your business."

"*She* is my business," the figure said with a firmness that did not invite debate. "You have your charges. I have mine."

The captain's hand dropped to the hilt of his sword. An outmoded habit, but he hoped that it successfully communicated his seriousness. "And, what 'business' is that?"

"Nothing of consequence."

"Anything in my house is of 'consequence' to me."

The stranger turned to take in the copse of trees opposite the house, fidgeting with the cuffs of his long velvet coat. "I was there the day you received your assignment to this place."

Danforth was feeling less and less at ease. "You have me at a disadvantage…"

The man turned to address him, his angular jaw set firmly. "I knew our paths would cross in the future. I knew you were to play an important role in my charge's development."

The meaning of the stranger's presence now became clearer.

"You mean…her." The soldier frowned. "Well, your 'charge' has more work to do…someplace else."

"Not…*quite* yet."

"She is disrupting the order of this house," he growled. "That is an order I take seriously."

"I'd be questioning your diligence here if you didn't." If the expectation was for the stranger to feel threatened, he couldn't have appeared less so. "My responsibilities are just as important to me. No physical harm will come to her while she stays here. Are we clear?"

The captain took a step forward, his nose scant inches from the newcomer's chin. Neither man flinched.

Danforth's jaw tightened. "I guess that will be up to her."

The spectral officer brushed by him, continuing his rounds. He paused briefly prior to rounding the corner to cast a look behind him.

The stranger had vanished, without a sound. It unsettled him. As a soldier, he wanted his adversary in view at all times. No, he didn't like it. Not one bit.

Young Bridgette Talbot sat cross-legged on the floor, the brown and white checked ruffle of her calico dress brushing against the dark barn wood of the floor. She stared at the junk heap of all that was left of the magic box from the nursery, dutifully having gathered all the broken pieces at the captain's command. But something made her reluctant to just…toss them out. The strange form that had emerged from the energetic field was terrifying enough, but now, with the house settling down in to quiet, it all seemed a little less threatening and a little more…curious.

She ran her small fingers over the bundle of wires that attached to the shattered remains of the speaker assembly. What was it about this device that alarmed the captain so?

There was a strange feeling growing between her hand and the collection of ratty wires. She wondered what might happen if she just…

A static charge arched from her fingers and into the wires, setting her fingers tingling. The small cone housing the speaker amplifier sizzled and popped.

"Hello?"

Bridgette scrambled back from the pile of debris, as if it had burned her, her dark eyes large with alarm. There was a voice—a young voice—emerging from the pile of junk.

"Please...I'm scared. I don't know where I am..."

Eyes still large with anxiety, the young girl edged closer to the discarded device.

"Who...who are you?" the young girl asked, reluctantly.

"Sam," the young timid male voice answered. "Who are you?"

"Bridgette."

"Please help me. I'm all alone. Can you talk to me awhile?"

Bridgette blinked. Such an odd request. No one ever wanted to talk to her. The adults just found her under foot, and the children were bored with her, wanting to play games. And Uncle Charlie...Uncle Charlie was becoming more preoccupied with other things. Lately, it seemed to involve the young living woman that had arrived.

Something deep down within her felt for the young voice. She certainly knew what it was like to be lonely. How many times did she wish to have someone closer to her age to talk to?

She eyed the pile of wires suspiciously. "Where are you?"

"I don't know. I'm lost," the little voice explained, the tone of it edged with anxiety. "Please. Don't leave me."

"Okay," Bridgette Talbot muttered softly, kneeling down with a healthy three feet between her and the broken box. "I won't."

Corporal Hampden smelled the smoke before he saw the fire. The trees in this area next to the river were thick, but he was grateful to find water. Light had a hard time filtering its way through the canopy above, but now that it was night, there was barely any light at all. He couldn't recall when the sun had gone down, but it felt as if he had been picking his way through the fallen timber and strewn boulders for hours. He was cold; that damp, bone-chilling cold. Regardless of who was tending the fire, he was ready to barter anything for time next to it. He just had to know who he was dealing with first. There was no one to cover him. No telling if this party was of the enemy. The rest of his unit had been picked off...how many hours ago was that?

Hampden pressed his lanky 5'8" form against the rough bark of an old rotted oak tree, his Enfield powder musket held tight against his chest. Was it loaded? In the chaos of the fighting, he couldn't remember if it still was.

"Stand down, soldier," a lazy tenor voice drawled from the clearing.

"Come on outta there. I ain't gonna bite ya."

Hampden's blue eyes went wide, darting around the woods. Was he talking to him? How did he know he was there? Did he have hidden comrades, watching him in the woods?

"No one here but us two," the voice called, as if to answer his unspoken questions. "Or, stay out there an' freeze. All the same to me."

Hampden eased out of the shadows and into the fringe of the clearing, musket at the ready. His eyes darted around the empty space, his eyes falling upon the figure of a man before a crackling campfire. He caught the whiff of coffee boiling and immediately craved some. The man didn't move, his back still to the youthful Union gunner. He wore a long, dirty duster and a dark slouch hat that had seen better days. He was of slim build, not overly tall. His blonde hair was heavily transitioning to gray and was far too long to be regulation length. His chin sported a day's worth of stubble. The wide brim of his slouch hat obscured any more of his features.

The soldier took a bead on the stranger with his weapon. "It true? You alone?"

"Why would I lie?"

He couldn't help but feel somewhat puzzled. This man. Out here alone, without even a horse. He lowered his weapon and hovered over the stranger. The firelight washed over his well-weathered face, and he took a sip from his own tin cup.

"Have a seat," the stranger muttered. "It's cold out. Help yourself to the java."

Hampden crouched down, one hand still on the musket. Placing his mess tin on the ground, he reached across for the hanging pot. While leaning forward, his eyes looked to steal a better look of the stranger's face. The host seemed to sense it, the man turning his head slightly to the right, just out of the firelight. It did not make the soldier feel any more at ease. Regardless, he topped off his cup.

"Mighty grateful," Hampden muttered, finally reaching back to rest his musket against the tree behind him. He wrapped eager fingers around the tin and took a long draw. "I just…can't seem to get warm."

"Always happy to help for the benefit of the Union. They've been of good service to me," he stated, cavalierly. "I was a brother in arms once. You look like you're on your own hook."

True, Hampden thought. He was without orders. "Nah. Got into a row just west of Columbia. Line broke. Everybody skedaddled. Trying to find my way back to the unit. You?"

The man took a long draw from his own cup. "I'm trackin'."

The soldier felt a chill run through his already cold body that sent his scalp tingling. Bounty hunter. He'd heard the men talk about them. He'd never met one.

"Runaways?" Hampden queried, taking another uneasy sip from his cup.

"Whatever is worth fetchin'," he muttered down into his drink. "Maybe you can help?"

"Maybe."

"I'm looking for an officer. They say he's a shirker," the rough-hewn man explained. There was something unsettling how he managed to keep his face, expertly, in the shadows. "Charlie Danforth. You know 'em?"

Hampden bristled openly, his jaw tight. "Do I *know him*? I dream of killin' that bastard day an' night!"

"So, you know 'em?"

"He's the reason my brother's dead!" the young soldier spat through gritted teeth, his eyes dancing with embers of their own. For the first time in the whole day, he felt his body warm with rage.

"Sounds like you and me could do a bit of business."

The young corporal said nothing, not exactly sure he should commit to this stranger. He wrapped his fingers even tighter around his tin cup, wondering how he could be so close to the fire and still not feel it. Even the cup felt cold in his hands.

"Perhaps it would be good for me to know who I'm doing business with?"

The youth thrust an eager hand into the firelight. "Corporal Daniel Hampden."

The stranger finally turned into the firelight, affording the young cannoneer a good look at his host. Hampden wished he hadn't. One eye was of a riveting blue-green, while the other…the other was of no use at all. A deep scar cut from his forehead all the way down to the stranger's left cheek. The left eye was nothing but a useless cloudy white.

Even as the man held out a leathery hand to the corporal in friendly greeting, it was still everything the young man could do, not to flinch from it.

"Jackson Carter," the man introduced, with more of a hint of a Southern drawl. "At your service."

BRAMDEN HOUSE

10

Lieutenant Moore stood at the side window of his post on the upper floor of the house. He was on time to be relieved, but he still couldn't help but take in the swollen encampment outside with wide-eyed surprise. The size of the camp city had, practically, doubled overnight.

Captain Danforth took up position next to the blonde-haired officer, his facial expression, along with his projected energy, carrying an air of satisfaction.

"Are we expecting *visitors*, sir?"

Danforth didn't look at him, gazing down into the face of his pocket watch, instead.

"Reinforcements," he muttered. "A precaution. Has Sergeant Solomon reported in, yet?"

"No, sir."

He looked down at his watch, as if he had to look again. A half an hour late. "That's not like him. Send out reconnaissance."

Moore snapped a sharp salute of acceptance. "Sir."

As the young officer disappeared, Danforth snapped his pocket watch closed, depositing it into his right breast pocket. He was only two steps behind young Moore when the last person he wanted to see fell into step next to him.

Catheryn pivoted mid-step on slipper-padded tread, to keep up with him. She tried to shed the self-conscious feeling of the fact that she was still dressed in her yoga pants and t-shirt.

"Captain Danforth, about yesterday…"

"No time," he snarled, keeping pace with the young corporal as they exited the house by way of the side kitchen door. "More important things this morning. Embry!"

The bark took Catheryn by surprise, forcing her back a step as a white-haired sergeant dressed in a blue sack coat and black slouch hat, answered the call.

"Get the men at the ready. Prepare for additional sentry assignments," he snapped.

"Sir," Embry acknowledged with a crisp salute. He only took four steps before freezing, an inner-knowing seizing hold without even looking. "Captain, rider!"

The small group turned to see a familiar chestnut stallion trotting slowly up the gravel road. Two privates scrambled to the sides of the animal to help down a slumped form from atop the mount.

The captain rushed to the side of his missing scout as the privates eased the new arrival onto his back on the flat dusty road. "Solomon! What happened? Report!"

Blood ran from the non-commissioned officers' nose, traveling in a crimson rivulet down his dark skin.

His brown eyes were wide with shock as he gazed up at his commanding officer. "Capn'…I'm sorry…"

"Solomon, what happened?"

"S'pose to be gone!" Solomon breathed; his voice edged with panic. "Gone from here…long time now. I saw him die. Never s'pected…to see him again!"

"Solomon, I need you to snap to!" Danforth pressured, his voice soft, but firm. "Report!"

"He's comin'," he said, weakly. "He's comin'…for ya. No one's safe!"

Danforth did his best to mask his shock, but Catheryn felt the emotional instability ripple from him.

The captain turned on Embry. "Get the surgeon over here. Double-quick!"

"Who?!" Catheryn demanded softly. "Who's coming?"

Danforth grimaced at her voice. "Get back to the house. You're safer there." He turned to Moore. "Double the guard around the house. And the nursery!"

Moore didn't even take time with the salute. He was gone in a flash but was quickly replaced with another man with a gaunt face, gray moustache and neatly-kept short beard. He wore a straw hat and cream-colored, knee-length linen coat. In his dominant hand was a black leather satchel, identifying him to Catheryn as someone medical. Together, they knelt next to the young sergeant, the surgeon unbuckling the side compartment of his bag to gain access to supplies. A young private rushed in, offering the injured man a tin cup filled with water.

"Sergeant," Catheryn whispered, laying a comforting hand on the scout's shoulder. "What happened?"

"Someone in the house…" he said, weakly. "They gave Capn' away. Says they tole 'im where to find us."

"Told who? Who is this person?"

"I met 'im. Years ago. He took my kin and sole 'em back into slavery." He slumped into the arms of the surgeon, too tired to go on. "He's comin'."

She brushed some of or stray auburn curls behind her ear. It was obvious that her fact-finding would be limited.

"I'll be sure to tell the captain," she murmured, empathetically.

As orderlies swept in to whisk the injured man away, she couldn't help but gaze up to the window of the room she had just come from. *Someone in the house.* God! Who could it be?

Andrew Baldwin didn't like waiting. Maybe it was his Adult Deficit Disorder, but he couldn't stand waiting around to find out what was happening. He had taken his usual care, putting his blonde coif together with generous amounts of pomade, but the faded blue sweatshirt and matching jean assortment was the only outfit that was convenient. His hands needed to stay busy. He put himself to work in the kitchen, cleaning coffee mugs, and staging them in the perfect position back on the kitchen shelf. He wanted this place back in the showcase condition that it was a week ago. It would take some time. He was determined to get this place back on the market, as soon as possible.

210

But then, there it was; that unnerving feeling at his back. There was that...*tingle*.

The same tingle he felt along his left side, the very moment he had entered the house. The tingle he felt, usually, just a fraction of a moment before something happened. Something *otherworldly*.

He turned his back against the iron shelf of the pine pie safe, his gaze drawn up to the upper corner of the kitchen. His hazel eyes widened as the white dish rag fell to the floor. The ceramic realtor's mug in his other hand, joined it on the hardwood in an unceremonious crash.

He stared, agape, as the miasmic black ooze spread across the white plaster of the ceiling, like an invading hostile host. It writhed and twisted like a thing alive.

Because, it was. He could feel it. It was a crawling colony of blackness that appeared to eclipse all light from that corner of the room. Every inch of the realtor trembled, riveting him to where he stood, unable to move.

"Dr. Greye..." he attempted, hoarsely, unsure how it would react to any sudden noise. "Dr. Greye..."

The Blackness seemed to churn and shift toward his position, spewing forth in a violent, attacking fury that terrified him. He was no longer worried about volume.

"*Catheryn!*"

The door to the back of the kitchen flung open, the sunlight streaming into the small space. Catheryn gazed down at the man in the corner of the kitchen, practically in a fetal position against the far wall.

"Mr. Baldwin?"

The Blackness did not seem to like the intrusion upon its space, retreating into the corner from which it had come.

Baldwin, in direct opposition, did not move, his mouth still agape at the roiling absence of light.

"There!" he breathed in a throaty squeal, his eyes a direct line to the area in question.

The young doctor turned, gasping at the corner of the kitchen. The Blackness boiled and churned, seeming to hum like a hive of angry bees. Her green eyes widened as she watched the mass move and pulse.

"What is *that?*" the young therapist breathed.

"I don't know!" Baldwin whimpered, feeling only slightly more empowered by her presence. He stood up, finding the stability of the pine pie safe against his back. He moved along the kitchen counter, inching toward the outside door.

The windows.

Catheryn could hear the familiar voice in her mind; the whisper that had always made itself known in moments of alarm. Her eyes darted around the room, looking for the source as a matter of reflex, although she knew she would never find it. She never had.

Light!

Her eyes fell upon the roller shade eclipsing the kitchen window. She dove across the kitchen, yanking down on the dangling cord. The mechanism went to work, retracting the white vinyl upward with a loud snap.

Light! You need the Light!

She moved to the dining room, yanking at the window blinds there. As each blind gave way, more light streamed into the dark room. She observed as the Blackness sailed along the white plaster ceiling, just out of reach of the creeping sunlight that emerged from each open window.

"Open all of the blinds!" Catheryn ordered, moving onto the parlor.

Andrew dove after her. "Are you kidding, it will fade the carpet—"

"Now!"

One by one, each of the blinds rolled up, the rays of outside light swallowing up the cracks and crevices for the Blackness to hide. With an echoing, spine-chilling, howl, the Blackness retreated into the upper left corner of the parlor.

The realtor witnessed its departure, trying to find his breath. "It's gone."

Catheryn stood next to him, her mind racing. It was gone, but something still didn't feel right. Still not at ease. It wasn't gone. Her memory kept replaying something. Something said earlier.

" *'Someone in the house'...*"

She gasped as the sudden realization hit her.

"The children," she gasped. "We just drove it upstairs!"

A bigale Bramden hurried the shrieking children down the hallway toward the nursery, taking note, every few feet, how quickly the blossoming black tide erupting across the ceiling was gaining on them. A perfectly good morning of needlepoint blown. Dressed in her casual brown cotton wrapper, and doubling that down with an apron, she wasn't exactly dressed to receive visitors, but duty called. The screaming of the children was unsettling, setting her teeth on edge. If she had any. She wished there was something she could do to calm the children down. There appeared to be a direct correlation between how large and fast it moved in relation to the children's excitement. Abigale realized she may be feeding it with anxiety of her own. Most of her stress was centered on one thing: where was Captain Danforth?

The herd of stampeding children filtered through the door of the nursery. She managed to fetch the old broom from inside the doorway before slamming the door shut behind her. The only thing that stood between the children and the Blackness was just her, and a straw-wound broom.

"You!" she growled, bitterly, holding the broom before her like a bat. "You get out of here!"

The matron swung at the cloud of black before her. It dissipated, but only temporarily, as it reformed in the corner behind her.

She glared, much like a maid would at an annoying pest. The older woman swung again, the instrument passing through the swarm and slamming into the wall. Catheryn and Andrew found her like that.

"Get out of my house!" Bramden snapped, swinging the broom at the roiling dark form once more. "Get out! Get out! GET OUT!"

Catheryn jumped to the window, snapping the roller blind up. Sunlight spilled through, illuminating the dark hallway. For the second time that day, the noiseless mass loosed an ear-splitting shriek that took all witnesses by surprise. The Blackness fled along the joint between the ceiling and the wall before squeezing through an unseen escape route in the upper corner of the hall.

"Vermin!" Abigale Bramden grunted disgustedly, glowering at the ceiling as she tossed the broom to the floor. "And don't you come *back!*"

The therapist and the realtor both blinked at her, incredulous. Here they were; feeling as if the children were in some danger, and there was the matron of the household acting as if she had just missed cornering a rat.

"Come into *my* house?" the older woman spat, wiping her hands on the apron in her lap.

Baldwin was the first to speak. "What *was* that?!"

She looked the realtor up and down as if he were no better than the thing she had just helped scare off. "Parasites. They feed off the basest of emotion. That's for lower beings. Not in *my* house!

It was Catheryn's turn to be confused. " 'Lower beings'?"

"Those..." Ms. Abigale sneered, waving away at some unseen reality outside the antiquated window. "Those that don't know that they're dead and lost in a tide of negative emotion that they won't let go of. They are not welcome here. They attract...pests. Only those that are looking to evolve can enter. The captain and I see to that."

Catheryn watched as the lady of the house moved to the window, gazing out at the world below. Her visage may have been standing in the house before them, but the older woman's mind was not present. Catheryn could feel that.

"Was it drawn here by the children?" Catheryn asked the matron, her voice low enough to not disturb the party she was implicating.

The matriarch's expression changed from agitation to one of solemn contemplation.

"Most of us are old enough to know what it means if we stay here on this plane of existence," the matron reflected. "We know the price. They—the young—barely had a chance at life. They barely have a sense of self, let alone the experience necessary to make their own decisions. That makes them easy prey to those that would manipulate them. They deserve our protection. For that reason, and that reason alone, we brave this chaos—for them."

11

"David! You didn't even call!" It was everything Catheryn could do to hold back from hugging the man, but things were surreal enough without adding to it. "What...no clients today?"

David was dressed in his usual business casual khaki pants and gray fisherman's knit sweater. He eyed his colleague with a measuring gaze. "Dressed for work, I see?"

Catheryn was suddenly very aware of the t-shirt/yoga pants ensemble that she had been practically living in all week. She, desperately, needed to ask Andrew where the washer and dryer were located.

"Yeah...uhmm, sorry. You need coffee, and we...," she murmured, stepping aside to let him in. "...we need to talk."

Andrew and Catheryn could tell David was struggling to absorb it all as he sipped his coffee with one hand, and thumb and forefinger of his other hand, massaging his temples.

"How many children upstairs?" Faustus inquired, somewhat incredulously.

"Twelve," Catheryn validated.

"And a battalion outside…"

"Actually, more like a regiment," Baldwin corrected. "Battalions are much larger, and, generally, consist of more disciplines...and a colonel, so since we don't have a colonel—"

It didn't take too severe of a gaze from Faustus to silence him. It was pretty clear the seasoned mentor was already topped out trying to analyze the situation he could neither see nor perceive.

David slid his mug onto the table, resting back into his high back chair as his thumb and forefinger dropped to the bridge of his nose.

"What do I do with this?"

Catheryn was confused. "What do you mean?"

"Do you know how this sounds? This all sounds completely..."

The elder doctor paused. There were just certain words his profession didn't use.

Catheryn felt like she had been emotionally sucker-punched. She stared back at her colleague, a thousand feelings welling up at once. She pulled away from the table without a word, heading in the direction of the front entryway.

David winced, suddenly realizing a misstep. "Catheryn, I didn't say you were—" As he followed her through a propped-open front door, he found her on the front step, arms folded tightly against her chest, jaw set in defiance. "Catheryn—"

Dr. David Faustus found himself in the rare moment of not finding the perfect words to say. Although that gift was very much his livelihood, at this moment, it was difficult. He closed his eyes, planted his feet on the stone step and let loose a cleansing sigh. Taking a moment to collect himself, he recognized he was mirroring her defensive posture, and unfolded his arms from across his chest. He rested a hand on the iron railing in an attempt to appear more relaxed.

"You're right," he muttered. "I never should have spoken to you that way in front of the client—"

"The *client*?!" She turned on him, her green eyes sparking, riveting him to where he stood. "We have worked together for *fourteen years*— that's more than I've ever worked with *anyone*. The reason we've worked together for so long is because you were the one to convince *me* that my abilities had merit. That *I* was not crazy."

220

"And you know we don't use that word. Ever." He took a measured breath before stepping forward and taking her by the shoulders. "I'm just concerned that you are getting too emotionally invested in this case. I want you to consider that we've reached the limits of what it is we can do here."

She twisted out of his hold. "You have not been here the last few days!"

Faustus refused to flinch, holding his ground. "…and, I was really reluctant just to leave you here. I really was! It was not fair to leave you here without means of escape."

Faustus realized his voice was rising in volume. He threw a cautious look back through the propped open door and into the parlor. Baldwin was doing all he could to look as if he was not paying attention to the two of them, however Faustus did catch him peeking over the edge of the business newspaper that he pretended to read, albeit positioned upside-down. It would have been comical if the situation wasn't so dire.

David gazed into her eyes, beseeching her for any patience she might have left. "What is Rule Number One when we do these long-term investigations?"

She sighed, her stone-hard gaze breaking from his. "Never

investigate alone."

"And why is that?"

"To have a witness to activity."

"And?"

"To offer a reality check, when needed." She hated when he was right; damn him. "But Andrew has been here the entire time—"

"—and is a client, who is not *grounded*," her colleague reminded. "It is our job to be that for him."

Catheryn turned away from him, hands on her hips as she began to pace back and forth along the steps, partly in irritation and partly in frustration. She froze, mid-stride, to look at him, a challenge in her gaze.

"Stay through Sunday."

He felt his shoulders tightening again, and he gave a tired sigh.

"If we don't make any headway…" She sighed, resignedly. "I'll leave with you."

He drew back to study her expression to see if she was serious. It was a fruitless exercise. She always was.

"Fine. Case closed. No more time spent on this." He turned, hands in the pockets of his khaki pants, fixing her with his steely gaze. "Sunday it is."

Danforth pressed two fingers into the soft ash of the inactive charcoal left behind by the campfire, and frowned. Catheryn and David were only a few short paces away, but as per usual, Catheryn was the only one to observe him.

"There's something wrong here," the soldier muttered to no one in particular.

Catheryn was reluctant to come out with the spectral captain this morning, but since he roused her at an ungodly hour of the A.M., she assumed it was important. She roused her partner to join her, but this wasn't what she was expecting to find. It didn't help that she was not able to take in her usual amount of legal stimulant before leaving the house.

The young doctor stifled a yawn, as she turned to a patiently-waiting David. "He says there's something off with that campfire. How a campfire is suspicious is beyond me…"

Faustus knelt before the dust and what was left of the incinerated wood. He fished through the ash and picked up a twig. He snapped it and observed the core of the charred material.

"Not unusual," the elder scientist muttered. "Not for something that was incinerated in a microwave."

Catheryn blinked in surprise. "What?"

"This combustion occurred from the inside out."

Catheryn's jaw dropped. "How…how is that even…?"

"Not natural." The captain frowned, turning away from the site with the wince on his face that indicated *something* out of place, even for his world.

She fell into step alongside the irritated spirit. "What do you mean?"

"Too organized to be a random lightning strike." Danforth didn't break his stride, his jaw set. "This was kindling collected to burn, but not with flint or match. Only someone from my kind can do that. And there's only one reason they would go to the trouble of making a fire."

Catheryn was at a loss, shrugging. "To keep warm?"

"No such thing as 'warm'," the spectral officer snorted. "We're dead. Only reason they would do that would be to…get attention."

Catheryn stopped, feeling helpless in keeping up with the pace of his reasoning. "Attention? From who? For what purpose?"

"I need to get back to the house."

Faustus caught up at the side of his exhausted protégé. "What's going on?"

224

She gave an exasperated sigh, shaking her head. "Like *he* would tell *me?*"

After regrouping at the house, and downing a few cups of coffee, Faustus and Greye exchanged notes with Baldwin. After doing so, David withdrew to unpack his bags. That left Catheryn with time to think. She was far from figuring out the logistics of it all, but it frustrated her that the spectral captain was the only one that regularly crossed over into her world. Perhaps it was time to try to connect with the camp outside, again. If Danforth wouldn't talk to her, maybe some of the others would.

She found a comfortable spot on the parlor settee. Finding even footing on the barn wood floor, she closed her eyes. Concentrating on her breathing, she allowed it to slow. In. Out. In...

She felt the familiar buzzing in her head, pushing it aside so as to not disturb the depths of consciousness into which she was entering. Instead of the buzzing fading off, it continued to increase. Louder. Louder. Until...

"Hello."

Catheryn's eyes snapped open, suddenly aware of a presence directly to her left. On the vacant space next to her on the settee, sat a young girl, barely a teen, if a day. She gazed up at the young doctor with wide brown eyes. Her brown hair was wrapped up at the back of her head in an elaborate braid. She wore a purple and pink floral print, knee-length dress. The drawstring neckline and shorter puff sleeves showed off more skin than the older ladies, but it was appropriate for a girl her age, out of the 1800s.

Catheryn smiled, cordially. "Hi. What's your name?"

"Bridgette," she answered, earnestly. "We met up in the nursery."

"I remember," the young doctor recalled. "What are you doing down here?"

"The menfolk are nervous," Bridgette noted, matter-of-factly, casting a gaze out the window. "Something's going on."

Catheryn followed her gaze outside and did her best to hide her surprise. She had been pulled back into the other Plane of Existence, and it was obvious that she was looking at the plan's architect. It shocked her that a girl of her young age could have, psychically, pulled her so forcefully into her little world. It was a rather advanced talent for an entity.

The houses across the street from Catheryn's reality, had dissolved, giving way to the familiar open expanse of green. She expected to see the standard number of soldier campsites but was surprised to see the dramatic increase in their number. As her eyes swept over the encampment, her attention was drawn to a small presence standing directly across the street; a familiar boy with scarecrow-style hair, crowned with a brown slouch hat. He stared back at her with unsettling intensity, almost as if singling the medium out. He was still dressed in his heavily-patched butternut-colored uniform.

"Isn't that Andy?" Catheryn observed, realizing she wasn't using the nickname she was invited to use. She'd leave it to the rest to call him that if they so wished. He was a boy. Not a farm animal.

She wasn't prepared for the young girl to turn, brusquely, away from the window. The brown-haired girl folded her arms, haughtily, against her chest. The young doctor tried to search the little girl's face for meaning.

"Bridgette, what is it?"

"I don't wanna talk about him," the young girl replied, her lip in a firm pout.

"Why?" Catheryn asked, mystified.

"He's done bad things!" she retorted, sharply, re-folding her arms, even tighter. "You don't know what he's done. *I* know."

"Is that why he's out there, and you're in here?" the medium asked. She was struggling with the hierarchy of this place. "Because of what he's done?"

"I don't want to talk about him!"

"Well, *I'm* going to talk to him. I'm sure he's a nice boy…" Catheryn stood up from the couch, looking down upon the sulking child. "You sure you don't want to come with me?"

Without a word, the young girl turned away from her, resetting her crossed arms in defiance.

Catheryn sighed, and with a shake of her head, she got up and moved to the front double-doors. She gave a surprised start as a young corporal in blue wool with cavalry stripes hopped out ahead of her to open the door before falling back into his sentry position with musket at the shoulder. Now the *inside* front door had sentries? Very curious.

She smiled politely, still trying to decide if she appreciated the intensity of protection as she exited the door. Before she even got a step out into the sun, the young voice of her person-of-interest rose to greet her.

"Good morning, Miss Catheryn!"

The young Andy-named-Rooster started in an enthusiastic jaunt toward her before he froze. The little private took a measured step out of the street and back onto the green.

The young doctor followed the boy's gaze over her shoulder, toward the picture window of the parlor. And, abruptly, the curtain of the ground floor picture window snapped shut. She didn't have to guess who that had been. Catheryn pasted an amiable smile on her face as she crossed the gravel street toward the boy.

"Andy, what's the matter?"

His head was down, but there was no missing the shame on his face. "I'm not supposed to cross the road."

"Why?"

He looked away from her. "I'm not supposed to. That's all."

"Is it because of Bridgette?" she asked, searching his downcast expression for any clue. "I'm sure she'd like you if she got to know you—"

His large brown eyes snapped to hers. "She wouldn't."

"Is it because you were a Confederate?"

His eyes avoided hers, again. "I don't want to talk about it."

"Okay," Catheryn replied lightly, hoping to remove some of the weight from the conversation. "So, what's happening today?"

He proceeded to walk along the road, a pause in his step inviting her to join him. "Sergeant Solomon is better now. We finally got a full report. It wasn't good. They've increased security around the house."

"Why?"

He paused; his freckled nose tipped up to reveal an expression of seriousness too old for his young face. "Somethin's comin'. Somethin'...bad."

Catheryn felt the chill. It wasn't exactly a chill, but it made the hair stand up on her arms. She rubbed the bare skin in an attempt to get it to subside. She may have dismissed it as minor, but something was churning in the pit of her stomach; an unpleasantness she could not quite describe. She could feel it, also. And if the Dead were afraid of it...

"Andy," Catheryn said, placing her hands on her knees to come closer to his level. "What is so important about this house?"

"We don't talk about that."

She sighed. She was beginning to take all of this silence, personally. But when a child has been told not to tell, she learned—especially in her profession—it was time to talk to a grown-up.

"I think we should go check on Sergeant Solomon," she suggested. "What do you think, Private? Would you escort me?"

The young soldier's face brightened as if happy to have been trusted with such an important task.

"This way, Miss Catheryn," the young soldier directed, taking her hand as he stepped off toward the encampment. "Follow me."

12

"Miss Catheryn, please!" Lieutenant Moore pleaded.

The Confederate officer held down his gray slouch hat by the crown to save from losing it, as he did his best to keep up with the young therapist's determined pace.

"You are not permitted to enter without an escort!" Moore called out.

She stopped just short of the large wall tent, marked with a ground-planted green flag emblazoned with the letter "H", and turned on the lieutenant.

"And what is wrong with the one I have?" she countered, indicating her young guest.

"It's no place for a lady such as yourself," Moore protested. "Please, ma'am!"

She fixed him with a withering glare. "Lieutenant, my first year of residency was in the emergency room down at County. Trust me, Lieutenant—we are not going to find anything in that tent that is going to shock me!"

Before the officer could even find his voice to ask what an 'emergency room' even was, the young private charged ahead and held back the tent's canvas fly. Emboldened by the private's action, Catheryn ducked inside.

Lieutenant Moore forced a sigh through pursed lips. A corporal dressed in Union blue saluted the senior officer upon approach. Moore answered the gesture with an added command.

"Corporal. Find the captain."

"Sir!"

The blonde officer in Confederate gray watched as the smaller man went scurrying on his way.

"He's gonna kill me," Moore muttered to himself. "Again."

The wall tent was over two hundred square feet, and boasted an eleven foot high peak, but even with all the roominess, the heat of the mid-day sun made the place stifling with both front and back flies closed. The light was surprisingly dim, however, with the aid of the gray-haired corpsman on duty, Catheryn managed to find her way to the military cot holding the mending body of Sergeant Nathaniel Solomon.

As the young private stood guard behind her, she knelt at the cavalryman's side. The sergeant's cavalry shell jacket and vestments had been removed, allowing the collar of a blue checked shirt to peek out from under the hem of a patchwork quilt. The man's steady, slow breathing shifted. As if aware of being watched, his brown eyes snapped open. He started slightly, noticing the previous female vision he had witnessed before, kneeling next to him.

"Stand down, Sergeant," Catheryn spoke, soothingly, motioning with her hand to lay back. "I'm just here to talk."

He turned to look away from her, his eyes riveting to the canvas wall. "I said all I meant ta say ta the Officer of the Watch."

"And the captain, too, I suppose."

His head snapped back to her, reading the all-too-knowingness in her aventurine green eyes.

His resolve eased, somewhat. "I suppose so."

She chose her next words carefully, using the crafted words of a therapist. "He's a hard man to get to know. How do you know him?"

"Cap'n Danforth?" The young sergeant struggled to pull himself up more comfortably on the pillows behind him. "I met him when he was with his Missouri family."

Catheryn moved to prop up the pillows to make him more comfortable. He maneuvered one behind his shoulders as the young doctor took a more attentive position next to the cot.

"His granmama...she own us—Mama, Papa, and me," he stated, matter-of-factly. "She...sent the cap'n to school in Columbia. Havin' no child'n of her own, she doted on the captain and her nephew, Rufus. Rufus didn't take to schoolin', so it was up to the cap'n to go to school to become a gentleman farmer. Take over the family business." The first hint of a smile crossed Solomon's lips. "Jus'...they forgot to ask him first."

Catheryn shared a chuckle with the young scout, adjusting the quilt more securely about him.

"He didn't want the farm." Catheryn's words were more of a statement than a question.

"He saw enough of that kinda life while he was there to knows he wanted nothin' of it," the sergeant said, dismissively, not meeting the young woman's gaze. "He wanted to see the world. Caught the Army bug early. Went in to...science and engineerin'. Although, he didn't exactly tell his granmama."

"How did he know you?"

"At first, he didn't." A smile tugged at the corner of his mouth, the look in his dark eyes looking somewhat nostalgic. "The family threw a shindig for the cap'n. He had come home for the summer. One year left to go. Some of us…we planned to slip away. Felt the house would be too preoccupied with the 'goins on."

He shifted his shoulders into his new position, and as he struggled, Catheryn moved to shift his pillow.

"My papa and mama grabbed me, and snuck down to the creek. We knew we would be cuttin' it close to the main house. That's when we saw him."

"Who?"

"The cap'n. Standin' on the back porch, lightin' up a cigar, dressed in the evenin' finery. We weren't expectin' him to be there. We froze. We didn't know what to do."

Catheryn remained enthralled, edging closer to the cot. "What happened?"

"He saw alla us. Didn't take much to figure what we was up to, I suppose," the young sergeant shrugged. "We didn't know if he was gonna ring the bell, or shoot us. Instead…he reached in his vest pocket

236

and pulled out this gold watch. He looked at it, and then…he threw it at me. 'Could fetch a good sum,' he said."

After all the time that had passed, the sergeant still managed to look amused at the memory. "You know, I think that was the only time I saw him outta uniform. He tole us how to cross the creek so the hounds couldn't catch us. We didn't waste no time to think why he did it…" His distant gaze returned to Catheryn, a smile tugging at his lips. "Never did sell that watch. Us havin' that—raise more questions than it was worth. Sent it back to him as soon as we got settled up here in Ioway. Couldn't make us citizens, here, but they let us work. Good thing, too. Papa didn't last the winter."

"I'm sorry."

"It is what it is." He looked down. "I met up with ole' Doc Watson. He took care ah me and Mama. Made up papers in case there was questions, too. Lotta folks down there liked to help our kind, all quiet like."

"What did you do?"

"I helped the doctor when I could," he mused. "That's how I met up with Cap'n Danforth, again. Doctor was helpin' soldiers on their way up to Keokuk Hospital way. The cap'n was wounded. Orderlies weren't takin' care of 'em, so I brought him food up when I could. Took a bit but he finally recognized me."

The young officer's face darkened. "When he passed, I made sure they knows how to get him home. After that, I told Doc Watson I wanted to sign up. Keokuk was takin' coloreds. He spent four days tryin' to talk me outta it. Didn't work."

She smiled, warmly. "Of course, not. Nathaniel…may I call you Nathaniel?"

He nodded, reluctantly, as she nudged the covers more closely about him. When she met his gaze, again, her eyes were more serious.

"What happened out there?"

Solomon's dark eyes narrowed, doing his best to recall. "We were runnin' scout along the perimeter of the house just like he tole us. And there he was…"

"Who?"

"Jackson," Solomon frowned. "The man was an ugly son a bitch when he alive…We didn't see 'em comin'. Took us out one by one. Like they knew where to find us."

Something in Solomon's demeanor seemed almost chilled. Catheryn moved to pull the blankets up more securely about him, but the young sergeant shrugged her off.

Solomon spat out, wincing, as he adjusted his posture. "He's got some score to settle with the capn'."

The young doctor's eyes squinted, uncomprehendingly. "What 'score'?"

The sergeant rolled away from her, his gaze on the canvas wall. "I dunno."

Catheryn had a thousand more questions, but Solomon had already softened into the embrace of the pillows, exhausted. There was more to know, but she would have to find it out on her own.

She stood up and took a step away from the sleeping soldier, just in time for the tent flap to be folded back. She was surprised to see Ralph duck through the entrance, sporting a brown frock coat and matching vest that went well with his light brown hair. A green silk cravat around his neck finished off the look, making him look quite smart in appearance.

He turned to acknowledge the considerably-shorter, gray-haired corpsman who rose from his seat as he entered. There was an apparent flash of recognition across the poor man's face as his pale eyes grew wide with astonishment.

"Stand down, Corpsman," the guide offered in his gentle tenor voice, smiling his usual serene smile. "I just happened to be in the neighborhood."

This did not remove the shock from the older enlisted man's face as he struggled with the proper response. He finally settled on a brisk salute before quickly exiting the tent.

Ralph turned, rubbing his palms together. "And where is our sergeant? Ah, there you are."

The guide had no trouble navigating the darkened tent, and Catheryn sat back with amazement as the sergeant turned, giving him an almost identical performance as the corpsman. As he turned in his cot, the young cavalryman's eyes grew quite large, his mouth open in astonishment.

"It's okay, Nathaniel," Catheryn assured, somewhat puzzled by such a severe reaction to her guide's presence. "He's here to help."

"Quite alright," Ralph muttered softly, taking the young man's hand in his own, stroking the back of it, soothingly.

His eyes never left Nathaniel's. Distress seemed to leave the injured man as the sergeant's body fell, content, into the pile of pillows, once more.

Ralph seemed pleased with the response, his eyes not leaving his new charge. "Catheryn, would you mind leaving us for a moment?"

After a moment's hesitation, she stood, crossing the floor to fling back the canvas tent fly. Before coming to a sudden stop as she, unexpectedly, found herself nose-to-brass buttons with a familiar bristling energy. Captain Danforth's gauntleted fists were resting on his hips, leaning, imposingly, into her personal space.

"Why don't you leave the poor man alone?!"

"What business is it of yours?"

"Since he's under *my* command!"

"Being under your command doesn't mean you rule his *life*."

"Actually, it's *exactly* what it means!"

In the middle of the disruption, the tent fly parted, and Ralph emerged.

"Ah, Captain—we meet," he greeted, warmly, his smile ever-present, but there was no mistaking the edge to his tone as he continued. "Again."

The captain peered past the tall arrival and inside the darkness of the tent. His dark gaze traveled between the new arrival and his resting sergeant.

"What are you doing here?" Danforth muttered, the usual commanding edge to his voice, noticeably, absent.

"House call," Ralph responded, as he turned to regard Catheryn. "Sergeant Solomon should be recovering nicely." He paused for a moment to address the corpsman behind him, the little man rising from his seat, watching the new arrival with an intensity bordering on anxiety. "Corpsman, you are a healer beyond compare. Never doubt your skill. It was a pleasure to meet you."

The gray-haired man fell into his chair, his gaze focused on a stunned emptiness before him, blinking incredulously. Catheryn gazed at her guide, expectantly, but his attention had already swiveled back to the captain.

"You are to be commended, Captain. Your staff is most *attentive*."

The auburn-haired therapist was beginning to see shades of the same awe in Danforth, as the captain offered a single nod, and stepped back, eyes downward as Ralph passed. Catheryn fell into step beside the tall, lithe figure.

"What was *that*?"

The guide smiled warmly, but just enough to set his brilliant blue-green eyes to sparkle as he took in the path before them.

"A reminder. I don't think you shall be threatened by him anymore."

B ridgette hadn't realized when she'd fallen asleep. All she was readily able to process was that she was no longer in the parlor of the house. She still wore her calico dress, but she was now out of doors. It was dusk, and the trees of the forest were closing in on all sides. Outside? She was not to be outside. That was against the rules.

No.

She could hear the horse hooves beating along the hardened dirt of the forest path behind her. He was coming.

Sprinting along the dirt path, she only spared a quick glimpse over her shoulder as she darted through the dense thicket and brush of the forest. Fallen branches and twigs snatched at her booted feet, briars and thorns grasping at her long brown hair. And all the while, the beating of the hooves.

She shrieked, plunging forward in the dim light as her pursuer rode her down. She glimpsed back at the silhouette of horse and rider inching ever closer. She sensed a hand snaking out toward her, and she screamed.

The shot rang out; like a miniature explosion really. The dark horse reared, the rider thrown to the hard earth. The noise sent her scrambling for the cover of the tall grass. She panted, fear clutching at her as she peered through the tall blades of cover. Laying a breath away, his hat thrown several feet from his form, was the body of her beloved adopted uncle. His eyes were open, frozen in a deathlike gaze. She screamed. Screaming and screaming as if she would never stop.

Until she did, finding herself staring into the uncomprehending, concerned faces of Captain Danforth and Dr. Greye.

Out of reflex, she sprang upon the officer, her arms wrapped around his neck, tears streaming down her face.

"I'm sorry!" she sobbed, burying her little face in the crux of his neck. "I'm sorry, Uncle Charlie! I'm sorry! I killed you! *I killed you!*"

The bewildered officer, reluctantly, accepted her embrace. "Of course, you didn't, sweetheart! I'm right here!"

"I did!" she insisted, her voice muffled by the blue wool uniform. "I did! I did!"

Catheryn didn't know what to make of the scene. She'd seen Bridgette's temperament before, but not like this. She turned to the window, gazing across the street at the encampment. And to her surprise, saw someone looking back.

Andy stood, directly across the road, appearing to look right at her. He stood, the crown of the slouch hat set high enough on his head to reveal an eerie, vacant, expression.

She didn't know if it was the intense emotion of the last few minutes, or something else, but she felt a moment of vertigo sweep over her. She jolted upright, blinking her eyes slowly. The room. She staggered to find a handhold on the arm of the settee. Stop the room. It was…moving.

Danforth seemed to notice something amiss, but he didn't want to release his hold on the child. "Catheryn, what's the matter with you?"

"I…," she stammered, swaying slightly. "I…"

"Catheryn…"

A child's nursery rhyme began to play in her head. A child's voice was singing. But it was wrong, something was wrong. The child's voice was cruel, almost mocking. She didn't know where it was coming from. It only made her dizzier.

"All around the Mulberry Bush, the monkey chased the weasel…"

Where was up? Where was down? She couldn't tell.

"The monkey stopped to pull up his sock…"

"Pop—"

The only thing she was vaguely aware of was someone calling her name. She gave up, her eyes closing, her body falling into the soft embrace of darkness.

Dr. David Faustus was feeling owly. He snapped through pages of the daily paper with increasing annoyance. Catheryn had gone off into another one of her meditations, leaving him to wait. Why, exactly, was he here, again?

He was immediately snatched from his agitation by a resounding crash, coming from the direction of the kitchen. It was a clatter of something metal. He heard a familiar voice yelp, just before another crash of shattering, breakable, dishware.

Faustus stood up, abruptly. "Andrew?"

"Help!" he whimpered, his voice barely audible through the wooden door.

David bolted forward, leaving the paper at his feet. He pushed the swinging door into the kitchen and ducked, just as a heavy ceramic mixing bowl heaved itself off the open-faced cabinet shelf and hurdled through the air in front of his face. He blinked in astonishment. Andrew Baldwin sat in the far corner of the room, arms wrapped, defensively, over the top of his head.

The doctor didn't know whether to be agitated, or amazed. "What's going on in here?"

"It just...started!" the realtor muttered, tightening his arms over the top of his head as a wooden spoon leapt off the counter and landed at his sneakered feet.

Faustus crawled on his hands and knees, knowing he was going to have to replace his designer slacks, but there was no other choice. He shuffled across the culinary war zone to find a space next to Baldwin. "Andrew, you've got to calm down! Take a deep breath—"

The realtor took a deep breath, and despite David's best intentions, held it.

"No," the doctor coached in his best soothing tone, "you have to let it out."

A carving knife slid across the counter, embedding it into the pantry door, just inches from Baldwin's face. Baldwin let the air out in an ear-splitting shriek. Much to Faustus's dismay and discomfort, it was, indeed, a girly scream.

David took the man, brusquely, by the shoulders. "Andrew! You've got to get a grip on yourself! This won't stop until you do!"

"It's not me!" he protested.

The doctor was in the midst of organizing his lecture notes into the most elementary explanation of poltergeist theory when Andrew grabbed both sides of the older man's head and forced him to look up.

The ceiling was alive, buzzing like a swarm of angry bees. The plaster of the ceiling could not even be witnessed through the churning blackness that swirled in a counter-clockwise motion above them. David's own mouth could not form words. He could only stare in amazement at the storm a few mere feet above their heads. He, reflexively, ducked, throwing an arm up over his head as a cast iron skillet leapt from its resting place in the sink. A sauté pan unhooked itself from its place on the wall. A glass pitcher slid off the open-faced cabinet shelf. All of the items remained suspended in mid-air, as if held there by invisible hands. Both Baldwin and Faustus wrapped their arms over their heads, awaiting the inevitable.

And suddenly, the buzzing stopped.

Andrew and David slowly lowered their arms, daring to take a look up.

And just as they did, the implements came crashing down like some absurd form of rain. Reflexively, without thinking, David dove forward to grab the pitcher, catching it with both hands. The metal utensils weren't as fortunate, clattering noisily to the barn wood floor.

The doctor caught his breath, the temperature of the glass finally registering on his palms. He let it tumble from his grasp, still close enough to the floor not to shatter.

"It's…it's *cold!*" Faustus managed, incredulously.

Andrew reached out, and gingerly, touched a pot. He snatched back his fingers. "It's hot!"

Faustus' gray eyes were wide with incomprehension for a good thirty seconds, before a lopsided grin began to tug at one corner of his mouth. "This is…incredible!"

Andrew drew back in shock. "What?!"

David gripped Andrew by both shoulders, glee dancing in his eyes. "Congratulations, my friend. You just witnessed your first PK event!"

"Great!" Andrew responded, a growing smile emerging as he tried to find the doctor's enthusiasm contagious. "That's great!"

"I know, right?!"

"Yeah!" As the adrenalin started to wear off, Andrew felt his head starting to shake back and forth, uncomprehendingly. "What's 'PK'?"

His energy spent, Faustus collapsed to the floor, his eyes darting along the ceiling. Bewilderment returned to his expression. "Wait a minute…where did it go?"

BRAMDEN HOUSE

13

"Catheryn?"

The images were swimming in an awful mess before her eyes. Things were melting and swirling into grayish, nonsensical blobs.

"Catheryn!"

The shapeless forms wheeled away, and she felt her stomach lurch with the sensation of falling. Falling down. Falling fast.

Her eyes snapped open. Ouch! Her solar plexus felt as if someone had knocked the wind out of her. She sat up, gasping. Wait. Her eyes were…closed? How did she see…?

Her partner was supporting her body into a seated upright position, his face a mask of dire concern. She could read it with utter clarity. It puzzled her as to what vision she had been attempting to use previous to coming awake. She would have to analyze that later.

She ached, but she couldn't tell what ached more—her stomach or her head.

The young medium brought a hand to her head, still blinking away the strange vision. "Where's that creepy kid?"

Andrew Baldwin hovered close over her partner's shoulder. "What kid?"

"The one singing that stupid song," she said, wincing. "You didn't hear it?"

The realtor shrugged. "Must have been from another zip code. We didn't hear anything."

"Great. Now I'm hearing things…"

Baldwin exchanged knowing looks with Dr. Faustus. "Wouldn't put it past *this* place! You wouldn't *believe* what we just went through."

"What happened?" she asked, sitting more solidly upright.

Baldwin frowned. "Let's just say we won't be using the kitchen anytime soon."

"Catheryn, I don't want you doing that anymore," the elder doctor said firmly.

"I don't even know what I did," she said. "It's like I was here, and then…someone *pulled* me across."

David Faustus looked puzzled. "Pulled you where?"

"To where they are," she said, the look on her face registering that she was still working through it herself. "There's so *many*. Andrew, does this place feel different to you?"

Baldwin made a noise that didn't, at all, challenge her assessment.

"Something's coming," she muttered to no one in particular. "I just don't know what…

The strains of the violin woke Catheryn out of a sound sleep. She rolled over in her bed to spy the time on her phone.

2:49 A.M.

At first, she was annoyed. She liked to sleep. It was making her feel better. It was helping shake off the weirdness of the day. But as she continued to listen, she seemed more aware of the tone.

The melody was low, sad. The pitch wavered in the form of a Scottish lament. The choice of the music wasn't the captain's usual jaunty self. She swung her legs off the bed, her feet feeling around the floor for her slippers. Eventually, her feet slid into them. Dressed in her t-shirt and yoga pants, her auburn hair trussed up in a top ponytail, she trudged out into the hallway. The music was hypnotizing, so familiar, But so sad. She couldn't quite place the tune, but she couldn't resist its pull. She started, gingerly, up the staircase. She did not turn the light on;

254

fearing if she did, it would break the spell of the music weaving through the house. It wasn't long until she found herself at the top of the staircase, pausing, uncertain whether to approach.

The captain was partially illuminated by the light of the moon shining through the tall attic window. The instrument was molded to its normal position beneath his chin, as if part of him. The music continued, uninterrupted, and finally, the tune's identity triggered in Catheryn's mind.

He issued another one of his trademark frustrated sighs, his hand that had been gripping the bow falling to one side.

"Don't stop," she urged. "That was beautiful. *Hector the Hero*, right?"

If he was impressed, his energy didn't suggest it, as his dark eyes took in the captivating night sky before him.

"The lady knows her Scottish," he murmured to the window.

He turned to the stack of moving boxes to his left, carefully placing the instrument into the black, home-made coffin-style violin case perched atop the towering stack of cardboard. Catheryn seemed to recall her uncle having a similar case; it was different from modern cases in that it made no effort to conform to the instrument's silhouette. It looked like an elongated triangle with rounded corners. The inside of the coffin case had to be carved and sculpted to the shape of the instrument to secure it from sliding around. It was a beautiful art form lost to more manmade materials and modern practicalities.

Catheryn braved a few more steps to emerge from the shadows. "So, I'm curious as to how you've come to learn such a...*variety* of music."

"A lot of musicians travelled through this town. This house had a *lot* of parties."

Catheryn watched as he diverted his attention toward the bow, twisting the screw at the base of it to release the tension on the horsehair. Feel. They had no bodies. No nerve endings. No sensation of temperature. No bones in the inner ear to vibrate, translating into sound.

"We may be dead," he smirked, as if reading her thoughts. "...but we're not deaf, either. We hear; just in a different way. It's more of an experience. One of the few things we can still *feel* in this existence."

He noticed her interested expression, and to her surprise, didn't respond with the usual acerbic remark. He pulled up a box next to her.

"So, you hear new tunes? Memorize new songs?" she theorized.

"For someone who still has ears to hear with, you don't do it very well. We don't hear music. We *experience* it."

She managed a slight smile. *There.* There was the tone that was missing. The slight childlike reprimand.

"Pick up the violin. I'll show you."

She blinked at him. It was the last thing she expected him to say. She got up and moved over to the open case. Her fingers traced over the rough-hewn strings, almost half-expecting for her hand to melt through it. No, it was there. Quite solid. She, carefully, gingerly, picked up the instrument, watching him closely as she did so.

He sensed her nervousness. "Don't worry. It's not going to explode or anything."

She smiled at his attempt at humor. "I just know it's important to you."

"Are you right- or left-handed?" he asked.

"Right."

She was somewhat startled to feel his presence directly behind her, but not so much as to lose her grip on the instrument.

"Take the instrument in your left hand, by the back of the neck, and tuck the end of the body under your chin," he instructed. "See how your chin fits right into the chin rest?"

"Yeah," she responded, not sure how comfortable she felt with his presence so close, and still, unable to see him.

"Now, wrap your fingers around the neck like you're cradling it."

Catheryn obeyed, wrapping her fingers around the slender carved end of the crafted piece, all the while feeling his presence move closer. Her scalp tingled, as if exposed to a static charge. She was expecting cold radiating from him, as she did with most of the Dead, but he was not. Everything radiating from him was warm. It enveloped her torso in a comforting calm that didn't feel, at all, unpleasant.

"Press your index finger down onto a string. Any string. It doesn't matter."

His voice was soft, next to her ear. She swallowed hard. The low, intimate tone of his voice, so close to her neck, activated a flutter in her stomach. To hear a disembodied voice that close, almost always filled her with anxiety, but not now. She forced herself to focus, as she felt his right arm come around her right side with the re-adjusted bow.

"Don't loosen your grip on the string. Keep it tight against the fingerboard."

It was hard to concentrate. His presence now almost totally engulfed her. Her old impulses would have told her to run, yet, she steeled her resolve as he moved to draw the bow across the strings.

The most beautiful vibration flowed through the body of the instrument, directly into her, the maddening flutter in her stomach vibrating in time with the vibration of the string. Her senses were already at high alert to communicate in her unique way, but now she felt as if the tremor of the musical note flowed directly through her and into him. It triggered a feeling of shared intimacy that made her catch her breath. She closed her eyes against it, feeling her cheeks flush. Could he feel it? Could he feel what she was feeling? Could she even hide it if she wanted to?

"See," he said, with a note of finality, breaking the spell. "You feel that?"

Her eyes snapped open, not exactly sure which *feeling* he was referring to. It was almost a relief when he took the instrument from her hand, and she felt his presence recede from her. She nodded, her voice feeling somewhat overpowered to speak.

He placed the instrument back into its molded space within the case. "*That* is how we experience music."

She couldn't turn to look at him, afraid he could read the emotional turmoil in her expression. She forced herself through her breathing technique, a grounding exercise to bring her energy closer about her.

That would do it. That would steady her. It always did.

"I used to play at all the parties on campus at school," he said nonchalantly, loosening the tension on the bow, once again. "Made almost more money doing that than almost any job. Not that my grandmother was that happy about it."

Catheryn was relieved to find that her energy was flowing back into a regular pattern, and she found herself more comfortable to use her voice again. She still wasn't ready to look at him.

"Why not?" she asked.

"Classically-trained," he stated, packing away the bow into its proper compartment. "She wanted a nephew she could show off to her high-society friends."

Catheryn found a compromise and turned toward his voice without looking directly at him. "A prodigy in her progeny?"

He shook his head as if she was speaking Latin. "She wanted a trained circus animal for parties. I wasn't for it. They liked *classical* music."

The distasteful tone in the way he mentioned the common instrumental form finally intrigued her enough to look at him, directly.

"What's wrong with classical music?"

"Anyone can play the notes," he reflected, "but only the really talented ones can express the music. I don't have that. It never sounded right."

He turned and closed up the case. "…and I suppose it would have helped if I showed up for the lessons. The parties kind of…kept getting in the way."

"We had dances *every* weekend. Sometimes two." He warmly chuckled at a memory. It was a rare sound, coming from him. "If you didn't know how to dance then you were *truly* living under a rock. That's how you met people."

"Did you?"

He responded to her question with a brow furrowed by confusion.

"Meet anyone," she clarified.

He seemed to ponder the question, before turning away from her to place the instrument case behind a box. "Always time enough for that, right?"

She could feel the tinge of regret in his voice. His whole life ahead of him, just beginning. And then…

She turned to look at him, her eyes clearly mirroring the compassion she felt. "I'm sorry."

A mixture of emotions struggled for dominance over his dark features, and he turned to secure the case in a safer crevice.

"Well, I had my chance."

The therapist did her best to ground herself against the tide of growing empathy rising within her. He was the patient and she was the doctor, after all. She chose to shift the direction to something less emotional.

"What do you miss the most?"

His gaze took in the moon beyond the attic window, the moonlight dancing in his dark gaze.

"Waking up in the morning."

And then she felt it. The steel walls rising about him, again. The moment for sharing had passed.

"Speaking of that; I have a job to do," he muttered, before turning to address her directly. "And *some* of us need sleep. Best be off."

She turned to go when something outside the window caught her attention. From the vantage at the window, it gave a clear view of the bridge, almost all the way to the other side of it as it spanned the river. This time of night, it should have been empty. Yet, someone was there; one solitary figure standing at the rail, looking down at the churning waters below.

"Hey, who's that?" she muttered, not taking her eyes from the curious presence.

Danforth peered over her shoulder. "What's *he* doing out here?"

It was pretty obvious by his banal reaction that he was more than familiar with who *he* was, but her therapist training was already kicking in.

"He's not going to jump, is he?" she said, hastily, not waiting for an answer.

"Catheryn—" the soldier called out, his voice tinged with annoyance as he watched her race down the stairs. "Damn it!"

Catheryn was halfway across the rough gravel of the street before she started losing traction. Hard-sole slippers didn't do well on marble-sized gravel. She was in the middle of stabilizing her balance when a voice next to her almost made her lose it, again.

"What. Are. You. *Doing?!*" Danforth growled, folding his arms across his chest, curtly. "Get back in the house. You're hardly dressed."

"I can't stand here and watch a man jump," she said, anxiously, renewing her stride.

"He's not gonna jump." His answer was tinged with more than a little annoyance. "You're not even…decent."

"What?"

"It's not exactly for a gentleman to comment on, but shouldn't you be wearing your corset?"

She looked down at her t-shirt, and it was obvious that the cool night air was having an effect that, in her excitement, she hadn't quite considered. Before she could even respond, he *blinked* out of existence. A moment later, in the position he once stood, lay a crumpled robe. She had heard of the Dead being able to spontaneously transport objects without physical means. Her researcher friends had even coined a phrase for it; apporting. But she had never actually witnessed it.

"Handy," she muttered, as she thrust her hands into the armholes of the garment and hiked it onto her shoulders.

Wasting no time in wondering where he had gone, she gathered the fabric about her and secured it with the matching tie as she sprinted toward the bridge.

"Wait! Please!" she cried out, not slowing her gravel-impeded gait toward the bridge. "Don't!"

The moonlight of the evening glinted off of the lean, silver-haired gentleman who stood at the metal rail of the bridge. He wore a dark vest, the moonlight making his white collar shirt glow. His shirt sleeves were rolled up, baring sun-kissed skin. He turned abruptly at her approach, his gray eyes regarding her with intense curiosity.

"Please don't jump!" she called out breathlessly, catching her breath as she slid to a stop less than ten feet from his position.

" 'Jump'?" He seemed to chuckle at the thought. "No. I wouldn't do that. Do you know how *cold* that water is?"

Catheryn blinked. "No."

"Neither do I."

As the man chuckled, good-naturedly, the young doctor was able to ground a bit more to observe him more completely. Although rail-thin, the older man had an ethereal being about him. Even though his hands had withdrawn from the railing to speak to her, it was becoming increasingly obvious to her that he was not completely *there*. The rustling weeds that grew from the sparse soil around the antiquated bridge girders stirred in the slight night breeze, but he did not appear to have mass of any kind to impede the flow of air. She could see the action of the stirring foliage directly *through* him.

He placed a hand to his chest before bowing, formally, at the neck.

"I am Elias Bramden." The man cocked his head to the right, ever so slightly. "I understand you are familiar with my daughter?"

The doctor brushed a lock of her auburn hair behind one ear as she processed the rolodex of people she had met in the last few days. It suddenly came to her.

"Ms. Abigale?"

"Yes," he replied, casting a razor-lipped smile down at the ground as he did so.

He moved back to the railing, gazing up at the waning moon. The sparse light danced silver in his eyes.

"I'm the reason she is in danger."

Catheryn was puzzled. "From what?"

"Jackson. Jackson Carter."

The therapist could tell by the set of Bramden's jaw that it wasn't a pleasant memory.

"He was a crude man; lived off the ground and whatever meager scraps he could muster," the older man said, grimly. "Most he managed off human misery. It was a curse the day that man came to town."

Catheryn moved closer, wondering if he could feel the intrusion into his personal space. If he noticed it, he didn't flinch. She reached out a hand to feel his energy field, and was rewarded with a sudden jolt of vision she hadn't expected.

She could see Jackson, astride a dark mare that had seen younger days. A threadbare blanket was the only thing that separated the animal's fragile back from the saddle. Astride the mare was a tall man, thin in stature. Graying, straw-like brown hair peaked around a brown, low-domed slouch hat, almost, but not quite, obscuring the patch that stretched across his left eye. His cheeks were sallow, as if the life, itself, had been sucked from him. No care had been made to shave the two-day stubble from his face.

Bramden continued to narrate the vision that spread out before her, his voice echoing in her head.

"Carter had heard of the existence of the Underground Railroad in our area, and came to find more bounty. Many runaway slaves had come across the border from Missouri, and sought refuge here. Most moved on North on their way to Canada, but some stayed."

Bramden seemed to ignore Catheryn's hand at his wrist but turned to regard her with a stern look.

"We sheltered them. Gave them work, but we knew the risk. Anyone that harbored runaways could carry a heavy fine; livelihood, land, and property seized. It had been done before down here. However, God's law was above that of Man."

Catheryn recognized the philosophy of the abolitionists; those that fought and forged clandestine networks to see slavery's end in the United States. It became a cause adopted by particular churches common to the region, years ago, as many saw the freeing of the slaves to be the will of a benevolent God. She allowed him to continue, uninterrupted.

"He would not leave. He stayed for days in a room above the general store, waiting for someone to slip him information, or to find some evidence of collusion. He was frustrated. And then…"

She blinked, the close contact with his consciousness projected the scene before her vision.

"I found myself with business at the stables. I heard low voices from one of the stalls. I found him…He had my Abigale on his knee! That man…that creature…had my little girl!"

She could feel the flow of the man's shock and horror at the memory, entering the dark shadows of the hay-strewn floor, and finding the nightmare of a man with his youngest daughter upon his knee. The child could not have been more than eight, but discomfort and fear were painted on her cherub-like face.

"I ordered Abigale away to the safety of the house and demanded the man leave.

He begged forgiveness for trespassing and taking liberties, but even as he passed me to leave, I could feel the chill of the Devil upon him. That night…was the beginning of the end."

Catheryn's vision was disrupted by a sudden flash of lightning, hinting at the dampness of rain from years in the past; rain she could not, physically, feel.

"It was late into the night. Most of the town had already retired when a voice rang out in the darkness of the cold September rain. I remember lights springing on in windows from neighbors around our house. Little Abigale and I bolted to the window overlooking our backyard, but we didn't dare raise a light."

Elias Bramden's jaw ground tighter, a glisten forming over his eyes as he recalled the frightful memory.

"Carter was in the back yard. He had young Nathaniel by the neck. Nathaniel was an escaped slave from Missouri some years before and was a help to the country doctor who had lodgings at our house. He had a noose around the boy's neck!"

"Listen!" Catheryn heard Carter proclaim from the nightmarish vision. "And listen good! I know you nigger-lovin' folk are here among this town! You have one chance to tell me where they are, or this boy dies!"

Recognition stabbed through her as if struck by lightning. That face…it was a few years younger, but she knew that face. It was the very 'Nathaniel' she had met on horseback, days before. But this was not the strong, proud cavalry scout that she had met with the captain. The boy before her in the soaked white muslin shirt was awkward and afraid.

Her vantage point seemed to shift as she viewed the spectacle from the second floor, looking down into the yard alongside the Bramdens. She watched as the spectral rain cascaded down the stubbled face of the rage-filled man as he spun slowly toward the lit windows surrounding him for any sign of a response. His movement yanked the young boy with him, causing his captor to gag on the unfeeling movement. She could see Bramden's horror at the presentation before them, the man pressing his child's face to his nightshirt front, not allowing his youngest to see. Nothing. He could say nothing. The most affluent in the town all aided and abetted in helping the less fortunate. If they were exposed, the whole town, and all those that depended upon them, would fall.

All the past Elias Bramden could do was watch helplessly, holding his daughter's face to his breast, as the bounty hunter threw the rope over the lowest, most secure branch of the old oak tree in the backyard. It was the same old oak that Elias had fashioned a swing to for Abigale last summer. Watching it being used in such a way caused enraged tears to flow from the old man's eyes, as Carter pulled.

She felt the rage, helplessness, and disgrace ripple from the visage of the older man before her, watching as the young dark-skinned boy that was her daughter's friend gasp and choke, fingers digging into the rope about his neck. He clung to his daughter desperately, turning her face away so she wouldn't see, or hear the creak and strain of the hemp as the weight of the body was drawn higher and higher. Finally, and as if the horror of the moment was witnessed by God himself, in a clap of thunder, the body landed on the ground with a grotesque thud, barren of life.

"This blood!" Carter proclaimed, turning to all who witnessed. "This blood is on your hands!"

The bounty hunter threw the remaining coil of rope on the ground in disgust, not even pausing to admire the carnage he was leaving on the ground behind him.

"You know where to find me," the stranger muttered into the mud, trudging off into the darkness of the night.

Catheryn found herself gasping for air over the wave of emotion she was feeling, emotions alien to her intermingling with her own. The terror, the agony, the confusion. She drew back from the overwhelming emotional field from the specter before her. Nathaniel. My God. Nathaniel.

"We couldn't let that go. We couldn't…We all had to make a decision. Either we do away with Carter, or he would end us."

The vision continued, unaided, before her eyes, relentless in its telling. Catheryn witnessed as men, under cover of darkness, ascended the staircase of the general store. Their faces were obscured by pillowcases, with eye holes cut in the fabric, to carry out their mission in anonymity. She observed as Carter struggled, managing one cry before one of the members could gag him with a torn piece of homespun fabric. Securing his stocking feet with another length of fabric, they carried his thrashing form to the bridge.

All of the "conductors" were there; three of the citizens in charge of their Underground stations, including Bramden. Carter struggled, violently, against his bonds, hurling muffled insults through the gag as one of the leaders declared his crimes aloud. The remainder of rope from the night previous, was fashioned into a noose. Ironically, it proved to be just enough rope to do the job. Tied securely to the iron railing, the nightmarish man, noose about his neck, was flung out into the blackness of the night. With more mercy than was shown the boy, the bounty hunter's neck, snapped. The past Bramden watched, his jaw set in defiance, as a man pulled a utility knife. With cold diligence, the corpse was cut loose. The body fell with a resounding splash, the generous river current speeding the evidence away down the channel.

"The water was much higher then. It was before the reservoir had been formed upstream. I doubt anyone ever found the body before it made it to the Mississippi."

The present Elias Bramden's horror from that moment still clung to his face like the phantom he was. Catheryn was still trying to shake off the chilling effect of the vision, rubbing her bare skin through the thick comfort of the robe.

"And now, he's coming," she surmised, flatly.

"I know," the vigilante muttered, still gazing into the water. "It's all my fault."

The therapist wished there was something to say. After all, wasn't it her job to comfort those in pain? What was done, was done. There was no taking it back now.

"Does Abigale know about this?" she asked.

"No." The older man's eyes closed. "How do you tell your child her father is a murderer?"

Catheryn moved to the side of the apparition, this time, taking care to avoid the entity's emotional wake. "She needs to know—for both your sakes. She's in danger. And she needs to know why."

Bramden sighed with a resigned nod. For the first time in the long course of the evening, he looked at her.

"Are you…an angel?"

She wished her touch could do something to soothe him, to bring him comfort. This would be the point where she would reach out and hold a client's hand. Unfortunately, he was beyond that now. All she could do was be present.

"No," she smiled, compassionately. "I just help people."

With that, she bid Elias Bramden a good night, and turned to trudge down the gravel road. She found the area behind the house that was twin to the nightmarish vision she had witnessed. Emotion rose, forming a lump in her throat, and she closed her eyes against it.

"It has been so long that I'd almost forgotten."

She started at the voice to her left, turning her head to find the familiar form of Sergeant Solomon standing there, the gold brocade on his shell jacket glinting in the moonlight.

"You never made it," she breathed, her green eyes sparking with the start of tears.

He removed his wool cap, scratching the back of his head as if it would awaken the memory.

"I left Doc Watson's that night with ten dollas in my pocket," he said to the ground before him. "He couldn't talk me out of it, so he thought it was the next best thing. I was gonna see about payin' a supply wagon for a ride to Keokuk, so I could enlist. Jackson found me first."

She swallowed hard to press the emotion down before she spoke, but her voice still shook.

"Nathaniel, where did they bury you?"

He shook his head, turning to move away, but Catheryn stepped before him to cut off his retreat.

"Nathaniel—"

He paused, his eyes taking in the house across the street. Had that been there before? He didn't recall seeing that before.

He didn't look away. "You were just looking at it."

She turned to look at the plot of land they had been taking in. No marker. No headstone.

Her voice trembled, tears springing from her eyes. "You deserved so much more than that."

He turned, regarding her with a look that beseeched understanding.

"Miss Catheryn...no one could know. It would be the end to alla it. So many more were saved after me. It makes it okay."

He stood back away from her, tugging on the leather brim of his kepi-style blue cap, the brass crossed-sabers emblem on its front, glinting in the sparse light.

"Besides," the young soldier smiled. "I ain't lost. I'm a sergeant in the cavalry now. Couldn't be any prouder to serve."

BRAMDEN HOUSE

14

Corporal Daniel Hampden removed his blue forage cap, and ran his fingers through his blonde hair. They had been on the move since they broke camp, but he still hadn't broken a sweat. It was odd. So...odd.

He picked his way through the underbrush, following after his evening host. Along with them, the bounty hunter had eight captives in tow, cuffed at the wrists in a linked fashion that allowed them to follow along single file. It was a large group for one man to handle, and he was somewhat surprised at how meek and docile they all appeared to be. He studied the lot as he moved past them. The soldier wasn't too surprised to find a ragged group of runaway male slaves in their lot, since it was well known among his comrades that there was money to be had in their capture. It was the *others* that bothered him. Some of the captured wore blue federal army uniforms, not unlike himself. Two even wore the butternut color of Confederate. Others wore soiled and tattered civilian wear. And to his strange recollection, he had never seen Carter *feed* any of them. Even though he had never met anyone of Carter's profession before, the whole thing just seemed abnormally cruel.

The young gunner caught up with the bounty hunter who did not seem to be in any mood to stop and chat.

"Mr. Carter, uhmm…sir. Where are we going?"

"Following the river," the grizzled man said, bluntly, forging on without losing a step. "Just as you said."

"Well, that's where he was before," the lad said, distracted momentarily as he freed a booted foot from a fallen branch snare. "What says he's still there?"

"A hunch."

"Aren't we going to need…" Hampden managed, in between breaths. He had been on long marches before, but not as fast as Carter was moving. "…more help?"

Hampden started when Carter came to a sudden halt, one scarred, milky eye riveting the soldier where he stood. "How many we need to take one man?"

"Well…some say he's a wily one." The soldier didn't know exactly what to say, but since he now had the grizzled man's attention. "He's had schoolin' an' such."

Carter snorted, before giving the lead chain a yank and starting forward once more.

"I'm just sayin'—if we need help, I know where we can get some."

The unsettling milky eye of the bounty hunter fell on the boy once more. Something in the way the man's upper lip curled in a half-sneer made the corporal wonder if he had been best to keep that bit to himself. Too late now.

"Where?"

"Corporal, where the hell have you been?" Second Lieutenant Miles Stacey barked at the two individuals being ushered into camp.

A picket sentry had come racing into camp, rousing the lieutenant from a shave. Unhappy about having his routine half-finished, he had just enough time to wipe the soap from his face and throw on a blue wool shell jacket, emblazoned with the red piping indicating his artillery status.

He slammed his kepi-style hat over his mess of short-cropped, auburn hair and marched toward the new arrivals.

Corporal Hampden was feeling ill at ease since the pickets drew on
280

them, and still had their guns at the ready in case either he or his guest tried anything. In stark contrast, Carter couldn't have been more at ease. He found a toothpick and worked it, cavalierly into his teeth. He observed the actions in front of him, with detached interest, as if watching a scene from a play.

"I...got lost in the skirmish, sir," Hampden explained nervously, standing at strict attention as the lieutenant circled them, like a hungry shark. "Honest. I'm glad I was able to find you."

The corporal looked around the camp. It was not very lively. And was it just him, or hadn't there been a few more tents before?

"Sir...," Hampden managed to say, with more than a degree of nervousness.

"What?!" the officer barked threateningly, his nose scant inches away from the corporal's own.

The second lieutenant was so close that the youthful gunner could smell the hair cream in the officer's rust-colored hair. It didn't help the young boy's nerves.

"Where is everybody?"

Lieutenant Stacey had already moved on, measuring Hampden's comrade up and down. "Who is this?"

The bounty hunter shifted his casual stance to offer a hand to the senior officer. "Jackson Carter—at your service."

Stacey ignored the hand, coming to stand before the young corporal.

"Sir, if it hadn't been for Mr. Carter here, I may not have found you," the young boy answered quickly. "He's an excellent tracker, sir."

The lieutenant circled round the pair, this time taking in the rough-looking character a little more approvingly. "Well…maybe we can help each other out. Seems I have more than a few soldiers that have gone *missing* in the last week."

The corporal grew wide-eyed. "On the hook…I mean, *deserted*, sir?"

Stacey pulled the hat off his head and dug his nails into the back of his scalp. "Every morning we call for reveille, fewer and fewer show up. We check their tents, and everything is still there; uniforms, everything. I don't get what's happening. If a man's gonna run—wouldn't he take his stuff with him?"

Hampden's expression was one of mystery and shock. His comrades wouldn't just *leave*. That would be dishonor, cowardice.

Like Captain Danforth.

The memory of it lit a fire under the boy. "Sir, Carter can help. He's offered to go track down the captain."

The senior officer wheeled about. "Danforth? Where!"

In the dim firelight, he could just make out the vein in Stacey's neck throbbing alive with anger.

"It's bad enough we're missing this batch, but an officer?" The second lieutenant spat at the ground, in disgust. "No doubt where this bunch got the gumption to leave!"

Stacey came in close to Carter's face, smelling the foul breath off the man, and then, there was that eye. That scarred eye.

Stacey did his best not to flinch. "If you can help us find him, I can make it worth your while."

The corner of Carter's lips turned up in a half smile as he threw his splintered instrument on the ground. It was a smile most unpleasant.

"Happy to do business with ya."

"David, please!" she pleaded. "You don't understand what's at stake here."

She rounded the rental car as he opened the driver's side door of the silver sedan, the glass window serving as both an emotional and physical barrier between them.

"No," the silver-haired mentor retaliated. "I *do* know. Our business.

This has been an entertaining side income to help keep things going, but that is all it is! You are getting too emotionally invested in this!"

Catheryn took a deep breath and closed her eyes. He made more than a valid argument. It hadn't been the first time her partner had accused her of getting too close. But that was the pitfalls of being a medium; seeing, feeling, and hearing things well beyond the normal spectrum. How could she explain that to someone who was vacant of those abilities?

In all honesty, the brutal truth of it was that these cases helped with rent and utilities in a high-profile district of town. It did not replace revenue from clients, and if Baldwin hadn't been paying the modest sum he was, they wouldn't even have come there.

Catheryn returned to her room and started stuffing her travel bag, doing her best to try and ignore the sick feeling in the pit of her stomach. This house had really gotten a hold on her.

At least, she *thought* it was the house.

She wasn't certain how to feel about that. Maybe she needed some time away to sort that out.

"It's safer if you go anyway."

She looked up from her packing to see the familiar silhouette of the

Civil War officer in the window, his hands folded behind his back, his eyes forward. At a time such as this, she wished she had a reflection in the glass to read his expression.

"I'll watch after…House Boy," he said with a snicker, his voice laced with begrudged sentiment. "But if it comes between him and the care of this house—he's on his own."

She sighed resignedly. Andrew Baldwin was not at all happy, but he also realized there was no way this could be a full-time gig to replace the day job. With the promise of a retainer, the two of them agreed to return on the weekend. As luck would have it, it included a holiday. They would have more time here, although she was certain her partner would rather be, just about, anywhere else.

She started out the door with a bag over each shoulder, when her gait was impeded by a tiny forlorn yowl. She looked down to find the gray tiger-striped tabby rubbing up against her jean pant leg. She put her bags down and sat back on her haunches to give the cat scratches around the ear.

"Don't do this to me," she murmured to the small animal, as it looked up at her with eyes not unlike her own.

"If you're asking me to look after that one, you can forget it!"

She rolled her eyes at the retort and petted the cat one more time.

"He doesn't mean it," she whispered quietly to the tabby, the cat purring in response.

She hoisted the bags onto her shoulders again, and quickly made her way down the staircase and through the front door.

Captain Danforth watched her, intently, as she put her bags into the open trunk of the car. Perhaps she felt him watching. What if she did? What did it matter? Why did *he* care?

He passed a tight-lipped frustrated sigh. The house was better off without her. Maybe things might quiet a bit, so they could prepare the defenses. He would have been doing nothing but tripping over her, anyway, in that annoying way that she had.

He watched as the car pulled away, and something in his midsection seemed to pain him as the car headed up and away from the valley. He could feel every inch of their ascent, as if it were a taut rubber band. He closed his eyes and shook his head to clear it. When had she managed to get her hooks into him so deeply? Swatting away at the sensation as if it were a mosquito, he turned back to address his work at hand.

So absorbed was Danforth in the actions outside that he had no idea he was being watched; a freckled face from around the corner, with a pair of intense brown eyes drinking in his very mood. Bridgette had mixed feelings about Catheryn's exit. The woman was pleasant enough, and she was interesting to talk to, but she didn't like the way the young therapist made her feel. She was equally bothered by the way she made the *captain* feel. The captain didn't *feel*—period. That was reserved for the children, and the children only. Since she wasn't exactly a child anymore, she found herself receiving less and less of his attention, but she graciously drank up whatever she could receive.

"Why do you listen to her?"

Bridgette jumped, suddenly realizing the little voice was emerging from the cobbled-together remains of the box the strangers had brought into the house. She had been carrying it around for days. It helped, in lonely moments when everyone was asleep. Little Sam's voice was a trusted confidant when everyone else was too busy to listen to her. It was almost like his voice wasn't coming from the box at all. It was like he was right there with her.

"Why do you listen to her?" the little boy's voice repeated, edged with impatience.

Bridgette frowned down at the ground. "She's nice. She makes me feel…important."

"She's not your friend. *I'm* your friend," the voice named Sam, insisted. "She's a grown-up. You can't trust grown-ups."

Bridgette blinked at the box, her brow knitted together in confusion. "But Uncle Charlie is a grown-up—"

"You can't trust him anymore!" the boy's voice countered, belligerently. "She broke him. She *changed* him. When is the last time he even *talked* to you?"

The girl frowned, her brown eyes falling to the barn wood floor. She couldn't remember. It had been, at least, a few days now. Whenever she had come to talk to him, he was preoccupied. Busy.

Talking to *her.*

It wasn't right and it wasn't fair. The girl fought to repress the dark emotional turmoil within her.

"I'm your friend," Sam's voice insisted. "I will never leave you. Never leave me, okay? They'll never understand you. Not like I do. I won't forget you like they do…they have no idea how special you are. I wouldn't be coming to find you if you weren't."

She returned her gaze back to the box in surprise.

"Find me? You're coming here?"

"I've been trying extra hard," the little voice explained. "The more you talk to me, the easier it is to find you. I no longer feel lost. Neither one of us has to be alone anymore. And then they'll know. Then we'll remind them."

"Remind them of what?"

"How special you are," little Sam stated, matter-of-factly. "And they'll be sorry. And then..."

"What?"

"They'll pay for ignoring you..."

Bridgette's gaze looked warily at the mangled box. " 'Pay'?"

"Pay for hurting my friend. They'll be sorry."

Bridgette returned her gaze to the bedroom, her brown eyes squinting at the captain—the totally distracted, and distant captain—that gazed out the window at the departing car rolling down the gravel.

They would all pay for ignoring her. She was important. They would see. And they would see soon.

The car ride was abnormally, and awkwardly, quiet. There was little to say that hadn't already been covered, and it would take them getting back to their professional lives to move past it. By the time David had come to drop her off at the front door of her apartment, Catheryn felt something akin to a sense of relief.

She proceeded into the lobby, a bag on each shoulder, sparking the memory for the umpteenth time to invest in a roller bag. Maybe she could order one online. She keyed the lock to her door, and deposited the one bag with the dirty laundry into the laundry room to her right, while discarding the other, with the promise to deal with it in the morning, in the living room. With that, she busied herself in the kitchen making a cup of tea. She was doing that when her video call chimed on her phone. It was Andrew Baldwin.

So soon? She picked up the phone and flipped open the active screen with her finger.

"Miss us already?" she quipped.

His grim face was the only answer required, as he swung the camera away to an untidy pile of books on the brick hearth of the front parlor. Some were splayed open while others just lay in unorganized piles.

"All of them leapt off the mantle and to the floor, right after you left."

Her eyebrows arched in curiosity, sensing the timing of the event was less than coincidental.

"Wow," she muttered, pursing her lips. "Did you check the house for any other disturbances?"

"Ironically enough—your room."

Catheryn blinked in surprise. " 'My room'?"

"All the drawers to the dresser were open, and the blankets were ripped off the bed," he reported, glumly. "Everything on the bedside table was on the floor, including the parlor lamp…which I won't need to tell you *I* wasn't happy about. That's an expensive piece—"

The young therapist was a little exasperated about his attention to staging over that of his own safety.

"I'm sorry to hear it," she interrupted, pushing aside her agitation enough to sound sincere.

"Oh, it's okay. It didn't break or anything. Which was really…weird."

That did warrant another raised eyebrow. The base and the globe were made of frosted antique glass. All that destruction. Whatever it was chose to be deliberate in its damage.

"Be sure to keep a journal and note any events," she instructed. "No matter how small."

The anxiety in his expression wasn't lost on the young therapist.

"Already counting the days…" Baldwin muttered.

BRAMDEN HOUSE

15

Catheryn returned to the living room, tea in hand, standing before the tall picture windows and taking in the dreary dusky skies hanging over the downtown district. The building and streetlights started to spark to life across the cityscape, like twinkling lights from some automated universe. She wrapped her fingers around the mug to fend off the chill. Was it the cold from the outside radiating in off the windows? Perhaps she had turned the thermostat down when she left, and forgot about it.

She moved across the room to the thermostat, and as she did so, she felt an uneasy feeling. The chill felt as if it was *following* her. As she stood before the thermostat, she could feel as if the sensation was rolling up her spine and settling about her shoulders. She eyed the thermostat—the normal 68 degrees Fahrenheit.

She didn't want to turn around, but she knew she had to. She would do it in a slow, deliberate fashion. She did not want—whatever it was—to know it was getting the better of her.

The dusky light from the window stretched elongated shadows of the living room furniture, which in any other time would feel benign and explainable. Now, it just resembled creeping tendrils rolling up the load-bearing wall that separated the living room from the sleeping area.

Her green eyes scanned the ceiling above her, clenching her jaw, anxiously. In her hurry to leave, had someone followed her home? It wasn't the first time, but nothing about this felt like the normal energy of the old brick house. This was cold, evasive, calculating. She reached out with her Awareness, and it would slink out of range. The moment she would withdraw her probes, she could feel it right at the margin of her perception. She didn't like this. She felt…stalked.

"Who's there?!" she barked, authoritatively. "Don't keep hiding. Show yourself to me!"

The feeling subsided, shrinking back from the challenge. So intent was she on probing for it, she nearly jumped when the furnace finally checked on. She took a few deep breaths and settled down, finishing off the rest of her tea. She moved to the kitchen and placed the mug in the sink, before retiring to her bedroom.

Maybe it wasn't from the house. Maybe something followed her in from outside the building. The city was large and old, which meant a lot of cycles of birth, life, and death to come back around. But usually, everything of a negative context tended to stay out. Ralph helped her figure out ways of dealing with that long ago. This presence—this thing—was a bit too bold for her comfort.

She kicked off her shoes, changed into a fresh pair of her favorite yoga pants and t-shirt, and crawled under the luxuriant warmth of her gray comforter. She must have missed the comfort of her own bed, since she nodded off, quickly.

The dreamscape was odd, dark. She remembered smelling the mustiness of old wood. It took her a moment to associate it with the house. Bramden House. She recalled how odd it was that she smelled *anything*. It was very rare for her dreams to have that kind of detail.

She looked down at her hands, and she found herself holding the old violin, cradling the neck of the instrument that settled into the crux of her elbow. Looking down, she saw the familiar coffin case that she had remarked on before.

"Are you right- or left-handed?" he asked.

"Right."

The memory seemed to be playing back without her interaction, the voice not coming from her, however, she felt the same unsettledness of someone behind her.

"Take the instrument in your left hand and tuck the end of it under your chin," he instructed. "See how your chin fits right in the chin rest?"

"Yeah."

Instead of the anticipated warmth of the captain's presence engulfing her, it was disturbingly cold. No. This was not the memory. Something was very wrong here. She attempted to recall some of her lucid dream programming. She needed to wake up.

"Now, wrap your fingers around the neck like you're cradling it."

The coldness wrapped around her being, creating panic to well up inside her. As her memory played out, her fingers moved of their own volition, wrapping around the neck of the instrument, her index finger pressing down upon the string.

But the tightness was no longer on the string, it was around her neck, tightening, squeezing, like fingers. She gasped, choking, allowing the instrument to fall from her grip to fight off the unseen foe. The instrument cracked against the barn wood floor, splintering into hundreds of pieces, but it was far from her concern. She fought in vain with the invisible assailant, but there was simply nothing physical for her to fight. Abruptly, a force spun her around, pinning her back against the packing boxes behind her.

The face was crafted from a nightmare, laughing maniacally, echoing in an insane fashion around and into her head. The floppy hat obscured part of it, but from what she could see, its flesh was worn and tattered, hanging in sheets from a skull that would no longer support it. One glowing red eye seemed transfixed upon her, the cruel mocking laughter mimicked there. But the other…While the other had an ugly slash across it, it peered down at her behind a film of cloudy white. From the loose skin around its mouth appeared a ghoulish grin, frightening teeth honed to such razor-sharpness, it terrified her.

At that point, she suddenly came to the realization that the hands had now released from her neck, in exchange to pinning her down by the wrists. She screamed the most blood-curdling scream as the laughter continued, unabated.

Just as suddenly as it started, she was back in her bed, bolting upright and gasping. Her heart was pounding as she forced her breathing to slow. She had never been so relieved to wake up.

And that's when she felt the hair on her arms raise.

The cold. The room was unnaturally cold. Colder than it was before. Before her brain could even process the insanity of it all, a force slammed into her body. It held her down in a vice-like grip, pressing her hard into the mattress. She heard the maniacal laughter, echoing in her head. Although the nightmarish mocking tone was no longer in a dream; it was in the reality and sanctity of her bedroom. She shrieked as the comforter was ripped off of her, but it was choked off as lighting-sharp pain intruded in the most intimate of places in between her legs, ripping the air from her lungs. Helpless, unable to find anything physical to battle, her left hand flailed against the bedside table, feeling for her phone.

She had left it in the kitchen.

It was at that moment, through the pain and the panic, that she felt it; an opposing force blast across the bed, right over her. Whatever it was seemed to rip away the unseen assailant, for she felt nothing atop her anymore. In a fear-laden state, she shrieked as another face floated before her vision. She stared back in shock, melting into incredulity.

"*Captain?!*"

Looming before her, his dark eyes wide with panic, was the face of Captain Danforth.

"Catheryn! Are you alright? Are you hurt?"

She felt the semblance of warmth enveloping her entire being, tinged with even greater concern; an almost alien expression from him. Even with his presence so intentional in comforting her, her body continued to shake. The violation of her most sacred space; not only her home, but her own bed. And now...*he* was here? She was going to have to have a chat with Ralph about their lack-of-spectral-security system.

"Catheryn, are you alright? It's gone. It won't be coming back here."

She could only whimper partial words, her body still cold from the shock. The whole bearing of the spectral officer radiated a mixture of overwhelming regret and concern. Such a change from his stolid, unyielding behavior.

"Are you *hurt?!*" he repeated, firmly.

She couldn't respond. She sat up from the bed, rolling off of it and staggering in the direction of the light in her bathroom. Her eyes had to adjust to the garish light of the vanity, and eventually, she was able to take in her reflection.

Her hands fell to both sides of the sink, bracing herself as tears streamed down her face. It was too insane to be real. It couldn't possibly be true. Never in her years of working with the Dead had anything like this, remotely, happened. She didn't want to look. Didn't want to acknowledge what she had just seen. If it was real, could she ever feel truly safe again?

She breathed through her grounding technique. This had to happen. The scientist in her had to assess. She managed to raise her head to look in the mirror, and began to shake.

Around her throat, unmistakably, were a full set of bruised finger marks.

🔫 🔫 🔫

"Catheryn, we have to call the police," David said frantically, hovering over her as she sat on the couch, cross-legged, another mug of tea in her hands.

Her partner felt helpless. Not knowing what to do, he did the only thing he could think to do and that was to make her tea. He settled into the spot next to her on the sofa.

"No," she answered, quietly.

She was grateful, wrapping her fingers around the mug, that she could feel physical warmth again. The numbness of the event was wearing off. It took some firm affirmations to send Danforth on his way, although now that he was absent, she rather missed the sense of security she felt from him being there. Ralph was only there when he felt he needed to be there for her, doing his best to teach her self-reliance. The darkness of night had been such a strange place for her; full of apprehension and fear. But with him there, his presence nearby as she slept, it was a slightly…different place. She never realized how much she truly craved that sense of comfort.

"No?! How can you say that? You've been attacked!"

"And tell them what?!" she raged. "I fought against someone I could not see? No description whatsoever?"

"There's something assault survivors go through—it's a defense mechanism. The mind doesn't allow you to see—"

"David," she said in the most solid tone she had been able to muster all evening. "You are not helping."

"I can't just sit here—"

She looked at her partner, her sympathetic side finally reaching through the trauma. She simply, quietly, handed him her empty mug.

He retreated to the kitchen, finding two more tea bags and retrieving the kettle from the stove. He poured the hot water over the selection of chamomile and lavender tea and let it sit on the counter.

He leaned through the cutout that allowed a view of the living room from the kitchen, resting on the frame with his elbows. "How do we know it's gone?"

How did she explain that *another* person, that not everyone could see, told her everything was going to be okay? And she had a churning deep doubt within herself that it wouldn't happen again. It was common. She saw it in abuse victims. She saw it in victims of violent hauntings. The truth was: there were no absolute assurances that it wouldn't happen again.

All you could do is prepare yourself better—mentally and physically–if it did. It was strategy time. Strategies that her partner could not help her with. Even with all of his surprising abilities, even Danforth was limited in that respect. There were defenses only one person was capable of helping her build. She had a feeling her and Ralph were going to have a long talk about this.

Danforth perched on the edge of an attic crate, hands folded in intense contemplation; the dim light of the setting valley sun failing to attract his military diligence.

"Captain?"

The spectral soldier did not need to turn to know Catheryn's guardian had returned. The enlightened vibration of the being announced itself without any needed introduction.

He only acknowledged the new arrival with a partial turn of his head before returning to his own innermost thoughts.

"She's recovering. In case you were wondering."

Despite the brooding energy rolling off the soldier, Ralph could still read through it to the core issue.

"You blame yourself," the guide stated, with an empathetic tilt of his head.

"He found her, because of me," he muttered through gritted teeth at the wall before him. "She became a target, because of *me*."

"And that really bothers you."

It was an observation. A recognition of vulnerability the officer did not want.

"I got there too late—"

"You saved her," Ralph countered.

For the first time since the visitor appeared, Danforth turned to him; his face a mixture of pain and anger. An anger, misdirected.

"And where were *you*!" he spat.

"I was not allowed to interfere," the guardian replied in his soft, unassuming manner.

304

It grated on the captain's last nerve. As if he had one. "And what purpose did *that* serve?"

To Danforth's continued frustration, the being refused to take the bait.

"You did not come from that fight, unscathed."

It was true. The officer was energetically drained, compromised. It took a lot out of him to confront that ugly, yet determined, ghoul. But he was loathed to note it. There were deeper wounds inflicted.

"I'll…," he began, stopping to snort at the irony of the uncompleted sentence. "I'll live."

Even though he knew the soldier would be reluctant to accept it, Ralph placed a comforting hand on his shoulder. And in that instant, Danforth felt the healing energy flowing from that touch. Jagged cuts in his ethereal field, fused, and mended. He felt his energy restored to him.

The being removed his touch. "You'll need that for the battle to come."

"I thought you couldn't interfere?"

"The needs of the many outweigh the needs of the one. Whether you wish to admit it, or not; you are required to be at peak performance."

"But what about her?" Danforth reflected.

"She knows the risks of crossing over into your world," he stated. "As you are learning about the risks of crossing into hers. You saved her—"

"But I couldn't help her!"

Danforth's memory of that evening was sharp; the fear in her eyes, the chill, the vulnerability. He caused that to happen. And he could do nothing to help her with that. To comfort her. To take that fear away. Return her to the innocent peace that she had once known. It drew a need out of him that he hadn't expected. A need that threatened to overwhelm him.

Ralph set his jaw, the dim light of approaching twilight casting severe shadows over his angular face.

"All is as it should be. We learn. We grow. It doesn't stop with our bodily death. You know that."

Danforth closed his eyes. Of course, he knew that. Even his time with the children had changed him. Grew him in ways that no other experience would. This. This was different. And certainly not expected. And certainly, not comfortable.

"What am I supposed to do with this?" the soldier muttered at the floor.

"What we all do. We choose. We either become a victim to circumstance," the guardian stated, blithely. "Or, we evolve."

The week had been quiet, Catheryn observed. Ralph remained no more than a call away, like he always did, but he was much more available without being summoned. As she expected, they had a long chat about the horrific event. He listened with intense concern, but that expression never wavered, even when she mentioned the captain's untimely arrival. It was almost like Ralph *expected* it.

It was likely the creature had bypassed all alarms by coming through her dream state. It had happened before, but not with this sort of tactical precision and never resulting in harm to her. It had taken advantage of the element of surprise. That wouldn't happen again.

She had carefully chosen, as part of her wardrobe that week, to wear a silk scarf around her neck, cravat-style, tucked into her tailored vests. David thought she looked like Watson to his Sherlock Holmes. Even though she argued the roles were the other way around, it was a style that suited her. No one would have guessed there was bruising around her neck. A good deal of it had subsided by week's end, and she could have touched it up with makeup had she wished it, but it would have just messed up her collar shirts.

Catheryn folded her arms atop her work desk, staring down the magic eight ball sitting in the middle of it. It was 3 P.M. on a Friday, and she was eager to leave.

David had exited his consulting room, bidding his last client of the day a good holiday weekend, when he turned and found her like that.

He planted his hands in the pockets of his gray tweed slacks, the action opening up the front to his matching suit jacket to expose his black argyle sweater vest. He sauntered casually up to her work space.

"You are one of the most talented and gifted clairvoyants and mediums I know," he said, scratching the back of his head in wonder. "Why you would ever consult that thing, I'll never know."

She didn't look up. "I am more than capable of screwing up my own life without consulting the sacred wisdom of the magic eight ball."

Resting her chin on the edge of her desk, she reached over to give the round black sphere a shake before tipping it up, allowing the oracle die to float up to the surface of the viewing window.

Without a doubt.

She planted the object, window down, upon the surface of her desk. "It's just the 1970's answer to the fidget spinner."

She pushed herself away from the edge of the desk, allowing the exerted force to roll the antique leather and mahogany swivel chair backward. She gazed up at him with a self-assured smile as she took a moment to relax in the leather chair's comfortable embrace.

It managed to draw a tight-lipped chuckle from him. No doubt, he was happy to see her getting her humor back—even if it was heavily-laced with sarcasm.

He turned toward the office exit. "The car is packed. Ready to go?"

She rose, drawing out her Celtic-themed gold and green-styled tote before wheeling out her newly-purchased purple, hard-sided weekender. Pulling up the telescoping handle, she rested the tote on top of the case, easily wheeling them both along at once.

"Why, after the drama of this week, you are in such a hurry to return..."

She paused for a moment to consider that.

"I kind of feel that...I owe it to them to come back."

David snorted. "Baldwin?"

"Least of all, Baldwin. But, he *is* paying us."

Catheryn felt guilty that her partner was burning well-earned vacation to go back down, and she offered to go alone, but he shut that down immediately. He was still concerned about her. He was very careful to watch her interaction with patients and called every night before bed. He even offered to sleep on her couch, but that was just a little too much encroachment into her personal space. A part of him felt guilty exposing her to this, even though she, willingly, went along. It was the everyday risk of her living her life. She dealt with her *special* perception, in her own way, every day—way before he had come along.

Besides, the real estate agent had admitted to missing the company. Even Abigale Bramden and the surly captain had remained, stoically, silent. On occasion, he had heard giggling and the sound of little feet gracing the upstairs floor, but it was a sound he had grown accustomed to. With the exception of the dramatic energy outburst upon their departure, not much else had really happened.

But even the elder doctor had her wondering why she was in such a hurry to go back. She did feel morally obligated, but as her fingers brushed the royal blue silk scarf at her neck, the stakes of that obligation were rising. Something seemed to be pulling her—commanding her—to return. It had haunted her all week. She really couldn't explain it.

She paused, picking up her desktop toy. She gave it a brutal shake before flipping the device to read its offering.

Better not tell you now.

If that didn't sound foreboding…

16

Andrew Baldwin was at the door to greet them as soon as their rental car pulled up in front of the house. Unlike the usual artificial smile that had met them in the past, this one looked genuine. His usual modern-styled hair, jeans and t-shirt were a bit more lackluster, speaking to a more relaxed side of him than Catheryn was used to seeing.

She slid out of the front seat and moved to the back door of the sedan to claim her luggage. The gravel was damp from a recent rain, turning the road in front of the house to a dark gray mud. She was grateful to have chosen her black combat-style boots for the trip. As her hand fell on the car door handle, she felt the all-too-familiar tingle along the back of her scalp. She turned back to look up at the house.

Just in time to witness a curtain dropping back into position from the second floor. Apparently, the agent wasn't the only one awaiting their arrival.

David, Andrew, and Catheryn escaped the house for a time, driving over to the neighboring township for a pizza joint Andrew had discovered. Being a holiday weekend, the place was overrun by locals, as well as a fair share of bikers taking advantage of some of the last good weather of the season. Over a good beer and even better pizza, they strategized the remainder of their stay. By the time they had wrapped up, it was late. She was more than relaxed for the drive back.

As they crossed the river bridge out of town, she felt her attention pulled to the red-bricked, lovingly-restored multi-storied historic steamboat hotel. As she took in the wrapping porch trimmed out in the stark white railing indicative of the Steamboat Gothic architecture, she noted the hotel was more *occupied* than the owners were probably aware of. She made a mental note to ask Andrew about it later.

Catheryn took in the weekly report from Baldwin as they entered the house, but she was only half-listening. She felt her attention drawn to the upstairs and was eager to go there. When their host finished, she excused herself to head up the front staircase. There it was again; the tingle. Someone was up here, watching, but their identity, intentionally eluding her. She continued her way up to the second floor and turned into her regular room, keeping her senses open about her.

A door slammed somewhere at the back of the house and she paused, listening for any changes in the downstairs conversation between her partner and Baldwin. They also seemed puzzled by the sudden sound, so she knew the sound hadn't originated from them. It was an unseasonably warm fall day. Was a window open? Did a breeze take a door?

She turned the round, chalk-colored knob to enter her room. The familiar male outline was standing in the large, antiquated, horizontal-hatched glass window. She could tell by his posture that he was observing something in his hand. Whatever he held appeared to fit in his palm and closed with an audible snap before depositing it inside his coat. In the generous light of the late day sun, she could make out he was not wearing his usual attire. Instead of his long military frock coat, he wore a short navy wool shell jacket trimmed with red piping, belted at the waist. Light blue trousers with red welting at the outer seams, were tucked into black leather knee boots.

"Back again?" the familiar gruff male voice commented.

Catheryn reached out with her senses to judge his mood but was unsuccessful.

"No one warned me off this time," she countered with an arched eyebrow.

"The cat missed you."

"I'm sorry to hear that."

He turned, not disappointing her with anything different than his regular dark scowl. "How long are you staying *this* time?"

"Tuesday. Is that a problem?"

He returned his attention to the window. "Only if you expect to sleep. There's a party this weekend."

Catheryn blinked. "What's the occasion?"

"I wasn't aware we needed one," he said, not turning. However, he seemed to feel the young therapist's expectant gaze. "It's Ms. Abigale's birthday."

The young therapist was a bit mystified. Ms. Abigale seemed far from the 'birthday party' type, but then again, Catheryn had the feeling that parties were a regular thing here, whether the living could witness them, or not.

"I wasn't aware you still celebrated birthdays."

"Well, maybe if you'd ask before just *inviting* yourself over you'd know we did. For some strange reason, she felt obligated to invite you, so I'm extending the invitation." His head shifted to the left, momentarily. "I'm needed elsewhere. I'm considering the message delivered."

With that, he *blinked* out of sight.

She sighed, turning her attention back to the belongings on her bed. Was it just her, or was he even *more* agitated than the first time she was here?

Catheryn chose a gown of dark green silk this time. Of course, in her lucid dreaming state, she could choose anything she wanted, so her imagination was the limit. Trimmed out in ornate black lace at the open neckline, and scalloped layered skirt, it showed off her complexion and complimented her red hair and light green eyes. She made sure to conjure a thick black lace choker, as well as a matching fan and black silk reticule-style purse. Pulling on her white short kidskin gloves, she reached for the doorknob of the dining room when she stopped herself. How did you enter a room with people that used no doors? She closed her eyes, taking a few deep breaths before walking right into the door. Her head smarted as her body rebounded off the solid material, or what her mind *accepted* as solid material. This was going to be harder than she thought. She decided on a different strategy. Instead of phasing through solid material—something that she couldn't even perceive doing—she

316

simply imagined no door there, at all. Closing her eyes and taking another deep breath, she stepped forward.

More rapidly than she expected, she heard music swirling all about her. Upon opening her eyes, she found herself among a very crowded dance floor. Catheryn managed to scurry out of the way, avoiding a collision with a couple waltzing to the left of her. This event appeared to be even grander than the one she had previously attended. Backing her way toward the safety of the punch bowl, she ran, unceremoniously, into someone. She began to apologize as she turned, and found herself face to face with, none other than, Andrew Baldwin. He looked so different dressed in a tan frock coat and pleated collar shirt. His brown wool trousers matched his notched collar vest. He still managed to wear his pomade but in a different manner; affecting a part in his blonde hair right down the middle.

"Catheryn!" The agent stopped just short of hugging her before stiffening his posture with one arm around his back. "I mean, Ms. Catheryn. A pleasure to see you."

He took her gloved hand in his own and bowed slightly at the neck. The therapist couldn't help but laugh, but to her relief, Baldwin did likewise.

The agent fussed with the lapels of the long suit coat and shook his head, still smiling. "Not...my idea, but Ms. Abigale helped me out."

"So, you got the invite, too?"

"I guess we're one of the few *living* people in the house that she actually *could*."

Catheryn smiled, gazing in wonderment at the full accommodations around her. "As if she could fit any more people in here!"

She shifted away from another whirling couple when she bumped into someone else. Sergeant Solomon picked up his kepi-style hat from the floor before realizing who it was that he had collided with.

"Oh, good evening, Ms. Catheryn!"

"Sergeant Solomon," she greeted with a smile, allowing him to take her hand, formally. "Are you here for the party, too?"

The young officer tucked his cover under one arm. "No, ma'am. I'm afraid I'm on official business. I mean to find the Cap'n."

Baldwin gestured toward the musician's area. "I think he's getting ready to take a break along with the band."

Danforth was dressed down to his dark vest and white rolled up shirt sleeves. The sergeant found his way to him quickly. She watched as the captain's expression seemed to shift from the gaiety of the event, to seriousness at the cavalry officer's approach. As she watched the exchange, she saw his dark eyes grow wide, his hand catching Solomon by the arm. The two swiftly left out the side door and into the night, leaving Catheryn curious as to what was going on.

"Can I get you some punch?" Baldwin offered.

It snapped the therapist back to her sudden surroundings.

"Thank you, Andrew, but I think I'll pass." She touched him, appreciatively, on the shoulder as she passed him. "Maybe later."

She made her way through the bustling crowd, and moved, tentatively, toward the back kitchen door that someone had propped open. She didn't want to intrude upon what could very well be a private conversation, but she did not have long to wait until Sergeant Solomon entered the room, again.

Catheryn's therapist empathy emerged as she saw the troubled look on the cavalry officer's face. "Sergeant, is everything okay?"

He studied her face for a moment, as if to find the right words. "He…might need a talkin' to."

Before she could ask anything else, he shouldered past her and disappeared into the sea of merrymakers. As she observed his wake, one face caught her eye. A charmed Abigale Bramden turned from a well-wisher and seemed to spy her. The cordiality seemed to drain from her expression, as if reading Catheryn from afar. The young doctor gestured toward the door and for the hostess to stay where she was.

Still using her lucid dreaming skills, she conjured a black wool wrap from the night air before stepping out onto the cement platform. If Danforth knew she was behind him, he didn't acknowledge it. He remained standing with his back to her, hands thrust into the pockets of his sky-blue uniform trousers.

She attempted to peek around him in an attempt to gauge his mood. "Captain, are you alright?"

He seemed to start slightly at her approach before returning his gaze out to the sparse evening campfires across the street.

"You shouldn't be out here. It's cold tonight."

She shrugged the wrap more securely about her shoulders as she moved closer. "I thought the Dead didn't feel cold?"

He didn't say anything, but she could feel the turmoil of emotions rolling off of him. His tone not *quite* being dismissive, she took up the view alongside him. She spared a sidelong look at his face and felt an extra chill at his vacant expression. It was so unlike him.

"I'm not sure why more of 'em didn't come to the party," he

muttered, his expression unchanged. "They know they're always welcome here."

Her eyes followed him among the campfires dotting the landscape before them. "It's a full house. It's crowded."

"They never come. They serve as faithfully as any soldier, believe firmly in our mission here, but when it comes to these things…" His voice trailed off as his eyes fell to the gravel at his booted feet. "The responsibility is mine. I need to work harder at inclusion."

"You think they still haven't gotten over it—the war, I mean."

"No one's hands are clean in this." He shook his head, ever so slightly. "It's hard. The things we did to each other."

She moved closer, feeling her therapy skills awakening as she gazed up into his face to draw him in. "You want to talk about it, you can with me."

"I remember my first large engagement. We were on Oak Hill in August of 1861. I was just a sergeant. A gunner. Formulated as back-up artillery for Totten's Battery," he explained, his eyes further away than just the camps in front of him. "The cannon had been firing nonstop since eight that morning. The guns were so hot that you couldn't touch them."

She could feel it coming off of him in waves. The guilt. The shame. It was breaking her heart to look at him. She reached out to touch his shoulder.

And instantly, regretted it.

She heard the whistle first before the explosion hit. The ground trembled beneath her, and she lost her footing. As she landed on an unceremonious pile on the ground, she was aware she was no longer an observer. So absorbed was he in the recollection of it that she had been pulled into it *with* him.

She found her eyes adjusting to the sudden light of day, but the light was so choked with dirt and soot as the guns around her erupted, again, and again, it was difficult to tell what time of day it was.

In between blasts, she could hear his familiar voice barking the cannons to turn. It wasn't the voice in her head any longer. It was present, in front of her, as the actions played out in real time. It was somewhat disconcerting, as if he were two places, at once. Privates and corporals scrambled to leverage their weight against the trail spikes; long sharp, iron rods shoved into the earth to pivot the guns to a different trajectory. Danforth stood behind the two-cannon section, his brown leather field glasses held up to his eyes. His attire mirrored much of what she had seen in the previous day; dark blue shell jacket trimmed in red piping and belted at the waist, but the markings at the bicep-level of his sleeves were different. Not the captain's rank she was accustomed to seeing. She could observe a fine sheen of perspiration on his brow and forming along his neck as if during the intense heat of summer.

"Who is that?" he yelled over the din, still peering through the field glasses, taking in the field in front of him. "Corporal, do you see their colors?"

"No, sir!"

He swore aloud, as he saw the sea of gray uniforms moving forward, less than three hundred yards away.

"This is a damn folly! Can't even tell who they are! Load canister!" Danforth barked, straining for one last look through his field glasses. "As a precaution."

"Captain gave us orders to hold!" the corporal yelled, more out of need to be heard above the din than to countermand a superior officer. "He thinks it's the Iowa Greyhounds!"

He swore again, field glasses pressed hard against his face, hoping against hope it would give him some clue.

"Impossible situation. Early in the war, states were still fighting in militia gray.

You couldn't tell who was on the battlefield until they opened fire. Earlier in the day, the enemy stole our colors, and advanced on our positions with no warning. We couldn't trust anything we were seeing. It was chaos."

Catheryn still felt grounded in the alternate reality, staggering back, startled, as a federal infantryman in dark blue clawed to the top of the battery hillcrest, right at her feet.

"Rebels!" the man bellowed with as much air as he could muster. "Those are Rebels in front of us!"

The Danforth to the side of her swore openly, turning to a corporal next to him. "Run this to Captain Totten, with my compliments. *NOW!*"

Why anyone would complement an officer at a time like that, Catheryn didn't know, but she didn't like what approached from across the field.

The gray uniforms were one hundred yards, and closing.

"Load double canister!"

"But Sergeant—"

Danforth turned and grabbed the cannoneer by a handful of blue wool on the front of his coat, the action by the much taller man clearly etching fear into the subordinate's face. "Don't make me relieve you,

Corporal."

The other men didn't wait for the conversation to right itself, racing for wooden cases at the back of the wagons and lugging the heavy canisters to the forward position. Catheryn could feel their anxiety as if it were her own, stumbling back with her hands over her ears.

Fifty yards, and closing.

A horse and rider raced along the ridge behind them, the message-bearing adjutant reigning in hard to bring the horse to a stop before Danforth, offering a hasty salute.

"With Captain Totten's compliments—fire at will!"

Thirty yards, and closing.

The words had barely left the messenger's lips.

"Ready the piece!" Sergeant Danforth called.

The forward cannoneers manning the gun, fell away to the sides, ears covered.

"FIRE!"

The corporal yanked the lanyard from the rear position. The weapon discharged at full effect. The ground shook, but somehow, Catheryn was able to find her feet, again, long enough to see the canister's steel shot rip through the advancing Confederate line of the 1st

Arkansas Volunteers. The first line of human beings, literally, evaporated into a horrific mist of red; so close was their advance that flecks of blood blew back and struck the only officer still facing forward.

Catheryn recoiled in horror as she witnessed Danforth standing, too far forward, frozen at the nightmare he had just witnessed; his face blanched white, giving the spray of blood against his skin a more ghastly effect.

The young doctor lost her balance, tears stinging her cheeks as the full effect of what she had just seen—what he had been forced to live and relive over and over—was rammed home, as he gave the only order left to him.

"Double canisters. Reload!"

"Those mothers? Those wives? They had nothing left to bury. I did that to them."

She staggered back, gasping for air, coughing and sputtering as she felt hands reach out for her. She had disengaged from the officer's energetic field, leaving her unsteady. The scene before her vision had melted away, giving way to the blackness of night, flashes of orange and red vacillating in her peripheral vision. All the while, she could hear a muffled sound of someone trying to talk to her. Another form rushed into her field of view. Was that Baldwin?

She was back. It was all coming back to her now. The party. The house.

The captain's face was floating before her vision, a face now clean from the past ravages of what she had just seen. She could not stop the tears, her eyes still wide with anxiety and fear as to what she had just witnessed. What he had witnessed. And it was only a fraction of his experience.

Danforth pulled away as Baldwin took over. Ralph had appeared, also, on her opposite side; concern clearly etched in his bright blue-green eyes, but the glances he exchanged with Danforth appeared laced with something more hostile.

The captain backed away, his eyes a mixture of horror and shame as he allowed others to tend to her.

17

When Catheryn awoke the next morning, Andrew Baldwin was at her bedside with coffee and toast. It took a moment for her to realize how he was aware of her need, but it wasn't until she accepted the steaming mug with grateful hands did the memory of the night before come flooding back to her.

She held the mug in her hands, allowing the warmth of the ceramic to permeate through to her fingers. "Have you seen him this morning?"

Andrew knew what she meant without any further prodding. "No...no, I haven't."

It was a dagger through her heart. Her reaction...her response was a reflex. Experiencing the event, as intensely as he had—as *she* had—caused a sensory overload. It put her in literal shock. It was nothing more than that. But how he interpreted it...

Gazing over the top of her mug, she saw Ralph. He sat in a chair, off to her left, sympathy etched in his startling blue-green eyes and sharp facial features.

She shifted her words to Baldwin without looking at him. "Thank you, Andrew. Could you…give me a minute?"

He stood up from his seated position at her right. "Sure."

It left her and Ralph to consult, alone.

She managed to raise her eyes to regard her guide, directly. "Have you talked to him?"

There was never a morning that the captain wasn't there, waiting with his usual brooding air, in her room. It was annoying, at first, but now that he wasn't…His absence was keenly felt.

"I wanted to make sure you were alright," her guide said, softly.

"Better than he is. I'm sure."

The therapist in her was ashamed, overwhelmed with guilt; unable to do much else than to study the inside of her half-filled coffee mug.

"It was my fault. Not his," she muttered. She paused for a moment to look at Ralph. "I reached in when I shouldn't have. It was a rookie mistake, and no reflection on anything he's done. Can you tell him that?"

"Catheryn—"

"Please."

The earnestness of her voice drew him out of his own sense of duty, and he looked at her face. It matched her voice. As it always did.

"Alright."

He drew up from his chair, and before he even turned away, his form vanished.

Danforth sat on the edge of a box in his usual spot in the upper attic, his dark gaze taking in the view from the attic window. Lieutenant Moore's morning exchange with him was minimal as he relieved his commanding Officer of the Watch. No doubt even his second-in-command was aware of the evening event. A day, or two, and the incident would blow over. With everyone, but himself.

So deep was he in thought that he hadn't realized he was no longer alone.

Danforth turned to the shadowy form that sat to his left, not bothering to look directly at them. He knew who it was already.

The captain managed his words without malice or weight. "What are you doing here?"

"You really should consider stitching that motto into a battle flag."

The form stood, and stepped into the early morning light. The tall, lithe figure's light brown hair shone like spun gold in the sun, his blue-green eyes aglow. It made him wonder if he was in collusion with the Architects of the Universe to give him such splendor.

"She's worried about you."

Danforth didn't bother to fathom what the new arrival meant. He knew. "She thinks me a monster."

"Had you been doing your duty and monitoring her thoughts, instead of being lost in your own, you would have realized the contrary," the guide observed, dispassionately. "Instead, you erred in acting emotionally."

Ralph moved out of the shadows, his gait toward the officer, casual and non-threatening.

"Society has evolved in the way they think of the trauma impacting its veterans. In this country, it started with your war," the guide corrected, the morning light revealing more of a directness in his demeanor. "She thinks only of you. You underestimate her compassion. She wouldn't be able to do her work if she were without it."

He snorted softly. "A shrink."

"She's a *healer*, in more ways than even *she* knows." Ralph said, firmly. "But you...you keep her at arm's length."

"I only succeed in hurting her; first her apartment, and now, the party." He slapped his knee with his white leather gauntlets in frustration, rising to put some distance between himself and the guide. "Both times she became hurt...because of me."

"It's easier to hurt the ones we love, because through love, we make ourselves vulnerable. It's impossible to avoid without closing yourself off to it," the spiritual assistant mused. "But you've done just that through most of your life, haven't you? You have an opportunity here to...make a different choice."

"I guess you've got me all figured out, don't you?" For the first time since the guide's arrival, the officer found the audacity to stare him down. "But then again—she doesn't know who *you* are, does she?"

Ralph didn't meet his withering glare, setting his jaw as his own gaze shifted toward the window. "She knows me well enough. That is of no importance. And you are avoiding the subject."

The soldier didn't flinch. "We're talking about our innermost secrets, aren't we? How is it that she doesn't know about you?"

"Fine." A shadow of reminiscence seemed to settle over the guest's finely-chiseled features, and a serene smile of recollection formed as his gaze dropped to the barn wood floor. "She was only five years old when

I met her. Her guardian spirit reached out to me for help. Her little charge was too close to the pond at her grandmother's house. Of all projected outcomes in her linear timeline, there was a high likelihood she would come to harm before it was…her time."

The guide took a seat on a box, offering him the seat next to him. The officer, reluctantly, took it.

"That's when I met her for the first time, quite surprised she could *see* me. Not too unusual for children to see us, but she approached me with no fear. I knew, even then, she was special. Not only strongly psychic but a healer."

"As her grandmother raced to the pond to fetch her, as I expected, she also saw me…the *gift* tends to run in families. However, her grandmother's reaction toward me was more…fearful. But I was so intrigued with the child that I visited her numerous times after that." Ralph looked up into the window, and he chuckled at the memory; the action in conjunction with the sunlight causing his blue-green eyes to dance in brilliance. "Dearest little Catheryn never could *quite* pronounce my name right, but I still knew when she called."

" 'Doesn't matter what you call me…as long as you call me'?" the officer smirked. "Maybe I should try that."

There was something in the vibration of the guide's sidelong look that hinted to the captain that he may be treading close to impertinence, but the usual serene smile was still, ever-present.

"I'll allow that in you seem to have worked your way into her present…affections," the luminous being said, his voice as smooth as silk, holding Danforth's gaze a moment longer to emphasize his point. "But make no mistake; as long as I am her guide, there will only be so much carelessness I will tolerate on your behalf. Step *cautiously*."

Danforth was only mildly surprised to see the guest had chosen that dramatic moment to vanish. He arched a bemused eyebrow.

"Thanks…Dad," he muttered to himself.

He supposed he should have been grateful that no one chose to *smite* the arrogance out of him at that opportune time, but it did give him some relief that he had provoked some favorable emotion in Catheryn, despite what had occurred last evening. Why he felt relief at that, he couldn't quite say, but the shift in her feelings must have been considerable.

Otherwise, he wouldn't have been paid a visit.

It was enough to give him the confidence he sorely needed, to leave the attic and go about his day.

Corporal Daniel Hampden found a quiet secluded spot in a cluster of trees near the river, far enough from camp as to not be seen. He stripped out of his woolen blue uniform and down to his long cotton drawers that had once been white a long time ago. The drawers most likely needed more of a wash than he did, so he waded out into the shallow portion near the bank of the river that came up to his waist. He was rather surprised the water only came up that high, but it was enough to do the job. After giving himself a sound scrubbing, he returned to the bank to conclude with shaving. Hanging his drawers out to dry a bit, he took his soap dish, brush and straight razor with him back to the river bank, squatting down to wet his brush and work the soap in the dish up to a froth. The corporal found himself wishing for the umpteenth time this trip that he hadn't lost his pocket mirror. As it was, his reflection in the water would have to do. As he leaned over at the water's edge to take in his reflection, he froze. The reflection was blurry, and difficult to make out. He didn't understand it. The water was still and unmoving in this tiny pocket. He should have been able to make out his facial features with no trouble. Perhaps there was something wrong with the water. Maybe he shouldn't have bathed in it. He'd have to ask the other soldiers to see if they had a piece of mirror to complete the task.

His drawers were still damp when he redressed for camp, but perhaps that would keep him cool for the day's march. But yet, he didn't recall being *hot*, yesterday, even though they had marched several miles. Maybe it was the day before that...

A freshly-shaven Lieutenant Stacey met him as he came up the river bank, already dressed for the day. The corporal offered a hasty salute. The lieutenant returned it, as Hampden observed the senior officer hiking a single-button canvas haversack onto one shoulder.

"Fall in, Hampden, we're moving out," the ginger-haired officer ordered, sparing a look behind the corporal as he did so. "Where's your 'friend'?"

The younger man offered a hasty salute. "Yes, sir! I'll see if I can find him, sir."

Hampden scrambled to where Carter had pitched his tent the night before, only to find it already taken down. Puzzled, he peered into the woods behind the tent and backed up, in surprise, as the bounty hunter emerged from the brush.

"We're on the move," the corporal relayed, looking over the roughly-dressed man's shoulder. "Where's your bounty?"

Carter spat at the ground, causing the younger man to recoil in mild disgust.

"Cashed 'em in last night," the man grumbled in his low gravelly voice. "Don't worry about it."

Something seemed aggressive in his tone, as if not to ask anything further. Swallowing down his intimidation, the soldier turned toward camp without a word, but he couldn't help but feel something was amiss. When had he found time to slip out of camp to complete his transaction, and return so quickly? On the other hand, it relieved him not to have him transporting the ghoulish-looking lot along with the soldiers any longer. It was already drawing distasteful looks from other members of the company.

Corporal Hampden chose to file it under 'not his business' and fell in with the rest of the crew.

Stacey approached Carter, planting his black leather wallet into his haversack. The bounty hunter extended his palm, expectantly, and the officer plastered it with currency.

Stacey didn't spare any pleasantries. "Lead the way."

Reading the flavor of the exchange, Carter eased his own personal sack onto his shoulder more comfortably, and moved onto the head of the troop formation, without a word. Stacey met him there.

The ginger-haired officer fastened his kepi more securely atop his head as he turned to address the tracker. "How far we got left to go?"

The grizzled man paused momentarily, as if reading something unseen in the air. A smile seemed to tug at the corner of his mouth before he turned to Stacey.

"Not far," he responded, confidently trudging out ahead of the troops. "Not far, at all."

Catheryn returned to the house after another evening out with Dr. Faustus and Andrew Baldwin. Baldwin and Faustus were heavily engaged in the topic of psychokinesis and the unassisted, anomalous movement of objects. Realizing her partner was in 'teaching' mode, and not likely to need her, she hung back as they entered the house. That's when the familiar *tingle* struck her, again. It was from the same second floor window, but when she looked up, she saw nothing—just the uneasy feeling of being watched. So focused was she on using her Awareness to probe the source that she missed the presence next to her when she heard it.

"Good evening, Ms. Catheryn."

She recognized the unmistakable drawl of Lieutenant Moore before she saw him. "Oh, good evening, Lieutenant. I wasn't expecting you out here."

His smile was all Southern charm, removing his gray wool kepi hat, the intricate scrolled gold braiding at its crown signifying his rank. He still dressed in his gray officer's frock coat with standing collar, and redundant scrolled gold soutache braiding at the sleeves. She found it fascinating that, after all this time, they still wore their uniforms with great pride.

"The captain has changed the watch," the officer noted, his eyes shifting out to the water across the road with an air of alertness. "Something's on its way."

"Yes, I feel it too."

Catheryn had to admit, as she pushed her Awareness outward, that she could sense the same. She wasn't entirely sure if this was a good time to address the situation, but it had been plaguing her mind since her last encounter with the captain.

"Lieutenant—"

"William. Please."

She smiled at the intimate gesture. "William. How do you come to work so closely with the captain? The others seem so…distant."

"Oh, the captain," he repeated, his eyebrows going up at the change in topic. "Oh, he killed me."

Catheryn's eyes went wide. He was so cavalier in his delivery that it took her completely unawares. "What?!"

He squinted upward, as if trying to remember. "Bentonville? Oh, yes. Bentonville." He chuckled. "We were audacious enough to charge the battery, if you can imagine."

She didn't have to. A chill roiled up her spine at the memory of her previous vision.

"Thought I had the drop on him," he said with a smile. "Didn't take into consideration that he knew how to use that sword. Ran me clean through."

He shook his head, chuckling so casually as if it was a fumbled pass at the high school football game while Catheryn was still getting over the first part of his delivery.

"He *killed* you," she repeated, as if needing confirmation of the statement. "And you accepted the position as his second here?"

"Anyone that knows how to use a saber is well worth knowin'," he chuckled. "I think the cap'n said somethin' similar—anybody bold enough to charge a battery was either a fool or someone worth knowin'. Fine line between courage and stupidity."

Sure, Catheryn mused. He could laugh about it *now*.

"I best be off," the young doctor said with a bemused smile. "I shall sleep well knowing you are on the job."

He tugged at the black leather brim of his kepi in a respectful salute, as she passed him to enter the doors of the house.

She paused in the entryway, hearing Andrew and David's voices carrying from the side parlor, smelling the hint of a burning fireplace as she passed. She thought of joining them, but not wanting to disrupt them, she opted for her room, instead.

Slipping into her favorite long-sleeved band t-shirt and yoga pants, she crawled under the comforter of her welcoming bed. As she did so, she heard the solemn strains of the violin playing in the attic. She recognized it as an old Celtic lullaby. Combined with the fragrant smell of the burning fire and the good-natured murmuring from downstairs, she found herself drifting to sleep in no time.

18

Danforth was just loosening the tension of the horsehair on the bow of his fiddle when movement outside the attic window caught his eye. He reached down to retrieve his pocket watch out of the breast pocket of his discarded shell jacket.

4:56 A.M.

"Who in the blazes…"

He left his jacket behind, tucking the timepiece into his blue wool vest pocket before he *blinked* to the second floor. It was there that he found Catheryn's bedroom door wide open, with no Catheryn in it. His attention was pulled down the hallway where he found, discarded, the fluffy white belt of her robe.

"Damn it!" he muttered.

Reaching out with his Awareness, he found her. He *blinked* again, his destination outside the house and in front of the pedestrian bridge.

There, he found Catheryn standing, completely still, the night air stirring the long, unkempt tendrils of her auburn hair. Her fluffy white robe was open, revealing her regular night dress of yoga pants and t-shirt. Her vacant green eyes were staring down river, the moonlight dancing in her unnatural, unblinking gaze.

"Catheryn!" Danforth snapped. Receiving no reaction, he tried louder. "Catheryn!"

Still no response. Not even a flinch.

He finally reached inside her mind. *Catheryn!*

The young doctor blinked hard, and then, a few more blinks before her hand rose to her head. "What…"

Her grogginess wore off with the surge of adrenaline as she realized she was only a few steps from the churning water beneath her. She gasped, stumbling back a few steps further inland. Feeling a gaze on her, she turned to find the captain standing there, his expression one of concern and bewilderment.

Her throat was dry, words raspy. "What am I doing out here?"

"Was hoping you could tell *me.*" Danforth's lips were pursed thin. "I, literally, had to get into your head to snap you out of it."

Now it was her turn to be confused. And alarmed. "I *don't*

sleepwalk."

"Helluva time to start!"

Her agitation at his sarcastic tone was beginning to clear away the fogginess. Her hands went to both sides of her head.

"I don't...all I remember is you..." She looked up at him, still feeling somewhat dazed. "You were calling to me."

"I know. I just said that. I had to get in your head to—"

"No," she replied, cutting him off. "You were calling my name, over and over. Calling me...outside."

The officer looked perturbed. "Why would I do that? I was in the *house*."

"Oh my God," Catheryn muttered to herself, looking away.

"What?"

The bedroom event back in Chicago. The attack. All of it used her familiarity with Danforth to gain access. Was it doing it, again?

Her anxiety rising, she shrugged her robe away from her neck, exposing her jugular to him. "Do you see anything?"

"What?"

"Do you see *anything?!*"

He peered down at the skin of her neck, the moonlight casting shadows across the peaks and valleys caused by the strained tendons, but…there. Almost imperceptible. A discoloration. But he didn't need full view of it to feel the residual energy of the malice that inflicted it.

"Just a little…" The realization was upon him, anger slowly registering in his dark eyes. "When did this happen?"

"The night you came to my apartment. That thing…in my bedroom."

"It was actually able to do *this* to you? And you didn't think to tell *me*?!"

"I thought you knew!"

Her defensiveness was beginning to grow into aggressiveness. She knew it was caused by her own feelings of vulnerability, but she didn't care.

"It's not as if we are on intimate terms—*Captain*." She pulled the robes more securely about her, her defenses rising, again. "Besides, it happened in my house. Not yours."

Her words stopped him cold, forcing him to reflect inward. Ralph was right. He was keeping her at arm's length. His authority. His rank. Even keeping her from using his own first name, even though, without permission, he was using hers. Repeatedly.

"I thought it wasn't 'my house'?" he muttered.

The rare attempt at humor broke through her embroiled emotion, and she cracked a smile she was grateful he couldn't see.

"And it's Charlie," he muttered, crossing his arms across his chest. "If you don't mind."

She froze. Feeling so frustrated and helpless, she hadn't realized she was throwing up barriers of her own. And yet, here he was, dropping his.

"I'm practically living in your bedroom any other time. You might as well," he grumbled sarcastically, rolling the gravel underneath his booted foot. "Just don't use it in front of the men."

He turned toward the house. She watched him walk away, the moonlight setting the sleeves of his white collar shirt aglow, musing that he could have just as easily *blinked* into the house.

But was suddenly glad he hadn't, or she would have been looking the wrong way and missed the huge black mass charging down at her from the second story of the house.

Eyes wide with fear, she backed up, losing her footing on the uneven antiquated barn wood planking of the bridge. Catching the railing, but not wanting to have another misstep, she instinctively, turned and sprinted from the bridge and down the river bank.

Away from the house.

She hadn't even realized where her intuition had led her until she had entered a small cluster of trees, cursing at the overgrowth of branches snatching at her hair. Somehow, while under the spell of whatever drew her out of doors, she had managed to put her shoes on, but now, she was sorely missing her hair ties.

After freeing her hair, she chanced a look over her shoulder. The thing was gaining like a swarm of deadly bees. She could almost hear the agitated buzz as the mass neared. She darted into the grove of trees, pressing through the resisting overgrowth. The bare branches of fall were pulling and snagging at her robes. It came to a point that she discarded the frustrating garment altogether. As she emerged into a sparse area of green, she nearly collided with the image of Danforth.

"Where the hell do you think you're going?" he blustered. "Take the path to your left."

She dodged him, turning to run down the path. She had only gotten ten yards when his visage erupted before her, again.

"Your *other* left!"

"That's *away* from the house."

"*Now* you wanna play scout? *Left!*"

Against her better judgment she turned, braving a look behind her. The tree canopy had nearly eclipsed all available light, so it was difficult to see her pursuer, but she could definitely hear it following, relentlessly.

As she took in the area ahead of her, she was beginning to see ample light breaking through the shelter of trees. Early dawn was setting the sky aglow, which she hoped would allow her the benefit of recognizing her surroundings.

It was at that point that she soundly tripped over a block of sandstone. The block was likely left over from a structure long gone, but it was serving as a dangerous nuisance now. She looked up from her sprawled position to see Danforth before her.

"Do *something!*" she said, breathlessly.

"What do you expect me to do? I can't transport you back to the house—you're too heavy."

She stood, brushing the leaves and moist dirt from her yoga pants, the indignance clearly registering in her voice. "I'm *what?*"

"I can only do that with the cat."

She continued to pick her way through the branches ahead of her at a determined pace. "You *apported* the cat?!"

348

"The cat didn't seem to mind."

She breezed past him. Ahead of her, she could see a thinning of the trees, yet, at the same time, the incline was increasing. Her sneakered feet were beginning to lose traction in the muddy soil; the fallen leaves keeping any of her tread from finding purchase. She stumbled a few times before emerging through the brush.

And right onto a protruding section of bluff overlooking the river.

She caught herself short of lurching forward. The stars above the valley were beginning to melt away from a darker hue of blue and giving way to pink. Any other time, she might have appreciated the view, but not now.

"You brought me *here?!*" she snapped, incredulous. "This is no time to admire a sunrise!"

The officer's form snapped into existence, standing at the very edge of the bluff with his back to the valley. He had removed an item from his vest pocket, which he appeared to be scrutinizing. All the while, Catheryn could hear the angry buzzing behind them getting louder.

"You are seriously not proposing that I *jump!*" she snapped.

He glanced up from his study, barely paying her any attention. "No, I suggest you get down. Flat on the ground."

Bewildered, she got down to her hands and knees, the mad tingle of her scalp proving her senses at full alert. As the volume of the buzzing increased, it was becoming clear to her that it was not just a thing, but it appeared to be conscious. Otherwise, it wouldn't have tripped her Awareness alarms.

As the black mass surged through the tree line, Catheryn flattened herself to the ground, straining to look up, witnessing the captain still examining the article in his hand. The pink hues along the ridge of the valley behind him started to glow brighter into a more golden shimmer.

The mass started to undulate. At one point, it even seemed to recoil slightly, before reorganizing and flushing forward.

"Captain!" she yelled, her anxiety at full peak.

He did not move, still absorbed in the object in his palm.

"Charlie!"

In an instinct of self-preservation, the young doctor planted her face in the mud, her hands securely folded over the back of her head. The mass burst forth, charging directly for him. As it blew past, Catheryn raised her head to watch in panicked silence as the spectral officer, his outline aglow with the first rays of the sun, closed the something in his hand with an audible click. With an utter air of

350

calmness, he placed it in his vest pocket. The charging mass had now reached him, and as Catheryn observed, he seemed to regard it with the same air of nonchalance as he had treated her, moments earlier.

And the mass blew past him, as if a harmless puff of smoke, disintegrating over his shoulders and vanishing into nothing.

He raised a smug eyebrow, his expression one of self-satisfaction.

"Six twenty-five," he muttered, to no one in particular.

He strolled, casually, past Catheryn who was just beginning to collect herself from her sprawled position on the ground.

"*Seriously!*" she exclaimed, managing up on all fours.

"Better follow me," he stated, his voice carrying from the brush behind her. "With your sense of direction, you'll likely end up in the neighboring township!"

Channeling her aggravation, she slammed her palms into the leaves with a frustrated grunt before rising up to go after him.

19

David Faustus was already up, outfitted in his dress khakis, white collar shirt and sweater vest. He decided to go casual and skip the tie, settling into a comfortable chair in the back of the living room, near the kitchen.

Andrew joined him, mug of coffee in hand as he watched the town goings' on outside the picture window. Baldwin's blond hair was a bit unkempt, wearing a red sweatshirt emblazoned with, what David assumed, was the agent's college alma mater. The bottom half of him sported a flannel pair of plaid pajama bottoms. It was becoming rapidly aware to the senior therapist that the little group of them were becoming quite comfortable with one another.

As Faustus read the morning paper, he flipped his wrist up to read his watch. It was a little after seven and a bit early for Catheryn to be up, but it concerned him that he heard no stirrings from upstairs. It was then that he noted a change in Andrew's demeanor as the realtor's focus seemed to shift to a different view outside the window. It must have been of some importance to make the agent lower his mug.

"Uh-oh," Baldwin muttered.

It was at that point that the front door opened, and then slammed close with such force that the display pieces in the china cabinet rattled. A disheveled Catheryn emerged from the entryway, still in last night's clothing, tossing her robe over the back of a wooden dining chair.

David didn't stir, focusing on his newspaper, offering nothing more than an arched eyebrow of curiosity. "Learn anything interesting today?"

She, brusquely, collected a coffee mug, filling it with coffee.

"Never put your life in the hands of a dead man?" she spat, sardonically.

With no apparent further explanation required, she marched back toward the main staircase, mug in hand, to head upstairs.

"Sounds like a productive morning," Faustus sighed, as he flipped the page to the business section.

Unbeknownst to Faustus, the energy of a flustered Danforth blew into the parlor, receiving only a nervous glance from Baldwin over the mug of his coffee.

"Well, I kept you from walking off the bluff, didn't I?!" the officer delivered toward the ceiling.

He glanced over at Baldwin, who was still eying him; the realtor looking more than a little unsettled. It didn't look like positive feedback to Danforth.

"Not good?" the entity inquired.

Baldwin wasn't sure if he was qualified to answer that, or was even accustomed to being directly addressed by the soldier. But since he was the only one capable of hearing...

"Yeah," the agent muttered. "Kinda 'not good'."

The answer elicited a disgruntled sigh from the officer before he stormed out of the room for destinations unknown.

Hampden was hunched over a campfire, after filling his tin cup with coffee. He cast off his wool sack coat over a large boulder, leaving him rather exposed with no vest over his red checked collar shirt. Of course, he was among comrades with no ladies present, so that was fine, but he still felt ill-at-ease. They had seemed to be marching for hours. After mid-day, a frustrated Stacey broke formation for rations. Didn't Carter say they were close? He spared sidelong glances at his fellow soldiers, wondering if any were holding him to blame for bringing this tracker into their midst. Where did Carter go, anyway?

The corporal got up off his haunches, brushing some imaginary dirt off on his light blue wool trousers, while still holding his mug. He tossed the remnant of the liquid off into the bush.

The snapping of twigs in the nearby brush drew his attention first. The sound of someone gasping, and the rustle of a struggle, piqued his curiosity enough to pick his way, carefully through the underbrush. He wasn't at all certain what he was feeling but it didn't feel right. He got down low and pushed some of the branches aside. What he saw riveted him to the spot, his whole body going cold.

One of the privates from the camp was suspended several feet in the air, his leather brogans flailing desperately for purchase on something, anything. Holding him by the throat, closing off the private's windpipe, was Jackson; still dressed in his threadbare collar shirt and tan slouch hat. As Hampden watched in terrified silence, Jackson Carter managed to force his own bony fingers into the private's mouth to force it open. As if something out of a nightmare, Carter's own mouth opened, but it was grotesquely misshapen. Nothing about how the jaw was hinged made any anatomical sense for a human being. The captive began to struggle more violently as something seemed to draw through the soldier's mouth, and into Jackson's own. It appeared to be some sort of essence being drawn from his body; draining, pulling all sustenance until the victim barely resembled a live human. The captive's cheeks grew hollow, his eyes wide as Jackson continued to feast with no regard to the man's struggles. Hampden recoiled in horror as there appeared to be very little mass left within the army uniform to hold a shape, and with a sudden note of finality, the uniform collapsed into a pile on the ground.

It now occurred to the corporal; the men in his thrall, the men in chains. He wagered that he didn't "cash" them in at all. At least not in any regular currency he knew. And the missing soldiers? How many of them had been nothing more...than a meal for this nightmarish thing wearing a human likeness. He had no idea just how violently he was trembling until the branch he held in his hand snapped.

The creature's head whipped about; its face nothing more than tattered remnants of skin, draping from a skull, as if borrowed from some corpse to construct a face. There was nothing left to even recognize the thing as Carter, except for the one milky eye that was transfixed upon the corporal.

Horrified, Hampden fell backward, scrambling away from the

stalking creature. His army-issued brogans slipped upon the damp leaves of the forest floor, but to his relief, he finally found enough traction to turn and run. The relief didn't last long.

Much like the victim he had just witnessed, his throat closed off, unable to breathe. He gasped, fingers reaching up to his throat to fight off the thing around his neck. He found his feet flailing for ground, only to find that he was no longer on it. With an unseen force that he could not comprehend, his whole body yanked back toward the creature, as if on a rubber band. Powerless, he watched, suspended in air as the tattered skin of his attacker began to mend and come together like some horrific puzzle. Muscle reformed to bone, new skin grew to glide effortlessly across the fibrous musculature of cheekbone and jaw. Now, there was enough there for Hampden to recognize, yet, it gave him no comfort.

"Well, Corporal Daniel Hampden," the low, familiar voice said in his familiar casual drawl. "What do we do with you now?"

David Faustus' gray eyes were fixed on Catheryn with grave concern.

"You said you found yourself on the bridge?"

Baldwin was listening intently, as well, from the seat next to her partner. Catheryn's elbows rested on the Duncan Fyfe dining room table, her fingers massaging each side of her temple. She knew how it sounded. She knew it would only cause her partner more worry, as well as more ammunition to just…leave this place. But she had to be honest. It was the responsible thing to report it. She was a scientist and a doctor, after all.

"I have no memory of going out there," she muttered down onto the varnished wood table top. "Not until Charlie woke me up."

David's thick gray eyebrow arched in curiosity. " 'Charlie'?"

She winced, inwardly. "Danforth."

"We're on a first name basis now?"

David's eyes hadn't left Catheryn's, a deeper concern now showing. She broke the staring match, looking away with a frustrated sigh. Yeah, a conversation of a different kind was coming.

Andrew studied both David and Catheryn's faces. "Well, that's good, right? Progress? They're beginning to trust us."

David Faustus fell back into the wooden barrel-back dining room chair, his arm draping casually along its curved backrest. "You think that this has something to do with what happened back in Chicago?"

Andrew looked puzzled. David felt it best to ignore the look. For now. Catheryn also noticed Andrew's inquisitive behavior, but she followed her partner's lead.

"Very likely," the young therapist muttered.

David turned to their host, who appeared more confused by the moment.

"Andrew, could you give us a moment, please?"

"Sure."

The partners got up from the table and stepped out onto the front steps. Catheryn chose that opportunity to steer the conversation.

"We owe it to him to tell him."

The elder therapist nodded, thrusting his hands into the pockets of his khakis. "Agreed. He's just as much at risk in this as you are. I'm just grateful nothing happened to him in our absence, but spilling too much, too soon may only escalate his anxiety. Best to get a handle on what we're dealing with, first."

Catheryn felt her partner's measuring gaze, and she looked away, sighing.

"There's more going on here than meets the eye," she muttered.

"Yes," he said, measuring his tone carefully. "There is."

She sighed, closing her eyes, feeling the lecture to come. "What?"

"You're in a unique position here," he said, softly. "You have individuals here that have suffered a…unique trauma."

"They are not my patients—"

"Aren't they?" he countered, his eyes still seeking hers. "They may have moved onto another…dimension, but their traumas are still, clearly, affecting them. There are…boundaries to consider. I'm concerned you are getting…too close to them."

She refused to meet his gaze, but the glistening in her eyes made it clear that she heard. She rested her hands on the iron rail attached to the stair step. "I…don't know how to help them."

"Them? Or, him?" he observed, frankly, gazing down at the oxblood-colored Oxfords that scraped against the cement of the step platform. "Don't think I haven't noticed. You are spending more and more time with him than any of the others."

She tried to tighten her jaw, fight against the emotion, but the best she could do was close her eyes against it. He said nothing more. He simply placed his hand on hers as he, silently, took in the churning river across the street.

He turned toward the front door, and paused.

"Oh…and one more thing," he stated, a hand raising up to his brow to massage it. "Can you do me a favor; turn down the radio tonight? It was a bit loud."

With that, he turned and entered the house, leaving her to smile to herself. She was relieved the house was *finally* beginning to have an effect on her partner, even if it was just the phantom music that played every night. She paused to take one last look at the remnants of the sun's glow playing on the rippling water of the river.

"I'll see what I can do," she muttered to herself.

C atheryn found Danforth in a peculiar position *outside* the attic this time. There was a platform just outside the window, a cast iron railing separated the edge of the platform from a several story drop. She found him there, hands resting on the cast iron rail while still maintaining the fiddle in one hand and a bow in the other. She managed out onto the tarred, flat surface, the night breeze whipping tendrils of her hair across her face. She brushed it back behind her ear as she approached him. Floating up from below them were the heart-straining notes of someone playing a guitar. She could not register exactly where it was coming from.

He looked down at the rail. "Reconnaissance report. Pickets picked up on movement in the outer perimeter."

"They determine what it was?"

"Yes," he said, with a sigh, shifting his stance to lean more heavily on the rail. "It's my old company."

Catheryn blinked. "What? They're still here?"

"Some. They didn't all leave with me the first time."

Shades of guilt seemed to come from him. For someone so self-assured, he seemed to have that, in spades.

"There was confusion. They didn't understand," he said, unwilling to meet her gaze. "They *chose* not to follow me. I couldn't just leave them here. That's why I came back."

"But I thought you came back for the house—"

"That came later."

She tried to catch his eye, to bring his gaze up to meet hers. "So, this is good, right? Perhaps they're coming to find...closure?"

"Not according to reconnaissance," he muttered.

He paused, his gaze casting out over the moonlight dancing on the water of the river. He was holding something back. She could feel it. Weighing information on whether to keep it to himself, or to share.

"They're coming to kill me."

An icy spear of fear shot through her. It wasn't the words, but the way he said it. He actually sounded worried, and somewhat ashamed.

That he would postpone his own personal peace to assure their proper life transition. Instead, the men he cared the most about, wanted him dead.

"That doesn't make any sense. You're already dead."

He snorted, as if any of it could be funny. "What's the saying—'it's the thought that counts'? I deserted them. That's the only thing they remember."

He pulled himself up from the railing, but still wouldn't meet her gaze.

"Maybe I did."

He turned, and entered the attic window with a practiced step.

"I don't want you leaving the house," he stated, bluntly, placing the fiddle and bow into their individual compartments within the splayed-open coffin case.

She gripped the outside window frame, feeling more than a bit indignant at the command. "Excuse me?"

"Jackson. He's already proven he can get to you—"

"—whether I'm in this house, or not," she countered. "Besides, after tomorrow, we have to leave."

He looked at her, as if that was not even a consideration in his strategy. He seemed to calculate something, and there was a flash of emotion coming from him that it was hard to pinpoint. Betrayal? Regret? A mixture of both? He shouldered past her, finding his way back to the railing. He gazed down below them, his arms planted rigidly on the rail to support him as the gentle stirrings of the music from the guitar strings floated up, unabated.

"There's something," he muttered down at the railing. "Something I didn't tell you. Show you. I may not get another chance."

"What?"

"It's about the cat."

She braced herself. He never liked that cat. And it never sat well with her that he was performing wild, and risky, experiments with it to improve his ability to interact with her world.

"I learned something," he stated, pulling back from the railing, his eyes locking with hers.

He held out his hand toward her; his palm out in invitation. She didn't know what to think of it. All she could do was blink at him.

"Would you do me the honor—☐

It took a moment for it to register to her. The gesture. The music below them. But what did any of this have to do with the cat? She swallowed a lump of dread. Surely he hadn't done anything to harm the poor thing...

"We're not in the dream state," she countered, knowing that in his ethereal form what he was proposing would be impossible. "I...we can't—

"Do you trust me?"

She hesitated. What's the worst he could do? He'd already proven he would put himself at risk for her safety. Slowly, reluctantly, she moved to place her hand above his.

And that's when she *felt* him.

It was jarring, but not enough to draw away from. It wasn't a physical human touch, with texture or temperature. It was more like...a tingle. As she analyzed it in her head, she felt something else. A pull. Almost as if there was a string to her torso, pulling her forward. Her body was betraying her, as if on automatic pilot. It was an intense pull, holding her in place before him. She was scant inches from him, all the while, his darkened gaze fixated on her with an intensity that both frightened, and intrigued her. She was lost in that gaze. So lost that she didn't realize how close she had become until she felt the static charge, almost strong enough to register as a physical touch, at the small of her back.

And they were…dancing.

She stared up at him, incredulous.

"This is impossible," she whispered, not able to take her eyes from his. "How did you…how—"

He chuckled softly with somewhat of a vulnerable smile cast down at the ground. "The cat and I had a lot of free time."

She smiled, a touch of humor reaching her lips. "You danced with the cat?"

He laughed, and for the first time, she saw the laughter reach his eyes. A light within the darkness.

"It taught me how to sense this reality in a way I hadn't thought of before. Everything vibrates…and if the vibration is just right…"

She felt the static charge at the small of her back increase. It roiled up from the base of her spine, spreading out and up until she felt dizzy. Her eyes threatening to roll back in her head, suddenly awash in vertigo. Her common sense was screaming for her to back away, but her curiosity and trust in him, allowed certain boundaries to be crossed. For a split second, she began to question her judgment in letting him get so close to her, past her normal energetic defense. Her senses were on energetic override. She staggered.

And he caught her.

The shock of it made her look up at him. His expression was nothing but a sea of tranquility, a certainty, as solid a grounding that she, herself, rarely felt. In his eyes, she felt a wonder; a question of just how strong a being he actually was. How wrong she may have been about how simplistic his evolution had been. It was at that moment that she chanced to look down. And gasped.

They were no longer on the ground. They were twenty feet up.

She floundered, trying to find solid purchase on something, but there was nothing there, just that pull lifting her up, and his eyes locked on hers with the continued solid certainty that he knew exactly what he was doing.

"You won't fall."

His hand let go of hers, gliding down to settle on the space above her heart, and the static charge *shifted*. It felt like a thrill, akin to that feeling of butterflies, but instead of her stomach, it was in her heart, shooting outward. It wasn't painful at all, growing and traveling. Tripping through every energy center in her body in such a way that it almost felt like…very akin to…

No. She wouldn't say it. It was impossible. But even as she felt wave after wave of the intensity, awash in the feeling of ecstasy, his face was nothing but a sea of calm. Energetically, she felt fine tendrils shoot from him, extending and wrapping like fine fibers into a cord that extended toward her. She felt it as the heightened vibration penetrated her heart, making a connection she didn't know could be had. She could only gaze up at him, wide-eyed, but in his eyes resided…something quite different. A vulnerability. A longing for things to be different. A wanting to express what he could not say. Instead, he made her…feel it.

And then, it abruptly stopped, plunging her into cold darkness. The warmth, the security, the pleasant feeling was all, mercilessly ripped away, like dropping into icy cold water.

She was no longer above the house. The music was gone. The moonlight was all but muted by the curtains in her room. She was on her bed, and trying as she could reach out with her senses, there was no one there.

But the tingle. Her fingers deftly travelled to the spot in the center of her chest. The energetic cord. It still felt as if…it were there. The residual of it still churned through her body like a pleasant afterglow. Had she had a dream? A strange, somewhat, erotic fantasy?

Or, was it a trick?

She recalled the psychic attack in her bedroom back home. Whatever that menace was used the familiarity of those close to her to gain access. Was it doing it again?

She glanced down at the clothes on her body. They were still from that day. She hadn't changed into night clothes, and her shoes were still on. Unless the deceptive powers-that-be were making her sleep walk…again.

The thought of it sent a chill up her spine, but as she recalled the evening, nothing felt like the previous episode, at all. This didn't feel at all harmful. There was no fear, chaos, or chill. It was the closest feeling of…warm bliss that she had experienced…well…she hadn't experienced anything to compare to it. Nothing *physical*, anyway.

She recalled their conversation. The coming reunion. His concern. Was all of that a dream, too?

"I may not get another chance."

What did he mean by that? Surely, he wasn't going anywhere. The house needed him. The *children* needed him. It was all too much to consider. Where was he?

She threw back the covers and moved to the window. It was an uncommonly warm fall evening, so she opened the window. The familiar night sounds of the crickets and churn of the water floated up to her on the slight breeze. And also something else.

The plucked strings of a guitar.

Her analytical mind took over. Ambient sounds were known to affect the course of dreams while the experiencer was in dream state. That was a documented fact. She pressed as far forward through the open window as safety would allow, but even though the screen had been removed, trying to look up to see if there was any sign of anyone above on the tarred roof platform just wasn't possible at that angle.

But there it was. That tingle. That feeling. That Awareness of what was, unquestionably, him. He was up there, but almost as if in anticipation of her probing, his emotions were, hopelessly, cloaked.

She shook her head in frustration, and was about to pull away from the window when she felt something…another tingle. Another *someone* else. This encounter was not pleasant, and the sense of it gave her something akin to a physical chill. Not only was she being watched, she was being mentally probed.

What was worse was that the cruel and frightening intelligence didn't care that she knew.

Catheryn gazed down below the window, and along the neighboring sills to the side of her. No one there. She swallowed hard, easing back from the open window, closed and locked it. She even went as far to pull the shade down over it, but it did little to sate her anxiety. She moved on to the other window on the east wall, but she couldn't take her eyes off the window she had just closed. The presence was still there, poking at her psychic defenses, prodding at her mental barriers. As she turned her attention toward the east window, she froze, her green eyes wide with terror. She had no voice. It was stifled by the fear rising up in her throat as she stared into a face.

That face. That nightmarish, ghoulish face from her apartment.

The floppy hat was still perched on its skull of tattered flesh, its glowing red eye burning a hole right through her soul. The feeling was in stark contrast to the pleasantness she had felt earlier. This was almost an intrusion; a violation as it dug into her energy with clawed ferocity. And if it couldn't possibly be any more disturbing, the tattered flesh seemed to part just enough to reveal that wicked smile and razor-sharp teeth, laughing, as it pressed its bony hands against the glass.

Somehow, against all the repressive feelings locking her down, she found the power within her to finally scream.

The piercing sound had no sooner left her mouth when she felt a presence behind her. The sensation sent her whirling about so quickly that she nearly fell against the east wall. The moonlight streaming in from the east window illuminated Danforth's anxious features.

"Catheryn, what is it? I could feel you…" He turned to the window, peering into the glass, his expression darkening. "Where is he?"

He made a motion as if he would try to open the window.

"Don't!" she countered, forcefully. "Just—"

She dove forward for the lock and twisted it into place, and as if the creature could find its way through the archival glass, she lunged forward just far enough to trip the release on the roller shade before falling back. She stood back to admire her work, folding her arms across her chest. She turned to him for some look of reassurance that wasn't mirrored there.

Danforth arched an eyebrow. "You really think the shade is going to help?"

The stubborn old oak door burst open, sending David and Andrew careening into the room. Andrew had a baseball bat raised, ready to do battle. Baldwin relaxed his battle stance, noting Danforth already there.

"Catheryn!" her partner barked, clearly alarmed.

"It was here," she choked out. "That thing from the apartment. It was here. Watching me."

Danforth looked on with an air of discomfort as Faustus embraced her, and uncomfortable with an alien, secondary emotion clearly stabbing at him—jealousy.

David pulled back to study her face. "Are you certain?"

The astonishment registering on her face that he could even suggest such a thing was answer enough.

Faustus ran an agitated hand through his salt and pepper hair. "I'm out of my element here. What do we do?"

Catheryn had nothing. Faustus sighed, agitatedly, folding her in a secure embrace for lack of anything else to do.

Danforth's jaw set. "I'm increasing defenses."

She watched him blow past a startled Baldwin from over her partner's shoulder. The realtor edged back from the door frame to let him past, exchanging concerned looks with Catheryn.

20

Daniel Hampden stared into the dancing flames of the campfire that separated him from Jackson Carter, although the barrier gave the soldier little comfort.

On the word of Hampden, Stacey turned the ration break into a camp stay, making up a story that Carter had business to attend to, and that he would soon return. In trade, Carter promised not to inflict his barbarism on anyone else in the camp. For the time being.

The promise came with an additional price; Hampden was to stay by Carter's side for the duration of the march. It was a deal with the Devil, but the corporal knew little else, what to do.

The bounty hunter felt the heavy gaze of the corporal in their secluded corner of camp as the mercenary creature speared some fresh catch from the river on some sticks, resting them, strategically over the fire so the sticks would not burn.

"You think me a monster," Carter snorted, a hint of a smile pulling at the corner of his mouth. "*I get it. But you* don't. You don't understand

what kind of ...*power* is needed to cling to this existence. If you don't

have it, then someone else will. You can be the fish—or you can be the

fisherman."

Even though he feared the man on the other side of the fire, the

corporal still kept a coldness to his stare. It was clear; Carter was the

predator, and they were prey. But if he thought he could bend Daniel

Hampden to betray his comrades...

"Oh, I know I can't," the creature muttered. "Don't you worry

about that."

Hampden's blood ran cold. What kind of...thing was this that

could invade his mind?

"But you see, there's a moral flexibility called for...in war," the

thing named Jackson Carter continued. "It helps people like me. Killing,

for example. You kill once, it gets easier. But still..." Carter tapped hard

at the side of his head with his bony finger. "There's this programming

you have to overcome. Your mama. Your papa. Family. Society.

Religion. It makes you less flexible. You stop. You think, before you do.

There's a limit. A line you won't cross."

The bounty hunter reached across to the stick that was roasting his catch. With a practiced swipe, he removed the fish and tore a piece of it open. So animal was it in action that it made the soldier cringe.

"Now, children," he droned on, pointing the other piece of fish at him for emphasis. "Children are different. You take children from the parents? You can mold them into whatever you want. They will do *anything* for any amount of affection you show them."

He popped the last of the fish into his mouth, the corporal's stomach turning at the audible pop and crunch of bone between teeth.

"The affection doesn't even have to be real. Your own private army—ready to do anything for you."

For the second time that day, Hampden felt horror. This wasn't about helping get Danforth. It wasn't about doing the job for Stacey. It was helping Jackson to remove the one obstacle, to get into the house.

He wanted the children.

The creature named Jackson smiled, a cold, unsettling smile. No doubt, reading the soldier's mind.

"With a little revenge, on the side."

Bridgette slipped out of the nursery room. The moonlight spilling through the hallway window at the far end lit the brown-painted barn wood planks before her. She pulled her cotton, wrapper-style robe around her body as her slippered feet made their way down the hallway.

She couldn't sleep, which was odd. Usually, she found the gentle violin

playing from the attic soothing, but tonight, it just sounded…off. She

pulled her white sleeping cap from her brown hair, allowing the curls to

fall around her shoulders. She moved to the window. The moon was

near full, lighting the camp across the street. The majority of the camp

fires had burned low, or completely extinguished, as most had turned in

for the night. But one lone figure remained. A small boy in patched jean

cotton trousers and worn blue collar shirt stood at the edge of the rough

gravel road separating the camp from the house. The slouch brown hat

he wore tipped up, his brown freckled face looking up at her. She felt a

chill and drew back. Why did he always stare at her so? It was unsettling.

It only fed her dislike.

She couldn't help but wonder how he would compare to Sam. He

was on his way and would be there soon. At least, that's what their last

conversation was. She was to leave the box on as long as possible, and

that would help him find her.

Her face rose toward the ceiling. The sound of the captain's fiddle

seemed sorrowful, but heart-achingly sweet; a tone very uncommon

from the lullabies he usually played. The abnormal, complex beauty in his selection didn't help her feeling of unease. She didn't like change, but this was too much, all at once. First, the Roberts'. Then, the funny little blonde-haired man. Then, *her.*

Why did *she* need to come here? Everything was just fine until *she* came...

Bridgette moved to the bannister and peered down over into the entryway. There were many of her adult house family below them. Not a member moved, all captivated in the music that weaved and drifted down throughout the house. They, too, noticed the change, causing them all to pause in what they were doing, their gaze rising toward the music coming from the attic. Lieutenant Moore stood next to Sergeant Solomon, slowly removing his gray, wide-brimmed slouch hat, as if the movement of displacing it would, somehow, break the spell.

"What is that?" the senior officer breathed.

Solomon only dropped his gaze temporarily, as in thought, before it returned to the white plaster above them. "It's...Sibelius."

"What? That's impossible." The lieutenant's blue gaze narrowed, uncomprehendingly, at the ceiling. "Captain never plays classical."

The bow danced over the strings in high-pitched, heartrending song, the effect of the music bringing many eyes in the household to a glossiness near tears. The crescendo rising, it pulled at the core of all present. For some of them, it was too much to bear; tears flowing, unchecked, down their cheeks, at the beauty and the sorrow of the melody moving through and around them.

As if the answer was somehow revealed in the melody, it finally occurred to Moore.

"He's leaving us," the lieutenant remarked, wistfully.

"No." Solomon shook his head, his moist brown eyes still riveted above him. "He's leaving *her.*"

Bridgette felt a cold settle upon her shoulders like a frozen mantle as the full meaning of the conversation came to her. Leaving them. Leaving Catheryn. What was the difference? The man she felt the most for, the closest she had to a father—the closest person she had to feeling anything for—was leaving the house. Why? Why would he do this to them?

Do this to *her.*

No.

The music switched to a brisk, hard, fervent pace; as if guiding her feet into a full sprint down the hall. Bridgette couldn't be here. She wouldn't watch it happen. She wouldn't be here when he…When he would walk away…Sam. She would find Sam. Sam would make it better. Sam would make the ugly feelings go away.

It was at that moment that she glanced behind her and saw it. The blossoming of black erupting behind her, growing and racing after her. The thickness of the darkness eclipsed the moon, making it difficult to see where she was going, but it made no difference. The only way was forward. Her rage quickly transformed to panic as she raced down the barn wood planks to the top of the staircase. Without a moment's hesitation, she plunged down the steps, not stopping to look behind her. She didn't dare check to see if it was gaining. Making it to the bottom of the stairs, she turned in the direction of the only option left to her. On old impulse, she grabbed the doorknob of the front door and flung it open, diving out into the night air.

And right into the arms of a waiting Jackson Carter. The scarred face gazed down at her from beneath his slouched hat, his lips contorting in a gruesome grin.

"Well, well. What do we have here?"

She attempted a shriek, but his hand was already over her mouth, another arm snaking around her waist and yanking her the rest of the way clear of the threshold of the house. Before any of the household could even react, the door slammed shut with a finality that rattled the

downstairs windows, leaving everyone speechless.

Whatever hold the music had, its spell was, irrevocably, broken.

21

Danforth came bursting out of the dining area after *blinking* downstairs. His senses already were alerted to the disturbance. Jessica, a petite blonde middle-aged woman who assisted in looking after the children, did her best to keep up with his deliberate pace as he stormed out of the dining area and into the front foyer.

"I don't know why she did it," the woman reported, anxiously. "The children know they never leave the house—especially at night. She's never done it before!"

"I've already called for the guard," Moore stepped up to meet his senior officer. "That thing. That...blackness. It was chasing her."

"You sure?"

All attention turned to the voice down the entryway. Solomon hadn't moved from his position next to the door, his lips pursed. His dark eyes were fixed with a hardened intensity up at where the young girl had just come.

When the sergeant's gaze met that of the two men, it was obvious, in his expression, that his opinion differed. "You sure that's what it was doin'?"

"Out with it, Sergeant," Danforth spat, impatiently.

"It's gone. It left *with* her."

Moore's eyes were wide. "Are you saying what I think you're saying?"

"It wasn't a thing apart. It *was* her," the sergeant repeated, his eyes not losing any of their assuredness. "It was her all along."

Young Bridgette was forced down to her knees in the mud of the river bank by a frightening figure of a man in the tattered remains of what once was general farmer's dress. He leered down at her menacingly, and forced her shoulder down any time she tried to rise up. Her favorite forest green homespun plaid dress was ruined, and she was damp, dirty, and covered in dirt and grime.

Her hair was worse. Ever since the scary man had ripped her away from the house, her curls were a mess. She attempted to braid them, but she gave up. All attempts to push the fly-aways out of her face only resulted in more mud and dirt getting on her face and hair. She didn't know why she was here, or who these strange people were. She just wanted to go home. Home to Ms. Abigale, and Jimmy, and Josie. She might even be tempted to talk to Andy. She had been mad before, and she couldn't even remember what about now. All she knew is that she didn't want to be here with these strange people that seemed intent on being bullish and intent on getting her dress all dirty. But what was more upsetting was what if Sam showed up to find her gone? What if he went away without her?

The Army soldiers that were guarding her seemed friendly enough. They made sure she had water from a canteen, and some of their rations. It was the *other* ones. They stood in stark contrast to the soldiers. Dressed in tattered rags, their skin carried a purplish hue, and their faces looked gaunt, as if undernourished. The worst of it were their eyes. Sunken and vacant. It was as if they were…not even there. Yet, they seemed to follow orders, albeit slower, than the soldiers.

The rail thin man with the eyepatch that had taken her away, pressed past the throng of bodies. Dressed in a dark blue hunter's tunic and long duster coat, he looked only in slightly better shape than the more sickly looking members. His whole presence made her exceedingly nervous. His energy felt like thousands of bugs crawling all over her. She didn't know what that meant, but she didn't like it.

The eyepatch man came to kneel down next to her. He produced an apple from his personal bag, and removed a long sharp knife from his belt. Her eyes grew at the size of the blade, making her even more ill at ease. However, he cavalierly went about slicing off pieces of the apple with it, and handing her a bite.

She took it from him, albeit reluctantly.

"How ya doin', missy?" the man inquired in his deep, raspy voice.

She looked at him, sidelong, before popping the apple piece into her mouth.

"I wanna go home," she muttered, her mouth full of apple.

"Sure enough," the eyepatch man replied, doing his best to sound soothing. He wasn't succeeding. "We just need some help from you, is all…"

"Me? What do you need me for?"

He leaned over to peer into her face, squinted with his one good gray-green eye. "You know why we're here?"

Bridgette shook her head, her loosening brown curls bouncing about her cheeks.

"We know you got…strangers here in the valley. People that don't belong. We're here to get rid of 'em."

This eased Bridgette's mind. Somewhat. She didn't like the new arrivals. They were staying too long and doing too much to change things. She wanted things to go back. Be the same as how they were. Things were so much better.

Better before *she* came.

"All we need is a way into the house," the man muttered, his voice smooth and calming. "You know...scare 'em a little."

Seeing no resistance in the child's demeanor, he carved out another slice of apple, and offered it.

"You know how to do that, don't you?"

Her brown eyes cast down at the ground, she still reached over and took it. And nodded.

She still didn't feel comfortable looking at him from anything other than sideways. "You promise...no one will get hurt?"

He did his best to placate her with as innocent a look he could with his one eye, placing a hand over his heart. "I promise. My word as a scout."

"Can I go home after?"

"Of course, little one. You can call me...Uncle Jack."

Uncle. No. that was reserved for one person, and one person only.

"Okay...Jack."

He reached across the space between them; a weathered hand reaching up to muss up the brown curls on the crown of her head. If he hoped the gesture would alleviate her concerns, it didn't.

She just wanted to go home; to the place where she really belonged. To the man she truly called 'uncle'.

The team of Faustus, Greye, and Baldwin convened in the familiar nook of the dining area, mugs plied with coffee. Early morning had, yet, to descend upon the valley. It was very early A.M. Way too early for Catheryn's liking, but it had to be done to bring David up to speed.

Her mentor had been awakened by the sudden slam of the front door, but due to his limited awareness of the situation, he had to be briefed on the 'why' of it all. By the time the explanations had been given, Faustus's expression was grave.

"We can't leave, yet," Catheryn stated, flatly.

Jaw set, the senior doctor's intense gray gaze threatened to burn a hole through the oak tabletop. They had clients—real, flesh-and-blood clients—that needed their attention back in Chicago. Clients that paid the bills. That paid the rent. That kept the lights on.

But there was something else here. Something of a higher cause. A higher opportunity for…

Faustus couldn't put his finger on it, but he couldn't ignore it either. He called the messenger service to start rebooking appointments.

Catheryn withdrew to the sanctuary she had grown to love; the pedestrian bridge outside. As she had so often observed, the light of day diminished early in the valley; setting the sky afire with hues of pinks and russet oranges. It was even more spectacular when there was a scattering of clouds, and the full moon danced along the rippling water rolling over the rocks of the riverbed below. She couldn't decide on when it was that she fell in love with its tranquility, and she doubted that she would discover that peace anywhere else on the planet.

She felt tears coming to her emerald eyes. Would it remain like this; unspoiled for generations to come? Who would come to claim this house once all was said and done? Could they respect it for the sanctuary that it was? Or, would others—like her old colleague, Peter—come to take advantage of its unique character and exploit it. She cringed to think of the "weekend warrior" ghost hunters, descending on the house like vultures, coming to pick its secrets clean. Poking and prodding the children with their questions and their equipment. It may be a curiosity to the entities, at first, but when would it cross that fine line between curiosity and nuisance? And, what would happen after that? Or, what if it raised the anger of someone such as Abigale or Captain Danforth.

Charlie.

The thought of him being under a specimen glass like that made her nauseated. What if such intrusive activity prompted her spectral family not to stay at all? How empty and *quiet*, it would be. She was suddenly reminded that it was David and her whole reason for being here in the first place, but it was also the one thing, drawing her back.

"I could leave *with* you."

She could feel him standing there right next to her. She felt herself choking back tears at the very suggestion. Something within her longed for it; the end to endless years alone. The end to no one ever truly understanding her. The awkwardness of having to explain who and *what* she was. The endless rejection once they *did* learn. And he could always be there for her—never growing old, never changing. It would always be just the two of them...

But only she would see him, experience him. Her family would never know him. Never understand. She could never share him with anyone else. The dream of a home and family would never be realized. And then there were the children and the house, under his care…

"I've been offered that opportunity to leave many times, but I said 'no'," he said, softly. "I've had no reason to leave here. Until now."

She turned to him, abruptly, her eyes glazed with tears. "I can't. I can't be that selfish. They need you—"

"It's only selfish if it's against my wishes."

That's when she felt it; the familiar ecstatic pull within her heart. The warmth, the very essence of it threatening to overwhelm her. That's when she realized the very difference between being told you were loved, and actually *feeling* it.

And then, he was gone. He left her with the offer. It was hers to decide.

Catheryn leaned her folded arms on the weather wooden railing and watched the waning moonlight dancing on the water, but then, she squinted. Something was disrupting the natural flow of the current. Something just beneath the water. Her eyes widened; not just perceiving with her physical sight, but the sight she was born with. There was something else there. Something else, churning underneath. Bubbling up from the depths.

Catheryn drew back, the choking feeling of anxiety rising in her throat as she stumbled backward. There was something down there. Something decrepit. Disturbing. And it was rising from the water.

Something seemed to repel her from the bridge, and she found herself stumbling back to the earthen supports, nearest the house. Once she found that grounding, she saw it.

The moonlight no longer danced upon the natural rock formations below. It danced along a shining, slimy surface of something breaking the water's surface. As the water drained away, it revealed more of a haggard shape, vaguely human.

But not human. The skin was a sickly pale white, veins working beneath the skin, but they were blue, as if deprived of oxygen. Hair hung in wet strands, mixed with seaweed, and other cast offs from the river bottom. Skin hung in patches on the skull, as if stitched in place by some mad seamstress. If that wasn't disturbing enough, there were its eyes. Or more specifically, the lack thereof. Where the eyes should have been, there were two vacant holes. It looked like the echo of something that may have been, at one time, human.

Her mouth fell open. She wanted to scream, but no sound would come out, as multiple other anomalies broke the natural churn of the river flow. Two. Three. Four more. What were those...those *things?*

Another of the strange entities broke the surface; a ghoulish face of what had once been a man. The skin of his face glowed an ashen gray in the dim light of the moon, but the skin had slackened away from the face in a grotesque way that revealed more of the bony protrusion of the skull beneath. Hair hung in wet strands about the face, but that wasn't the most present feature. Its eyes. Its eyes still seemed present. Filmy and gray. And riveted right on her.

Something about the movement drew her gaze straight up. Straight into the cross girders of the top bridge supports. Looming, in a nightmarish wrap of black, ragged cloth, backlit by the light of the full moon, was the thing.

The thing from her nightmare. The thing that had terrorized her in the sanctity of her own bed. Threatened her with penetrating the defenses of her upstairs bedroom of the house. The glowing red eye and the decayed flesh working over that frightening visage. Despite her fervent wish of it not to be so, it saw her. Its maw dropped into a hideous grin of recognition, its sharp white teeth gleaming in the moonlight.

Catheryn shrieked, repelled by the vision. She turned and ran

392

straight for the house. She didn't even recall her feet touching the gravel as she launched up the steps and slammed the door right behind her.

She fell against the strong oak wood of the double door frame, fighting to bring her breathing back to a normal state. She became vaguely aware of other bodies crowding her, and at first, she pushed at them, still locked securely in the grotesque vision she had seen outside.

Finally, she snapped to, aware of David staring down at her in dire concern, with Baldwin bringing up the rear.

"Don't go out there," is all she could bring herself to say in between heaving, panic-driven gasps. "They're coming. Don't go out there!"

22

Captain Charlie Danforth sat in the solitude of his attic, staring out at the waning moon sharing the sky with the morning hues of dawn. He closed his eyes. He said what he wanted to say. And now, it was up to her.

In that moment of closed introspection, he felt the presence to his left. He frowned.

"You know, I'm beginning to believe she doesn't corner the market on *skulking* as much as you do."

Ralph stepped from the shadows. If the guardian was surprised to be called out, he didn't show it. His face still radiated the same annoying calm and serenity that so bothered Danforth. And, as usual, his voice was as smooth as silk.

"Do I really need to say anything?

The spectral officer frowned at the floor, not bothering to question the being's omnipotence.

"It's her decision to make."

"It's yours, as well."

He gauged the guardian out of the corner of his eyes and noticed the ever-so-slight arch to the visitor's eyebrow. The expression was a nudge; much like a parent making a child rethink his behavior to change it to the right choice. He hated that. He wasn't about to say that just because he was dead that he knew what he was doing. He was just as capable of making mistakes in this state as he was while living. He was just beginning to discover his limitations in this world, and there was much more to experience than just the limitations of this valley. He was powerful here, but was he ready to test it out there with her? Was he willing to fail? Was he willing to pay the price for that failure?

"There are other ways," Ralph's smooth voice mused, making it clear that he was following the soldier's conscious stream of thought. "You could...come back."

Those on the other side of the veil had spoken of other *opportunities*. To come back to this world. To start again. To be reborn. But no. It held no interest. No draw. No meaning. Not without her.

"Your understanding of these things are limited. You could always ask for...help?"

Charlie frowned. "You. Would help?"

"We are always here but do not intervene unless asked," the guardian stated.

Danforth snorted cynically. "I would think you would need to recuse yourself from any decision-making, considering—"

"On the contrary; I would be perfect for the job." the enlightened being countered flatly. "You're placing human restrictions where they do not apply. Do I need to remind you who I am?"

"That may get you a table at some places, but it doesn't *exactly* work with me."

Ralph's gaze narrowed, perceptibly. "Time and space mean nothing to me. I can move forward and back any time I choose. Any *timeline* I choose. I can tell you exactly how each one will play out, and I am here to say—"

The captain's self-assured posture began to crumble under the weight of the guardian's words, and he refused to look at the asserted figure.

"—it will end. Badly. You will hurt her, unnecessarily, and I will not have that. Damage that may take decades to repair. Decades in which she could learn and grow. Evolve."

"*I* never got that. Was my guide sleeping that day?"

"Things happened as they had to," Ralph's explained, his words, and posture, becoming more rigid. "If you'd stayed on the other side of the veil long enough, it would have been made clearer to you. *You* made the choice to come here, instead."

"I would *never* hurt her."

"Not on purpose," the guide corrected, softly. "Would you like me to show you?"

With a graceful sweep of his hand, the enlightened being painted a picture, and he saw. There were several moments that he had to look away, and then, refusing to look, altogether.

"You've showed me what will happen," he stated, unable to meet the ethereal being's gaze. "Now...now I can change it. I can do something else."

"I could show you different variations all day. This one was the most kind."

Danforth winced, the emotion of it threatening to overwhelm him. If that was the least damaging...He sighed inwardly, eyes closed to form his next argument. He didn't have one.

Ralph's chin raised, just a fraction as he fixed the spectral officer with his sharp gaze. "And, for what reason *did* you return?"

He reflected on his leaving Source, why he was here in this reality. *Her* reality.

"To collect my men."

"And they are here now, are they not?"

Danforth wanted to rage against the argument. To shut it out. To push it aside. The unfairness of how his life had been taken, so mercilessly. Taken before he could…

But was that more important than the oath he had made to his men? Did he dare put his more selfish needs ahead of their own? Words from the past reverberated in his mind, undeniable. The memory of the final words of his best friend.

"For the good of the rest, you have to."

The attic felt dark and lonely. Isolated. He realized that Ralph had left him with his thoughts, and as he did so, he felt another emotion invading. So absorbed in his own dilemma, it had overridden his ability to perceive it.

Fear.

Not just any fear, but *her* fear. It stabbed through his energy like a spear. Something was wrong. Something had gone terribly wrong.

Out of the darkness, materialized an alarmed Lieutenant Moore, his face taut with urgency.

"Captain, we have a problem."

Lieutenant Miles Stacey watched through field glasses from his position on the pedestrian bridge, his kepi tucked into the belt at his waist. He watched the emergence of Jackson's so-called *reinforcements*, coming out of the water, with a dismissive air. None of them looked the least bit military-trained, and more than a little worn around the edges. Most likely fished from the local tavern. Or creek. Or both. Dawn was the perfect time for attack, while the house was asleep, but what these mercenary additions were capable of, was beyond him. He dropped the field glasses away from his face, securing them into the case at his hip as he heard someone approaching from behind.

A staggering, winded Corporal Hampden offered a weak salute before falling forward in fatigue, hands resting on the thighs of his worn, sky-blue trousers.

"Sir," was all that the corporal could muster, as he caught his breath. "All units present and ready to respond."

The Army lieutenant retrieved his field glasses from his belt and raised them to take in the town shoreline. The multi-storied Federalist-style house took up the majority of his view.

"Is Carter sure this is the target?" the commanding officer queried, the glasses glued to his face. "Looks quiet."

"Lost his location, sir," the young gunner managed between breaths. "But yes, sir. That's the target. There was movement earlier, but I believe they retreated back into the house."

"Any idea if they've been alerted to our presence?"

"None, sir."

The senior officer swore softly, dropping the field glasses to his side. "Bring the reinforcements along the right and left flanks of the house. We'll smoke them out if we have to."

Hampden watched the commanding officer storm off in bewilderment. 'Smoke them out'? Did he not know there were women and children inside? He wanted Danforth as much as the next guy, but not at civilian cost.

"Sir? Sir…wait!" the younger soldier declared, hobbling after the senior officer. "We have to secure the women and children. There are innocent civilians—"

"—that are harboring federal fugitives!" Stacey spat back. "We have to be prepared that they may be willing to fight. Could be a nest of rebel sympathizers for all we know. Now, go send the order, or I will find someone who will!"

The lieutenant charged forward, leaving his subordinate in stunned silence

L ieutenant Moore pulled down the creased crown of his gray, wide-brimmed slouch hat more securely over his eyes as the low angle of the morning sun threatened to blind him. His blue eyes remained riveted on the approaching Federal artillery officer dressed in sky blue trousers and red-trimmed blue shell jacket. At thirty yards, he couldn't make out much of the Federal's face underneath the kepi-style cap, but on the opposing man's shoulders, he could make out the rank as second lieutenant.

The Confederate junior officer, jaw set as he counted thirty soldiers bringing up formation behind the new arrival. He had no idea why an artillery officer, unaccompanied by cannon, would perform such a bold maneuver, but he wasn't about to let it go, unchallenged.

"Hold!" Moore announced, dropping a hand to his saber hilt. "Identify yourselves!"

The Federal lieutenant held up a white-gauntleted hand to halt the company's approach.

"We don't answer to Rebs!" the ginger-haired officer announced from across the gap, hand dropping to the handle of the revolver at his belt.

"You let me know when you find some," Moore drawled under his breath, his steel blue gaze not wavering from the Union officer.

"We just want Danforth!" Stacey barked. "Send him out, and we'll let the rest of you live!"

The lieutenant in gray held back an indignant snort, and was on the verge of firing back an acerbic remark when he was interrupted by a booming male voice from behind.

"Where the hell have you been, Stacey?"

Captain Danforth came to stand behind Moore, wearing his knee-length navy blue frock coat. The senior Army officer's hand rested on the grip of his holstered weapon but without any aggression in his posture. If Stacey felt threatened, he didn't show it.

"Captain Charles Danforth—you are under arrest for sedition, treason, dereliction of duty, and actions resulting in the unnecessary deaths of subordinates under your command," the Union lieutenant responded, curtly. "You are to return with me to Camp Douglas and await court martial by your peers."

Danforth felt the roll of his junior officer's eyes without seeing it. He silenced any further action from Lieutenant Moore with a sidelong look.

The captain frowned, drawing his fingers down over his thick mustache, in contemplation. " 'Court martial'?"

Miles Stacey glanced over his shoulder at his company, his assuredness somewhat compromised by his quarry's disaffected demeanor.

Stacey reasserted his stance, his blue eyes flashing. "Of course, court martial!"

"So, I'm sure you received a copy of the order…" Danforth arched a dark eyebrow at the lieutenant's faltering confidence. "You *do* have a copy of the order, right?"

The Confederate lieutenant's gaze narrowed. "These *are* serious allegations you are making."

"Like I would expect a natural-born traitor to understand!" the Union artillery lieutenant challenged. "We just sent in the request for assistance just…just last…"

Something in Stacey's confident demeanor seemed to deteriorate further, as he attempted to recall the chain of events.

Danforth's head tilted, questioningly. " 'Last week'? 'Month'?"

"Year?" Moore muttered, sarcastically, under his breath.

The captain shot his junior officer with another pointed look, and Moore fell quiet.

Danforth paced in front of the house, sporting a thoughtful expression. "Maybe we should…wait."

Stacey's brow furrowed in confusion. " 'Wait'?"

The captain frowned, introspectively. "Well, I'm not going anywhere…We'll…wait for the order to be confirmed."

Moore's gaze shifted from his commanding officer to the artillery lieutenant across from him, giving a minute shrug, searching the opposing officer for agreement.

Stacey was at a loss. He was expecting to release his rage in a strategic action, and here it was, crumbling before him. He expected panic, groveling, maybe a little weeping. No one here seemed the least bit concerned. He really didn't know how to respond. He heard his men, shuffling in their own discomfort, uncertain what they were to do, as well. The junior officer was feeling a creeping sense of embarrassment that was, slowly, giving way to frustration. It was about as unnerving seeing a junior Confederate officer taking orders from a Union soldier. None of it was making any ounce of sense. All was being played as to the game plan managed by himself and Carter. He just wondered what the bounty hunter was doing to hold up his end of things.

"Yes, I understand," Andrew Baldwin answered, reluctantly, into the smartphone in the palm of his hand, pacing anxiously in the house's dining area. "It's just...I know it was filed under MLM, but...twenty-thousand dollars *over* asking?! But the house is nowhere near...I see. Yeah."

David and Catheryn had been seated at the dining room table, working on independent mugs of coffee, when the call came in.

David was listening with detached interest. Catheryn had her fingers wrapped around her mug, waiting for the coffee to ward off the chill of the scene from the night before. She chose a different distraction as she focused on the realtor's conversation, but the more Catheryn gathered from the conversation, the less she was liking it.

Baldwin's hand dropped from next to his ear, his thumb hitting the terminating button to end the call. He buried his gaze into the Oriental rug at his feet. It was obvious that he was avoiding eye contact with his guests. When he finally did look at them, his expression was vacant of enthusiasm.

"The house. It sold." Something in his demeanor seemed honor-bound to explain, hurriedly. "It was listed as MLM—which means any realtor could pick it up for a shared commission. An offer above asking was put in...by Peter Elgin."

Catheryn felt her stomach bottom out at the same time she could feel her partner's eyes on her for reaction.

"Well...this is good, right?" David observed. "He won't care if it's haunted—"

"He'll turn it into a circus attraction!" Catheryn countered, harshly, standing up abruptly from her seat at the table.

Her mind racing, she looked about, helplessly for inspiration. Her gaze fell upon Baldwin.

"Certainly, there's something *you* can do!" she said, pleadingly.

The realtor was already running his fingers through his pomade-styled blonde hair, pacing anxiously.

"I...I can't! If I had put a hold on the listing, we would have had a chance, but..."

Baldwin dropped his hands, making his helpless, hopeless

expression all the more apparent.

Catheryn turned on him. "Tell them I already bought it. Technical issues. You couldn't find a fax—"

It was David's turn to get anxious, uprooting his body from his seat.

"Catheryn! What are you saying?!" her partner countered in disbelief. "You're not making any sense—"

"He can't have it! He just...*can't*!"

"It's too late. It was a cash offer," Baldwin noted, grimly. "Inspection was waived. He takes possession next week."

Catheryn winced, unable to look at him. She felt sick. No. Not again. Not *this* house. He could keep the house in St. Louis.

Not this house.

The helpless turmoil churning within her caused tears to spring to her emerald eyes, but just as they did so, a sound to her left caused her to jump.

Something heavy—something large—threw itself at the barn wood door of the cellar. She fell back from the door, her hand flailing to find purchase on one of the dining room chairs as she backed away. The second slam caused Faustus to flinch back from his secured footing, his gray eyes riveted to the door. It was as if someone was throwing their shoulder into the wooden structure; trying with all its might to rattle the drop latch loose.

"What the hell is that?" Faustus muttered under his breath, his back finding support in the wall behind him.

Catheryn couldn't speak, her eyes not moving from the door as it continued to take blows. The ancient hardware was sturdy, but the screws were backing out of the rustic wood as the assault continued. Even Andrew Baldwin was backing toward the doorway that was a quick sprint to the front door, but even he refused to take his eyes away from the direction of the pounding. Dust from the aged wood was lurching through the cracks in the door, and with each blow, could be heard the crack of that wood giving way. One final blow sent the iron fastener off the door, landing at Catheryn's feet. As everyone stood, agape, the door creaked open slowly on rusty hinges, without any dramatic fanfare, or any perceived visible assistance. The opening to the cellar was a gaping maw of black. No light came from the lower level, and nothing stood in the door frame, making it all the more frightening as to what force had caused all the commotion.

And where was it now?

Catheryn and Andrew, both, scanned the area all around them; the possibility of supernatural power at play, not lost on either of them. David, however, remained focused on the darkened entrance. He eased toward it, cautiously, straining his neck higher to get a better angle of view down the stairs. Seeing nothing to indicate danger, he eased the door back further for a better look.

He turned back to his startled companions. "Nothing. There's nothing here—"

No sooner had the words left his lips when something lashed out at his throat. The elder doctor struggled with a tightness around his neck, panic in his eyes as his hands thrashed about at something he could not see.

But Andrew and Catheryn both could. Emerging from the door frame of the cellar was a protruding human arm covered in sparse pieces of rotting flesh and cloth; its bony fingers having the elder doctor's throat in a vice-like grip. More of the body ascended from the depths like a nightmare from hell itself. The tattered black shroud hung from its bony structure, obscuring the tattered remains of human flesh clinging to the skeletal frame by mere fibers. Its head, which was not much more than a skull, glared down at its prey with black pits that had once been eyes. Catheryn couldn't speak; powerless to do anything but consider it a kindness that her mentor could not see it.

BRAMDEN HOUSE

23

Charles Danforth was suspicious as he continued to stare down Miles Stacey from across the span of gravel separating them. Stacey seemed almost nervous, as if waiting for something. There were a number of times that he caught the ginger-haired lieutenant seeming to gaze in the direction of the trees to the west side of the house.

And that's when he *felt* her scream.

Catheryn.

It wasn't just the sound. It was the emotion behind it. The terror of it ripped through his being like a hurricane, causing him to stagger. It did not go unnoticed.

"Captain!" Moore whispered, his arm going out to steady his commanding officer.

"It's a distraction," Danforth stated through gritted teeth, glaring down the Union artillery officer across the way. "They're already in the house."

The enemy did not miss the faltered step either. Stacey's face screwed up in anger as his grip transferred from his gun to his saber, withdrawing the blade, the steel pointing the way.

"Charge!"

"Damn it!" Danforth spat, reaching for the sergeant nearest to him. "Embry, go order the side flanks to pull in closer to the house."

"They're already engaged, sir!"

How the hell did they get around the defenses? He didn't have time to mull that over, and it was obvious he couldn't withdraw to help just Catheryn. He drew his own blade from its sheath to take on the only option left to him, and charged toward his old comrade.

The soldiers swarmed across the divide, but Danforth had no interest in hurting anyone today. The attacking boys had more bluster than horse sense, and it was easy to maneuver through the fray toward his intended target without inflicting heavy damage. His officers had similar orders, but the pressing of bodies was still overwhelming for their defensive numbers. He was hoping it didn't have to get rough.

It wasn't long before he found Stacey doing what he did best; commanding from the rear, and safely situated behind the biggest obstacle. Typically, in the case of artillery, it would usually include a cannon, but since there weren't any, the shoulder-high boulder off to the side of the pedestrian bridge was the next best thing. Danforth was about to jump the boulder and end this thing, when something strongly pulled at his Awareness. He tried to press through the distraction, leaping atop the boulder, but the pull was insistent. The nursery. He was needed there.

He *had* to get to the nursery. Grunting in agitation, he turned away from his cornered adversary and headed back toward the house.

Catheryn looked on in horror as more decayed and decrepit creatures poured out of the cellar. As the mass of them pushed forward, others swept up the walls and along the ceiling like a mad swarm of locust. The lead figure shifted its position, standing like a monarch among the chaos, lifting Faustus up from the ground, leaving the elder doctor's Oxfords kicking wildly at anything to get the creature to let go of him. The grotesque swarm continued past all in the room, seeming to vanish through cracks in the walls and ceiling. But as she watched, transfixed on the chief figure and her partner, a whirlwind seemed to surround them both as flesh and fiber seemed to congeal, crawling up the skeletal frame like some insane jungle of vines that had suddenly come alive. David cried out in pain as the creature leaned over him, its mouth wide as if to devour him, all the while, the creature seeming to take on a more solid form; a form that became all too familiar to Catheryn.

She watched, helpless, as Faustus continued to gag and cry out. At first, she thought it was an optical illusion, but the longer she watched, she realized it really was happening; the fringes of his dark gray hair appeared to turn white as the creature's mouth neared his face. No, that was impossible. It couldn't be...

Yet, it was. And damn if it was going to continue. Along the wall, her hand fell upon a stick-like object. It was a broom. Abigale's broom. She recalled how the bullish behavior of the matron had driven off the so-called 'vermin' from her house before. It was time to do the same now.

"Alright! You get off of him, you piece of shit!" she challenged, lunging forward, brandishing the broom like a bat with the bristles up toward her head. "I thought I was the one you wanted?"

The head turned, its face resembling a patchwork quilt more than an actual face. But she still recognized it; the same milky eye from her nightmares, fixed on her. And as it did so, the face seemed to transform

into a hideous grin of recognition. Faustus fell to the floor like a
discarded sack of potatoes, and before Catheryn could even respond, the
creature sprang through the air, with catlike agility, toward her. She
couldn't even get a swing in before it was upon her, pinning her to the
ground, its grotesque face inches from her own.

"You…the Dead like you, don't they?" the thing hissed. "I need
more of them. You can bring them to me. I always need more!"

"You leave her alone!"

The creature's weight shifted in the direction of the unknown male
voice, and it was just enough for her to be able to crawl out from under
it. Andrew had grabbed a skillet from the kitchen, brandishing the
kitchen implement like a weapon. Was that…Andrew shouting? She'd
never heard him so…forceful. Unfortunately, the realtor's plan of attack
met with the same fate that befell David, as the creature caught the
blonde-haired man by the throat and lifted him off the ground.

"I'll take from the Living, if I have to," the specter spat out, some
macabre exchange of energy happening between Baldwin and itself,
manifesting in more organic growth on the creature's face and arms.

And just like Faustus, the being discarded the real estate agent onto
the ground. The thing's black shroud coalesced into a ranch-style duster,

and the face, although still scarred and grotesque, took on a much more human appearance. A black leather patch materialized, covering the affected milky eye. Catheryn couldn't be sure which visage terrified her more.

He brushed microscopic dirt from the sleeves of his duster as he looked down upon his discarded prey, addressing it with a look of distain.

"…but the Living are so…squirmy."

He reached down to the floor and caught Catheryn by the wrist, wrenching her upward.

"Then, there's you," it sneered, its breath hot against the sensitive skin of her wrist, taking in a deep whiff of her scent. "I could do a lot with you. I could attach to you. Anywhere you went. I would be there. Ready to make a meal of the Dead drawn to you. I'd…never have to hunt again."

"I'd haunt you until the day you died, and then…" He wrenched at her wrist harder until she cried out in pain. "…I'd still be there to collect…what's left of you. But there would be a lot of fear and torment I could inflict until then. I could feed off of that alone, for a long time. Just think…you could be begging me to kill you."

For the first time in a long time, Catheryn felt dread. The idea of this creature—this thing—following her, tracking her wherever she went. Tormenting her in her dreams, whispering to her while awake…it was truly terrifying. And for someone with no support system on the Other Side, it really would be a nightmare. A fate worse than death, itself.

But he hadn't met her spiritual backup team, yet.

She glared at him through the mixture of adrenaline and pain, before finding her footing and ripping her wrist from his grip. The momentum of the sudden movement caused her to stumble to the floor, but the walking nightmare seemed already tired of his quarry.

"I'll deal with you later," he growled. "For now, I've got far easier prey. You're not going anywhere I can't find you."

Catheryn watched from her spot on the floor as the thing seemed to evaporate into a mist; writhing upward like smoke until it disappeared through the ceiling. She managed to crawl over to Andrew, who didn't seem as worse for wear as David. Her partner was still breathing, but unconscious. As Andrew knelt on the other side with a retrieved throw pillow for their patient's head, Catheryn locked eyes with him.

"The children," she whispered. "He's after the children!"

Andrew looked down at the inert man before him, making an instant decision.

"Go!" he ordered, sharply. "I got this. Go!"

Catheryn raced up the stairs at a full sprint, stumbling on a few steps along the way before rounding the banister toward the nursery.

And nearly colliding with a very dark-faced Captain Danforth. She gasped, falling back a step. The spectral officer stood at the closed door, saber drawn and at the ready.

"I wish you would stop just…appearing like that!" she protested.

"May I remind you that *you* are the guest here?"

The loud shrieking of children on the other side of the door silenced the argument. Sparing each other a singular glance, she grabbed the chalk-white door knob and thrust the door open.

The whole nursery was in disarray. The neat bookshelf kept at the opposite wall was cast down, its contents strewn all over the barn wood floor. The single beds lining each side had been flung aside, as if some gigantic arm had brushed them away in a fit of agitation. Cowering in the corner were eleven frightened children, and standing ahead of them, brandishing an iron claw-style garden rake, was Abigale Bramden.

The gray-haired matron was sporting a messy bun, tendrils snaking out in a curly mess around her face. Her face was smudged with black, as was her apron. Apparently, she had been in the middle of cleaning when the chaos began. Ringing in the tightened mass of innocents was the ugly, slime-ridden creatures that Catheryn had seen earlier that morning. They looked just as vile and pitiful in the daylight. Leading the rabble was the familiar figure that had cast her aside, downstairs.

"What are you dead-weights waiting for? Go grab them!" the lean man with the floppy brown hat, ordered. "I want all of them. Don't let any of them escape!"

"*Carter!*"

The bark from the side of her made everyone in the room jump, including her. Danforth's gaze was fixed on him, his dark eyes flashing beneath the brim of his blue wool hat.

"How…" the captain bit out, a flash of surprise flickering across his features, but it didn't last long before the tip of his saber came up to point directly at his foe. "You son of a bitch!"

Catheryn blinked, incredulously. "You *know* him?"

Carter pivoted, casually, toward the duo at the door, his face a scarred portrait of disdain.

"Well, well," he growled. "The return of the manor-born."

Catheryn frowned. The saying wasn't correct, but it was obviously, out of spite. Backing away, she brushed against the captain's sleeve...

...and found herself jolted to a whole new place. It was dark where she was, but she could still make out the captain was standing before her. His silhouette had become more than familiar. The floor of the rough-hewn building was littered with straw, and unfinished wood planking was constructed in the style of corrals. A stable. A lone light of a lantern hung on the wall ahead. It was enough light for her to make out that Danforth was still dressed in his Federal blue uniform and regulation Hardy hat, but there was a different rank insignia on the shoulder boards of his knee-length frock coat. His woolen trousers were a dark blue color, but they were still tucked into the familiar black riding boots.

There was a strange grunting sound, accompanied by the sobs of a woman. As the Danforth before her lifted a lantern of his own, everything became clearer.

It was Jackson. He had a very young African-American woman pinned to the barn wood of the stable wall, his hand grinding her cheek into the rough planking. Her tattered tan skirts were hiked up in a very vulnerable situation. Tears from dark eyes, wide with terror, streamed down her face, as Jackson continued ramming away, his open fly telling Catheryn all she needed to know.

A guttural voice projected forcefully from the Danforth before her. "*Jackson!*"

The visage of the Jackson Carter in front of her staggered backward into the stable aisle, losing the grip on his prey, allowing her to flee into the night. This Jackson was fresh-faced but still dirty, with a day's worth of stubble on his chin. His eyes were undamaged; eyes of a gray-green. However, he still wore his singular brown slouch hat.

"Well, the prodigal son returns home," Carter quipped good-humoredly, heaving his suspenders up from around his waist and tucking in the shirt tails of his white collar shirt.

The overseer held out a hand in greeting. The Danforth before her, refused to take it.

"I have no doubt you've gained certain liberties in my absence," the captain growled. "…but I will never see—or *hear*—of such a display, again."

"Well, there's no trouble here, Lieutenant," Carter replied light-heartedly, throwing up his hands in surrender. "There's plenty of tail to be had down here. You know, their women…you need to take care of 'em on a regular basis, or they just grow wild—"

Carter never finished his sentence as Danforth's left connected with his jaw. It was enough to send the letch of a man sprawling to the ground. The blow knocked off his hat, revealing short, straw-like graying hair that may have once been blonde. Catheryn witnessed as Carter rolled onto his backside, cradling the side of the jaw that took the hit. He spit out blood before turning to look at the soldier with a mixture of shock and rage. He sprung from the floor of the stable, hands around the officer's neck. Danforth kneed him into the groin, allowing some space between them. He pulled the saber from his sheath and pointed it at Carter.

The struck man flashed him a lopsided grin.

"I hope you know how to use that pig-sticker, Soldier Boy," Carter growled, stepping back to retrieve his own sword propped up in the corner behind him. "Because, I know I do! Plenty of pigs to be stuck around here!"

The man lunged at Danforth. The taller soldier easily blocked the lunge with his blade, however, Carter's weight upon the lunge pinned Danforth's saber, precariously, against his own chest. The officer threw him off to allow enough space between them.

"Comin' back here. Think you own everything," Carter said with his trademark drawl. "I'm sure your *meemaw* loves explaining to her close circle of friends how she has a grandson in the Union Army. Not exactly the education she paid for—"

The officer lunged forward with his sword. Too close. Carter countered by tossing his saber to his left hand and sucker punching his quarry with his right, folding the officer over. Danforth fell backward to the straw-strewn floor, catching his breath.

Carter edged forward, the tip of his blade before him.

"I have done what I can to keep this place from burnin' to the ground in your absence!" the farm hand challenged, an emotional edge to his voice. "You don't know what it's like to be in the middle of a secesh county, trying to defend this place, all because of *you*?! Just you bein' here draws unwanted attention. Others have lost everything out here—just for picking a side!"

He lunged, again, but Danforth batted the attack away with ease. As he did so, the soldier managed to get up from the straw; a supporting hand on the floor as he countered another emotionally-fueled, yet, ineffectual, blow from his enemy.

"I earned my place here, and it's *mine*! It's time you leave, and never came back—"

Danforth rolled backward, covertly, tossing his blade into his right. When he rolled, face-up, Carter did not expect the blow coming.

The blade sliced the overseer's left cheek, arcing upward toward a fated and familiar area. Carter howled, staggering backward, falling backside-first into the straw pile behind him. The man was still whimpering as Danforth staggered to his feet and cornered the cowering man with the point of his sword.

"I want you to leave," the soldier growled. "If I catch you anywhere near my family again, I will hunt you down, and kill you myself!"

Catheryn fell back, severing the connection to the past. The stumble caused her to hit the ground, staring up at the spectral soldier, wide-eyed.

"You did that to him?" she said, surprised.

Charlie Danforth's gaze remained unapologetic, glaring at his foe from across the barn wood floor of the nursery.

"I warned you," the captain said, menacingly, slowly advancing toward the tattered foe. "Never to come near my family, again."

24

Lieutenant Moore was at a loss as to what to do with the advancing enemy pressing forward across the gravel road to the house.

"Stand your ground, men!" he ordered, forcefully, wheeling his arm about in a circular fashion, saber in hand, just hoping he was being heard above the din of clashing sabers. "Forward the defenses!"

Sergeant Embry came alongside, the white-haired non-commissioned officer had his sword at the ready, also.

"Sir!" the older man shouted, parrying another blow that came their way. "We've been holding them back all morning, but they still keep coming. It's only a matter of time before they wear us out, while...*not* killing them!"

Moore winced, but not from the oncoming blow. Embry was right. They were expending just as much energy, if not more so, holding their enemy back, attempting not to hurt them. It would only be a matter of

426

time before Stacey's troops just…pushed past them.

"Are you sure we couldn't just…shoot a few of 'em, sir?"

Moore stared down at the older man, mortified.

"Out of the question! We can't just…" Moore's voice trailing off while blocking another blow, knocking the next man back with a kick to the groin.

"…But if they get into the house, what they believe about the captain may cause carnage we cannot afford. And belief is a powerful motivator," the Confederate officer stated as he glanced down at the gold brocade on the cuffs of his own uniform. "Belief is a powerful motivator…as we well know."

The adjutant rolled his eyes. "Well, they also believe they're alive, too."

Moore blinked at Embry as if the older man had just struck him. "They believe…"

The young lieutenant recalled how many soldiers on the battlefield died of their wounds. Their doctors were at a loss to explain it. Those that had a strong conviction that they would live would do so, and just as powerful was that belief if they *believed* they would not.

"We can't kill 'em, because they're already dead," the lieutenant muttered, a smile beginning to form across his face, "But they don't know that. Which means...if we shot them..."

"They would feel it, sir," Embry answered, a quirky smile crossing his lips. "It wouldn't be permanent, but it would give us the delay we need."

"Embry, I'm putting you in for a promotion." Moore sported a lopsided grin as he motioned for the courier to come forward. "Stand by for new orders. Ready the bugler. Offensive units forward—no quarter!"

Embry blinked. "Are you issuing a 'black flag' order, sir?"

"You heard the order!" Moore barked, sending the courier scrambling with a hasty exchange of salutes. "Embry, sound the call!"

Embry saluted before darting in the opposite direction.

The blue-eyed lieutenant assessed the field with the most assuredness that he'd felt all day.

"Let's end this thing," he muttered to himself.

Miles Stacey dropped his field glasses from his eyes, feeling rather pleased with himself. His men appeared to be holding a fighting presence, twice their size, to a stalemate. It was a real credit to the men of his unit. He was putting every single one of them in for a commendation. Placing his field glasses into his side pouch he set his hands firmly on his hips. Perhaps, there would be a commendation for him, as well.

When word got to headquarters, that is.

It was then that he seemed to notice a peculiar pattern forming in the front line of his company. His men. Were they...falling back?

He blinked incredulously. They were not just falling back; they were falling back *en masse*. One of his younger sergeants came running up the hill toward him. When he realized the lad was not about to stop, he collared the non-commissioned officer.

"Where the hell are you going?"

The young man still appeared to be floundering in his grip, his brown eyes wide with anxiety.

"Sir, they changed their approach! It's the 'black flag'! A 'black flag' order!"

It was Stacey's turn to go pale with anxiety. A 'black flag' order meant no prisoners. To the death. The opposing mixed force of Confederates and Union were beginning to push—rapidly—toward his position. In the clash, it would be almost impossible to tell who friendlies were. And by the time they figured it out...

Carter was on his own, damn him! Danforth wasn't worth these kind of losses.

"Sergeant. Sound retreat!"

It was at that point that the young man broke free of his commanding officer's grip.

"I'm sure someone else could manage that, sir!"

With that, the lad was gone, leaving Stacey to wonder if the skittish sergeant didn't have the right idea.

Bridgette peered, timidly, around the door frame of the nursery, anxiety flowing freely as she noticed Ms. Abigale with her arms outspread, pressing the flock of children into the corner. The slimy human-like creatures she had observed earlier were now in the room and advancing on Ms. Abigale's position. Uncle Charlie—Captain Danforth—appeared to be having cross words with the scary man who had put her up to helping them. She had made bad choices before, but she had a sinking feeling, this was a *really* bad one.

This wasn't meant to happen. None of the children were supposed to be harmed. It was only to scare the newcomers. And although the auburn-haired lady was looking properly scared…no one else was to be at risk. It didn't look much better outside. She had never seen Lieutenant Moore as terse as she had today. A lot of the soldiers, from

430

both camps, were poised for a fight with the other Union soldiers that had come with the scary man.

Yes, it was a fine mess, indeed, and she couldn't just stand by and let it happen. As frightened as she was, she couldn't just hide like a scared rabbit. She had to, at least, try and fix it. She, gingerly, walked across the floor, stepping carefully around the debris. A slight trip over a discarded teddy bear drew the room's attention in her direction. She couldn't recall a time where she had felt more vulnerable.

"Please," she said, her wide brown eyes pleading with the scary man. "This is not what was supposed to happen. You said no one would get hurt!"

"Bridgette!" Abigale Bramden shouted from her point across the room, her booming voice laced with relief and concern. "Where on earth have you been, girl? We've been worried sick!"

"I'm sorry, Ms. Bramden," the girl muttered, her head hanging in shame. "This is all my fault. No one was supposed to get hurt. We were only supposed to scare them."

The matron of the house, blinked in incomprehension. "Who, child?

"The new people."

It was Catheryn's turn to cast her confused aventurine green eyes in the direction of the freckled-face girl.

"Please, Mr. Carter," the girl pleaded. "We need to stop this."

The lean man cracked a smile, then began to chuckle down low.

"You don't get to call take-backs, little girl," he chortled. "It's not my concern that you are so...gullible."

The evil man's face contorted into a look of mock sadness, but the voice that emerged from his mouth wasn't his—but all too familiar.

"Please, Bridgette. Don't leave me all alone," a little boy's voice said, mockingly. "Only I really know who you are!"

The voice returned to the familiar mocking laughter of Jackson Carter finding great amusement in the girl's wide-eyed look of finally realizing she had all been part of a game.

"I know all about you, little girl," the scarecrow of a man said, leeringly. "I know all the bad things you've done. Bad things that even your friends don't know!"

Bridgette's lower lip protruded as her eyes began to well with tears. Her hands plastered against her ears as she backed away. It was a joke. A trick. All on her. So gullible. And now all her friends were in peril. All because she was so awful.

"Aww," Carter mocked. "I think she's gonna cry!"

As Catheryn watched, the puzzle pieces were starting to come together in her mind. Sergeant Solomon's warning—the threat from within. It was Bridgette, all along. The girl had been played; lured into collusion. All because of the scariest thing to threaten her world.

Change.

And now the child looked flushed, shaking. Catheryn wagered it was mostly from embarrassment, but now a rising anger was growing within her as the man continued to laugh and laugh.

"It's not funny," Bridgette said flatly, fixing the scary man with her brown eyes aflame. "Stop laughing."

She was beginning to become so angry that even Catheryn could feel it in her Awareness from across the room. It was a feeling Catheryn had felt before, but she couldn't quite place her finger on when.

It wasn't long before everyone could hear it; the buzzing, like a thousand angry bees about to swarm. A black darkness seemed to enshroud the child's shoulders, her brown eyes lit with a fire from deep within. The power that had been Carter's beacon to the house—the power that had been terrorizing everyone, including Catheryn—had been coming from this confused and enraged child.

And then, the rage launched from the little girl. Catheryn watched with utter amazement as a cloud of black raced across the room, closing the distance between Carter and the little girl before anyone could count.

"Poltergeist," the researcher breathed. "This child…is a poltergeist."

Recurrent spontaneous psychokinesis; it was a term that her and her colleagues had coined to describe a haunting where a living person was the focal. The slang term was 'poltergeist'. It was surmised that the unleashed energy tossing and moving object about, came from repressed anxiety, resulting in a sort of 'psychic explosion'. She had a few cases during her career that she would label it as that, but she had never witnessed it in the Dead to such a damaging degree.

The black mass hit Carter like a gut punch, sending the vile man flying against the far wall. Their leader down, the action caused his grotesque companions to stare at each other, unsure what to do. It was in that moment of confusion that Abigale ushered the children, swiftly, across the room and out the door.

"Get out," Danforth said to Catheryn, quietly, his eyes refusing to move from his combatant.

"But—"

"Now."

There was a deadly earnestness in that quiet voice, and Catheryn knew not to question it. Danforth shifted his fury on the ugly, sludge-drenched henchmen that had been terrorizing the children. Without leadership and their lack of agility, the spectral soldier's sword was no match for them. Which ones the captain couldn't dispatch, fled the room. He would let Lieutenant Moore's men handle the rest.

Taking advantage of the distraction, Catheryn turned and was about to exit the room when the door seemed to slam shut by unseen hands. Catheryn did her best to steady her nerves, not wanting whatever had done that to know that it had gotten the better of her. She turned about to find the now risen Jackson Carter glaring across the open space, directly at her.

"Where do you think you're going?"

Danforth's eyes darkened. "Your quarrel is with me."

"Oh, the lady and I have an appointment," the rail-thin humanlike creature drawled. "She's mine. I *own* her."

The spectral officer glowered at his opponent, as the man across from him started a leisurely walk along the edge of the room toward where Bridgette was standing.

"You stay away from them!" the soldier ground out. "They are family, and are, therefore, under my protection. And you know what I said about family."

"Oh, or you'll kill me?" the bounty hunter muttered, taking on an overdramatized expression of mock fear, before dropping to a deadpan expression. "Too late."

Lieutenant Moore frowned, watching the continued fighting through field glasses. Ordering the Black Flag didn't work *exactly* as he'd hoped. Forcing the enemy to a fight to the supposed death only strengthened their resolve. Some of Stacey's troops were falling, but not enough. At this rate, they may be back at the point where they started. The house defenses were becoming fatigued. If this was to continue...

He sighed, resignedly. He really didn't want to be run through with a blade, again. He'd finally got Chester Melville to stop stabbing him with his hunting knife every time he beat the lad at poker. No doubt, it made Chester feel better, but it still hurt like the blazes and damaged and scarred his energetic field. He finally just told the boy that he would stop playing him if it continued, and since Moore was the only one in the house worth playing, they called a truce.

But a saber? A saber would be a different thing, entirely. Sergeant

Embry stood at his side, observing the carnage, grimly.

"Orders, sir?"

"We need more reinforcements," Moore muttered.

"We've called in all that could be spared," Embry replied, frowning.

Corporal Talbot, a lean, auburn-bearded chap from the Southern side of camp, waved his kepi hat to gain the lieutenant's attention from down the road. He couldn't help but notice that, unlike all the others, he sported a broad grin on his ruddy face.

"Sir, you're not going to believe this," the corporal called out.

Moore blinked as he noted rising dust stirring in the road just over the corporal's shoulder. There were horses coming. Lots of them. And the rider at the lead was a sight for sore eyes. Upright, and in good form, was the sorely-missed Sergeant Solomon. It was rather anticlimactic when Talbot finished his statement.

"The cavalry's here."

25

D anforth and Carter circled each other like warriors from the arena

days of old; both assessing each other's weaknesses and strengths.

Danforth moved, his saber out before him, as Carter stalked him with a

rusty blade of his own. All Catheryn and Bridgette could do was stay out

of their way.

The brown-haired girl had found her way to Catheryn's side. She

leaned into it for comfort and support. Catheryn did not deny it to her.

The child stared, blankly, down at the hands that had caused the earlier

disruption. Try as she might, she could not summon the power, again.

"I'm sorry, Miss Catheryn," the girl muttered, her small hands

clenching into fists. "You didn't deserve any of that. I just...well, I

felt..."

"Afraid?" Catheryn finished, her green eyes filled with nothing but

sympathy. She would have hugged the child if she could. "Change is scary, but we're not here to hurt any of you."

"I know that now," she observed, down in the direction of the floor. "It's just the captain—Uncle Charlie—he's really different when you're here. He's changing, too. I just don't think he knows it."

The therapist smiled. "You think so?"

"He likes you," the teenager said, finally finding the bravery to look up at the doctor. "He doesn't want to, but he does."

"Oh, I don't think he likes me all that much."

"He does," the brown-haired girl replied, her freckled face turning down toward the ground, again. "More than he likes me. But he *should* like you better than me."

Catheryn bent down closer to try and draw up the girl's buried gaze. "Bridgette, I'm sure the captain loves you very much. He was very worried about you."

"He shouldn't," Bridgette murmured. "I keep doing the wrong things. Over and over. And now it's going to get him hurt again."

The young therapist didn't know what to say to that. She didn't know what the young girl meant by "again". And it was clear by her avoidance behavior—and the event at hand—that, now, wasn't the time to ask. The medium could only flow as much positivity to the child as she could.

"You brought this on yourself, Danforth!" Carter called from across the floor. "Let's say we make things interesting; if I beat you, I get the girl. If you beat me, I'll walk out of here, and leave you to your…nursery school, here."

"…and you leave Catheryn alone," the captain amended.

"Oh, no. She's mine. Regardless."

"Then it sounds like I better beat you into an unconditional surrender."

The bounty hunter continued to circle, cracking a lopsided grin on his broken face.

"I'm stronger than I was when we first met," the fowl man boasted. "You and your little pig-sticker. I underestimated that you could actually, use it. Now, I've got my own secret weapon."

"We'll just see about that," Danforth muttered under his breath.

With that, the soldier dove forward, crossing the space between them in the blink of an eye. The energy of the spectral officer plowed right into Carter's mid-section, knocking the brutal man off his feet.

Danforth approached the crumpled form, with confidence. Perhaps a bit too much, as Carter turned, delivering a blast of energy so strong that it blew the captain against the far wall. Danforth could have let the momentum carry him through the wall, but he wanted the potential damage of this fight, contained. They had enough carnage outside. Besides, it wasn't as if Catheryn could walk through walls, and he wasn't about to chance leaving her alone with him.

Carter came to stand over the officer, an unearthly breeze playing with the edges of his long, knee-length duster. Danforth could feel the energy roiling off of him; energy that had once been dormant but now alive.

"I come with my own army, Danforth," the creature gloated, his head tilting, mockingly, "and I don't mean the one outside."

He continued to pace in front of the Union officer, much like a predator playing with its prey.

"Stacey was easy to get," Carter explained, with an air of nonchalance. "Flip a few emotional switches, and people like him are easy to manipulate, but still…not quite what I'm looking for."

He got down on his haunches to meet Danforth's dark gaze. "Now children…especially, *orphan* children…they're still rather a blank slate; still waiting for their authority figures to teach them right and wrong. But if I get there first…"

Danforth moved to pounce, but Carter simply raised his hand, and the officer felt as if he were caught in an invisible viselike grip.

The bounty hunter gave him a look of mild annoyance. "Now, don't get ahead of the story! I'm not done. You just stay put right there."

The cruel combatant continued, examining the dirt under his fingernails. "Now you get, say, one or two of these little gems, you could do a lot with them. But if you get a real diamond, like Bridgette here…the power that could be had. Those children will do what I tell them for a simple act of attention—a simple pat on the head—and they'll do it without question. And taking them into houses…now, who isn't going to trust a child?"

The ghoulish man stood, making a dramatic flourishing gesture at the ceiling.

"This world…they love their ghosties don't they?" he observed. "Some will even buy a house with ghosts just for bragging rights."

In the blink of an eye, Carter was gripping the Union officer by the lapels of his frock coat.

"I'm sick and tired of feeding off the Dead," the scarred man ground out. "I want a real meal. Now, that I've had a taste of it off your little girlfriend over there—I want more. And these living people will just welcome these little precious children ghosties with open arms; showing them off at parties and other festive holidays. Until one day, I have their little resident ghosties open the door for me. And I. Will. Feed!

He frowned at the soldier's look of disgust and dropped his grip from his uniform, letting him fall back, unceremoniously, against the wall.

"I can survive and grow on this plane of existence for a millennia. Even longer. And no one will stop me, because those humans are too stupid to even know what's going on," the creature named Carter drawled. "Don't look at me as if I'm a monster. I'm not the first to do this. And definitely, not the last."

Catheryn lay huddled with Bridgette, listening to the ravings of the madman, uncertain what she could do to help the captain. If the captain couldn't stop him...

"Catheryn!"

The therapist started, violently, turning to her other side to find the welcoming sight of her guide at her side.

Ralph did his best to remain small, hunkered down next to her and Bridgette.

"We've got to get you out of here!" he whispered, briskly.

Catheryn looked into those serene blue-green eyes, and couldn't believe what he was saying.

"Leave? Have you even been listening to this?"

"Of *course*, I've been listening," he said, with a touch of impatience. "This has nothing to do with us. We have to leave—"

"And leave the captain?" She gazed at the enlightened being with a look of incredulity. "No. No, I won't!"

It was Ralph's turn to be taken aback. "This is *their* fight. It's private. It has nothing to do with you. We need to get you and the girl out of here—"

Catheryn contemplated something on the floor, and finally raised her eyes to look at him.

"You're right. Take the girl."

"What?!"

"However this turns out, he can't have her. You heard him."

For an enlightened being, he was appearing more flustered by the moment.

"He is not the first of his kind to do this!" Ralph countered in a harsh whisper. "He has simply gotten a taste of something he hasn't had.

There are beings like him all over the world."

"Then do something!"

He shook his head, forlornly. "I can't"

"What?!"

He looked into her eyes with a sternness she rarely saw. "Even a creature, as vile as he is, has a right to exist. The opportunity to learn and grow and change. The opportunity to turn back to the Light that bore them."

"And the captain?"

Ralph's jaw set, his judgment unwavering. "The Dead know what it is to exist down here; the benefits and the pitfalls. It's something they agree to when they are determined to stay. My only concern is the Living. You! That thing hasn't harmed any of you. Yet."

"Tell that to David," Catheryn shot back, her gaze burning right into his. "I'm staying."

Ralph flinched as if she had burned him, looking away. It took a moment for him to look at her, again.

"Then, you stay here, on your own. I cannot interfere."

A part of her was taken aback. Her guide, her stern protector and confidant, the spiritual presence that had been with her since childhood, was turning away. The other part of her, no matter how shaken, accepted it.

She turned to the child at her side. "Bridgette, you go with Ralph, here. I trust him more than anyone. He will get you away from here."

"But the captain…"

"I'll stay," the young doctor said, trying to sound her best to be comforting. "I won't let that thing hurt him."

It was a promise she didn't know if she would be able to keep, and Ralph's sidelong disapproving glance called her on it. Regardless, he drew the child up from the ground and turned away, the pair vanishing into thin air.

In her entire life, she had never felt as alone as she did at that moment.

Andrew Baldwin had managed to find a small cot for Doctor Faustus.

He had been watching over the sleeping therapist for the last hour or so, occasionally peering out of the antique glass at the carnage outside. The attacking force seemed to be beating a hasty retreat with the arrival of Solomon's cavalry. He was grateful. He had had his full of hostile ghosts today.

His eyes swept the ceiling. The noises upstairs weren't lost on him.

446

He could only trust that Catheryn and the captain knew what they were doing.

But then, he heard another noise. Chatter. A pulsing sound much like a distant locomotive. It was coming from the slightly ajar door leading to the cellar. He swallowed hard. Why did it have to be the cellar? He dreaded the cellar.

Picking up his baseball bat, Baldwin moved, cautiously across the Oriental rug. He used the tip of the bat, as if the door handle might burn him, carefully nudging the door open.

"...battle...murder...kill..."

He'd heard that noise before. Easing down the wooden steps in the sparse light of the stairway, he dared to come closer.

"...Danforth...kill..."

It was getting more unsettling as he listened, but he moved stealthily downward until he finally saw it; a cobbled box with a nest of wires sticking out at odd angles. It looked like a child's science project, put together with chewing gum and sealing wax.

The box. The box the investigators had brought, and everyone thought, Catheryn had broken. It was alive and working! But who put it there, and who turned it on?

"…Carter…more…power…"

As he watched, he saw an odd billowing shadow emerge from the device. He watched it move, like a cloud of smoke, upward and through the ceiling. Now it was becoming clear to him. Now he understood how the horrible creatures had gotten access to the house. They were using that collection of wires to find a way through the defenses.

And helping Jackson Carter.

Andrew felt his anger growing. All this time he'd been staying on the sidelines while others fought. Violence was never his strong suit— even more so since he had a new mouthful of veneers. But this was it. Whatever it was had crossed the line. It was messing with his friends. His career.

His adjustable rate mortgage.

He recalled his little league days, and set a solid grip on the bat. Wiggling his hips to free them up, he gave a vicious swing, clocking the box right in its side. He was sure if he was outside, it would have been a home run. Instead, it smashed into the limestone walls of the basement, splintering into tiny—hopefully, irretrievable—pieces. Just for good measure, he began pummeling the pieces on the dirt floor of the basement, making sure the thing was devoid of all life.

The basement fell into abrupt silence, the only noise Baldwin could hear was his own labored breathing. Satisfied, he tossed the bat away, bouncing with a hollow clatter against the limestone and on to the basement floor.

Lieutenant Moore turned to run his sword through his twenty-third victim. He frowned as the private fell to the ground, lifeless. The private was one of the eighty, or so, littering the property.

Just as he turned his attention back to the road, a Union corporal came running up out of the woods, his kepi lost to the day, exposing a dampened mess of short brown hair. He couldn't have been older than eighteen. The boy had a revolver at the ready, a manic look in his eye as he rushed the lieutenant. He observed the Confederate only had his sword, and Moore could have sworn that his expression went from anxious to utter glee in a matter of seconds. The corporal thrust the pistol toward his perceived enemy, point blank, and pulled the trigger.

Click.

The incredulous look the corporal gave the weapon would have been entertaining any other day than today. The boy threw the weapon hastily away and struggled to unsheathe the sword from his scabbard, only partially succeeding.

Moore rolled his eyes. "Please don't make me do this."

And, yet, the boy did manage to successfully pull the blade from the sheath, holding the blade aloft, gazing up at the weapon as if it were a prize from the fair.

He dispatched the lad quickly, increasing the body count by one more too many as he stormed off down the road on his way to check the other side of the house. Embry rushed up to fall in step beside him, opening his mouth to say something, but noticing the dour expression on the lieutenant's face, closed it.

Moore continued ahead, his pace unabated. "This is incorrigible."

"Sir, may I suggest we withdraw the Black Flag order, since it didn't play out as we expected?"

Moore had stopped feeling bad about the faulty decision three hours ago when Solomon drove the cavalry through the clash, sending Stacey's men into a rout. Breaking up Stacey's forces made it easy pickings for the house's protection detail to round up stragglers. Requests were floating up from the field from other officers, like Embry, to cease the killing order. It was time. At least, unlike his previous incarnation, he wouldn't have to scrounge up a burial detail for these. The men of the attacking force would, likely, rise on their own accord, wondering what had happened. He had already dispatched for various clergy to deal with the matter. He hoped—prayed—this second exercise in mortality would pan out better than it had with Danforth all those years ago.

"I certainly hope they've gotten the point by now," the lieutenant muttered.

"I'm…sure they've received several points by now, sir," Embry responded, flatly.

He paused, abruptly, turning on the older man. "Was that an attempt at humor, Sergeant?"

Embry flashed his best comical smile, hoping it lightened the mood, if just a little. Moore just sighed, decidedly unimpressed.

As the two continued down the stretch of gravel, they noted two figures on horseback trotting toward them. The lieutenant, easily, made one out to be the celebrated Sergeant Solomon. Bringing up the rear, on a slightly smaller horse, was a small boy dressed in a well-worn Confederate uniform.

The junior officer greeted the cavalryman with a salute. "Sergeant, I couldn't have been happier to see you than I was this afternoon. How is it you knew to return?"

The sergeant tugged at the bill of his blue kepi, but nothing could hide the smile of pride on his face.

"Thank you, sir. May I add that the 1st Cherokee Mounted Rifles completed the pincer movement that won the day, although…" The cavalry officer looked about, dismally, at the carnage surrounding them. "I don't know if 'won' would be the right word to use."

The boy spurred his mount to come up next to Solomon.

"…an' as far as our alert, it was good ole' Rooster, here, that stole away from camp an' found us."

The senior officer reached over and gave the boy's straw-like hair a tousle. Rooster winced at the expected gesture, but his freckled face broke into a broad smile, all the same.

"Well done, Private," Moore added, offering a salute to the boy.

Rooster returned it, his proud smile not leaving him as he moved his mount on toward camp.

The junior officer turned, partially, to the infantry sergeant, on the ground, next to him.

"Sergeant, rescind the Black Flag order," Moore stated. "I believe it has done what was intended."

The white-haired sergeant had just pivoted to be on his way, when

Moore's arm flung out and stopped him.

Marching up the gravel, were some members of the 60th U. S. Colored Infantry. Being dragged, in tow, was a belligerent, but exhausted, Lieutenant Stacey.

"Get off me!" the officer declared brusquely, desperate to find his footing to stop the dragging. "Get...off!"

As the company came to a stop before the unamused Confederate officer, Stacey removed his kepi and took his frustration out on the article, beating the dust from it on his pant leg. He finally plastered the cover back over his red hair, not looking any more presentable than he had moments before.

"I'd like to file a grievance!" Stacey barked. "The inhumane treatment of captives is…unacceptable!"

"I'd say you're looking pretty good considering my last order was to shoot you," Moore replied, blandly. "You should be thanking these gentlemen."

The Union artillery officer broke into a burst of laughter, taking in the surrounding company with distain.

" 'Gentlemen'," he snorted, the chuckle still in his tone. "Just because you put 'em in a uniform…"

He noticed, quite rapidly, that no one around him was sharing in his sentiment. Moore's blue eyes simply drilled through the man in silent disgust. Stacey's smugness quickly vanished. The man stiffened his posture and raised his chin a fraction.

"The casualties today were excessive," Stacey blustered. "And completely unnecessary."

"I agree," Moore traded, blithely. "However, I think you'll find there aren't any."

Stacey swung about, taking in the fallen soldiers all around him, mystified by the Confederate officer's statement. "Wha...how can you say—"

Moore unholstered his Colt pistol, pointed it at Embry's check, and fired, point blank. Stacey staggered backward, stunned, as the white-haired sergeant brushed the slight char of the burning wool off the front of his coat.

"Ow!" Embry uttered distractedly, as his fingers sought the wool for damage.

"We're dead, Stacey!" Moore stated, bluntly. "He's dead. I'm dead. *You're* dead!"

"Did you really have to do that, sir?" the annoyed sergeant

muttered. "I'm gonna have to fix that."

Stacey still just blinked in incomprehension.

"Your men weren't deserting you," Moore drawled impatiently. "They were coming to. They were realizing their situation before you did. They crossed over!"

The Union lieutenant still looked defiant. "I don't believe it!"

A Union soldier a few feet from Stacey, stirred from his prone position. The lad sat upright, groggily, massaging the temple where the bullet had pierced him.

"Boy, do I have a headache," he groaned, glancing up to the officer looming before him. Surprised, he bolted up from the ground, snapping to attention with a sharp salute. "Lieutenant! I wasn't slacking, sir. Honest!"

Stacey's blue eyes just blinked as he stared at the young man, obviously bearing a mortal head wound, saluting him. Moore was noticing the first sign of wheels beginning to turn. He said no more, and offered no further resistance, as his escort led him away.

"Embry," the Confederate lieutenant called out.

The older man still looked rattled, brushing at his uniform. "I may have to file a grievance, sir!"

Moore pursed his lips. "Grieve away…after you rescind the Black Flag order."

After a brief exchange of salutes, the white-haired sergeant was on his way.

BRAMDEN HOUSE

26

Captain Danforth rolled over to sit upright, his back against the wall of the nursery. Jackson Carter hadn't moved from his position in front of him. He sat on his haunches before the officer, looking tired and impatient.

"Come on, Danforth. Get up!" the cruel man demanded. "You're not even making this a challenge!"

The rail-thin nemesis stood up, throwing his hands, frustrated, at the ceiling.

"I've been waiting for years for this day; and this is the best you can give me? Perhaps you need just a little more motivation…"

The bounty hunter marched across the floor, and to Catheryn's horror, he reached down and grabbed a handful of her long red hair at the crown. She cried out, the pain of it drawing her up from her seated position on the floor.

"What do you think? You think she would look better with gray hair?" He turned to gauge the captain's reaction. "We can make that happen."

"Get…get off of her!" he spat, staggering to stay upright. "Your quarrel is with me!"

"It is," the savage man agreed, taking a more assertive grip on the medium's hair. "But I tire of these games. Perhaps I need a snack…"

With a roar, Danforth charged, with whatever strength he had left, plowing into the man and knocking him to the ground. Danforth's vertigo only increased, wondering if the charge wouldn't be his last play.

Stop playing his game!

Danforth shook his head to try and clear it. What was that? Whose voice was it?

Stop playing to his strengths. Use your own!

The officer didn't understand what was happening. Was this some cruel game of Carter's; an attempt to get in his head? But no. This voice was male, but it was calm, soothing. He doubted Carter could imitate that, even if he tried.

What is your purpose here?

The voice was insistent, but he was tired. So tired. Feeling as if the life was being drained from him.

Because, it is!!

Danforth blinked. He had felt fatigue during the entire exchange. Even he was unimpressed with his own efforts. His wrestling with Carter hadn't taken that much out of him.

What is your purpose here?

"To move…," he muttered, drawing on what was left of his energy to try and think. "To move between worlds."

He could hear Carter cackling, as if he was looking at the biggest joke in the universe.

"Really?" the man spat out between laughter, picking himself up from the ground. "That's the best you got?"

Open the door.

"I can't make him go," the spectral captain replied, tiredly. "It's against the rules."

Leave that decision for others to make.

Danforth stopped questioning. He had to trust that the omnipotent voice was on their side. Somehow, he felt sturdier, as if a fog of fatigue was being lifted. Was the being doing this? He was feeling a surge of adrenaline, as if all his power switches were suddenly turned back on.

Drawing himself up onto all fours, glaring down the nightmarish creature.

"Maybe you should come over here, and try again."

"And show me what? How much more floor you can eat?"

Carter started across the small expanse between them.

"Let me enlighten you," Danforth ground out.

With that, Danforth planted his palm, forcefully, on the barn wood floor. The space before Carter opened up in a brilliant circle of light, extending halfway to the ceiling. The energy within it swirled and churned with spectacular brightness and a power, unmatched, radiated from it. Even as Catheryn stared at it, she became dazed and mesmerized. The beauty, the love that poured forth through that opening amazed her, filling her heart full with a joy that mirrored ecstasy. It was a portal; that much she could fathom, but where it went was a mystery.

Carter teetered forward, nearly losing his balance toward it. He staggered backward, chuckling.

"Oooh, you had one more trick up your sleeve, huh, Danforth?" the rival laughed. "Almost had me there, didn't you?"

The man creature's expression soured, glaring at the brightness before him.

"I'm not going in there. No chance!"

"You afraid what waits for you in there?" the captain called from behind the barrier.

"I don't know what's in there!" Carter shot back. "I'm gonna stay right here where it's safe. Thank you very much! I can manipulate this world and just about everything in it. I'm staying."

A thought crossed his mind, a thought that Danforth partially intercepted. And the captain didn't like it.

"You know what? I bet your girlfriend would love a look," the bounty hunter mused, marching back over to Catheryn's side. "Whattaya say? You're such a big fan of what's over there. You keep selling it, even though you've never been. Here's your chance!"

Carter's hand clawed into her hair once more; the pain, once again, drawing her up from the floor. Even though he was forcing her head at an odd angle, she could still see the roiling whiteness of the light in her peripheral vision. She could feel the pull. The melodious vibration that tripped through all her energy centers. It was heartbreakingly beautiful. A call to…home. No. That portal wasn't for her. As lovely and ecstatic as the energy was, it was incompatible with her physical body. The churning forces within that vortex may tear her asunder—or worse, maybe yank her soul right out of her physical body. Even though that feeling of joy and ecstasy would probably haunt her for the rest of her days, it was not her time to learn its mysteries. Not yet.

But how did she fight back against the strength of this monster?

And in a flash, something came to her. A memory. A memory involving Abigale Bramden. She recalled Abigale chasing the vermin out of her house, fearlessly charging it with her broom. Demanding it—no, ordering it—to leave, with the strongest of assuredness.

She summoned it up from deep within her; the disdain, the outrage, of Carter, and all that he stood for. How dare he invade the sanctuary of her bedroom back home. How dare he invade her innermost thoughts.

How dare he have the audacity to place his hands on her!

Her eyes flashed with heat, as the rage built within her. She managed a hand on top of his that still clung to her hair.

Catheryn wrenched the hand off of her head, much to Jackson Carter's surprise. As she rose from her awkward position on the floor, he could read that her expression had grown quite feral. His one good eye widened perceptively, as he took an unsteady step backward.

"You!" Catheryn bit out, marching a step toward him.

The power behind that word, the emotion within it, sent Carter staggering backward, against his intentions. Unbeknownst to him, stepping one step closer to the open maw churning behind him.

"Don't!"

Again, the anger, the power, the groundedness of her certainty, hit him like a wave from an atomic blast. He fought against it, but when he called upon the power he had been using all afternoon, he suddenly found that it wasn't there. He couldn't stop his backward progression.

"YOU DON'T TOUCH ME!"

The blast of energy that came from those words were like nothing else she had ever witnessed. Carter's feet left the ground, caught in the energy blast that was her own self-autonomy. The power behind that one, unalienable right, not to have her space invaded. The energy of it sent him sailing, wide-eyed, toward the swirling vortex behind him. He had not even neared the event horizon of the effect when something snaked forward from the light. Catheryn had to blink her eyes against the brightness, holding up a hand to shield against it.

Something else broke through the portal. It was pure energy, but it looked like some sort of tentacle. Both of the snakelike tendrils lashed outward, wrapping around Carter's body. He screamed, helplessly, as more of the same deterrents erupted from the effect, attaching to his hands and legs. As powerful as Carter had become, he was no match for these…these things. The look of pure terror on the face of the man that had haunted her nightmares, rendered completely powerless, struck Catheryn dumb. For a split second, Catheryn Greye almost felt sorry for Jackson Carter.

Almost.

It pulled the body of its prey into its gaping maw, and all Carter had time for was one last blood-curdling scream as the anomaly pulled him fully inside.

And then there was silence. Blissful silence.

Feeling like an exhausted, frazzled mess, she could do nothing but stare into the blinding white mass for several seconds. It took about that long for her to register the presence on her right.

Ralph stood, gazing into the same vortex, the light emanating from it playing shadows against the sharp, yet serene, features of his face. He turned to look at her, his eyes full of love and pride for his charge. She felt the power of it travel down into her heart. She felt as if it would expand to fill her entire rib cage. The utter joy transmitting throughout her body. She glanced toward the churning vortex, something about that sensation feeling oddly familiar.

"Good job," he said, quietly.

With that, he turned his attention back toward the distortion. Raising his hand to trace the circumference of the anomaly, Catheryn felt a change in the energy emanating from the effect. It was almost as if it was a heightening. A frequency change. So engrossed was she in the shift that she didn't see Ralph's shift in attention.

"Captain," he greeted, simply.

The umbra effect of the swirling portal had hidden the figure trudging out from behind it. Danforth looked weary, but color was returning to his face. His uniform, however, still was disheveled compared to his near regulation perfection. He glanced over at the tall serene figure next to Catheryn.

"About time you showed up," the captain managed.

The guide said nothing as Catheryn moved away from his side, and over to the officer.

She wanted to help him, to support him in his broken gate, but there was nothing she could offer.

"Are you alright?" she questioned, concern clearly registering in her aventurine green eyes.

For a strange moment, Danforth found himself lost in them. The reflection of the portal in them made them almost hypnotic to look at. Perhaps he was just tired.

"I'll live," he finally muttered. "Of course, I was dead before, so, I guess the whole point is rather moot."

She sighed at his attempt at humor, gazing up at him. She got lost in his own dark eyes, wanting so badly to brush that wayward lock of wavy hair from his forehead, although she knew she could not.

"I don't know how to thank you," she whispered.

She could read the discomfort in his demeanor before it registered on his face. He didn't know how to answer her, and that was okay. She knew words, such as that, did not come easy to him. And between the two of them, they were unnecessary anyway.

"I'm glad I've proven I can take a beating for you," he said with a succinct nod, as if that was the most perfect thing to say.

The officer brushed past her to go stand next to the enlightened being, gazing into the brilliant abyss together. Ralph spared him a sidelong glance, ever so briefly, before returning his gaze straight ahead.

"There have been developments," the guide said, softly.

"I'm aware."

Ralph didn't need to ask if he was aware of which ones since he knew the communication channels of the house flowed freely back and forth between each inhabitant's Awareness. It really was quite the hive mind. It reminded him of that same interconnectedness within his own home.

"Then, you know what needs to be done."

There was a slight lilt to the guardian's tone that suggested a question. The captain's silence, and unwavering forward gaze, suggested no need for an answer. The two did not speak for a time, simply taking in the magnificent beauty of the churning power before them.

27

Captain Charles Danforth stood on the front steps before the house.

He waited, patiently, for his men to assemble the prisoners, reading the timepiece in his hand.

7:42 A.M.

He was late starting the day. Of course, it had been a very long night, with many of the field "dead" coming to. Some were in shock, and needed to be tended to for the majority of the night. Others wailed, insisting their wounds required attention, only later to find that those wounds had, mysteriously, disappeared. It was a literal godsend to have the clergy starting to arrive last night.

The first of them to arrive was a familiar face. Still dressed in his signature tweed frock coat, spectacles and brown slouch hat, not much about the preacher man had changed. He still carried his black book under one arm, and his hazel eyes still managed to dance with joy every time he smiled. He also discovered the preacher man had a name, now that the captain had enough clarity to accept it. The spry little man introduced the members of the relief corps who had volunteered for assistance.

They were numerous and varied as to background. Some were from the venerated Christian Commission and Ladies' Aid Societies—those that were very active in service during the war he remembered. Priests, those of the sisterhood, and dedicated nurses, were also among their numbers.

The captain also found himself talking to those soldiers he remembered. Some were more willing to speak to him than the other volunteers; someone that had shared their trials and tribulations. He was also happy to see that others within his protection detail had taken to the task, as well. Even Lieutenant Moore's good humor seemed to be in abundant supply, and it wasn't unusual to see him sharing a laugh, and shaking hands with some of the "convalescing" soldiers. For many, it was the first time to encounter a "Reb" of such a compassionate nature. For others, there was too much of a perceived divide to overcome.

Moore found his way to the front of the crowd, taking his place on the step below his commanding officer.

"How is the mood this morning?" Danforth inquired, covertly.

"I believe you will be moving a fair number of them along," the lieutenant murmured.

Danforth was aware of an inner conflict within the junior officer, and he was not readily sharing it.

"Your thoughts, Lieutenant?"

His blonde-haired adjutant seemed to reflect inward for a moment, before responding.

"I like this work, sir."

"Can you be more specific?"

"I think I could be of even greater service," the young officer mused. "...to men like these. No disrespect to our service together. No, sir!"

"No disrespect taken," Danforth replied, his eyes taking in the growing sea of soldiers before him. "Where we're going, I would assume you'd have your choice of assignments."

"You are...familiar with this process, then?"

Among the assembly, he caught the hazel eyes of the preacher man. An unspoken conversation seemed to pass between the two men, even from that distance, concluding in a minute nod of understanding.

"I know who helped me with mine," the senior officer said, quietly.

Gazing out over the throng, he was grateful that so much varied help was available to them.

"Wait…" Danforth's brow furrowed, as his head tilted, perceptibly. "There is someone missing."

From Moore's returned puzzled expression, he could tell the answer wouldn't be coming from his adjutant's direction.

"No one is being left behind," the captain muttered, his eyes dark with serious intent. "Not again."

S ergeant Solomon rode his mount down by the river bank, exchanged salutes with one of his pickets that had requested his presence: someone of "delicate need" down by the river. His first thought was that the person in distress may be female, and that Miss Catheryn should be notified, but the closer he got to the individual, the more he realized that would have been a poor choice.

A lean figure of a man was seated next to the riverbank, his arms wrapped around and the knees of his gray woolen trousers, hugging his knees to his chest. His hair was short and choppy, looking the color of graying straw. His collar shirt that had once been white was dirty and unkempt. A pair of suspenders held up his pants as he rocked back and forth, his eyes wide and transfixed on a point of the rolling river before him, muttering anxiously to himself. So far was he gone in his distress that he didn't even notice the African-American cavalry officer had dismounted from his horse and was standing next to him.

"Sir? You alright? I'm respondin' to a report a someone needin' assistance."

The pitiful man snapped out of his anxiety, staring, fearfully, up at the officer. Looking deep into his panic-ridden eyes, something about the distressed man felt overwhelmingly familiar.

No. It couldn't be.

The nervous man scrambled backward on all fours, doing what he could to place distance between him and the cavalry officer.

"I...know you," the man said in a harsh whisper. "Are you...Nathaniel?"

"Yessir? I'm afraid you have me at a disadvantage—"

"Are you here...to torment me?" the man questioned, the fear still very present in his gray-green eyes. "So many...so many..."

The man resumed his fetal position, rocking and sobbing loudly.

"I keep feeling the torment over and over, from so many. So many!" he cried, pausing only briefly to look up at the soldier. "I can't...I can't take it."

The non-commissioned officer finally came to a cold realization. The pitiful creature before him was Jackson Carter.

But this Jackson Carter had changed. The scraggly beard was gone, as well as the vicious slash across his face. Both of his eyes were intact and free of defect, but his mind. His mind seemed...broken.

The man's eyes still plead with him from his position on the ground.

"Please...please, kill me!" he pleaded.

"I can't do that," the cavalryman whispered. "Did you go to the place? The place where you were supposed to go?"

"There was people. They were kind. They healed me. So much love." Carter's gaze broke from his, his vacant stare cast out upon the river once more. "And then, they showed me what I'd done. I couldn't stay there. I couldn't...I didn't deserve it. I couldn't stay there. I couldn't stay there!"

The affected man choked on another series of sobs, burying his face in his arms, unable to look at anyone or anything, rocking to and fro.

Solomon had to admit to feeling empathy for the man, despite himself. Despite their brutal history, the cavalryman's pain had come to an end with his healing on the other side. The accounting of his previous life, and the reasons for it, had been complete. He had closure. A small part of Solomon was satisfied that the reaper of men's souls was feeling the pain he had doled out to others, but even the torture Solomon had suffered at the man's hands, was finite.

Without intervention, Carter's could last in this state, forever. There was no greater hell than the one an individual created for themselves.

Sergeant Nathaniel Solomon gazed down at the man, stone-faced, as the man on the ground still rocked back and forth, like a child, and still whispering his fervent wish that someone kill him. End the pain. End the anguish.

"I can't absolve you of the crimes you committed. Only you can do that" the army officer said, flatly. "…and there are ways to work through it; even down here, but I'm not the man to help you."

Solomon felt the presence behind him as the words left him. He turned and looked up to the top of the embankment. A familiar silhouette of a shorter man, with a floppy hat stood above him, observing in the silent way he often did.

It was time for the best person for the job.

Catheryn searched behind the furniture and in the closets near the downstairs parlor. Danforth had *blinked* down to the lower level to help her.

"We can't leave. I refuse to leave anyone behind," he said, sternly. "Not again."

"Where is she?" Catheryn muttered. "Bridgette!"

She seemed to instinctively know, or maybe it was a side effect of being plugged into the hive mind that was the house. The name just whispered itself back to her. Young Bridgette was missing. Where could she be? Where in this house would a young girl be hiding? Something seemed to pull at her Awareness; tugging her, with insistence, toward the open basement door. Of all places...

Danforth came to the same realization as her, and he *blinked*, leaving Catheryn to transport herself to the darkened room below.

There was one lone window to illuminate the damp, cold cellar. Fortunately, on a storage box, next to that window, she found the little girl. Next to her, scattered in pieces along the dirt floor, were the remains of the spirit box device.

"Bridgette—"

"I let them in, you know," she confessed to the dirt floor, cutting

Catheryn off. "I wanted to put things back as they were before. It's too late. It never will be now."

Catheryn knelt before the little girl, searching her expressive brown eyes for a hint to the mystery.

"It's alright, sweetie. I understand—"

"Don't you get it?!" the young girl erupted. "I'm no good! You have no idea what I've done. I nearly killed *you*!"

Empathy drawing the young medium in, Catheryn's hand brushed the part of the field where the child's cheek would have been.

Catheryn felt the darkness around her shift and change. The restraints of the four walls fell away as she found herself staring down a lonely country dirt road. A horse whinnied behind her, and she dodged aside just as a small number of riders on horseback, trotted up from behind her. Behind them followed an artillery supply wagon. Several other members of the artillery battery walked alongside the wagon. Whether they were on horseback or walking, everyone appeared nervous.

The riders ahead of her proceeded to engage in some playful banter she couldn't quite make out; a banter which their terse commander put an abrupt end to. There was something familiar about that terseness.

Something about that voice…

The same commanding officer raised his white gauntleted fist, the sparse light of the waning moon nearly causing it to glow in the dark. The procession halted, and the commander turned sideways to a sound in the bushes. She covered her mouth as she nearly eked out a noise in surprise as it dawned on her who it was. It was Captain Charles Danforth.

Although, it wasn't *Captain* Danforth. The insignia on the shortened shell jacket he wore was different. She watched with curiosity as a young child's voice called out from the brush. There was a perceived moment of reluctance, seeming to acknowledge something in the palm of his hand that flashed a brilliant silver. Catheryn jumped as she heard an ominous click in the bushes to her right just as Danforth dismounted with an order to cover him. Within seconds, the fruitlessness of the order was all but clear as fire rang out. Muzzle flashes opened up from the bushes all around them. For the second time that evening, she found herself dodging out of the way of a horse and rider, as it, recklessly, drove through the procession at high speed. The rider appeared to be wearing a cavalryman's jacket, but the rest of the uniform looked very homespun. Something about the presentation wasn't right, and those fears were confirmed as she saw Danforth's knees buckle from the rear. She saw the man go down, landing hard on his knees, slumping over onto the hard, cool earth. A child screamed out over and over, but Catheryn couldn't see enough through the brush to make it out. The wild rider let out an unearthly howl, driving his mount into the woods, drawing the fire with him. The ruse became more apparent, as a pair of men dashed out of the brush to pick a young child up by the arms. The child continued to scream in alarm as the scene before the medium fell into silence. Bodies of soldiers were splayed on the ground. Some of the fire took some of the riders right off their mounts. Another horse screamed, staggering from severe wounds, but out of all of the carnage, she couldn't take her eyes off the fallen commanding officer at the end of the trail.

It was at that point that she felt the young presence next to her. She looked down at a child dressed in butternut gray, a slouch hat perched on top of its head. She recognized it almost immediately. It was Rooster. Dark brown eyes vacant, the emotions flowing forth were that of numbness. The child reached up to remove the brown slouch hat.

As Catheryn watched, a cascade of dark brown curls fell about the shoulders. She stared at the transformation in alarm, but alarm gave way to clarity.

Standing before her, in homespun gray, was Bridgette.

Of course, now it made sense. The self-loathing. The denial. The inability to face the embodiment of what she had done.

"I was there that night," she whispered, as if she spoke any louder, it would break the spell. "The land owner's son where we rented our farm, came down to our house. I was sleeping in the loft above, so I could hear them talking. He first asked my papa if he would conscript into the Confederate Army on his behalf. It was good money, but with his responsibility to us, Papa couldn't even think of leaving."

She looked down at the ground, hat in hand, too ashamed to meet her gaze. "After a while, it was no longer a request. The land owner's son made it a condition of our rent. I remember Mama crying by the fireplace as Papa pulled his squirrel rifle down from the mantle, and began to clean it. To think of running the farm without him, with three other brothers and sisters. Mama wouldn't know what to do...I couldn't let him go. Mama's heart would break in two, while me...I was just another mouth to feed. In the middle of the night, I grabbed his leather bag and gun, and I signed up in his place."

Catheryn knelt next to the small child, her empathetic eyes looking for any emotion around the numbness. "How old were you?"

Her answer was deadpan. "Twelve."

"I cut my hair. I was young enough not to worry about hiding much of my body, so that helped. Before I knew it, they were moving us up north, helping our Missouri kin with guerrilla raids to stop the Yankees from invading. Up until that time, I did nothing but run messages and help the cook with meals. That night..."

The young girl, for the first time, seemed choked with emotions. When she turned to Catheryn, there were generous amounts of tears in her brown eyes.

"I didn't know what they were up to," she responded, her voice edged with defensiveness. "I swear, Miss Catheryn. I didn't know!"

"Of course you didn't know," a male voice contested from behind them. "You were just a child."

The male voice behind them caused them both to jump. Bridgette recognized the voice a hair faster than Catheryn, forcing the therapist to turn and find the young girl throwing herself into the arms of a very-much-present, Captain Danforth.

"I'm sorry, Uncle Charlie! I killed you!" her muffled voice sobbed as the captain held the girl to his breast. "I killed you as if I pulled the trigger myself!"

"No, no, sweetheart," the captain soothed in low quiet tones. "It was not your fault."

"But I'm no good. I'm just bad. I'm sorry!" Bridgette drew back, tears still staining her cheeks. "I won't blame you if you...if you...never forgive me."

His large calloused hand rose up to her cheek, wiping away tears. For once, Catheryn was jealous that he could perform such a sweet gesture. She wanted so much to comfort the child, too.

"Sweetheart, there's nothing to forgive," the captain said in hushed tones. "You've come to be the daughter I never had. I can't even think about leaving without you."

The girl called Rooster continued to cry in her adopted uncle's embrace. The night scene evaporated before Catheryn's eyes, and she found them all back in the cellar. The captain continued to hold Bridgette, tenderly, in his arms, until all her tears were spent.

28

Catheryn dropped into the vacant chair at her partner's bedside.

Andrew had filled her in on David's condition, and it didn't appear to warrant any medical attention. As for the rest of the report, he felt it best she received that from her partner, personally.

Dr. David Faustus was propped up on pillows in the twin bed, his reading glasses and his regular regimen of book discarded on the bed stand next to him. It was fortunate that the house appeared to have a great many of them in just about every room.

"Well, it's about time you came to visit," her partner mused, sitting up to interact with her more socially. "I was beginning to think that you had abandoned me."

The startling white tips to his gray hair had subsided, and despite the fatigue etched in his gray eyes, he didn't look the worse for wear. She brushed some of his shaggy hair off his forehead. He still needed a haircut.

"I knew you needed some rest," she murmured. "Andrew has been a saint looking after you. We may end up owing *him* money soon."

The older doctor chuckled at that as he adjusted his seated position to be more comfortable.

"Well, I don't know about that. It was quite a spill I took down those stairs."

Catheryn blinked at her partner. " 'Stairs'?"

"Honestly, I don't recall half of it. Maybe it's the concussion."

She glanced over her shoulder to Andrew, who happened to be lingering in the doorway. The realtor shrugged, his expression suggesting cluelessness as to where he would have gotten such a notion.

Had his memory of the whole event been erased? She had heard of the brain filling in gaps of trauma with less painful fallacies, in order to live through it. She had witnessed it in her practice, many times. But now that it was happening to the colleague that she worked with, she wasn't sure how she felt about it. Was it healthy for that fantasy—that spill down the stairs—to remain? Would it really forward the work that they did?

She drew back and pondered it. No, she decided. She would let him keep that. Reality was just too fantastical to even describe, and probably a blessing in disguise.

"It's about time," he muttered, throwing his legs over the side of the mattress, "to get out of this bed. We have to get moving…and Andrew has new owners to meet."

Concussion or no, Faustus recognized the look of melancholy in his partner's green eyes. He reached across the space between them to take her hand.

"It's for the best," he said, knowing full well the words did very little to put her mind at ease.

It was at that moment that they both heard a commotion upstairs. It sounded like a whole army was marching up the stairs and down the upstairs hallway. Her partner exchanged quizzical looks with her.

The elder doctor raised his gray eyes to scrutinize the ceiling. "What is that?"

A glance over her shoulder found Andrew noting the same disturbance above them.

Quickly dressing him in something more presentable, Catheryn offered her partner a shoulder to lean on as they moved to the main staircase. The noise continued, unabated; the sound of heavy and numerous footfalls on the barn wood floor. Andrew met them, looking apprehensively, up the stairs. It was clear to Catheryn that the realtor really had his fill of the paranormal, but his curiosity looked to be getting the better of him, and with David having Catheryn to lean on, the whole party moved up the stairs.

Catheryn was drawn to the nursery, and trying as they might to do a stealthy approach, the creaking barn wood gave away their approach. Despite the noise, no one came out of the room to meet them. With her arm still supporting David, she nudged the door open, slightly. The scene before her, took her breath away.

The portal from last night was still alive and pulsating with its brilliance. It had grown to twice its normal size. The room was full of soldiers, all standing in formation, with Captain Danforth taking up position on the left side of the portal. Flanking the anomaly on its right, to Catheryn's astonishment, stood Ralph. The guide seemed to sense her strong emotion from across the room and offered her a serene smile before returning his attention to the assembly. Her attention was drawn away from the scene by a grip on her shoulder. She turned toward her partner to find his gray eyes wide.

"Where did all these people come from?"

It was hard to tell who was more surprised at his words; Andrew or herself. Of course, she and Andrew could see the event with their special sight. But David?

"You can see it?" Andrew asked, incredulously.

"...and that bright light; what is it?"

Catheryn warmly chuckled to herself, but at the same time, she couldn't help but feel tears gathering in her eyes. Her partner, after years of working together, was seeing it. Really seeing it. She wondered if the combined presence of Andrew and herself standing next to him might have triggered some sort of heightened perception; a shared experience. She brushed those scientific thoughts aside. More to ponder at a later time.

The soldiers started toward the event horizon, in neat, orderly lines of four abreast. As the first four neared the opening, military decorum seemed to falter with each individual.

"Mother? Father? Is that really you?" a young corporal called into the abyss, at something Catheryn could not see.

"Delia! Delia, sweetheart!" a brown-haired private hailed, addressing something within the void. "I'm here. Here I am!"

The soldiers behind watched in heightened anticipation, all their eyes reflecting the brilliance of the anomaly, watching as each of their comrades found something enticing them through. They all seemed to eagerly await their turn.

"Miss Catheryn."

She turned toward the voice, knowing it was Lieutenant William Moore before she even turned. He was wearing his wool frock coat and white, wide-brimmed officer's hat. He reached up and removed his cover, respectfully.

She smiled a heartfelt smile. "Bill."

"It's about time you used that," he said proudly, his smile all charm. "I'd offer you one last turn around the dance floor, but..."

She knew he couldn't. Not on this side of reality, anyway.

"The dance floor seems a bit full anyway," she muttered thoughtfully.

She tried to think of something more appropriate to say, but she could find no words. The southern officer didn't seem bothered by that. He replaced his hat, tugging the front brim down slightly in his familiar informal salute, and he moved on to be absorbed into the crowd.

She felt the moment pull at her heart, and she sighed. The moving moment was short-lived. In the stillness of the room, it made the slightest noise apparent. She heard a stifled sob coming from behind her.

Huddled against the far wall, was a soldier, curled up in a fetal position. The blonde-haired corporal pressed himself into the wall to provide as much distance as he could between himself and the anomaly, his blue eyes wide with fear. She recognized the markings on the lad's coat as belonging to a Union artillery unit. Catheryn knelt next to the boy, who appeared to be trembling, uncontrollably.

"Hey," the therapist said in her most soothing tone. "What's your name?

He spared her only a solitary glance before receding into his emotional cocoon.

"Daniel," he stuttered. "Daniel Hampden."

Catheryn smiled, warmly. "Well, Daniel Hampden. My name is Catheryn. Can I ask…why do you seem so scared?"

"That thing. Over there. Everyone says it's good. That it's safe," he said, shakily, his trembling increasing along with that of his lower lip. "I don't trust the feelings I get from it. It scares me. It's a trick. I know it is!" The corporal found it within himself to lock his blue eyes on hers. "I've seen evil. I know what it can do. If it can trick me, it can trick them!"

Catheryn sighed. "I know it's scary, but it's no trick."

The corporal resumed his fetal position, shutting her out, until they both felt a presence directly behind them. She turned slightly, first taking note of a pair of tall riding boots. The two gazed up at the face of the new arrival. He could have been a younger mirror of the corporal huddled against the floorboards, sporting slightly lighter hair, but the kind, expressive, blue eyes were definitely a family trait. He wore a similar Union blue sack coat, like his brother, as well as the familiar sky blue trousers.

"Hello, brother," the young guest said.

Daniel Hampden's blue eyes went wide. "Joe?"

The younger man broke out in a warm smile. "Where have you been? Mother and I have been waiting for you for so long!"

"No, you can't be Joe," the corporal said, turning away from the figure. "This is some kind of trick. Joe has a stutter."

"It *is* me, Daniel. They fixed me over there when my physical body died," the young man said, soothingly. "Don't you remember? That day near Palmyra?"

The corporal's nerves were shot, his darting eyes showing that he was searching memories but was having a hard time connecting.

"You yelled for me when the bushwhackers hit," the young man continued. "In the thick smoke, you couldn't find me. You couldn't find me 'cause it was too late."

Catheryn could see something of the memory registering on the nervous corporal's face.

"But Danforth," the corporal said, anxiously. "He got you killed. He was reckless!"

"You're confused. Nothing could have changed the outcome of that day, Danny," the young man named Joe, offered. "It was just our time. It took me a while to understand what was happening, and I tried to get you to come with me, remember? That night we were lost in the woods?"

It was all beginning to click. Daniel Hampden closed his eyes as all the puzzle pieces started to come together in his head. He remembered Palmyra. He remembered the ambush, and then he remembered...what was it? He couldn't quite grasp it...

It didn't matter. The young man claiming to be his brother, Joe, could be no other. How else would he have known so much?

Joe reached a hand out to him. "Come with me, brother."

Daniel stared at the offered hand a moment, his uncertain gaze shifting from the offered hand to his brother's welcoming smile.

"Come with you where?"

The younger man's smile did not falter. "Where you'll never need your gun again."

The corporal hesitated, but only a moment. He reached up and grabbed his sibling's hand. Catheryn watched from her kneeling position as the two disappeared into the throng of people. She could already hear them joking and laughing as they moved through the crowd.

"Another satisfied customer," she muttered to herself.

Or, at least, she mused, no one ever returned to complain.

She looked up to find Andrew hovering over her. He caught her by the elbow to help her up. She found her feet, brushing the imaginary dust of her hands off on her pantlegs.

"You need to come," he said, quietly, trying not to break the spell of the moment. "They're going."

"Well, of course, they're going," she responded, perplexed as to why he was stating the obvious.

"No," Andrew replied, fixing her with as hard a look as he had ever given her. "*All* of them."

Catheryn blinked, staring at Andrew Baldwin as if he had three heads. He could see the question in her expression.

"You'd have to ask the captain."

She drew back, closing her eyes. The house without the regular noise. The constant patter of little feet. The music. The dancing. It would just be another ordinary house. It would break her heart, but she could understand them moving on in the face of what the house's new management would be like.

But him? She couldn't fathom it. She picked her way slowly, deliberately, through the crowd, not wanting to ruin the momentum of all going. After a while, she ceased caring; pushing through at a run. Explanations. She needed to know the reasoning. Perhaps, she could argue it. Come to a different decision. She just about reached her destination when something at the event horizon made her pause.

There was a black Union soldier peering into the swirling vortex before him. The brilliant light of the event horizon played across his facial features, revealing an expression of wonder and joy.

"Althea," he whispered. "My sweet girl! Is it really you?"

For a moment, the churning surface gave way to a small body emerging; a child sporting long braids on both sides of her head, her gingham dress a checkered brown. Her dark eyes were filled with an expression of such love that Catheryn felt it tug at her own heart.

This was the moment she was trying to argue against. And there were hundreds more stories out there. This was what she was intending to keep them from. All the reasons for doing so, suddenly, felt so selfish and two-dimensional.

The crowd was swelling. It not only consisted of military. Some were civilians; some noticeably from the past and others more recent. They ranged from the very old to the incredibly young. Some peered at the gate warily, while others were happy to pass right on through. She caught a side glimpse of a familiar face. Abigale Bramden paused, hand in hand with the man that was her father. They both turned to look at her, an unspoken thanks before moving on. Catheryn started as a small creature barked, scampering up to the portal. A beautiful terrier. He didn't even pause. With a joyous leap, he was gone. She couldn't help but find the humor in such simple trust, and amidst all the somberness, she laughed.

"Catheryn."

The young medium turned to find the captain standing next to her. Of course, even in the midst of all this chaos, he found her. He always could. She gazed up into his eyes, her own brimming with tears. She could feel the turmoil within him; the deep-seeded need to touch her. Wanting to touch her. Wanting to wipe the tears away. She didn't even need to feel it to know it. It was so plainly etched in his dark eyes.

"With Peter taking possession of the house, I can't protect them," he said, flustered. "How the living have forgotten the war I come from. No one owns people. They don't own us either."

She nodded, an attempt to take the burden of the explanation away.

"My job here is done. I have to leave."

The tears flowed freely from her aventurine green eyes. She had nothing to cling to. Nothing to relieve her pain. All she could do was cover her face with her own hands.

As she did so, the turmoil within Danforth grew, and the soldier looked past her to the enlightened being on the far side of the portal. Ralph was watching them, intently, the fire of the opening dancing in his compassionate blue-green eyes. And was something else mirrored there? Did the elevated being *feel* something? Sorrow, perhaps?

The officer gazed down at her; helpless, hopeless.

"I can give you nothing," he admitted, his voice gruff with emotion. "I can't give you a house. I can't give you my name. I have nothing to offer you. Perhaps, in another life…"

Andrew and David had made their way through the crowd to her. He looked back to them. David stared back in wonder, finally able to see him. And then there was Andrew, his face sympathetic as he gazed up at the specter that had cause him so much trouble. Resting a hand on Catheryn's shoulder, he nodded a subtle nod. Yes, they would take care of her, so he could do what he must.

He turned away, pausing at the event horizon. For a moment he locked eyes with the portal guardian, sharing the rage and grief that he would not burden her with. And he walked through.

Catheryn gasped, crying out in agony; the suddenness of it hurt more than she ever thought imaginable. It was as if someone had reached in and pulled her heart out of her chest. She fell to her knees. David and Andrew at her side, in an instant, reaching down to her, their faces etched with concern. The cord that had connected her to him was straining, pulling apart. There was a last brief moment that flooded her, sharing a love that could not be expressed with words.

Then it was gone.

29

Catheryn spent the majority of the car ride in silence, curled up against the passenger-side window in the back seat. She felt empty and hollow. David let her have her space, knowing the eccentricities of the grieving process, better than most.

He helped her carry her bags up to her apartment, knowing full well she was more than capable. She let him. She was going to have to take her time with it and deal with it in her own way. As colleagues there would always be work, but he would be there for her when she was ready for him.

She turned on the bathroom light, and threw herself into the bed, not even bothering to change clothes. Rolling on her side, she gazed at the far wall. The intense boomerang feeling of loss threatened to overwhelm her, and she felt herself choking on tears.

Would it always be her burden to walk this life alone? No one ever truly understanding? For one brief, shining moment, she had that.

Catheryn felt something warm against the small of her back, and she turned to find Ralph standing next to the bed. His blue-green eyes gazed down at her, some of her own pain was reflected in them.

Part of her, the healer within, pushed through her own pain, looking up at him in concern. She had rarely seen him so affected. She took a deep breath to steady herself before she spoke. She did not want her voice to shake.

"Are you alright?" she whispered.

"No," he whispered, heartfelt, his brilliant eyes shining from something other than his natural luminescence.

"But why?"

"Because, you are not." He took a breath to center himself, some of his natural serene expression returning. "But I am here," he said, warmly. "I will *always* be here."

She didn't say anything, and she knew he didn't mind. She rolled on to her back, propping up pillows to gaze out the door way of her bedroom to the oversized glass windows of the living room.

She wasn't aware when she fell asleep, but when she did, she awoke with a start. Early morning was painting the cityscape in early morning hues, and wait…

She blinked, and then, rubbed her eyes. It couldn't be. A familiar silhouette standing before the glass. She rubbed her eyes, again. No one was there. Grief did funny things. She'd heard if from patients over and over again. Now she was living it. She sunk into the embrace of the pillows, trying to push it from her mind. She turned, and Ralph was still there, seated next to her, smiling compassionately.

"Was it him?" she asked.

"Was it who?" he queried.

Knock, knock, knock

The sudden sound made her start. She exchanged worried looks with Ralph, whose gaze shifted to the door and back to hers, almost expectantly, but as per usual, never demanding. It was a moment for her to decide. Life could remain safe. Remain the same.

Knock, knock, knock

Who was she kidding? Life was *not* the same. Life would never be the same. She had looked into the Darkness and stared it down. Stood her ground. She had survived and was the stronger for it.

And the Darkenss knew her now. She would have to live with that. But she was not alone. She was never alone.

Catheryn Greye sat back in her bed, taking a deep breath to center herself. Pulling back the bedsheets, she swung her legs over the edge and walked, barefoot, across the plush pale carpet of the bedroom.

Knock, knock, knock

Crossing the linoleum of the kitchen and across the vinyl simulated planking of her entry way, she paused before the door.

Knock, knock, knock

She took another deep, cleansing breath before she twisted back the deadbolt, and placed her hand on the door knob. She peered out the security eye hole. No one there.

Knock, knock, knock

She pulled back, startled. She swallowed, re-centering herself. With that, she twisted the door knob, and opened the door.

Coming Soon:

Bramden House: Echoes

www.ingramcontent.com/pod-product-compliance
Lightning Source LLC
Chambersburg PA
CBHW020823030726
47496CB00001B/70